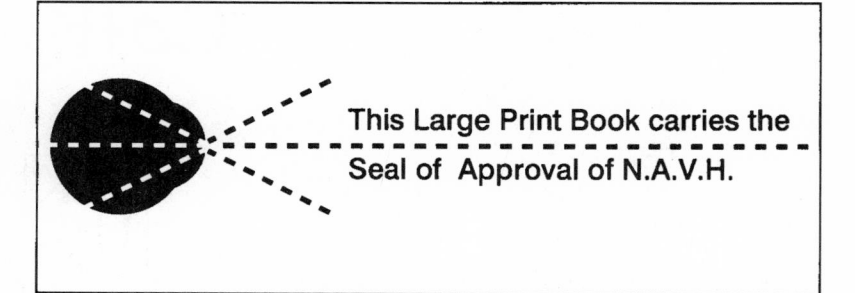

This Large Print Book carries the Seal of Approval of N.A.V.H.

G·K
Hall
&Co.

IF YOU
LOVE ME

IF YOU LOVE ME

Elaine Coffman

F
Coff

G.K. Hall & Co.
Thorndike, Maine

5/97 G.K. Hall 26.95

Copyright © 1997 by Elaine Coffman

Published in 1997 by arrangement with
Fawcett Books, a division of Random House, Inc.

G.K. Hall Large Print Core Collection.

The text of this Large Print edition is unabridged.
Other aspects of the book may vary from the original edition.

Set in 16 pt. Plantin by Rick Gundberg.

Printed in the United States on permanent paper.

Library of Congress Cataloging in Publication Data

Coffman, Elaine.
   If you love me / Elaine Coffman.
     p.   cm.
   ISBN 0-7838-8122-3 (lg. print : hc)
   1. Large type books. I. Title.
PS3553.O39I5   1997
813′.54—dc21   97-1887

Friends are like melons. Shall I tell you why?
To find one good, you must a hundred try.
CLAUDE MERMET

For Sally Salners:

Dear friend of many years,
who has withstood the test of time.
Was it really twenty-five years ago
that we taught school together?
I don't know about you, but I think I
was fifteen . . .

▣ PROLOGUE ▣

England, 1857

It was Christmas Eve at Emberly Hall.

The last notes of "God Rest Ye Merry Gentlemen" drowned out the sound of approaching footsteps that echoed down the long hall leading to the grand salon. As the man and his companion passed by, the members of the household staff stopped what they were doing and turned to stare at the strange sight, many pausing to whisper, asking just who he was.

" 'Tis the viscount," whispered the under-butler to the chambermaid. "Saints preserve us. The prodigal son has returned at last."

The butler reached for their coats. The man's companion allowed him to take hers, but the man waved him away.

Without waiting to be announced, the Earl of Warrenton's long-absent son threw open the great carved doors of the grand salon and walked in — garbed in a great coat of grizzly fur, flakes of melting snow clinging to his long hair and shaggy beard.

The sight of him was enough to pull anyone up sharp, even those who had known him when he was a striking figure. It was not so much his great height that marked him, but the careless powerful look he had. There was something raw and unapproachable in his face, where the marks of a deep and profound sadness lay.

He was accompanied by a woman, the likes of which no one gathered at Emberly Hall had ever seen, for she wore her hair in two long plaits that hung down her back, and her dress was made of antelope skin, decorated with animal teeth. On her feet were leggings that reached almost to her knees. She walked like a cat on padded paws, entering the room as silently as a breeze drifting through an open window, passing undetected.

In spite of the gasps of surprise, the whispers of speculation, the shocked looks, the man spoke not a word but strode purposefully to where the Earl of Warrenton stood. He did not remove his great bear coat but merely slipped it back over his shoulders to reveal the worn buckskins beneath.

The woman followed him, walking a respectable distance behind, her head bowed slightly, as if it would be an insult for her to raise it and take a look at her surroundings.

The silence stretched on. The Earl of Warrenton's long-absent son was home at last, and no one in Emberly Hall dared to breathe.

The silence was broken at last, when the earl's wife, Octavia, spoke through the fingers she had spread across her shocked mouth. "William? Dear God above! Is it really you?"

A slight, teasing smile broke through the reddish beard and played about his mouth. "A man can fool anyone but the woman who gave him birth. How are you, darling mother?"

Ignoring the exchange between his wife and son, the Earl of Warrenton's red, mottled face showed the extent of his outrage. "How dare you come in here . . . among your mother and your sisters and their families, dressed like the heathen you have become."

Octavia put her hand on her husband's arm. "Charles, please . . ."

Charles jerked his arm away and spoke to his son. "What is the meaning of this?"

"Why, Father, I have come home for Christmas, as you can see. You did send for me, as I recall. Urgent, I believe the missive said."

Nothing moved. No one dared to speak. The room grew painfully quiet. Outside, even the wind that had been so bravely pelting the windows with icy snow only moments ago seemed to have grown meek and timid.

The only sound that could be heard at all was the heavy breathing of the earl, as anger flared deep in his gray eyes and his neck seemed to swell above his perfectly tied cravat. His nostrils flared as he gave his son a look of disdain. "You've been drinking."

William took a slight bow, wobbled a bit, then righted himself. "I have indeed, but not as much as I plan to." He pulled a bottle out of his coat and brought it to his lips.

9

His father reached out and slapped the bottle away. It fell with a splintering crash. Bits of glass went skittering across the highly polished floor. The strong smell of whiskey rose from the puddle of liquid on the oak floor to blend with the scents of Christmas that filled the room.

William appeared unfazed, his words coming slow, almost lazy. "I have more bottles."

Once again, a hush fell over the room. For the longest time, no one said a word. The discomfort stretched on . . . and on . . . to the point of snapping.

On tiptoe, the younger children were led from the room. Other members of the family began to whisper as they moved back, as if trying to become one with the background as the battle lines were drawn.

Octavia looked from her husband to her son, as if she fought some inner battle. Then, without a word, she stepped forward and put her arms around her son and hugged him to her. "This is the most splendid Christmas present I could have had. I have prayed for your soul and your safe return since the day you left. I thank God that my prayers have been answered." She kissed his cheek. "Dearest William, I have missed you terribly."

"Thank you, Mother, for your prayers. I have missed you, too," he said, with none of the harshness, the anger in his words that had been present when he spoke to his father.

Octavia's gaze left her son's face and went to

the strangely dressed woman who stood forgotten behind him. Only a curious sort of kindness showed in her eyes. "And your friend? Whom have you brought with you, William? Is she from America?"

"Yes, she . . ."

Charles fingered the Masonic emblem on his watch chain, then stopped suddenly. "What are you doing, bringing a filthy servant into the midst of our family at a time like this? It is Christmas Eve. Have you lost your senses? Has that wild country caused you to forget your manners, your upbringing? Get her out of here! Now!"

"Charles . . ."

"Stay out of this, Octavia. This is between William and myself. It is no concern of yours." He turned back to William. "Did you hear me? I said get her out of here."

"I heard what you said, but I am afraid you misunderstand. Walks Fast is not my servant."

"I don't care if . . ."

"She is my wife."

A gasp went up around the room.

"Your wife?" Charles's face grew stormy. "By God, is there no limit, no depth to which you will not sink?"

William shrugged. A smile played about his mouth. A spark of triumph gleamed in his eyes. "Apparently not."

And with that, William Woodville, Viscount Linwood, the only son and heir of the Earl of Warrenton, turned and strode from the grand

11

salon in Emberly Hall, and left his wife behind.

Everyone in the room turned to watch William go.

Everyone, save one person . . .

Only Octavia turned to look at the girl he had left behind and made an astounding discovery. For it was apparent to anyone who took the time to study her, that although the girl was dressed in the garb of an Indian . . . she was white.

The girl was Margery Mackinnon, and this is her story.

CHAPTER
▣ ONE ▣

Crow Territory, September 1857

Armed with pencils and paintbrushes, William Woodville, Viscount Linwood, came from England in the fall of 1854 to hunt Indians.

And find them he did.

For the next three years, he traveled throughout the upper plains painting and sketching pictures of tribal life, a moody perfectionist with an English title and a past he was running from.

It was late September and William and his party had been in the Yellowstone valley since early May. The weather was unusually warm for this time of year, but up here it could change overnight. He knew it was time for them to go; time to migrate farther south, or they would risk being caught by a sudden snow and not being able to leave until after the spring thaw.

Yes, they should leave, and yet he continued to stay on, riding out each day to make a few more sketches. Already he had decided that tomorrow they would move their camp farther up river so they would be closer to the winter camp of the River Crow.

He sat before a small campfire, his brooding

gaze fastened on the exotic dance of flames. He felt the artist in him come to life as surely as the dried wood had burst into flame before him. With a million voices, the whole of creation called out to him, and his soul listened. Tremendous feelings coursed and howled within him, as strong and fierce as the winds that blew down from the Rockies. Even now, the need was there, the pressing need to express the things that stirred in his soul, and he wondered if he would live long enough to paint them all.

He knew now that he would paint tonight, that he would go to his tent and paint feverishly, furiously, with a speed that seemed unnatural, even to him. Maddened by the splendor of color and hues, he would give himself over to his passion, until his arm ached and the colors ran from his canvas to drip on the floor. And then, only then, would he sleep.

" ' 'Tis said of love that it sometimes goes, sometimes flies; runs with one, walks gravely with another; turns a third into ice, and sets a fourth in a flame; it wounds one, another it kills; like lightning it begins and ends in the same moment; it makes that fort yield at night which it besieged but in the morning; for there is no force able to resist it.' "

The two men sitting across from the fire from him looked up. One of them, a Scottish scout who called himself Festus McGillvry, said nothing and went back to eating the last bit of meat off the hind leg of a rabbit. The other man, a slender and gentle Englishman named Daniel Boardman, tossed the remains of his rabbit into the fire. He was William's oldest and dearest friend. "Are we waxing poetic again?"

William put his plate of food down beside him, uneaten. "And if we are?"

Dan whistled. "Three nights in a row. That's a new record, isn't it?"

"Are we keeping a tally?"

The sound of Daniel's laughter drifted over the camp. "Not I . . . but perhaps I will consider it. What was it that you were quoting? It sounds familiar, but I cannot place it."

"Cervantes."

"Ahhh, *Don Quixote*."

A slight smile played about William's mouth for a split second, then it was gone, leaving behind only the hint that he had been close to something he seemed to have forgotten: humor. "A good guess. Are you familiar with any other works by Cervantes?"

Daniel laughed. "Come to think of it, no, but then you were always the scholar in school, not I."

William said nothing.

A few bites later, Festus dumped the remains of his food into the fire and stretched. "I will see to the horses." Another stretch and he walked toward the string of horses hobbled nearby.

Daniel watched Festus move around the horses. "Are you going to eat?"

William looked down at the plate beside him. "Later."

15

"If it makes you feel any better, I'm not particularly enamored with eating rabbit three times a day, either."

When Will remained silent, Dan frowned. "What is bothering you? You've been brooding for days."

Will was silent for a moment. Then he said, "I'm not sure, but I can't seem to shake this feeling I've had."

"What feeling is that?"

"Something is going to happen."

"You aren't getting morbid on me, are you?"

"No, I don't think so, but in a way, perhaps I am. You remember the night before Anthony was killed?"

"Of course. It isn't every day that one of my friends is killed in an avalanche. Is that what's eating at you? Anthony's death?"

"No, but remember how we sat around a fire, very much like this one, the night before he died? Anthony was despondent. He had been having the same dream every night . . . a dream that he was dying."

"And the next day he was killed. You aren't having dreams, are you? Like you are going to die?"

William did not answer.

"Well, if you are, that would be perfect, just perfect. Drag me along to this wild, godforsaken land and then die on me, leaving me here all alone, to fend for myself among a bunch of scalp-crazy savages."

16

William managed a wan smile. "No, I don't think I'm going to die, but something is going to happen. Something that will change my life."

"A perfect opportunity for me to recite the only quote I know. 'The readiness is all.' Shakespeare, I think, but don't ask me to tell you which play."

"*Hamlet.* 'There's a special providence in the fall of a sparrow. If it be now, 'tis not to come; if it be not to come, it will be now. . . . The readiness is all.' "

Daniel shook his head. "I have never understood your powers of recall."

Will heaved a copious sigh. "I can spout lines of poetry, but I cannot remember the last time I slept in a bed, or lay between a woman's legs."

"Now that I can remember . . . well, not the bed exactly, but the other is vivid in my mind."

"When was it, then?"

"A couple of weeks back. How about you?"

"I told you, I have no idea."

Dan seemed to mull that over in his mind a bit. "Well, to tell you the truth, I can't remember either." He groaned as he came to his feet. "I wonder if I'll ever become accustomed to sitting on the hard ground. After five minutes everything forgets how to function." He walked over to where William was sitting and clapped him on the back. "Cheer up, old chap. The way your life has been going, a change can mean only one thing."

"What?"

"That it's bound to get better."

William watched Dan walk away, then he turned his gaze back to the fire. He listened to the sounds of Dan settling down for the night. A few minutes later, he heard Dan sigh deeply and begin to snore.

How he envied Dan his ability to sleep, his nights free of the haunts of his past.

As the moon above drenched the world below in loneliness, Will picked up the sketchbook lying beside him and began to draw the angled lines of his boyhood home. Not the fashionable town-house on St. James Street, but the sprawling country estate in the Midlands. Emberly Hall, with its slate roof and walled gardens. He drew the ancient old oak that had branches enough for the six swings that belonged to him and his five siblings — his brother, James, and his four sisters; the two eldest, Marianne and Caroline, and the two younger than him, Elizabeth and Emily.

He turned the page again and sketched his mother, giving much lavish detail to the vividness of her eyes and the love and understanding he always found there, the fine lines around her mouth, the black hair that was turning gray in a becoming manner. He scooted closer to the fire, wanting to capture the last reflections of light upon his sketch pad. He quickly added a bunch of fine lace at her throat, shading the fullness of her lower lip.

Next, he found himself sketching his cousin, John Woodville, who was two years older than Will. John and Will were as close as brothers.

18

Brothers. The mere word seemed to pierce his heart. He thought about his only brother, James, the younger brother he had always looked after. James, laughing and announcing his betrothal to their childhood playmate, Lydia. James, the brother who lay in a shallow grave in the Crimea; the brother Will betrayed before his handsome, lifeless body was cold.

He tried to sketch James's face, but, as always, the pain got in the way. He could not bear the grief and the guilt, nor could he hold the memory for long without going mad. And so he tucked the vision away, dulling the pain with the driving need to paint.

In quick succession, he turned the pages, sketching his sisters, one by one, capturing the memories of them, the spark of life, the characteristics that were as familiar to him as his own: the exact placement of Caroline's mole to the left of her lip; the smallpox scar between Marianne's eyes; the widow's peak that was set off by the blackness of Elizabeth's hair; the mischievous smile on Emily's face.

Those completed, he turned the page to sketch the one person he had been avoiding: his father. For several minutes he stared down at the blankness of the paper, willing his father's likeness to appear there, feeling the same old mixture of pain and anger.

He slammed the sketchbook closed and pushed himself to his feet. He leaned over and picked up his plate of food, and with a quick movement, he tossed the joint of rabbit into the fire, watching a shower of sparks rise into the air accompanied by fierce popping.

Then he turned away and went into his tent, where he painted through the night, losing himself once again in the serenity of sunlit, golden plains.

CHAPTER
▦ TWO ▦

Margery . . . Margery . . . Margery . . .

The words haunted her — scattered bits of a lullaby, a song that surrounded her with the warmth of a mother's arms and a long-forgotten time, fragments of a part of her life she could not remember, secrets to her identity that came down twilight paths woven of countless threads; threads that shimmered just beyond her reach; brightly colored ribbons for which she would reach, trying to grasp one narrow streamer, one connection to who she was and from where she had come.

But as always, they were elusive, just beyond her grasp.

The moment she reached for them and had them in the palm of her hand, the voices would disappear; the bright colors of the ribbons would fade away, and she would wake, her heart pounding, her breath coming in short gasps, the answer she searched for no closer to her now than it had been on that day so long ago when it was sealed away.

Her eyes flew open. In a rush of rampant feeling, she could not, for a moment, remember where she was. Trancelike, she raised a hand to her forehead. She recalled the dream and wondered why it always ended the same way, without her knowing anything more than scattered images about the parents that had given birth to her: bodies without faces; voices without names . . .

She saw an old Indian woman watching her, and she remembered.

A short while later, Walks Fast perfumed her hair with bear's grease and sweet-smelling herbs and plaited it into two long braids. She took one last look around the tipi that had been her home. Old Grandmother, the Crow woman with whom she had lived for the past five years, asked her if she was afraid.

"I am not afraid," she answered, speaking the language of the Crow perfectly, "but I fear the unknown. I would rather stay here, with you." She glanced at the ancient-looking woman and felt the only human connection she had felt with an Indian since her captivity over twenty years ago. Old Grandmother was the only one who had been kind to her during her captivity.

How many changes had come into her life, how many transformations? And yet, she had survived each one. She learned at a young age that nothing in life was accomplished without a great deal of pain. She learned also that survival did not always outweigh that pain. She thought about the new life she was beginning and wondered what would happen to her now — not that it mattered, for there was nothing that could be done to her that had not already been done. She had paid the price. Only the pain of remembrance remained. For the third time, she was to be traded to another Indian tribe. This time it was the Mandan Sioux.

Old Grandmother took Walks Fast's face between her aged palms. "Do not be sad, and do not be afraid. You are a *bii'tsi*, a good woman. I have had a revelation and do not worry for you. In my vision I saw a woman with yellow hair being carried away by a great and powerful eagle."

"What does it mean?"

"Perhaps you will catch the eye of some handsome Mandan warrior and he will carry you away to a new life."

"And like the others, he will grow fearful of me and I will be traded again."

Outside the tent, a brave spoke, telling Old Grandmother the Mandan warriors had assembled. "They wish to see the captive."

Her heart began to pound, and Walks Fast suddenly felt terrified by the prospect of being traded again. Dread forced her to close her eyes for a moment, to concentrate on the uncertainty of her future. There had been many times like this in her life when she was called upon to sell her very soul in order to survive. She was nothing more than a thin shell, a lost soul; a body without a spirit, a heart without a beat . . . alive, but with no beginning . . . no family . . . no past.

Long ago, she learned to compromise, to give up that which was important to her in order to survive. Because of that, she had no knowledge of who she was or from where she had come.

Her identity was as lost to her as the family from whom she had been stolen twenty years ago.

Whenever she looked at her reflection in the river, nothing stared back.

"Do not worry," Old Grandmother was saying. "Some of our finest and most prized horses have been traded many times. Now, go. Two Leggings has come for you. Do not anger Many Coups by being late. He would not deal kindly with you if he were to lose face before the Mandans."

To honor Old Grandmother, Walks Fast did not cry, but held herself proudly as she lifted the flap of the tipi and stepped outside.

Two Leggings waited for her and she fell in step behind him. She watched the back of his head, not needing to see where she was going. She had made this trip many times and knew the way to the tipi of the chief, Many Coups.

Only today was different. Today she would not join in the celebration after the Crows finished trading with the Mandans. Today, when the Mandans left the Crow village, she would be going with them.

Once again, she would have to adapt.

Her torment was adaptability. It was also her strength, her saving grace. Part of her life had come to a close, and like the changing of seasons, a new life for her was beginning. Once again, she was calling upon her inner strength, her ability to change, to adapt — just as the coat of the varying

24

hare turned from summer brown to winter white when the time for snows came.

Once again she would have to submit.

The torment had begun. . . .

CHAPTER
❖ THREE ❖

William and his men rode away from the place where they had camped the previous night, leading the packhorses along the river, before turning east. When the sun was high in the sky, they came upon two men riding toward them. Even from this distance, William could see that one of the men was a gentleman; the other an Indian guide.

What in the name of hell is a gentleman doing out here?

The moment the strangers spotted William and his party, they spurred their horses forward and broke into a gallop. When they were just about even with William's party, one of the men called out. "I say there, one of you chaps wouldn't happen to know Viscount Linwood, would you?"

They pulled their horses to a stop, then Daniel and William exchanged glances. Dan leaned forward and crossed his arms over the horn of his saddle. "What business do you have with the viscount?"

"It is of a family nature," the older of the two men said. "Are you Viscount Linwood?"

"I am the viscount," William said.

"I am Sir Reginald Fitzwalter, and this is my guide, Joshua Dupree. I cannot tell you how delighted I am to find you, your lordship. Dupree and I have had a deuced difficult time locating you. We have been combing these bloody hills for weeks now."

"What brings you in search of me?"

The man reached inside his coat pocket and withdrew an envelope. "I have a letter from your father."

William did not take the letter. "What does it say?"

The man looked a bit taken aback, but he recovered quickly. "Your father is quite ill with lung fever. He wishes you to return to England immediately."

"And?"

The man's face grew dark red, his discomfort obvious. He offered the letter to William again. "It is all in the letter, your lordship."

"I prefer to have the news delivered in person."

Sir Reginald cleared his throat. "Your father says in his letter that it is high time you were married, and since you have not shown any inclination to do so before now, he has taken it upon himself to arrange the terms of your betrothal."

"I'll be damned," Daniel said.

William ignored that. "And if I choose not to return?"

Sir Reginald squirmed in his saddle. He cleared his throat again, careful not to look William in the eye. "He said that if you do not return to England, he will be forced to disinherit you. He further states that he will sell or give away every parcel of property and every last shilling of his money so that when you come into the title, you will inherit nothing."

"You may tell my father you found me and delivered the message." Will lifted the reins to turn his horse.

Sir Reginald cleared his throat then extended his hand. "Your letter, your lordship."

This time William took the letter, but he did not open it. Instead, he handed it to Daniel. "Put this in the pouch with my other papers, will you?"

Daniel nodded and took the envelope.

"Is there any message you would like me to take back to your father? Will your lordship be returning home? Shall I give him an estimated time of arrival?"

William did not say anything. He was overcome once again by the intensity of the ongoing conflict between him and his father. The same conflict that had caused him to leave England in the first place. Part of him wanted to tell Sir Reginald that he could take his letter and stuff it down his pompous throat. At the very least he wanted Sir Reginald to tell his father that he would never return to England. Yet another part of him, a gentler part he had thought lost, did not want to cause his mother and his sisters any more grief.

William found himself torn between his desire

to control his own life and his duty to his family and his title.

Since birth, he had been groomed to become the earl when the time came. He still believed in the system. And if he failed it, he would sink into oblivion. He sighed, cursing his indecision, which was nothing but a measure of his own imperfection. If he didn't heed the obligations of life, he was afraid he would sink into true debauchery.

"Have you reached a decision, your lordship? Will you be returning? What shall I tell the earl?"

"I will return, but at the time of my own choosing." William did not wait to see what Sir Reginald's reaction would be. He spurred his horse forward and rode off, leaving the members of his own party behind. He needed to feel the sun on his shoulders and the wind in his face. He had to know he was free.

If only for a little while.

CHAPTER
◉ FOUR ◉

Walks Fast followed Two Leggings into the circle
where the Mandan warriors had gathered. A low
murmur of voices arose from the group, but none
of them looked up when she approached.

ˇ The bartering had been going on for some time
now, for she could see that already many horses
had been traded. Upon the ground, the blankets
were spread with an array of handicrafts made by
the Crow, and many of the Mandan warriors were
already wearing finely made Crow breastplates.

She glanced at Two Leggings who indicated
where she should stand, and she took her place
with the respect she had been taught to display,
knowing well what would happen to her if she
did not. Silently she stood before them, her head
lowered in submission.

When the trading for war bonnets, leggings,
and moccasins was finished, Many Coups rose to
his feet. He did not look at her, but indicated by
a motion of his hand that Two Leggings was to
bring her forward.

Without hesitation, she followed him. Once she
reached the designated spot, Two Leggings

stepped back and she was left to stand alone. With a deep, indrawn breath that she did not exhale, she lifted her head and stared out at the group of Mandan warriors, not really looking at any of them, but fixing her gaze upon the earring of one brave. She did not listen as Many Coups spoke about a white captive who they had taken on a raid against the Cheyenne five years before, or how this captive had been taken by the Cheyenne, who had kidnapped her from the Comanche.

She had lived with many tribes, stolen like a valued commodity. But this was worse. Today, she would not be taken as a prize in a raid — she would be traded, as horses and blankets and moccasins were traded. She was no longer considered a prize but something disliked and feared, something to be discarded. She would be scorned and looked down upon.

The thought of more humiliation saddened her.

She did not hear what was said or what stories were told about her. She did not look at the Mandans to see what their reactions to Many Coups's words would be. As she had done many times before, she retreated into herself, into that private place that she could go where the pain and misfortune that had become her lot in life could not follow.

And for a moment, she knew peace.

After leaving Sir Reginald and his guide, William rode for half an hour before Daniel and the rest of the party caught up with him.

Reining in beside Will, Daniel slowed his horse to a pace that matched William's. "Do you still want to visit the Crow encampment?"

Will nodded. "Of course. Nothing has changed."

"What about your father? Are you going back?"

"I don't know. I haven't decided."

"Your father is ill."

"My father doesn't give a damn about me. He never has. Aside from wishing I had never been born in the first place, his greatest regret is that it wasn't me who was killed instead of James."

"Perhaps he doesn't feel that way now. Old age can change a man, you know."

"Not even you can color the truth enough to make it believable. Can you give me one reason why my father would suddenly care?"

"He is dying. He wants to see his title secure."

"He knows what he can do with his title."

"Will, by English law the title is yours, regardless of what you or your father want."

"I know that."

"Besides, I don't think you really want to thumb your nose at the title. I think there are still parts of you that are English to the core."

"Right again." Will looked at Daniel. "Now, if you are through playing the sage, done badly, I might add, can we continue on to the Crow encampment?"

Dan grinned and nodded. "After you, your lordship."

Will nudged his horse forward, moving into a

gallop. Dan rode beside him. Before long, they came upon a narrow ridge and paused. Below them, the Yellowstone curved around a bend, as crooked as a dog's hind leg. In the middle of the bend lay the Crow village.

There was much activity there today. Even from where he sat, William could see that the Crow were trading with a band of Mandan warriors. This would prove to be an added bonus, for now he could capture some of the trading scenes on paper and paint them later on.

Dan's horse snorted and began to paw the ground. "Are we going into the village?"

Will held his own horse in check. "No. I want to do some sketches from here first."

William was about to dismount so he could remove his sketch pad from his saddlebag, when he heard one of the French guides swear.

It was Pierre that said, "*Mon Dieu!* They are going to sell a squaw."

"I doubt it is a Crow squaw. I canna see them selling one of their own," Fergus said, riding up. "She is probably a captive they have taken in a raid."

The other guide, Etienne, looked at Pierre. "By all that's holy, I would swear the girl is white. Look at her hair. It's brown."

Fergus didn't bother to look. "I ken she may be a half-breed, then."

Daniel, who had looked at the squaw, glanced at Fergus and shook his head. "I doubt she is even that."

Hearing Daniel's words, William turned around and stared down at the scene below, watching dispassionately as a young woman was led forward to stand in front of the Mandan warriors.

Pierre reached out and put a hand on his arm. "Monsieur, she is white."

There was a time in his life when William might have cared, but that was a long time ago; a time when he cared about himself.

Daniel kicked his horse and rode closer. A moment later, William and the rest of the party followed, riding down to the place where Daniel waited.

"Will, I think Pierre may be right. She doesn't look Indian to me. She is taller, and there is something that marks her as different."

"The Crows are a handsome people."

"It isn't that . . . there is something . . . Oh, I don't know. Why don't we go in now? You can still get some impressive sketches there."

William nodded and the five of them rode across the river. As they approached the camp, William could see there was some sort of disagreement going on. Suddenly one of the Mandan warriors began shouting as he sprang to his feet and walked toward the girl.

Just as they reached the outer edge of the trading circle, his attention was drawn back to her. He watched as the Mandan warrior stopped in front of her. Suddenly the Indian reached out and grabbed her dress by the shoulder. He gave it a yank. The buckskin lacings gave way and the dress fell away from her body, baring her to the waist.

"Would you look at that," Pierre said breathlessly. "She is beautiful."

"She also happens to be white," Will said. He was about to turn his horse and ride off, when the girl lifted her head and looked right at him.

He was struck by the vividness of the green eyes staring out at him. The moment their gazes met, she glanced down and William saw the hauntingly proud carriage. He sensed the embarrassment she obviously felt. She was definitely white.

Something about that moment reached out to him, touching him in a way he could not explain. He felt as though he were standing there, feeling the humiliation, the shame. He was swept back to another place, another time, a time in England when his own future seemed every bit as bleak as this girl's. A time when he, too, knew humiliation and pain.

When the woman he loved chose money over him. When his father cursed the day he was born and blamed him for the death of his brother. "Buy her," William whispered.

Dan's head whipped around. "Buy her? Will, what are you saying?"

His voice was hard and flat. "You heard me. Buy her."

Dan looked back at the girl. "Think about what you are doing. The girl is more savage than white."

Fergus, who normally maintained his Scots tendency for not showing emotion, turned a stunned face to William as well. "You want to buy her?"

"Give them whatever they want for her." Without waiting to hear if anyone had anything further to say, Will turned his horse around and rode off.

Daniel spurred his mount forward and rode ahead, catching up with him.

"Will, you can't buy that girl."

"Why not?"

"What will we do with her?"

"We'll take her with us."

"Take her with us? Are you out of your mind?"

"Probably."

"Look, if it's a woman you want, we can camp out here for a few days and you can take care of that . . . urge . . . with her or with some other squaw. The Crows are very open about their sleeping arrangements, you know."

"I am not buying her for that."

"You're not? Then why? What do you intend to do with her?"

Will stopped his horse and turned to look Daniel in the eye. "I intend to marry her," he said. His impulsive reply surprised even himself, for in truth, Will had no idea from where the thought had come.

"Marry her! Good God above, Will! Have you taken leave of your senses? Why would you do this?"

The answer to that was suddenly clear in William's mind. "Maybe I'm doing it out of benevolence. The girl is obviously white. She deserves to be rescued. She deserves to be with her own kind. She deserves more of a future than she will have if we leave her behind. She is being sold, for God's sake, and I . . ." William stopped suddenly, the color draining from his face.

Suddenly, Dan's expression relaxed and his voice turned soft with understanding. "And you of all people know what it's like to be sold out, don't you?"

William said nothing.

"It's because of Bess, isn't it? You are doing this because of what happened with Bess."

"Bess was a long time ago."

"True, but you've never gotten over what happened."

"I've gotten over it. I never think of Bess anymore."

"Maybe not, but you think of what your father did. You think of how he went to her father and how he offered them money if she would marry someone else. You think of how they took your father's bribe, of how she loved the sound of your father's coin more than she loved you."

"I told you, I don't think about that anymore, and if you know what's good for you, you won't mention it again."

"I'm your friend, remember? I've known you since we were boys. I was there, Will. I saw what her rejection did to you. I was with you the night she married the blacksmith."

"And why shouldn't she marry a blacksmith? It was fitting, was it not? She was, after all, a lowly miller's daughter, and not, as my father said, 'the kind of girl a viscount should marry.' "

"You're pretending it doesn't mean anything to you."

"It was easy to forget."

"You can believe that if you want to, but don't try to make me believe it. I was there. I saw the way you reacted to the news that she had married. You went crazy."

"Only for a little while."

"Yes, after three others and I held you down until you returned to your senses."

"The point is, I did return to them."

"Only to turn around and try to drink yourself to death."

"Only for one night."

"You were never the same after that, Will. And then there was James . . ."

"I don't want to talk about my brother."

"Why not? It would do you a world of good. My God, you've grieved for years."

"You call coming here grieving?"

"I know why you left England, Will. You came to America to keep from doing something that would tear your family apart. It was either you or your father. If you didn't kill yourself, you would have killed him. I think your mother knew that. I think that's why she didn't try to stop you from leaving. She knew the demons that chased you. She knew you had to get away from England in order to save your soul."

"All of you can stop worrying about my wretched soul now. Whatever devils haunted me are long gone. I never think of it anymore. Bess has been married for five years and my brother has been dead for four. It's been a long time since I left home. Things have changed."

"Say what you will, but I know you. There's only one reason you want that girl."

Will turned in the saddle, his gaze locked on Dan in a way that said he had gone this far, so he might as well finish it. "Which is?"

"To get back at your father. I have to hand it to you. He sold you out, as sure as Judas took those thirty pieces of silver. I would have never thought there was anything you could do to equal that betrayal. I see now that I was wrong." Dan paused and looked out over the prairie. He shook his head. "God, to marry for revenge. I never thought you had it in you, Will. I never thought you did."

Will turned his horse away. "Go back and help Fergus. You are much better at bartering than you are at divination."

"It's your life." Daniel spurred his horse and galloped off.

Listening to the sound of his retreat, William thought about what Daniel had said.

Did he want the girl for the sole purpose of getting back at his father? Why marry her?

Part of him said he was doing it for altruistic reasons, out of sympathy. If he had to marry someone, why not her? At least, by doing this, he would be rescuing her. And he would be in control of his life. He was the one making the decisions, the one to make the choices he would have to live with. Not his father.

At last, he laid the turmoil to rest. He was doing the girl a tremendous favor by marrying her. He was saving her from a life no white woman should have to endure. She would be back among her own kind. He knew why he bought her. He didn't need Dan painting it with colors that were not there.

He turned his horse around and rode back. He wanted the girl. He had better go back, just to make certain they bought her. He did not want this bungled.

Well, what was wrong with helping them both out a little bit? It was bloody perfect, as far as he could see. He would marry the girl and take her to England, to his family, and show his father he could not live his life for him. The girl wouldn't suffer. As his wife, she would be provided for in a manner any woman would covet.

It was the perfect revenge, and all by accident. How he longed to see his father's face when he told him he couldn't marry the woman he had chosen for him, simply because he was already married.

How bloody perfect.

CHAPTER
◉ FIVE ◉

Walks Fast saw the Mandan warrior approach, saw his upraised hand. A moment later, she felt her dress being ripped from her body, then falling to her waist. A low murmur went up around the gathering of warriors.

She lowered her head in shame, feeling this was the worst degradation of all. She reached for the tattered remnant of buckskin, raising it to cover herself, but the warrior's hand shot out, capturing hers and shoving it back down. There was nothing she could do now. She had to wait, to suffer the pain, the ignominy, the shame she felt because it had to be this way. She had no choice. With this final humiliation came a sense of futility. Deprived of human dignity, she experienced her own annihilation.

Now that she had endured the stripping away of every sense and fiber of body, mind, and spirit, what else could they do to her?

She heard the sound of horses approaching and lifted her head to look over the heads of the warriors sitting in front of her. From a cloud of dust, five riders emerged. Five white men, coming

41

to witness her debasement.

They stopped a short distance away. She did not duck her head, nor close her eyes to spare herself further humiliation. There was something that prevented her from doing so. She stood before them, a captive filled with fear, self-loathing, guilt, and a death wish.

Her gaze locked with the hard stare of one in the group, and as she looked at him, she saw a man such as she had never seen before: whole, complete, and beautiful in his very creation — something of which she had no understanding, no part.

"There she stands, in all her beauty, the naked truth," one of the others said.

The one who exchanged glances with her said, "Keep your poetic utterances for later, Daniel."

"Sorry, Will," the one called Daniel said, then dismounted. He joined another man in his party and the two of them walked up to greet Many Coups.

Much discussion followed.

She could not hear everything that was said, but she heard enough to know they were bartering for her. Fear crept up her spine.

She knew why white men bought squaws.

It had been her good fortune that she was considered bad medicine by the Crow, a curse that made her undesirable for marriage. The whites, she knew, did not harbor such beliefs. If they bought her, she would be theirs for the taking.

She lifted her head higher, not wanting them

to see her fear. The man the others called Will did not join in the talks, but remained on his horse, his gaze fastened upon her. She told herself she would survive this, just as she had survived everything else. Without any choice, she stood before him, in her shroud of nudity, her nakedness on display.

Her humiliation was seen by everyone, and she found it strange that it was this fact that made her lift her head high. She had never felt such pride, until they sought to bring her low.

At last, the talking stopped, and the two men returned to the others. While they spoke, Many Coups raised his hands and said, "What the Comanches have taken from the whites, I give back."

It was over.

She pulled her dress up to cover herself. A man with red hair on his face rode forward, leading a string of six fine ponies. It would have been a good price for a bride.

It was unheard of to pay such a price for a captive squaw.

The one they called Dan came toward her. He put a blanket around her shoulders and motioned for her to follow. She went with him, following him to where the horses waited with two men she identified as French scouts. She knew this because it was quite common for French trappers to hunt in Crow territory, and often they would live in the village during the cold months.

After telling her to gather her belongings, Dan — who spoke the language of the Crow — led a horse forward and told her to mount up. He had light brown hair and his eyes were almost the same color. He looked at her with kind understanding.

There was neither kindness nor understanding in the eyes of the man called Will.

Turning her head away, she gave her attention to mounting her horse, finding it difficult, for the torn dress and the blanket she used to cover herself afforded her little freedom with her hands, but no one seemed to notice.

Following the men's lead, she turned her horse and went with them as they rode slowly out of the village; Dan and Will were in front, the red-bearded one riding beside her, the two French scouts behind. When they reached the rolling hump of a hill, she turned and took one last look back at the home she had known for five years. She wondered if she would ever be able to forgive the Crow for humiliating her. But even then, she realized, it was not so much her shame that would haunt her, but that *he* had seen it.

She heard Dan chuckle. When she looked at him, he said to Will, "She looks like she could eat your heart with garlic. What did we do to incur her wrath so soon?"

Will said nothing, but the red-bearded one spoke. "Breathe, more than likely. Her kind dinna need a reason to carve out a man's heart. Once a savage, always a savage."

Dan gave him a scolding look. "Now, Festus, you don't know that she was raised by Indians, although I am a mite curious as to how long she has been with them. Do you suppose she speaks any English?"

"I wouldna think so, but I ken there is a way to find out."

"How is that?"

"Ask her."

Dan shrugged. "Good idea." He turned toward her. "Do you speak English?"

She did not answer him. She continued to listen to what they said, for she had learned a long time ago that her survival depended more upon what she heard and learned than it did upon what she said. Keep quiet and you live longer.

Although these men were white and her own kind, she decided to behave the same way around them that she would have if it had been a Mandan warrior who had paid the price of six ponies for her. She would do as she was told. She would give them no cause to be displeased with her. At least not yet — not until she learned if they would beat her.

It did not take her long to realize that Will, the one who purchased her, was the leader of the group, for there was something of the chief in him, a confidence, an air that made him appear perfectly at ease commanding those around him. Still, she could not help wondering why he traded six fine ponies for her if his intention was to ignore her completely.

᷎ Perhaps that was confirmation that he did not intend for her to be his woman, which seemed reasonable, since he did not look at her as the warriors who desired her did. In fact, he did not seem to notice her much at all.

If not to warm his bed, then why had he purchased her? Perhaps he had taken pity on her because she was white and one of his own kind. That could only mean one thing . . . that he intended to give her freedom.

The thought of gaining her freedom caused her body to relax completely and she moved with the rhythm of the horse that carried her — something else that was new to her, for as a slave, she had never been allowed to ride when the camp was on the move. She walked, carrying a load, just as the horses and dogs did.

The two Frenchmen urged their mounts into a faster gait and rode around her. Soon they rode out of sight. She fell into a comfortable pace behind Will and Dan. Festus rode a short distance behind her. She knew now, after hearing him speak a time or two, that he was a Scot, for Scot trappers from the north often visited the Crow village almost as frequently as the French, speaking in that same soft manner of speech that this man had, a sound that had always been hauntingly comforting to her, although she did not know why.

Soon, she stopped thinking about her new owners, for the thought of gaining her freedom occupied her thoughts for most of their journey. She was quite taken by surprise when they stopped.

"We will camp here."

46

She looked up and saw it was Will who spoke. As he dismounted, she glanced at the sky and saw the sun had dropped lower. They had ridden much longer than she thought.

The two French scouts rode up just as Dan dismounted. While Will talked to them, Dan came back to where she waited on her horse. He motioned for her to get down, indicating they would water and rest the horses.

She nodded. Once she was down, she held her dress as she had before, with one hand, watching to see what he would do. Without a word to her, he turned and removed something from his saddle packs.

"Here," he said, tossing it at her, "put this on."

She caught the bundle and gave it a shake, realizing it was a dress. She held it up. The fine craftsmanship, the stitched decorations indicated it was of Crow design. It was a very beautiful dress, even by Crow standards, for it was decorated with many elk teeth and not the more common bone imitations. A dress such as this would cost much, and would only be worn by the daughter or wife of the most prominent warrior.

She had never owned anything so fine.

She rubbed the soft antelope skin with her fingers, her gaze searching the riverbank for a place to change.

He must have understood, for he smiled at her and said, "Go ahead and change. No one will bother you."

Unconsciously, she glanced at Will. He was

incredibly tall and slender, with hair as black as any Crow warrior. But the similarity stopped there, for his eyes were the color of the sky when the snows came, and the expression in them was just as cold. Self-conscious now, she ducked her head and tucked the dress under her arm before she slipped quietly away and made her way down to the river.

Before putting the dress on, she dipped her hands into the cool water and washed them, bringing a little water to her face. That done, she rebraided her hair, wanting to look her best in this fine dress. When she finished, she walked back to where the five men waited with the horses.

Only there were three men now, the two Frenchmen having ridden on ahead to scout. Festus was adjusting the pack on one of the horses. He glanced up as she passed by, then went back to what he was doing and said nothing, which did not surprise her. The Scot trappers that visited the village were not very talkative, quite unlike the French, who always had an abundance to say.

Suddenly, without any thought as to why she did it, she paused a moment. Festus turned his head to stare at her. How strange that the sight of this man was something familiar to her — not that she had ever seen him before, but that she had seen his ilk. She realized then that what she was feeling was loneliness, a sort of disconnection. She found it odd that, although the Crow were not her people or her friends, they were all that was familiar to her, while these men were of her own kind, and yet they were strangers — people who made her feel lost and afraid.

She was drawn to this Scot, she assumed, simply because she had seen many like him in the village. This small grasp of familiarity prompted her to overcome the silence she had vowed to maintain. "Do you speak the language of the Crow?"

He did not stop what he was doing. "I can speak it . . . when I have something to say."

Will and Dan suddenly stopped talking. Dan smiled. Yet, in spite of his friendly gesture, her gaze was drawn to the other man and a pair of eyes that regarded her in an cold, aloof manner. There was something about this one called Will that was compelling, and she stared at him, unable to look away, even though her pulse began to pound in alarm.

"You know," Dan said, "cleaned up and in a stylish dress, she wouldn't look too bad. She has nice features."

Impassive and aloof even to his friend, Will gave her a quick glance. "It would take more than a dress to get the savage out of her. Save for her skin and the color of her eyes, there is little of the civilized white in her."

"That isn't her fault, Will," Dan said, his expression as kind and soft as his words.

Will let out a sigh. "No, I suppose it isn't her fault. It's a pity she can't speak English. It would be interesting to hear how old she was when she was taken . . . how it all happened. I would imagine she would have quite a story to tell."

"If she was older when she was taken, then perhaps she will be able to recall some English."

Will studied her, allowing his gaze to move over her slowly, as if he could learn about her past simply by looking. "No, it's my guess she was taken when she was quite young."

"What makes you think that?"

"Have you ever known a woman who could speak that did not exercise that right to the fullest? Look at her, Dan. Observe her actions, the way she moves . . . Indian to the core. And there is the look in her eyes, wary; yet if you look just beneath the surface, you encounter a cunning fierceness, a will to survive." He glanced at his friend. "Poor Daniel, you never dig that deep, do you?"

The softness was gone from Dan's voice now. "No, I have a tendency to accept people on the basis of what they show me. I meet kindness with kindness, and in her case, fear with understanding. Why don't you try . . ."

"Putting myself in her moccasins?"

"Exactly."

"Perhaps I have. Perhaps that is why I bought her."

"Don't embellish on it, Will. You cannot embroider your actions with altruistic reasons. Not with me. We both know why you bought her, and if you cannot admit it, I can. You bought her for revenge."

"But that is not the point, is it? The reason why

is insignificant. What is important is how it will affect her. I have saved her from degradation and a life of slavery. She will live the life of a princess, well cared for and free from worry. You may be the kind-hearted one, but there is little doubt that you would have ridden on by and left her to her fate. Now tell me, which of us is the real bastard?"

"Perhaps leaving her to her fate would have been the kindest thing to do."

"I'm not convinced. She is white . . . savage, but white."

Dan turned back to the girl, searching her face. She looked back at him but gave no hint that she understood what they were saying.

At last, with a shake of his head, Dan said, "All I see is fear and uncertainty."

"Which will pass as soon as she realizes we mean her no harm."

"She is like a trapped animal, Will. A fish out of water. Leave her out too long, and she will die."

"Believe me when I say you have nothing to fear. She will evolve. I told you, the will to survive is in her eyes."

Dan looked at her again, then shook his head. "I don't have your artist's sensitivity. I don't reach my hand out to grasp things I cannot see. But I cannot help wondering if you would have bought her if she had been more white than Indian."

Will smiled. "You will never know the answer to that, will you?"

Dan shook his head again. "I have never been

able to understand you any more than I could understand how you could take a piece of canvas and a few paints and turn it into a living, breathing thing."

"And I have never been able to understand your levelheaded, analytical way of looking at things. Maybe that is why we have always been such good friends."

"Because we are so different?"

"Yes."

Dan laughed. "Then you better be careful, my friend. I cannot think of anything more different than the two of you," he said, nodding at the woman.

"Then, above all, it should be interesting."

She watched in silence as the two of them laughed. Then Dan slapped Will on the back as they turned away.

It was a good thing they did not look back. For if they had, they would have seen her fists clenched at her sides. Perhaps then they would have known that she spoke English.

CHAPTER
◈ SIX ◈

The man called Will had ridden completely out of sight before she realized she had not been set free, that she was expected to accompany them. Holding the pain of disappointment inside her, she mounted when Dan and Festus did, pretending for a moment to be one of them.

She often pretended to be someone else, someone with a past. A past was something she wondered if she would ever have. The yearning for it was always there, sometimes lolling around in the background, like a buffalo at a wallow, content and anxious to go nowhere. At other times it became more intense. It was something she felt every time a stranger rode into camp; each time she spotted evidence of the white man.

They rode for another hour, until they reached the place where they would set up camp. Excitement beat like tiny trapped wings in her heart.

Now he would tell her she was free. . . .

At last, she would go where she pleased, be whoever she wanted to be, able to find the family she had lost long ago.

As it often did, whenever she thought back to

that day, the present began to fade. She could hear the prophetic war cries and taste the dust of their ponies' hooves as a band of hawk-faced Comanches with black, braided hair and war feathers rode into her life and changed her destiny.

There was not much that she could recall; it had been over twenty years ago and she had been quite young. Mostly she remembered the fear: the fear of being separated from her mother, a woman for whom she could not find a face in her memories, but one she thought of as kind and soft-spoken.

The horror of what she had seen that day also remained vivid in her memory. The Comanches suddenly appeared out of nowhere. She had been unable to move and stood as if frozen, unable to scream or run. She could only stand there and watch what was happening around her, hearing the pitiful screams and the sound of tearing flesh, smelling blood and feeling the amazing warmth of it as it spurted across her face. She would never forget what she had seen: the smashed skulls, brains splattered on the walls, bellies ripped open as dead bodies were mutilated.

Even now, she could recall the smells, the sounds, the warm feel of blood, the dust settling upon her as the screams and moans began to fade away. How strange it was that these things stayed with her, while she could not remember anything that had happened before. It was as if the mutilation she had seen had somehow destroyed her own memory, the blood that was spilled covering the facts of her life before that moment. The only recollections of it she had now were vague snatches of shadowy faces and softly muted voices that came to her in the depths of sleep. And as always, whenever she awoke, the vision would fade away, like an eagle feather born upward on the wind, the melodious chant of a single word ringing in her ears.

Margery . . . Margery . . . Margery . . .

Her name.

All she had left of her past. Her only connection to a family that was lost to her. Her only proof that for a time, at least, she had been white.

She glanced down at the skin on her arms and saw the brown flesh, and she understood why the Mandan warrior had not believed the words of Many Coups when he claimed she was white until her dress had been ripped away from her flesh.

The sun had changed her white skin as surely as the Comanches, the Cheyenne, and the Crow had changed her life.

"We're here. You can get down now."

She looked up to see that Dan had spoken to her and realized then that she was still on her horse, when everyone else had dismounted. She slid to the ground, glancing at Will, looking, hoping for some indication that she was free to go, that the moment she had awaited for many years had come.

He looked at Dan when he spoke. "Tell her she can put her belongings down over there, then . . ." He stopped talking suddenly and turned toward her. "You speak English."

She did not know how he knew, but he did. She decided she did not want to risk his anger, for if angered, he might not set her free. "I speak English . . . and some French."

His dark brows raised to pointed arches. "English and French. Well, well, well. A literate savage. How bloody unusual."

He turned once again to his friend. "She is perfect, is she not? Look at her. So perfectly savage. So hopelessly dirty. And yet, she speaks two languages. . . ."

"Three," Dan said, "if you count Crow."

"Five," she said, "if you count Cheyenne and Comanche."

Will's gaze was back upon her. "I understand how you might have learned the Indian dialects, but how did you manage to learn French and English?"

"I have English from Father Marc Edouard. . . ."

"Who is?"

"Catholic . . . a priest."

"A French priest, out to save the heathen souls. Tell me, little savage, did he convert your heathen soul?"

"I am Christian."

He glanced at Dan. "A Christian savage. Full of surprises, isn't she?"

"If he was French, why did he teach you English?" Dan asked.

"So I would not lose the words of my fathers."

"You speak English, but I assume your French

is better?" Will asked.

She nodded. "I have spoken it more."

"How so?"

"I take many words from the French trappers who spent the long winters with us."

Will snorted. "I wonder what else she took from the trappers."

"Will . . ."

Will shrugged. He did not look at Dan, but he did soften his words when he spoke to her again. "Since it has already been established that you are white, do you remember your name?"

"Margery," she said, carefully pronouncing it Mar-gerr-y.

"Margery . . . Margery what?"

"I do not remember anything more. Only Margery."

"How old were you . . . when you were taken?"

She frowned, trying to remember. "I have twelve winters with the Comanches, four with the Cheyenne, and five with the Crows."

Daniel whistled. "Twenty-one years. Then she couldn't have been more than four or five because she looks to be somewhere between twenty and twenty-five to me."

"Twenty-seven," she repeated, the number sounding almost the same as when Father Marc had said it.

"Twenty-seven?" Dan sounded surprised. He looked at Will. "Did you hear that Will? Twenty-seven. That would make her born in 1830 and captured when she was six." He shook his head again. "Twenty-seven. She sure doesn't look it."

"Don't get overly ecstatic. I doubt if she knows how old she is. She probably just liked the sound of the word."

"Father Marc has written." She turned back to her horse and pulled her bundle down. Once it was on the ground, she opened it and took out a book. She started to hand it to William, then changed her mind.

She handed it to Daniel.

"A Bible," he said, turning it over in his hand. "How's your French, Will?"

"It's a French Bible?"

"Down to the last *bon mot*." He opened the Bible and read out loud. " 'Margery, child of God, baptized in the name of the Father, the Son, and the Holy Ghost, on this thirty-first day of August, 1851. Taken captive in the year of our Lord, 1836, by the Comanches, most probably in Texas. To the best of my ability, I have calculated her year of birth to be 1830. May God in his infinite mercy see fit to reunite this lost child of God with her family. God's servant, Father Marc Edouard.' "

Daniel was obviously touched by what he read, for he closed the Bible and stood silently.

Will was not moved in the least. "Baptized, were you? I suppose that makes you only half savage."

Dan looked distressed. "Will, don't."

"I am no savage. I am Christian!"

He did not seem to be paying her any attention. He took a canteen from his horse and tipped it back, drinking deeply.

She did not know what possessed her to speak up when she should have remained quiet. "God protects widows and orphans."

"A scripture-quoting savage . . . my, my, Father Marc was a busy old soul, wasn't he? Did he make Christians out of any of the other heathens, or were you the only one?"

"The others would not listen. He help me because I am white and an orphan."

"And God protects widows and orphans." He looked her over as if he were just now seeing her for the first time. "An orphan and a widow, hmm? Tell me, how many braves have you known, sweetheart?"

"Will, I don't think you should be talking to her like that."

Will shrugged. "Perhaps you are right, but if she is as old as we think, then it stands to reason that she isn't as pure as the driven snow. She admitted to being a widow, didn't she? So what's wrong if I ask her about it?"

"I am an orphan, not a widow," she said, poking herself in the chest.

Dan laughed. "You may have made a bargain with the devil, Will. This one seems to be holding her own with you."

Will ignored Dan's ribbing. "Tell me this, just how is it that you have reached the age of twenty-seven without being some brave's wife?"

"Walks Fast is bad medicine."

"Walks Fast is bad medicine." Will raised his

brows and glanced at Dan. "Now, why do I believe that?"

"Because it is always your nature to believe the worst."

"Why, thank you, dear loyal friend," Will said, then gave his attention back to Margery. "Where did you get a name like Walks Fast?"

"From the Crow warriors. Whenever they would try to talk to me, I would walk faster."

"How utterly clever. However, from here on out, you will not call yourself Walks Fast. If your Christian name is Margery, then use it."

"What do you mean, you are bad medicine?" Dan asked.

Margery went on to explain how the son of the Comanche chief wanted her for a wife, and how he was killed in battle the day they were supposed to marry. Considered bad medicine after that, she was distrusted and treated as a slave. "When spring came and the band went north, we were attacked by the Cheyenne."

"And you were taken by the Cheyenne?" Dan asked.

She nodded. "On the way to the Cheyenne camp, the warrior who captured me wanted to make me his woman."

Will, who had appeared uninterested up to this point, suddenly looked at her. "You mean he tried to rape you . . . to force himself on you."

"Yes."

"And what happened after he raped you?"

"He did not. I fought him and he tripped. He

fell over the side of a ravine, taking me with him. We rolled to the bottom. It was a long way. When we stopped rolling, I was dizzy, but I got up. The Cheyenne brave could not. His neck was broken."

"And you were bad medicine to the Cheyenne after that," Dan said. "What happened then? What did the Cheyenne do with you?"

"I was a slave to the Cheyenne. Four years after they took me from the Comanches, I was taken in a raid by the Crows."

"And obviously managed to get yourself considered bad medicine by them as well. What did you do this time?" he asked. "Kill someone?"

"After I come to live with the Crow, many in the village became sick. They said the big sickness came from me."

"Smallpox," Daniel said. "You did not take the sickness?"

Margery shook her head. "No, and because I did not have the sickness, I was blamed for causing it."

"And made a slave again," Dan said.

Margery looked down.

Dan leaned toward her and lifted her head. "You have nothing to fear from us. You will never be a slave again."

Her eyes burned. The lump in her throat seemed suddenly too large to swallow. She looked at Will, her eyes expectant, hopeful. "Then I am free to go?"

"I think not, little savage. I have other plans for you."

61

CHAPTER
 SEVEN

Will watched her walk off. He did not understand himself. He saw the look in her eyes and understood what she was thinking. Even if he hadn't bought her to set her free, he didn't have to reveal the awful truth to her in such a callous way. It was something he did not understand. Because he hurt, he hurt everyone around him. He felt like putting his hands on each side of his head and pressing until he crushed the devils that tormented him. He had abused someone innocent. He had used her to get back at his father. If he hadn't been so quick to rationalize, it would have been difficult for him to accept the truth of it. Ignoring the fact that he had used her, he focused instead on the fact that he had saved her. In his mind, one canceled out the other. But when he looked at Dan, he saw instantly that Dan did not see things the same way.

Dan's sarcasm didn't help. "How nice of you to bring yourself down to her level. I would have never thought of it."

"Down to her level? What do you mean?"

"I mean you've called her a savage so much

that you've become one yourself. You didn't have to crush her hopes. Obviously, she thought you bought her to give her freedom. Neither of us has any idea what it is like to be captive, to belong to someone and be their slave. Nor do we know what she has suffered all these years. I doubt there have been many things in her life to give her hope — and then, when something did, you ground it beneath your heel like a worthless insect."

"All right, so I'm a bastard."

"Of the first water." With a curse, Dan turned and walked away.

For some time after his friend had gone, Will stood there, watching Festus start the fire, wondering how he had lost control of the situation.

He went to unsaddle his horse. The gelding blew softly through its nostrils in recognition and Will scratched him behind the ears. Over the gelding's broad back, he saw that Dan was talking to the girl. He realized he had called her a girl again, and he vowed to use her Christian name from here on out. Margery, he said in his mind, remembering the way she pronounced it, Margerr-y.

Margery . . . Somehow the name did not fit the Indian woman he saw talking to his best friend. Margery was a civilized name. The woman was not civilized. He shook his head. No, a buckskin-clad Indian didn't look like she should be called Margery, but neither did she look like someone who would become the bride of a titled Englishman.

He folded his hands over the gelding's back and wondered if he should simplify things and walk over to where the two of them stood and tell her to mount up, that she was free to go. Hell, there were other ways to gall that bastard that he called Father besides hauling her arse back to England with him.

All right, I'll let her go, he told himself. How strange it was that he could not remember the last time he had had a twinge of benevolence.

He unsaddled the bay, then hobbled him before he picked up his saddle and heaved it over his shoulder. He started walking toward them, his mind swimming with thoughts. If he was going to set her free, then he supposed he should send her off to her first taste of freedom with a little money in her pocket.

Neither of them glanced his way when he dropped his saddle at the spot where he had rolled out his bed earlier. He hunched over the saddle-bags, then reached inside, intending to get his money pouch.

Instead, his hand touched paper and he froze. He knew what it was, even before he looked at it: the letter from his father. The summons. The paternal decree that he was to marry the woman of his father's choosing.

Whatever milk of human kindness that had been flowing in his veins chilled to an icy resolve. It all came back to him in a mad rush . . . the reason why he had decided to marry her in the first place.

He reminded himself that she might have been born a white, but she was raised Indian. She knew nothing about the ways of civilization. A woman like her would never survive on her own, not even with a little money. She wouldn't be accepted by polite society, and God knew what happened to a woman scorned, especially if she was pretty. She would find herself used by one man and then another, treated no better than a squaw or a half-breed, and once she was flat on her back, it was likely she would stay there — until she was too old, or too fat, or too ugly to be used anymore. It might be cruel not to give her the freedom she wanted, but in his mind, it was worse to turn her loose.

With a tightly clenched jaw, and resolve that was just as firm, he called out to Festus. "Pack everything up good and tight tonight. We break camp tomorrow."

Festus, as usual, showed no surprise. "Where do we go now?"

Pierre and Etienne stopped talking and looked at him. "St. Louis, I think."

He saw that Dan was watching him as well. Well hell, let him look. William had bought the girl, not Daniel. That meant she belonged to him. And that meant she was his to do with as he saw fit.

He was saving her, wasn't he? It would have to be enough.

When the two scouts resumed talking, Will called out to them. "Do you two Frenchies think you can find your way back to St. Louis?"

Pierre grinned. "*Oui,* monsieur. The way back is ever easier. When do we go?"

"Tomorrow morning. Early."

Pierre did not say anything, but his questioning glance flicked over to the girl.

"Naturally, she goes with us," Will said, not looking at Dan, yet feeling the prick of his disapproval.

Winter blew in the day they left, howling down from the mountains, driving snow flurries against them like icy fingers that seemed to serve as a preview of what was to come. Three days out of Crow territory, the first snowfall hit, freezing their hides and slowing their pace so that it took them three cold, miserable weeks to reach St. Louis.

It took only five minutes to make Margery William's wife.

When it was done, when the ceremony was over, she stood quietly beside him and he could not help wondering if she understood what it meant to be married. Well, enough of that, he thought. It was married he wanted to be, and married he was; where there had been one, there were two, and he had never felt more heartsick, more lonely, more loathsome in his life. He had bought another human being, made her his wife, and now he felt guilty as hell. But it was something he was driven to do, by a force even he did not understand. He could only ease the guilt and the pain of it by convincing himself that he had saved her from a worse fate at the hands of a Mandan warrior.

He turned his head slightly and looked down at her standing quietly, submissively at his side. His wife.

What in the name of all that is holy had he done?

The minister, a sleepy Methodist, aroused from the depths of slumber, looked at him. "You may kiss the bride."

As if sensing his gaze upon her she lifted her head and looked at him, uncertainty written in her eyes. It was obvious she did not know what to do.

And neither did he.

He stood there for a minute, thinking about his next action. The sparsely furnished room where they had assembled was small and way too warm. The clock ticking on the mantel sounded cheap and loud. He looked around him, seeing the expectant faces of Festus and Daniel and knowing they were waiting.

You may kiss the bride. . . .

He wondered if she understood what the preacher was saying. Her upturned face was filled with anticipation. Surely to God she didn't think he denied her freedom and married her because he had any feeling for her? Did he look like the kind of idiot who fell in love from the first sight of a woman? Maybe that isn't what she's thinking. But why else would she be looking at him like he had just walked on water? This won't do, Will.

You can't have her falling in love with you. . . .

How could he make her understand that this was nothing more than a business arrangement, that he was giving her far more than she could ever hope to have — wealth, prestige, a title, and what most married women would give their finest jewels for, a husband who did not assert his conjugal rights. And all he asked from her was her hand in marriage. Just her hand. Nothing more. He had no intention of ever touching the rest of her.

"Uh-hum!" The minister cleared his throat and Will knew he was the kind that had one way of doing things, and his way of doing a wedding was to finish up with the groom kissing the bride. He would probably stand there, waiting all day, if need be.

More to give himself time to think than for any other reason, Will leaned forward, his hands going to lightly grip her upper arms as he drew her against him. He brushed her lips with a chaste kiss.

When he looked at her again, he knew she did not understand, but she was smart enough to know something about this marriage wasn't going right. He saw the infatuated look fade to one of confusion.

Well hell, better confused than infatuated.

For some time, she simply stood there watching him, her expression one of blank surprise. Slowly, she lifted her hand and touched her lips with her fingers.

Oddly, he found that unconscious move endearing.

If she hadn't been such a grimy little savage, he might have considered doing more than kissing her. Of course, it was his fault that she had not been given time to take a bath or clean up, but then, he wasn't so certain that she would have known how to truly bathe, even if she had been given the time. The English version of cleanliness and a frequent bath were not, as yet, part of her code. It was something else he would have to teach her.

But then he remembered his father and decided he liked her better for the role he intended if she remained a dirty little savage — at least until he got her to England. Once he was gone, his family could have the pleasure of civilizing her.

"Congratulations!" Dan said in a voice so cheerful, Will wanted to punch him. "Well, now you're a married man. How does it feel?"

Will scowled. "How do you think it feels?"

"Since I did not understand the purpose of the wedding in the first place, I couldn't even begin to venture a guess. However, I do wish you and your viscountess a long and blissful married life."

"Go to hell, Daniel."

"Ah-hem!"

"Pardon me," Will said, looking back at the reverend, Mr. Pettigrew. Will took the money out of his pocket and handed it to the reverend. "Thank you for your services. I do apologize for waking you up this time of night."

"Morning," Reverend Pettigrew said. "It is half past five."

"Right," said Will, glancing toward the dark window. "We will be on our way then."

"Just a moment," the reverend said, walking to his desk, where he sat down. He picked up his pen and dipped it in the inkwell, then began to scratch his way across a sheet of paper. When he finished, he stood, blowing on the paper to dry it. Apparently satisfied the ink was set, he crossed the room and handed the document to Will. "You might have need of this."

Will looked down at the paper.

"Go on. You better take it. It's your marriage certificate . . . proof that the union is legal and binding."

Will took the certificate and put it into his pocket. He looked at no one in particular as he said, "We'll be on our way now."

He led his companions away from the minister's home, Margery falling in behind him in the customary squaw fashion. Once they were outside, they mounted their horses and rode up the street.

When they reached the Lewis and Clark Hotel, Dan dismounted. "Want me to get us a room?" he asked. His gaze drifted over to where Margery sat quietly upon her horse. "Er . . . a couple of rooms?"

"No. I'll take care of it. I told Festus and the Frenchies that I would leave envelopes with their money here in the hotel safe. I'll do that now, before I forget."

"I guess I'll wait here, then," Dan said as Will dismounted and walked off.

Will got three rooms . . . one for himself, one for Daniel, and one for Margery. As he walked back outside to where they waited, he wondered if Daniel would go and stick his nose in this, for Will knew Dan would make some comment about his decision to rent three rooms. Sticking his nose into Will's business is all Dan seemed to be doing of late, calling his hand on every decision he made concerning Margery and doing his deuced best to make him feel guilty.

And he would be doing it again, just as soon as he learned Will rented three rooms. Well hell! Daniel didn't expect him to sleep with her, did he?

Will was about to open the hotel door when he suddenly jerked to a complete stop. It had just occurred to him that he could not take her to England and leave her with his family if the marriage was not consummated.

The first thing his father would do would be to have the marriage annulled, and then, as always, Charles would be in control of Will's life, having the last word.

He shoved the door open and walked inside. A few minutes later he returned. Margery was still on her horse. Dan was standing beside her as they talked quietly.

Will looked from one to the other. It amazed him. It really did. Whenever he was around her, she hardly said a word, but the moment his back was turned, she and Dan put their heads together and chatted amicably, like a couple of old maids.

"Did they have any rooms?" Dan asked.

"Tonight, that pretty head of yours will have a pillow to rest upon."

"I can forgo the pillow, as long as I have a bed."

"They threw that in with the pillow."

Dan raised a questioning brow and glanced down at Margery.

Will tossed him the key to his room. "This will open the doors to paradise," he said. "You have some time to catch up on your sleep. Two days from now a steamer leaves for New Orleans. I plan to be on it."

Dan's amused expression drifted over to Margery. "In a hurry, are we?"

Will ignored him and walked around to where Margery waited upon her horse. He intended to help her, but when she saw him coming toward her, she slipped down off the horse herself.

"It's the end of the journey," he said to her. "Now it's time to show you your first bed in over twenty years. It will be interesting to see if you remember what it's for."

"It will be even more interesting to see if you remember," Dan said, stepping aside to let them pass.

CHAPTER
❋ EIGHT ❋

"Bed."

Will watched the way her mouth formed the word. He noticed once again that there was something enchanting about her in spite of her dirty state and her savage background. Perhaps it was her innocence, for it was rather nice to see things he thought of as commonplace through her eyes. He pushed away the thought. She was ignorant, not innocent.

"Bed," she said again, and he could tell by the expression on her face that she was trying to recall the memory to go with the word. He saw the light in her eyes fade to disappointment. He had not thought before of how it must feel to search for part of your past and not find it.

Well hell, she doesn't know how lucky she is. If only I could lose my past. . . .

He unlocked the door to her room and they walked inside. She paused and looked around, her eyes as big as the sun that was just rising on the horizon. He knew she was searching for something that she recognized, something that went with the word *bed*.

He felt her disappointment and knew how strange all of this must seem to her. Being inside a room again seemed a bit peculiar to him, too. "Just think of it as a big tipi." He walked to the bed and sat down, bouncing a little. "This is a bed. You sleep on it. Do you remember sleeping in a bed?"

She shook her head. "No."

"Come here."

She gave him a suspicious look, took three steps toward him, then stopped.

"I'm not going to ravish you." He could tell by the expression on her face that she did not comprehend the word *ravish*. That was understandable. He doubted there was such a word in the sanctimonious Father Marc's vocabulary. "You are as safe with me as you are with Daniel."

"Daniel is very kind."

"And I am not?"

"I do not know. I have seen no proof of it. . . ."

She was an outspoken little savage, he had to hand her that. So, Daniel is kind.

Well hell. He was not about to be outdone by Daniel, not if he had to get down on all fours and crawl around like an infant. "Be that as it may, I am trying to be nice now. Come here. I want to show you what you've been missing."

She came closer, clutching her bundle to her chest, and stopped next to the bed. She was standing beside him and he noticed she eyed him and the bed with the same sort of wariness.

He patted the mattress. "Sit down."

She did not move but stood looking suspiciously at the bed.

"Go ahead. Sit down. It isn't a horse. It won't throw you."

She sat down stiffly beside him, still clutching her belongings.

"Here," he said, and took the bundle from her. He tossed it on a nearby chair. "Now, watch." He bounced up and down a few times.

Her eyes followed him . . . up . . . down . . . up . . . down. . . .

"You try it."

She smiled and her face seemed to transform itself. Her eyes sparkled. How childlike she was, how utterly innocent. How deliciously dirty.

He almost regretted having to leave her in England. Given other circumstances, he might have enjoyed teaching her things. God! How he would love to paint her right now, to capture for all time that wide-eyed look of wonder upon her face.

"Go ahead. Try it." He bounced a few more times.

She raised herself up and sat down quickly.

He heard her indrawn breath, the way she released it with a gasp.

"That's it. A little higher this time."

She bounced again, raising herself higher, just like he said. She bounced again. And then again.

Soon laughter spilled from her in a musical rhythm he found he enjoyed. Strange. He knew he had heard women laugh before, and yet he could not remember ever having noticed.

She was standing on the bed now.

How fresh she was. How untainted. He could not imagine any woman in the whole of England finding so much pleasure in jumping on a bed. Show them a mattress and their thoughts went off in another direction entirely.

He would never understand why he did it — and he, a grown man who knew better. Perhaps it was because she lost her balance and bounced down on her fanny instead of her feet. And when she did, her startled expression was almost his undoing.

She blinked her eyes then opened them wide as she stared at him in utter amazement. He could not help himself. He started laughing and the next thing he knew, she was on her feet again, holding her hand out for him to join her. He climbed onto the bed with her to prove that he could be just as nice as Daniel.

But I sure as hell won't jump. . . .

Instead, he leaned against the wall, his arms crossed in front of him.

He learned one thing about beds, though: when two people are standing on a bed, and one of them jumps, they both go up in the air. Soon, she was bouncing in earnest, and he was bobbing along, trying to maintain his dignified pose, in spite of himself. She was laughing, and he wondered how long it had been since she had enjoyed herself like this.

He also learned something else: laughter is contagious. He found himself smiling along with her.

Suddenly, she bounced higher than she had before, and when she came down, she bounced against him. Both of them were knocked to the edge of the bed. Will landed flat on his back.

She bounced once more, then disappeared over the side.

He rolled over and peered over the side of the bed.

Margery was sprawled on the floor, rubbing her posterior. "You lied to me."

He blinked down at her like a drowsy owl. Lie? Him?

"You said it would not throw me."

He opened his mouth to respond to that when her hand lashed out and grabbed him by the collar. The next thing he knew, she had yanked him off the bed as if he didn't weigh more than two stone.

He landed with a thud, hitting his shoulder. Damnation! What had he married? A wrestler?

He noticed then that she was sitting up, looking down at him and laughing. Daniel was right. Cleaned up, she wouldn't be bad looking.

"Oh, you think it's funny, do you?" He grabbed her arms and rolled her over, pinning her body to the floor with his own. The action caused a very powerful reaction. She might look like a savage, but beneath him, she felt like a woman. All woman. And it had been a long, long time since he had been with one.

Well hell. Why not? She is my wife, he reminded himself. He looked down at her face, seeing the way her eyes sparkled, the bloom of color on her cheeks.

He lowered his head and was about to kiss her, greasy hair and all, when suddenly the door crashed open.

"Pardon the intrusion, but I heard a terrible commotion and thought I'd come and see if you were . . ." As he spoke, Daniel stuck his head around the door and froze.

He seemed to gain control of himself mighty fast. He looked first at one and then at the other. "Apparently she did not like the bed," he said dryly.

Will did not bother to hide his irritation. "What are you doing in here?"

Daniel grinned. "I thought you were in here alone. When I heard the noise, I assumed you might have encountered some difficulties . . . a thief, perhaps." He paused, humor dancing in his eyes. "Tell me, was she showing you the way to do it Indian fashion, or were you trying to impress her by showing her just how much endurance your elbows have?"

Will looked down and saw he was on his elbows with Margery lying quietly beneath him. She had an impish look on her face, as if she knew what was going on.

"Don't say a word," Will said, and rolled away from her.

Margery came to her feet, then said to Dan, "We were on the bed."

"Were you now? Was it fun?"

"Oh, yes. It was magic."

"Magic?" He arched a brow and looked at Will. "Seducing her with wizardry, were you? What did you have up your . . . er . . . sleeve? A magic wand?"

"Don't try to be funny, because you aren't."

"Well, not to worry. You are funny enough for both of us. Bouncing on the bed . . . at your age. I cannot wait until the lads in London hear about this."

Luckily for him, Daniel had the forethought to duck behind the door and close it at just that instant. Had he hesitated a moment longer, he would have gotten a pitcher of water in his face.

As it was, the pitcher crashed against the door. Water and shards of pottery flew about the room.

The spell was broken.

Without thinking, Margery bent down and picked up one of the bits of broken pottery.

"Don't!" Will shouted. "It's sharp. You'll cut yourself."

She jumped at his shout, instinctively clenching her fist. He saw the flash of pain in her eyes and he knew what she had done.

"Well hell!" He walked to her.

She had opened her palm and was staring down at her hand. Already it was covered in blood. He removed the jagged piece of pottery, then turned back to the table and grabbed a towel. He wrapped it around her hand.

"Sit down. I'll be right back."

She did as she was told while Will hurried

toward the door, kicking shards of pottery out of the way as he went. He reached Dan's room and knocked on the door. When it opened, Will's words came out in a rush. "Find a doctor. She's cut her hand."

"Bad?"

"Bad enough to need a doctor. Now stop talking, or she'll bleed to death and then we won't need the doctor."

Luckily, Dan hadn't undressed, so he took off at a dead run across the hallway, then disappeared down the stairs.

Will walked back into the room. Margery was sitting on the bed.

Sitting on the bed? Good God above! A woman who did what you asked? A man could grow accustomed to that, just as he could grow accustomed to those eyes so full of wonder, that face looking up at him with a touch of adoration.

"Keep the towel on it and press down on the cut. It will help slow the bleeding."

"It does not hurt."

"Give it time. It will hurt like hell tomorrow."

She watched him quietly, then made a move to get up.

"Where do you think you are going?"

"My bundle . . . inside I have my medicines."

"Oh no, you aren't going to filthy it up with a bunch of native herbs, buffalo dung, and God knows what."

"It was given to me by Batce Baxbe."

"Who is that?"

She frowned, as if trying to remember something. "In English, he is called medicine man."

He had a fine picture of that . . . a primitive man in a savage costume, brandishing a buffalo-tail rattle and feathers as he muttered, grunted, and chanted, jumping over the fire and throwing gunpowder into it.

"Keep the medicine bundle to show to your grandchildren. The doctor will be here soon."

Not more than five minutes passed before Daniel opened the door and ushered in a tall, thin man with two fuzzy gray tufts of hair.

"This is Dr. Ellory," Dan said.

Seeing Margery, Dr. Ellory gave a start. Obviously he was surprised to see an Indian, and for a moment Will wondered if he would see to her hand without him having to hold a pistol to his head. But then Dr. Ellory's gaze dropped down to the bloody towel in her hand and the healer in him seemed to overcome his prejudices.

"Let me see what we have here," he said, and crossed the room to where Margery waited. He put his bag down beside her on the bed.

She held out her hand. "It is a big cut. Much blood."

Dr. Ellory glanced at Will. "She speaks good English."

"Of course she does. She is white." Will was surprised at his own defensiveness.

He wondered if anyone else had noticed. He cast a quick glance in Dan's direction. Well hell! There stood Daniel, grinning like an idiot.

"My, my. This is a nasty cut. I'm afraid I'll have to take stitches." Dr. Ellory opened his bag and removed a bottle of laudanum. "Give her a couple of swallows of this. It will ease the pain."

Will took the bottle and unscrewed the lid. He put the bottle to her lips.

She turned her head away.

"You have to drink this."

She shook her head.

"Come on. Take two swallows. That's all."

She shook her head. "No."

"You need to drink it. It will stop the pain. The doctor must sew up the wound."

She nodded as if she understood.

Will saw Dan's frown. Well hell! What was it that he had thought a short while ago about a woman that did as she was told?

He took a deep breath and tried again. "You don't understand," he said. "It will make you feel better. You won't feel anything. You will get sleepy and when you wake up, the doctor will be finished and your hand will be on the mend."

She looked at him with an expression that was quite understanding and sincere. "I understand. He will sew my hand, as I sew a buffalo robe." She turned toward the doctor. "Sew it. Now, please."

Will put the bottle to her lips. She turned her head away. "I do not want the sleeping medicine." She lifted her hand and thrust it toward Dr. Ellory. "Sew it now. It is not good for so much blood to be lost."

Dr. Ellory looked at Will.

Not knowing what else to do, Will shrugged. "You heard her. Sew it."

Dan stepped forward. "Will, you can't mean . . ."

Will held up a hand. "Relax. I have a feeling she will change her mind soon enough."

He kept the bottle close by, while Dr. Ellory cleaned the wound. The doctor was surprised she did not change her mind when he poured the antiseptic. The stuff burned like fire, he knew.

Will gritted his teeth as he watched Dr. Ellory begin to stitch the deep cut. He pushed the needle through the torn skin.

Will uncorked the bottle of laudanum and took a sip.

"Let me have some of that," Dan said.

Will handed him the bottle.

Dan took a healthy gulp.

Ten times Dr. Ellory stuck the needle into one side of her raw flesh and ten times into the other side, drawing the thread tight to pull the skin together.

Not once did she cry out, or even flinch.

From time to time, Will would glance at her face. He could see the pain in her eyes, but she never shed one tear. If that had been Will, he would have polished off the whole damn bottle of laudanum and still be howling his head off.

When Dr. Ellory finished, he wrapped her hand. "Leave this on. Whenever you bathe, you may wash it with soap and water, then put a clean linen back on. In a few days take off the bandage and let the wound dry out. I will need to remove the stitches in one week."

"We are going to New Orleans tomorrow," Will said. "I will have them removed there."

Dr. Ellory snapped his bag shut, then stood. "She is a remarkable young woman. I have never seen anyone, not even the toughest man, with her tolerance for pain." He looked at her and shook his head. "Remarkable. Quite remarkable."

Will handed him five dollars.

"This is way too much."

"Keep it. Who knows? We may need you again."

Dr. Ellory thanked him and departed.

When he was gone, Will looked from Margery to Dan. "Makes you feel like you're not the man you thought you were, doesn't it? Ten stitches and nary a peep out of her."

"I have had worse wounds," she said.

Dan and Will almost bumped heads turning to look at her.

"Worse?" they asked in unison.

She nodded. "I was cut by a wounded buffalo."

Dan asked, "You mean you were gored by a buffalo?"

She nodded.

"Where?" As soon as he said the words, Will knew he had made a mistake.

A big mistake.

Before he could stop her, Margery stood and pulled her dress up. She showed them a long scar that ran from the side of her left knee up almost to her waist.

It was a nasty scar, but Will hardly noticed it.

What he did notice was that beneath her buckskin dress, she was completely naked. Naked and quite beautiful.

He heard Dan gasp. "My God!"

Will looked at Dan, who, in true gentlemanly fashion, had turned his head away.

Neither of them saw anything but her bare leg and hip, but it was more than enough for Will. He whipped his hand out and grabbed her dress, yanking it down. "The first thing you must learn is not to display parts of your body to others."

"You are unhappy with me?"

"Yes, you damn well better believe I am, and if you ever do that again, I'll tan your backside until you can't walk for a week. I'm just thankful it was Dan that was with me and not some lecherous stranger. That," he said, "is a good way to get yourself raped, and my skull split open."

Margery sat down on the bed and burst into tears.

Stupefied, Will and Dan looked at each other.

Dan, for once, was at a complete loss for words.

"Well hell!" Will said. "I don't believe this." He threw up his arms and began pacing the floor. "She sits through ten stitches as calm as a widow's bed, and then when I tell her to keep her dress down, she starts crying. Women! Who can understand them?"

Dan chuckled. "Not you, apparently."

"Oh, and I suppose you can?"

"I can understand this one."

Will looked from Dan to Margery, then back to Dan. "I need a drink."

"That sounds like a grand idea to me," his friend replied.

Will put his hand on Margery's shoulder. "Dan and I are going downstairs for a bit. Will you be all right?"

She sniffed and nodded. "I am tired. I would like to sleep."

"Lock the door when we've gone, and don't leave the room."

She followed them to the door.

They waited until they heard the lock click, then they turned and walked down the hall.

"You really understood why she was crying?" Will asked.

"Only an idiot wouldn't."

Will didn't say a word.

Dan paused. "You don't mean to say you didn't understand?"

"Of course I understood. I just wanted to be sure you did."

Dan didn't say anything.

Will stole a quick look at him out of the corner of his eye. *If he laughs, I'll bust his nose.*

Dan, thankfully, had the gumption to remain silent.

CHAPTER
 NINE

The dreams visited her again that night. At first there was only the golden warmth of a sunny summer day, the musical lilt of voices, someone's laughter reaching out to her from far away. She stirred in her bed and moaned something in her sleep. The sun's warmth touched her, filling her with a drowsy sort of ennui. She heard the flapping of wings and looked up to see a giant eagle fly overhead, casting its shadow to the ground, blocking out the sun's warmth and light.

The world turned suddenly cold and barren, filled with shapes and faces that had no eyes. Through the darkness came a dozen arms, long and groping, grasping the air, searching and feeling, and she knew they searched for her. She could hear her voice cry out, "I'm here! Mama . . . Papa . . . I am here! Come and get me!"

But they did not come, and the image began to fade, turning gray, a thick mist that shimmered before a great source of light. From out of the lightness of fog a shadow emerged. Fearful, Margery whimpered in her sleep. Soft and warm was the touch of a loving hand that reached out to stroke her face. *Hush ye, hush ye, little pet ye. . . . Hush ye, hush ye, do not fret ye. . . . The Black Douglas shall not get ye. . . .*

The whimpering subsided, the eagle overhead flew on, and the darkness began to vanish. Margery felt the warmth of the sunlight upon her face once more. She reached up to touch the hand that caressed her cheek with such loving care, but when she tried to grasp it, the hand was gone. Only the faintest grayness of a hovering shadow remained, growing dim and dimmer still, until at last, it began to fade away.

"Nooooo," she screamed. "Come back! Don't go, Mama. Don't let them take me away."

She sat up abruptly and lifted her hand to her head, where a swift and violent pounding made her close her eyes for a moment. She heard noises . . . the click of a key turning in the lock, the creak of the door as it opened, the soft tread of silent feet as they crossed the room. The bed sagged under a burden of weight.

She opened her eyes. William was sitting beside her, his arm around her shoulders, a look of concern etched upon his face. "What is it? What happened? Were you frightened of something . . . or was it a dream?"

She looked at him, feeling a bit groggy. "Dream."

"Everything is fine now. Lie down and try to get some sleep."

She lay back, clutching the covers tightly over her breasts. "You won't leave me?"

He smiled at her and brought his hand up to stroke her face. She leaned into the warm reassurance of his touch. "I will stay here with you, until you fall asleep."

She closed her eyes. "I shall sleep then, for I trust you."

Her eyes were closed and she drifted off to sleep, having no way of knowing William stayed beside her until morning, a look of regret upon his face.

The throbbing in her hand woke her and Margery opened her eyes to a dull gray day. For some time, she lay in the soft bed, listening to the familiar sound of rain in unfamiliar surroundings.

This was nothing like the inside of a big tipi where the rain pelted the buffalo robes with a soft thump. Here, the sound was much louder, a *ping* . . . *ping* . . . *ping* . . . that tapped against the window glass, a reminder that her life would never be the same.

She looked around the room, seeing strange pieces of wood, not having a name for any of them, save the word *bed*, which she found to be a rather short word for something in which one spent such a long amount of time.

A strange thing, this bed.

Yesterday, it was an object of much laughter and joy, a place to bounce and enjoy life with another. Last night, it had been a place of refuge, a place to lay her head, to close her eyes and dream. Today, it was a place of sorrow and sadness, a place to lie and think in silence and solitude.

Someone knocked on the door and she gave a start.

"Margery?"

It was Dan's voice.

She hurried out of the bed and straightened her buckskins as she walked to the door. When she opened it, Dan stood on the other side, smiling down at her.

"Good morning. How was your first night in a bed? Did you sleep well in those clothes?"

She looked around him to see if Will was there, too, but save for Dan, the hallway was empty. "I slept on clouds. It is a very fine thing, this bed. Do they have them everywhere?"

"Just about everywhere, except tipis, that is."

She gave him a smile that did not come from the heart. Where was William?

"How is your cut?"

She held out her hand. "It reminds me."

He gave her a puzzled look. "Reminds you? . . ." Then he smiled. "Oh . . . it reminds you. It throbs?"

She frowned. "Throbs?"

He ran his hand through his hair. "Throbs . . . it is like . . . how can I say this? It is like the beat of a drum that is inside your hand."

"Ahhh, yes, I feel the drum."

He put his fingers on her forehead. "You don't have a fever. That is good."

"Fever is hot?"

He smiled. "Yes, hot."

"I have no fever."

"You probably haven't had any breakfast, either. Want to come downstairs and eat with me?"

"Oh, yes, I am most hungry. My stomach throbs."

"No, your hand throbs. Your stomach growls."

"Growls . . . like the bear?"

"Yes, like the bear." He mussed her hair with his hand. "Come on. Let's see what we can get to eat."

She followed him down the stairs.

Soon they were eating, her plate piled high with things that were unfamiliar to her, things she knew the names of, but had never seen. Eggs. Bacon. Biscuits. She liked the food of the whites. She could not help wondering if she had eaten these things before. She sighed. If she had, the memory of it was locked away with the other things she could not recall.

"Where is Will?"

"He went down to the river to talk to the riverboat captain."

"We go to New Orleans today?"

"I don't know. We may have to stay here another day. We got word this morning that the rain will delay things a bit. . . . It's turned the snow to an icy slush and that will make it slower to unload."

"There is tomorrow."

He smiled. "Yes, there is always tomorrow. But don't worry. Your husband will be back before long."

"Husband." She paused, reflecting on the sound. "It is a good word, I think."

His face registered surprise. "You mean you like being married? That is . . . I mean . . . What I'm trying to say is, I thought you might be unhappy with the situation — you know, being married to someone without your consent."

She thought about that for a moment allowing the English words to settle in her mind, for Dan spoke much faster than Father Marc. "I do not know if I like being married or not. My husband has not come to me."

Dan made a strangling sound.

When she looked at him, she saw the discomfort in his face. "I have said something wrong?"

"No, it's just that it isn't proper to discuss such things with someone other than your husband or other women."

"But he is not here, so I cannot discuss it with him."

He nodded. "Margery, you must not take it personally, as if Will is intentionally trying to hurt you."

"I think sometimes that he does not like me. If this is true, I do not understand why he took me for his woman."

"He married you to protect you."

"Protect? I am not safe here with the whites?"

"Of course you are. It's just that you are much

safer now that you are married, than you were before. He has given you his name. In the land where we come from, in England, his family is a very great family. His father is like one of the leaders of a tribe."

"He is a chief, then?"

"No, there is only one chief for many people, but Will's father is next to the chief in power and wealth."

"There are many buffalo robes and fine ponies?"

"There are no buffalo in England, but the ponies — we call them horses — are finer than any you have ever seen." He paused. "I don't think I should be telling you all of this. Will should be the one to teach you about England."

"Perhaps he does not intend to take me to England. Perhaps he will leave me here."

Dan gave her a look she could only call sad. "No, he will take you to England. I am certain of it." He still looked sad.

"You are not coming?"

"Oh, I'm coming. I have been gone a long time . . . too long. I'm anxious to get back to civilization."

"England is civilized?"

He chuckled. "Oh yes, the English are most civilized. We only enjoy ourselves for a noble purpose. Why, we haven't had a revolution in England for centuries."

"Revolution?"

"A war."

"You have had no wars?"

"None on English soil."

"Why?"

"There aren't enough white gloves to go around."

She did not understand what he said, but he laughed, so she laughed, too.

"At first, you might find the English a bit strange, but that will pass."

"Why will I find them strange?"

"The English are a bit like their weather . . . predictable, sodden, and staid."

"Staid," she said, repeating the word as if she were tasting it, committing it to memory. "I do not know this word."

"Staid is . . . well, it's serious."

"Oh. They have no humor?"

"They did at one time. It's been replaced with newspaper reading and drinking tea."

This time she laughed without waiting to see if he did. She liked Dan, and she was happy that she would go to England, that she would meet Will's family, this father who was powerful like a chief.

Out of the corner of her eye she caught sight of movement. "Will has come," she said. "He is not happy."

Dan looked up. "No, he isn't. That must mean we can't take off until tomorrow," he said, then added in a lower tone, "or else he isn't too happy that I'm showing you my charming side."

She heard Dan's words, but her eyes were feasting upon her husband and she did not respond. Instead, she watched Will as he walked toward them. She liked to watch him, to see the way his body moved, with all the beauty and poetry of a majestic river. She was very pleased with him, with this man she could call husband. She had never met a man that made her feel as strange as he did. To look at his face was pleasing to her. To feel his warmth next to hers made her hunger to know more. She thought about last night, when she had fallen off the bed and he had rolled on top of her. How strange he made her feel.

As she watched him, her heart seemed to grow lighter, bobbing in her chest as her hand had throbbed. A beat powerful and full of mystery like the Crow drums during the Sun Dance. Her heart did not seem to belong to her now, but to him, and she could not help but wonder if he had any knowledge of this.

As he drew closer to their table, she felt his presence as surely as she could feel the heat from the sun.

He sat down in the chair next to her.

Her gaze never left his face, not even when Dan spoke. "Bad news?"

"I'm beginning to think there isn't any other kind. The captain says they won't finish unloading until late this evening."

The lightness in her heart was gone. In its place was a heaviness, a sadness that threatened to pull her under, as heavy garments would pull one beneath the churning waters of a river. He had not spoken to her, nor did he look in her direction. She did not understand the whites' way of marriage. Was this all there was to it? You marry, then go on living your separate lives? She thought about this strange practice, her brows drawing together and a deep crease coming between them. If that were true, then how did they ever get together to make children?

She could feel Dan's gaze upon her, but she did not look at him. Instead, she glanced at the food on her plate. It did not look so good to her now. She put down the strange object Dan had taught her to use. Fork. There was no reason to hold this fork now. The bear in her stomach had quieted.

"Are you hungry?" Dan asked.

"No, I ate earlier. How is your hand?"

"It is good. It does not growl. . . ." She sensed her mistake as Dan gently shook his head. She corrected herself. "It does not throb."

Will nodded, missing the exchange of glances between her and Dan. "I am surprised it doesn't hurt," he said. "That was a nasty cut."

"I do not feel it." She silently thanked Dan for not mentioning the pain she had admitted to him earlier.

Will stretched and stood up.

"Are you leaving?" Dan asked. "You just got here."

Will glanced at Margery, then looked off. She could see the way his jaw moved, as if he were biting back his words, or perhaps his thoughts.

"Finish your breakfast. I'll be back in a little while. There will be plenty of time to talk then."

Together, Margery and Dan watched him walk off.

Her hand came up to touch the end of one long braid that hung over her shoulder. "He has many bad spirits in his heart."

"Yes, we call it being tormented by devils."

"He is not happy."

"No, there is . . . bad medicine . . . between Will and his father."

"Why?"

"I've never been certain, really. Will has four sisters, but he is the only son, the heir to his father's title — and before you ask, a title is an honor, like chief, that is passed on from father to son. In his case, Will's father is an earl, so that makes Will a viscount, and you, my lovely, a viscountess."

He must have seen the confusion she was feeling, for he smiled and said he would back up a bit. He then proceeded to explain all about the titles of honor in England.

When he finished, she understood much more, but still, she did not understand why Will chose to come to America if his place was in England. It was something she asked Dan.

"Let's see if I can make you understand," Dan began. "In the Crow village, when a boy becomes a man, he is consumed with the quest for a vision. He goes to a lonely mountain peak, to fast, to thirst, to wail. He strips off his clothing, covers himself with a buffalo robe, and lays down at night, his back to the east. At daybreak he rises, and sits down, facing east. As soon as the sun rises, he chops off a joint of his left forefinger. Am I correct, so far?"

She nodded, adding, "The joint is placed on a buffalo chip and offered to the sun. While the warrior asks for greatness, praying for a vision, something as great as what he has heard of in the legends."

"It is my understanding that many of these young men have visions that come to them very quickly, but others must go through much torture before they receive their vision. Will is like these young men. He is on his quest for his vision, but he is not one of the fortunate ones. His vision and source of power have not come to him quickly. He will continue to fast and go without water, to torture himself, until he receives his vision."

She frowned. "It is not good that he has taken a wife at such a time."

"No, but he likes to think he has done it for altruistic reasons. He thinks he has helped you by doing so."

She understood that, and it made her chest lighten again. "He is a very good man. His heart is kind. I will make him a good wife. He will not be sorry for what he has done."

"Margery . . ."

"Yes?"

"You need to understand . . . Oh, never mind."

"Why is there such bad medicine between Will and his father?"

Dan tilted his head to one side and bit his lip, as if he were chewing on her question before he answered it. "I knew you would want to talk about that," he said, "but I think Will should be the one to tell you."

"But he will not, so you must."

"How do you know he won't?"

"He is like the eagle. He flies alone. You are like the buffalo. You surround yourself with others of your kind."

Dan gave her an odd look.

"I have said something wrong?"

His eyes were soft, as soft as his words. "No, it's just that I find it amazing, that's all. Here I came to teach you something, but it is I who am learning. You are quite the most remarkable woman I have ever met. I pray to God that William realizes that before . . . Oh, bloody hell! I talk too much."

∨ " 'Bloody hell.' I do not know this."

Dan's face darkened. "I should not have said that. It is not something a woman should say."

"Oh. It is forbidden?"

"No, but it should be."

"I do not think you talk too much. There is much for me to learn. You talk. I learn. It is very simple. Tell me more, so I will learn about my husband."

"He is not an easy man to describe, but I suppose his most notable quality has always been his passion, a sort of shrinking away from himself. I know that doesn't make sense to you. It's something that is hard to explain. Logic means nothing to him. . . ." He laughed. "I can see it doesn't mean much to you, either. I am not making this easy for you to understand, am I?"

"I do not understand all the words, but I understand most of what you are saying."

"I will try to keep it simple. The most important thing for you to understand about Will is that there has always been a wildness in him, something in his spirit that would not let him forgive himself . . . or others. Not that there is any reason why he should forgive his father. Charles and Will have never gotten along. For that reason, don't expect his father to approve of you. Charles wouldn't like any woman Will married, unless Charles picked her out himself."

"I do not understand why they are enemies."

"When Will was much younger, he fell in love with a young girl and wanted to marry her. She was not the daughter of an important person like Will's father, and so Charles did not want Will to marry her. Will wouldn't listen, so his father went to the girl's father. He offered them a great deal of money if the girl would marry someone else. Four days later, she married another man. Will was betrayed twice, by his father and the woman he loved, and that made it twice as hard on him."

"And that is why he left his home?"

"Yes, that and the fact that Charles made certain that everyone knew what happened. He endured the teasing, the humiliation for a while, but it was hard to ignore the jokes, the songs they sang about him. Not long after Will's humiliation, his younger brother, James, was killed."

"He brought much pain with him to America."

"Yes, but it was good for him to come here. I truly think if he had not left when he did, he might have destroyed himself."

"It has been good for him, then? This country?"

"Yes. Will is very talented. Remind me, and I will show you some of his sketches. I think it was good that he came out West, where he could be away from all the reminders of civilization for a time. But he is torn with indecision. He was raised for a noble cause, to be an earl. I honestly believe he wants that very much. He loves England and everything English, but he carries his English weather in his heart."

"The weather is sad?"

"It is like the weather today. It rains frequently."

"Oh." She understood this idea of rain in a person's heart. There had been rain in her heart many times. "Life is very strange, I think. He has his family and he runs from them. I have no family and yet I pray that I will someday find them."

"Is there nothing you remember?"

She shook her head. "No. Only at night, I sometimes have dreams. I hear voices and see shadows, but no faces."

"Do you feel you came from a large family?"

"Yes, I think I did. And I know I was loved."

He smiled at that. "You will be loved again, Margery. Be patient. Love sometimes comes when you least expect it."

CHAPTER
 TEN

Will was sitting on his bed, staring at the sketch pad in his lap. For the past hour he had given more attention to a bottle of rot-gut whiskey than to what he had drawn.

He couldn't think. He couldn't concentrate. Every time he tried, he would find himself remembering the sight of a naked length of leg, a softly rounded hip, and satin-smooth skin. "Well hell!"

Dan, who was at a small desk, writing notes in his journal, looked up. "Did you say something?"

"No." Will took another swallow. Not even whiskey would rid him of her image.

"Is something bothering you?"

"Nothing that I can't handle."

Dan stared at him for a moment longer, then went back to his journal.

Will paid him no mind. He didn't want to pay her any mind either. In fact, he didn't want to think about her at all. Not that way. He was a man with a mission, and a man with a mission was a troublesome thing. Far too much confusion lay between his heart and head already. He did not need more.

He married her to save them both from a fate they did not want. It was something he needed to remember, something to keep before him like a map. Now was not the time to turn sentimental.

He picked up a pen and wrote across the top of his sketchbook. "To everything there is a season . . . a time to embrace, and a time to refrain from embracing; . . . a time to keep, and a time to cast away; . . . a time to love, and a time to hate. . . ."

This was his time to refrain from embracing, his time to cast away, his time to hate. He had a mission in life, one that would not be accomplished without a great deal of pain. He knew it was a gamble, and that the rewards in the end might not outweigh the pain.

"Why don't you try talking about it?"

"There is nothing to talk about."

"It's her, isn't it? You've bought her and married her and now you don't know what to do with her."

"No, that isn't it. You're wrong. I know exactly what to do with her. I've known since the moment I bought her. Nothing has changed. I still plan to take her to England."

"But you don't really want to, do you?"

"I really don't want to sit here discussing my life with you."

Dan grinned at him. "No, but you'd feel better if you did. It's easier to talk about it than it is to sit there drinking yourself into a stupor over her."

"I am not drinking over her, and I don't want to talk about her." He didn't want to *think* about her, either. He wanted to stick to his original plan: to marry her and take her to England, thereby giving them both a new life.

No, he did not want to think about her . . . her, with her quiet, matter-of-fact openness, her innocence, her gentle strength, her fresh approach to life. And that was damn hard. For when he was around her, he forgot the torment in his life, the demons that waited for him each night, the memories of a lonely childhood, a ruined love affair, the guilt over his brother's death.

"She doesn't understand why you avoid her."

"Perhaps it is better that she doesn't. I'm not a very likable man right now."

"No, you aren't. I'd be surprised to find you even liked yourself right now."

"Lay off, Daniel."

"Oh, Daniel, is it?"

Will stared at his companion.

Dan held up his hands in surrender. "Okay, I'll stop. First and foremost I'm your friend, remember?"

"Yes, but I was beginning to wonder if you did."

"How can you say a thing like that, Will? I've been your best friend since we were seven and I busted your nose."

"We were eight and I busted your nose."

"Well, whatever. Do you remember what we were fighting about?"

"Yes. Lady Mary Louise Braddock, who, at the ripe age of seven, had the bluest eyes and the blondest hair either of us had ever seen."

"We've been through a lot together, haven't we?"

"Yes, and I've a feeling there is more to come."

"When we get to England, you mean?"

"Precisely."

"Are you worried about seeing your father?"

Will was amused. "Wouldn't you be?"

He laughed. "Yes, I would have to say the thought of facing your father with an Indian wife in tow is not exactly my idea of a family get-together."

Will didn't say anything.

Dan stood up. "I've been in the out-of-doors so long, having a roof over my head makes me feel restless. I think I'll take this to my room, then I'll go out and stretch my legs a bit. Want to come, or would you rather stay here and look mellow?"

"Mellow becomes me."

Dan plucked a flower from a vase on the desk and stuck it in Will's hand as he walked from the room. "Want me to fetch the undertaker?"

"Wait a bit," Will said, trying to force some levity into his voice. "I've got a breath or two left."

Dan opened the door. "Too bad she can't see you now . . . you're the epitome of the brooding hero."

"I'm no bloody hero, brooding or otherwise." Will tossed the flower at Dan, missed, and hit the door.

"You're not a very good liar, either."

When Will did not come to her the second night of their marriage, Margery decided not to wait any longer, but to take matters into her own hands. Having been raised by Indians, she held to many of the Indian ways of doing things. Among these were her views on lovemaking and marriage.

Because it was her way to be very open and honest, she decided to seek Dan's advice.

It was not hard to find him, for he was walking toward the stairway just as she opened the door to her room.

Dan started down the stairs, saw her, and stopped on the second step. "I can see by the expression on your face that there is a big question looming in the back of your mind. What troubles you?"

"I should like you to explain to me the English way."

He raised a brow. "The English way?"

She nodded.

"The English way of what?"

She walked toward him and stopped at the top of the stairs. "The custom of marriage in your

107

country. When a man and woman marry, what happens next?"

"Well, they generally live together and raise a family."

"I cannot raise a family if my husband does not know me."

The light of sudden understanding darkened the color of Dan's face. He seemed relieved when she went on talking.

"I must know the English way of making children."

Humor danced in his eyes. "I have a feeling it is basically the same as the Indian way."

She frowned at that. She did not understand. It couldn't be the same, for the Indian way would have been for the man to come to the woman and make love to her. Will had not done that. He had barely looked at her.

"My, you are troubled. Is it because Will has not been a husband to you?"

"I do not understand why."

"Perhaps he is giving you time to adjust to him before he comes to you. You hardly know each other and . . ."

"If he came to me, we would know each other better."

Dan raised one brow and nodded at her, as if he were keeping score and giving that point to her. "True, but the English way is for the man to always be a gentleman, and being a gentleman means you don't force yourself upon a woman."

"I would be willing."

"Every man's dream." Dan chuckled. "You should be a member of Parliament."

"What is this Parliament?"

"It's a male sort of thing, difficult to explain, and not something given to much pleasure."

"Like marriage?"

With that, Dan threw back his head and laughed. "Come on," he said, taking her arm. "Let's go for a walk and we'll see what we can come up with."

She gave him a confused look.

"You want your husband to, uh, know you. Right?"

She nodded.

"Let's see if we can't find a way to make that happen."

"I know the way to make it happen."

Dan laughed and held up his arms in surrender. "You don't have to convince me."

They crossed the hotel lobby and passed through the doors to an overcast sky outside, but the weather was warm, and the streets reasonably dry, so they walked along the wooden sidewalks.

"If he won't come to me, then I will go to him."

"What a pity I didn't buy you first," Dan said. "A wife like that is worth a king's ransom."

But she wasn't listening. "I will go to him tonight and crawl beneath his robes."

"Blankets."

"I will crawl beneath his blankets."

They crossed the street, then turned right. Dan stepped behind her, putting her on the inside.

"You do not like this side?" She looked at the space he had just vacated.

"A gentleman always puts the lady on the inside."

"Why?"

"It's a thing called manners and to explain it would take a long time. Remind me to tell you some other time. Now, back to your going to Will. I think that is a fine idea, but there is something you should know, something that is part of the Indian way, that is not done in England."

She turned her face up to his, her eyes watching his mouth, as if she could see the words he spoke.

"I know it is the custom of the Crow to put bear grease on their hair . . ."

"Bear grease mixed with herbs."

"Don't do it."

"The herbs?"

"The bear grease."

"He likes the castoreum of the beaver better?"

Dan grimaced. "I think he would prefer it clean, with nothing on it."

"I should wash my hair before I go to his blankets?"

"Yes. You should wash your hair and bathe before you go."

"I had a bath this morning."

"This morning?"

She nodded.

He still looked skeptical. "Are you certain you had a bath?"

"Yes."

"A real bath?"

"It is the Crow way to take a bath each morning."

"A bath every morning? Are you certain?"

"Yes."

"In the river?"

"Only in the summer. In the winter, it is the custom to fill one's mouth with water and to squirt it on your hands, so you can wash where you are dirty."

"I'll tell you what. Let's go back to the hotel, and I'll arrange a bath for you — the English kind."

"This is the way it is done in England?"

"Cross my heart." And he did.

They turned back and walked toward the hotel. Dan kept talking, but Margery had a hard time concentrating on what he was saying. She was puzzled about this English bath. If you did not fill your mouth with water and spit, then what did you do?

As they walked back into the hotel, she made it a point to look at each woman they passed. Had they taken this special kind of bath this morning? She noticed the way they wore their hair, which was difficult, since it was usually up and tucked beneath a hat.

As she studied their appearance, it occurred to her that they were also noticing her. Now, as they walked through the lobby of the hotel, she was conscious of the fact that she did not look like the other women; that they all stared at her as if her antelope-skin dress with the rare elk teeth was not fine enough.

It was the same feeling she'd experienced when the Mandan warrior had stripped her dress from her. She straightened up, walking proudly, challenging the scorn in their eyes, even though she wanted to hide. She decided not to tell Dan how the women made her feel. She did not want to suffer the pain of humiliation again.

CHAPTER
⊞ ELEVEN ⊞

She had not been in her room very long when three maids came marching in, armed with a huge cooking pot.

She eyed the pot suspiciously.

Was she to be boiled in a cooking pot like a joint of buffalo? Was this what made the women's skin so smooth and white? She liked the Indian way better, and to prove the point, she backed out of their way and stood with her arms crossed.

"Where would you like the tub?"

Margery looked at the yellow-haired girl that had spoken. "Far away."

One of the girls said, "Did you hear what she said? Far away. That's funny." The three girls snickered and put the tub down near the bed. That done, they turned toward Margery.

"I'm Moll. This is Betsy and that's Sarah."

As Moll and Sarah poured the water, Margery heard a knock on the door. She turned just in time to see Betsy open it, then stand back as seven other girls walked in, each carrying a large pot of steaming water.

Margery had never seen so much hot water,

and never had she seen so much water in a pot. The seven girls emptied their pots then departed.

Margery stepped closer, intrigued with watching the three who remained as they began pouring bottles of oil into the water; oil that smelled as sweet as prairie flowers that bloom after a spring rain.

There was far too much water in that pot to put in her mouth and squirt on herself, and besides that, she didn't particularly like the idea of drinking water with oil in it — even if it did smell like prairie flowers. She was thinking that perhaps this bath wouldn't be so bad if she just washed her hands and face. . . .

The three maids slowly turned toward her.

Margery wasn't certain as to what they intended, but the look in their eyes was the same as the look in a warrior's eye just before he lifted a scalp.

She began backing away.

"Come here and we'll help you undress."

Margery wasn't about to go anywhere, except farther away from them. *Help me undress?* She did not like the sound of that.

She took another step back, then turned to gauge the distance to the door.

"You'll never make it," Moll said, folding her strong arms over her strong chest and taking a wide stance that made Margery think the Crow would have called her Stands-Like-a-Buffalo.

Sarah looked at Moll. "He said she would need a little encouraging."

Sarah had no more than finished the words when the three of them sprang for her. Margery gave a yelp of surprise and darted out of the way, but three to one isn't the best of odds, and Moll was second in size only to a bull elk, with an arm that was longer than the wingspan of an eagle.

"Let me go!" Margery shouted, then she began to curse in three languages: Comanche, Cheyenne, and Crow, with a smattering of French thrown in.

Later, she was to think she should have stayed with an English dressing down. At least they would have understood when they were being insulted.

Not giving her time to think further, they hauled her toward the bed, like a bundle of scraped skins, and she never knew until later just how close to the truth this was.

When they reached the bed, they threw her down and descended upon her like a flock of hungry buzzards. Fighting for all she was worth, Margery shouted, "Let me go! I'll cut out your liver! I will take your scalp and tie it to my medicine bundle!"

When that did not work, she tried a more civilized approach. "I've changed my mind," she panted.

The girls laughed, and Moll said, "He told us you would be reluctant."

Reluctant? Didn't they understand unwilling? Terrified? She couldn't have been more scared if they had said they were going to hold her feet over a fire. She scrambled to her feet, then bolted. She made a dash for the door, but Sarah caught her by her braid, slowing her down and giving the other two time to catch her.

They wrestled her to the floor, with Margery vowing to shave her head so they couldn't catch her so easily next time. She forgot about her hair when Betsy straddled her. Now they began to strip her in earnest, and the only thing Margery found she could do at this point was yell.

So she did.

She howled and kicked and screamed until a group of people, hearing the commotion coming from her room, began to gather outside her door.

It was about that time that Dan and Will walked up the stairs. They heard the tortured shouts and saw the crowd standing outside the door.

"What's going on?" Will asked. "It sounds like someone is being murdered." He stopped. "Isn't that coming from Margery's room?"

Dan, who was wearing an amused expression, said, "Yes, but don't worry. It's just a difference of opinion."

"Who is in there with her? Marquis de Sade?"

"No, it's another form of torture."

"Such as?"

"A bath. I believe the exact tally is three maids, a bathtub, hot water, and enough soap to scrub through at least four years of grime and dirt to get to the rosy skin beneath."

"Obviously you had something to do with this."

"Perhaps it was her idea and she just told me about it."

"Not bloody likely. Judging from the way she is howling, I gather it wasn't her idea at all."

"And that makes it mine?"

"Of course. You've turned into a bloody Mother Superior since she's been with us."

"My, my, are we jealous?"

Will gritted his teeth. "Go to hell."

"I don't know . . . hell might not be such a grand place to be. After all, you sure don't look like you're enjoying it too much."

"Daniel, I'm warning you."

"Not to worry. Things will soon change. I promise you that after these women finish with her, you will find yourself married to one hell of a woman."

"I like her just the way she is."

"Do you now? And here I was thinking you hardly noticed her."

"I'm the bloody bastard that bought her, in case you've forgotten. What do you mean I've hardly noticed her?"

"I daresay, old chap, that you don't even know the color of her eyes."

"Brown."

"Green as grass."

"I didn't marry her for her damn eyes."

"Now we're getting somewhere. Tell me, just what did you marry her for?"

About that time, Margery let out a loud howl

and Dan laughed. "Come on. There's no need for us to stand here attracting attention . . . not when Margery is the main attraction. Let's go downstairs. I'll buy you a drink."

"Now why would you want to do that?"

"Because I'm your friend."

"Oh, so now you're my friend again?"

"I'm always your friend, Will. Even on those occasions when I have to apply the sole of my foot to your backside."

Will gave a disbelieving snort, but he turned and followed Dan down the stairs anyway.

Meanwhile, back in the land of torture, Margery's skin had been scrubbed to a bright pink. She complained about the loss of hide and the miserable burning, finding herself mighty thankful when they left her with the last inch of skin on her body and stopped their horrid scrubbing.

She was just about to lie back and relax, glad the worst was over, when someone shoved her head under the water.

When she surfaced, one of the girls gagged.

"Gawd! What is that horrible smell?"

Margery wiped the water from her eyes, then watched the three of them sniff the air like they were trying to pick up the scent of something dead.

She sniffed, but she didn't smell anything.

Sarah leaned closer. "Lord above! It's in her hair!"

The other two girls took a whiff and almost fainted. Moll, being the strongest of the three, managed enough breath to say weakly, "What is on your hair?"

"Bear grease." Margery felt it was worth the burning pink skin just to see the expressions on their faces. She didn't get to think much of anything else, for her head was shoved underwater again, and when she surfaced this time, they doused it liberally with a flowery-smelling soap.

Bear claws were never this sharp, Margery thought as the three girls took turns scrubbing her hair. All the howls and yelps she could muster seemed to go unheeded, for they never slowed once, except to dunk her under the water two more times, lathering her up good and proper in between.

Just when she thought it would never end, Betsy said, "There! We're all finished."

Now I can relax, she thought, only to find herself unceremoniously yanked from the tub and wrapped in a towel. Next, her torturers set about drying her hair with a towel, with Molly exclaiming, "Well, would you look at this? Her hair isn't brown at all. It's blond." She clamped her ample arms on her hips and said, "Don't recollect that I have ever seen a yellow-haired Indian before."

"Maybe she isn't an Indian," was Sarah's response.

Molly looked Margery over with a critical eye. "She must be an Indian."

"Why is that?" Sarah asked.

"Because she was dressed like one."

"Oh," Sarah said. "I guess you're right."

Betsy eyed Margery's hair. "Do you have a brush?"

Margery nodded and went to her bundle. She removed her brush and held it up.

"My God! What is it?" Sarah asked.

"Is it dead?" asked Moll.

Margery looked at it. "Of course it's dead."

Betsy groaned. "You mean it was alive . . . once?"

Before Margery could answer, Sarah asked again, "What is it?"

"A porcupine tail."

"I'll be right back," Molly said, and hurried from the room.

A few minutes later, she was back with something she called a brush . . . which to Margery's way of thinking did not look any better than the porcupine tail she produced earlier, but it seemed to make the three of them happy, and Margery was glad to do whatever she could to get them out of her room the quickest way possible.

Not even torture can last forever, and finally Betsy exclaimed she was as pretty as a princess. Margery had never seen a princess, of course, so she had no idea just how pretty that was, but when Molly led her to the mirror and told her to look at herself, Margery understood.

I am pretty. . . .

While Margery stood there admiring herself, Betsy dropped a long white gown over her head and removed the towel. A few minutes later, they began gathering up their scattered things, the room looking, at this point, like a winter storm had just passed through.

While Sarah and Moll finished picking up, Betsy went to get help to remove the tub.

Margery was still staring into the mirror when they left. She lifted a section of her hair and brought it to her nose, inhaling the fragrance that was as sweet as river grass. She touched her skin, unable to believe the bath had turned it white.

This was nothing like the way the Indians bathed, but still, she had to admit that once the torture was over, the English way wasn't so bad.

Margery wondered if Will would like her better after her bath, as Dan had indicated. A knock sounded at the door. Afraid it was the three maids coming back for another raid on her person, Margery did not answer.

Another knock.

Silence.

"Margery? Are you in there?" It was Will's voice.

"I am here."

This time it was Dan's voice that asked, "Are you all right?"

"Parts of me are better than others," she replied, hearing both of them chuckle. But when she said, "I burn," it was Will that she heard groan.

English men were very strange, she decided, then turned away from the mirror and walked to the door. She found this thing they called a gown a bit awkward to move in, for its length kept getting under her feet. She was trying to decide if she was going to leave the gown on or take it off, when Will's voice came through the door.

"We thought we'd see if you wanted to come downstairs with us to eat."

She looked down at herself and felt suddenly unsure. She needed a little more time to adjust to things before she was around the two of them. She declined dinner, preferring to remain in her room so she could practice walking in her gown.

After they left, Margery waited, wondering how long it would be before she heard them come back after their meal.

She waited until the noise on the streets below began to grow quiet. Still, she did not hear them return. She was beginning to wonder if she was becoming so accustomed to the English ways that she couldn't hear something as loud as the two of them coming up the stairs, for they sounded remarkably like a wounded stag tearing through a stand of trees.

A sudden knock on her door nearly sent her jumping out of her skin. She hurried to the door and, putting her ear to the smooth wood, she answered softly, "Yes?"

"Will has gone to bed," Dan whispered. "You're sure you want to go through with this?"

After what she had endured, she wouldn't let anything short of a prairie fire stop her now, but she did not tell Dan that. "I am sure."

She thought she heard him chuckle. "Good girl."

A moment later, she heard something and she looked down to see an envelope slide beneath her door.

She picked it up, then opened it. Out fell a key. Dan had given her the key to Will's room.

She smiled and was about to thank him when she heard the soft sound of his footsteps going away from her door. A moment later, she heard the door to his room — which was next to hers — open, then shut.

Margery stood there, her hand on the door-knob, her heart pounding in her chest, her throat dry as desert sand, and everything else quaking like an aspen leaf.

She opened the door and looked out into the hall. It was deserted. She stepped out into the hallway and started to make her way slowly toward Will's room. As she walked, she was thinking that she should have asked Dan more about the English way.

For it suddenly occurred to her that she had no idea what happened after the bath.

CHAPTER
❈ TWELVE ❈

Will was sitting on his bed, his knees drawn up, the sketch pad in his lap. The room was quiet, save for the sound of the reed pen scratching its way around the paper or the occasional click of the pen against the bottle of brown ink.

He studied the drawing for a moment, then blinked to clear his vision. Tonight, he'd had a bit too much to drink. Yet he was compelled to finish his work, inspecting the sketch he was filling in. Perhaps this was due to his feeling particularly sensitive tonight — a mood that always seemed to lend itself to intricate detail.

He paused a moment at the sound of a soft tapping on his door. Before he could respond, the knock came again. It was louder this time, but not loud enough to be Daniel's familiar pounding.

Will frowned. He wondered who would be knocking at his door this time of night. "Come in. It's open."

He watched the door as it slowly opened.

He saw white.

Yards of white gossamer gown reflected in the

lamplight, swirling around a naked form.

Margery, as he had never seen her . . .

Margery the woman, the vision in white, the seductress, wrapped in little more than gossamer and long golden hair.

She stepped farther into the room, then closed the door behind her. She leaned back against the door, as if she needed it for support.

Long habit kept emotion from his face, and he knew that in spite of his looking at her, she had no idea how he reacted to her coming into his room, uninvited.

For some length of time, they remained this way, each of them looking at the other, neither of them bringing to life the thoughts they were thinking. At last, Will left the sketchbook lying in his lap and picked up his whiskey glass. Without shifting his gaze, he brought the glass to his lips, then tossed the drink down.

When he finished, he held the glass aloft, seeking out her image through the distortion of glass. Even then, she was lovely and quite desirable. He realized then that he had been holding his breath. He released it with a whisper. " 'License my roving hands, and let them go/Before, behind, between, above, below.' "

He slurred the words, to be sure, but she did not seem to notice. "I don't suppose the name John Donne means anything to you, does it, little savage?"

She stared at him curiously but said nothing.

He hated this look, for he could not tell if she

was looking at him with understanding or scorn. He put the glass on the bedside table. He had asked her something, hadn't he? Yes. Did the name John Donne mean anything to her? "Of course the name means nothing to you. And why should it? I doubt your pious and saintly priest was much given to waxing poetically, save in the Biblical sense."

She did not answer him, but then, why should she? She had no idea what he was babbling about. "You don't understand, do you? You have this primitive understanding, something that is very basic. You comprehend well enough that we are married, and in your backward little mind is a reservoir of daring. You rush in where angels fear to tread. You are like an unenlightened wanderer who walks along the beach and finds a golden medallion that has washed up from the deep, having no notion of the beautiful necklace of which it was once a part. You have no idea what your captivity has cost you . . . you have been deprived of much, much more than just your identity, your family. You, with your natural ignorance, your limited understanding. If you only knew . . . but your primitive little mind is as lost as Babylon. You come in here wearing your ignorance like an exotic flower, not knowing that once it's touched by knowledge, the bloom will be gone. You are so primitive with your simple logic and primary urgings. Your mind tells you that you are my wife and that calls up all kinds of thoughts of duty, doesn't it? Well, don't bother. I married you, but it wasn't for love, or even lust. It isn't your duty to spread your legs for me. That isn't what I want from you. Don't you understand that? I have my own demons to fight, my own reasons for doing what I did. I can't take on your battles, your demons. I'm not that strong and I'm too bloody selfish. I'm using you, my girl, but I am saving your wretched soul in the doing of it. Be glad that there was something about you that spoke to me, something that made me take notice of your plight. I felt pity for you, some emotional identification that reminded me of my own pain. But don't make it out to be more than it is. I bought you, but that does not mean I want you. Your lot in life will be remarkably easier from here on out, and one day, when you have learned knowledge, you will understand. Once you understand, you will thank me."

He sighed deeply and saw the blank expression, the fathomless look in her eyes. "God, if only I could make you understand. . . ."

She licked her lips and he found himself wondering what it would be like to feel her mouth against his. "God . . . there is no aphrodisiac like innocence," he whispered. "Come here, little savage . . . my angel in white. Come here and tell me what you are doing here, what it is that you want. Come . . ."

She pushed away from the door and the spell was broken.

Suddenly, it occurred to him that she had walked down the hall like this, with nothing on but her nightgown, which did precious little to hide everything relevant, and a whole lot to bolster the imagination.

"Did anyone see you come in here? Did anyone see you dressed like that?"

She shook her head. "No."

"What are you doing here this time of night? What do you want? Don't you realize what could happen to you . . . walking around looking as you do? You look like a blooming invitation."

He knew the Crow were the most promiscuous of all the Indian tribes he had visited. Had she come here to be seduced? Did she consider it her duty as his wife? The thought turned sour in his stomach. No matter how long it had been since he had a woman, no matter how desirable she was, he had no intention of making love to her all in the line of duty.

But his body sure as hell did.

He found it ironic that God, with his infinite sense of humor, saw fit to bestow upon his manly creation far more passion than reason. And if that wasn't enough, he ordained that this small speck of reason would occupy an insignificant part of the brain, while passion was given the rest of the body.

His body might desire her, but love, given in the line of duty, did little to stir him. "Go on back to your room. You should have been asleep long ago."

She did not say anything, but she stepped closer, coming toward him until she was beside the bed. When she stopped, she was near enough that he could feel the whisper of the softness of her gown as it brushed against the back of his hand.

"Did you understand what I said?"

She nodded but said nothing.

"Then do as I asked. Go back to your room. Now."

She remained silent, finding a way to answer him without saying a word. She began undoing the buttons on her gown.

His mouth went dry. He started to tell her it made no difference what she did, that he wasn't about to be seduced, but he knew it was such a pitiful excuse that even a blind man would see through it.

Buttons undone, she dropped one shoulder of her gown.

Her skin was smooth and unbelievably white. He swallowed. Dryness sucked at his throat.

She dropped the other shoulder and the gown slid downward, stopping at her waist.

" 'O mischief, thou art swift to enter in the thoughts of desperate men.' I am doomed."

He watched as she pushed the gown and it fell in a shimmer of reflected light to the floor. She was doing pretty damn good for her first time — if it was her first time.

All bare and bouncy, her body called out to him, and by heaven, he was man enough to answer the call. His first instinct was to grab her and yank her into the bed with him and give her what she was obviously asking for.

He was about to do just that when he remembered something his longtime tutor, Guy Montgomery, had once told him. "A gentleman doesn't pounce . . . he glides."

Trying to hold back the pounce, so he could glide a bit, he searched for a thought to help him slow down the clamor going on in his body.

Well hell! He had no idea it would be this bloody difficult. Never, ever had he seen a woman be so obvious. Not even the most practiced whores in Covent Garden were as blatant. He had to hand it to her: when she wanted something, she did not clutter it up with a bunch of talk or flirtation. She got right to the heart of the matter.

He gave her a good look, going from her head to her feet, lingering a bit longer in some strategic points than in others. Here was a force to be reckoned with, for there was nothing more arousing than a naked woman, built to perfection, standing not more than a handful, er, hand's length away.

He kept reminding himself of the old saying, "You have to penetrate a woman's defenses. Getting into her head is a prerequisite to getting into her body." Somehow that didn't seem to fit here, for Margery looked primed and ready for something, but it sure as hell wasn't conversation.

Well, a man does what he has to do. He dropped the sketchbook to the floor and placed the pen on the bedside table. His gaze never left her body as she stood proudly before him. Her legs were long and well tapered, her waist lissome, her belly flat and smooth.

She was a beauty all right, and he wanted her.

He had known all along that he would have to consummate the marriage if it was to be considered valid, but it wasn't his way to force himself on a woman. He was gentleman enough to give her time, time to know him, time to adjust. For that reason, he had waited.

Margery, however, didn't seem to need time to adjust to him or her new surroundings. She was his wife and she wanted him. And to top that off, she was damn desirable — enough so that no man in his right mind would turn his back on what she offered. She had a body like Aphrodite; one that would have sent a Donatello bronze hurtling off its pedestal.

And he was no bloody statue.

It occurred to him then that he wasn't certain as to what he should do next. He was unaccustomed to the woman's making the first move. In his past experiences there had always been a certain amount of seduction before actually making love.

Somehow, they had bypassed all of that. It was damn frustrating. Here he had a naked woman on his hands, and he wasn't certain what he should do next. It was one of two things: lie back and see what her next move would be, or yank her in the bed with him and ravish her.

Before he could think further, she took the

initiative once again. She dropped down on her knees beside him and began removing his clothes. One by one, her capable hands undid the buttons on his shirt. When she finished, she pulled the garment from him and dropped it on the floor. As she leaned over him, her long, blond hair fell in a cool wash of silk across the hot flesh of his chest. He twisted his hands in her hair, fighting the urge to wrestle back control by pulling her down on top of him.

The light touch of her hands on the buttons of his pants caused him to gasp. He held his breath then, afraid to release it. He feared that doing so might herald the finish of such sweet torment.

He needn't have worried, for the moment he began to breathe, albeit unsteadily, she was tugging his pants down over his hips, and he found he couldn't remain passive any longer, no matter how curious he was to see just how far she would go with this.

She was a strange creature, alive with curiosity and a thirst for knowledge. He could not help but pity her, for hers would not be an easy path to travel. Already she had many stripes to overcome. He watched her, studying her face, and he wondered what dark secrets hid behind her eyes . . . those remarkable green eyes, bright with humor and understanding. How could he ever have thought them brown?

He wanted her, to the point of desperation.

The only way to be rid of temptation was to give in to it. How noble he was, how wise. He had thought his troubles drowned in a bottle of whiskey. Now he saw how wrong he had been. He could hide his lust if he wished, but an evening of whiskey would always reveal it.

He reached out and took her hand as it worked to slip free the last button on his pants. Holding her hand still, he pressed her palm against him. He saw the shocked expression in her eyes but dismissed it. Her innocence was a seductive kind of chicanery. "Tell me what you want."

"I . . . am your wife."

"Granted. You are. But you didn't come in here to remind me of that, did you?"

She looked off. "No."

"Come now, don't turn suddenly shy. Every harlot was a virgin once. You seem to appreciate honesty. Tell me why you came in here. Tell me what you want."

"I want to lie with you."

Her honesty was seductive as hell, prompting him to remove the rest of his clothes with true military dispatch. He had no more than tossed the last boot to the floor when she lay down on top of him and began kissing him.

She kissed like a novice.

Something he knew she wasn't.

His first thought was that kissing must not be something the average Indian brave gave a great deal of attention to, for her kisses were rather chaste and misplaced. He had a brief vision of her — her white limbs intertwined with the naked, brown skin of a brave, his fringed leggings

133

up to his knees, the two of them making love in a buffalo wallow.

He could not hold on to the image, for the sweet smell of her hair, the satin softness of her skin, drove all sentiment from his mind. His only thought now was to finish what she had started. Digging his hands into the hair at the back of her head, he pulled her face down to his and kissed her, opening his mouth, forcing hers open as well. His hands moved across the smooth skin of her back, over the curvature of her spine, to cup the soft flesh of her legs, which were parted and lay to each side of his hips. Stroking her thighs, he felt her softness move against its counterpart. Desire stirred strong within him.

She whispered something in a language he could only recognize as Crow.

He wondered if she had changed her mind, if she was telling him to stop. Not that it mattered. He wouldn't have stopped . . . couldn't have stopped at that point.

Taking over now, he rolled her beneath him, pinning her against the bed with his body. He could feel her heart thudding against his ribs. He saw the way she was looking at him, with her eyes huge and trusting, and he tasted the bitterness of remorse. He had mocked her with talk of being nothing more than an ignorant savage, and yet he could not help wondering who was the real savage here. Was his civilized behavior nothing more than the lamb's skin hiding the barbarian in him?

He felt her move beneath him, but it was her words that stirred him.

"I have great hunger for you."

He brought himself up against her. She was ready. A second later, he felt the fragile membrane tear and heard her sharply indrawn breath.

Or was it his own? — for surprise at her virginity made him stiffen.

A virgin?

Impossible. Unbelievable. Indian braves did not let a woman, white or Indian, reach the age of twenty-seven with her virginity intact — not unless she was dog-faced ugly, something Margery was not.

He felt as though he had captured lightning in a bottle and he didn't know what to do with it. His first instinct was to apologize, to show her the tenderness and gentleness that he felt inside, but from somewhere in his subconscious came his father's words, reminding him that a titled gentleman showed no emotion.

But she was soft and warm and nuzzled up against him, and he was not the arrogant, uncaring, and cold son of a bitch his father was. With infinite care, he began to move, whispering words he was not aware he was saying, burying himself deep within her, feeling as if he had touched her heart.

The momentum grew within him, and he felt frustration. She did not come with him and he was too far gone to wait for her. He could not control his own body now, and a moment later, he arched wildly against her, compelled forward by the ecstasy of rhythm, the breathy flutter of her soft murmurings.

A heartbeat later, it was over and he lay spent against her. She whimpered and he felt disappointment that she had not found release with him.

He rolled off her, drawing her against him, touching her with his hand. He could not change what had happened, for there was no way to go back to the point where he had left her, but he could give her release. "Come," he whispered. "Come with me now."

She shifted against him in a hypnotic sway, her movement coming faster and faster until she cried out and her body jerked beneath his.

Her eyes fluttered open and their gazes met. " 'And ye shall be as gods, knowing good and evil,' " he whispered, his mouth lazy now as it closed over hers.

He had made love before. Many times. And yet, he could not help wondering what it was about this time that lingered like the words to an old song in the back of his mind.

"We have shared a blanket. I am your wife now."

"Yes," he said, kissing her gently, "you are my wife now."

"I will make you a good wife in your England. I am happy." With a sigh you could have heard in Baltimore, she nestled under his chin, her hair wrapping around him like a silken shackle. A short while later, he heard her breathing deepen and he knew she slept.

He continued to hold her, even after she had drifted off to sleep. How he envied her and her ability to fall asleep with such ease. He closed his eyes, willing himself to feel the drowsy comfort of slumber. He wished it to come as easily to him as it did to her, for only then, when he slept, would he be free from playing the hypocrite.

As he held her on into the night, he could not help thinking he had committed the greatest treason. He had done the right thing for the wrong reason.

CHAPTER
◙ THIRTEEN ◙

They left for New Orleans the next morning. A week after their arrival, they set sail for England.

It was not a good experience for Margery. She had never seen so much water, and never had she seen such a big ship. The Crows were Plains Indians, and they had many ominous legends about large bodies of water. Margery had plenty of misgivings.

At first, she refused completely to even board the ship. In her estimation, there was a reason why she had been born with feet instead of fins. Even after she was persuaded, she was uneasy. She did not like the rocking motion of the ship and the feel of water beneath her.

When they set sail, she began to feel her heart pound with a terrified sort of panic. She had not thought they would go so far from land. Not even the calm and steady assurance of both Will and Dan could ease her fears. It was strange to her that, in spite of being so afraid of living on the water and not being able to see land, she did not get sick.

But Dan did. The seasickness hit him the second day out.

"Will he die?" she asked.

Will looked back at Dan, who tossed on the small bunk in his cabin. "He probably would like to, but he isn't anywhere near death."

Dan moaned then, as if to contradict Will's words. Will laughed. "He gets seasick every time we sail."

"Why does he do it then?"

Will smiled. "Because he can't bear to be parted from me."

Margery looked at him, puzzled. To her, his words had been the most logical thing in the world.

"Come on," he said. "He is sleeping like a baby."

She followed Will up on deck. "When will we reach England?"

"Don't start asking that now. We've just started our trip."

"Why?"

"If I answered you now, it would make the trip seem overly long."

"I do not mind." His gaze moved over her, coming to rest upon her face. Something told her that he was thinking about the night she came to him.

As if reading her thoughts, he turned and braced his arms on the ship's railing, staring out over the water.

"You are displeased?"

"Displeased? About what?" He did not look at her.

"Because we have known each other. Because I came to your bed."

"No, of course I'm not displeased. Why would you think that?"

"You do not look at me. When I look at your face, I see shame."

"Are you always so bloody honest? Do you say everything you are thinking?"

"Honesty is not the English way? You would prefer that I speak falsely?"

"The English appreciate honesty as much as anyone, but there is a difference between being honest and being too quick to say what you think, too open with what you are thinking. The English are more reserved. They keep their thoughts on the inside."

"Ahhh," she said with sudden understanding. "That is why your heart is heavy."

"My heart isn't heavy."

"Your heart is heavy. I can see the burden you carry in your eyes. However, I understand now that it is the English way to say your heart is not heavy when it is heavy." She frowned, putting her arms on the railing as he did, and like him, she stared out over the water. "I do not understand all of this yet. Perhaps, in time, I will learn to say what I am not thinking, and to think what I am not saying, and to hide my thoughts and feelings, like a doe hides her young."

Well hell. She was such a charmer, he couldn't resist. He turned his head and looked down at her. "You don't have to change the way you are.

You haven't done anything wrong."

"But you and your ways are English, and I am your wife. Your ways will become mine. I have no wish to embarrass you."

"You don't embarrass me."

"I have seen the way the civilized women look at me. I do not behave as they do. I do not wear their clothes. When they look at me their eyes are full of questions. They wonder what a fine, English gentleman is doing with such a savage."

"If it bothers you, why don't you wear the clothes I bought for you in New Orleans?"

"It does not bother me enough yet. I am who I am. I see no reason to be ashamed of myself. I did not choose the life that I was forced to lead. It makes me no less a person because of it. I will wear the English clothes. But I will wear them when it pleases me to do so . . . when I *feel* English, not because I am shamed into wearing them. It is more important to me to become English on the inside before I try to look English on the outside."

"You are a very strange and unusual woman."

"I have led a very strange and unusual life."

"Yes," he said, "you have."

She looked away from him then, to stare once again over the water. "Whenever I look at the way the water seems to touch the sky in the distance, it reminds me of the way my past and present come together, seeming to touch, but the exact point at which they do so is hazy and difficult to see. I am the ocean, each wave searching for the one that went before it. My past is like the heavens, always above me, hidden in the clouds and beyond my reach."

"You have no remembrance of your childhood? No names, locations, nothing?"

She sighed. "Nothing. Only shadowy faces and blurred visions of a house. I try so hard to remember sometimes that my head aches."

"I suppose it is difficult . . . not knowing who you are, where you came from."

"Yes, we are very different, you and I. I am searching for a past I do not know, while you are running away from yours."

"I am not running away from my past."

She stared directly into his eyes but did not say anything. He was very handsome to her now, with his dark hair windblown and the kiss of sun upon his face. There was a mood of quiet reflection about him, almost of understanding in his expression, and it left her feeling vulnerable.

He was her husband, yet she knew his best friend better than she knew him. Will was a quiet man, private, sensitive, burdened. He was a gifted artist, insightful, capable of much emotion, and yet, she had only seen this in the art he produced. How could she get through to this man, to touch the heart that existed beneath the troubled exterior? "What made you leave England?"

"Don't look for things to make me a worthy husband. You won't find them. My worth can only be judged in terms of the fatness of my purse, the nobility of my title. If you look for other things, you will be disappointed. I am a disappointment to my family and an utter failure in my father's eyes. I betrayed my dead brother. My mother is the most loving and gentle human in the world and I have broken her heart more times than I care to remember. I am forced by law to inherit my father's title and all that it entails, but it is my cousin my father would choose as his heir, if he could."

"Why?"

He gave her a half grin, and she thought him the most beautiful man in the whole world. "You have the amazing capacity to ask short questions that involve a great deal of detail. Your English, by the way, is exceptional."

"Father Marc was schooled in England and I have benefited from that. He had no books, save the Bible, of course, but he had an incredible memory. He was quite a scholar and well read. It was no task for him to tell me the stories of many great books and ideas. For his knowledge, I had a great thirst."

"Why did he never try to take you back to civilization, to your own kind?"

"Father Marc could not take me with him and he had no place to leave me. His order was from Canada. He believed it was more cruel to take me there and abandon me than it was to leave me as I was. There were men, he would tell me, who would use me for their own purposes, men who would take advantage of my obedient ways."

She heard his indrawn breath, the softly whispered oath. She turned her head, but as always, his look was guarded. He showed her only what he wanted her to see.

"You should have listened to him."

"I did. That is why I tried very hard to remember everything he taught me. He would always say that there was something wonderful waiting for me, something that would make all I had suffered fade away. He believed I would find my family one day. That is why he took it upon himself to teach me as much as he could about the ways of the whites. He apologized much for teaching me more about England and France than America, but his travels there had been limited to Indian villages."

"Well, perhaps you will have the opportunity to put your knowledge of England to work once we reach there."

"I am eager to learn about your home and anxious to meet your family. They will think it strange, will they not, that you have taken to wife a woman held captive by Indians?"

"Oh, they will think it strange all right."

"Do you think they will like me?"

"Some of them will."

"Some . . . but not all?" She paused, remembering Daniel had warned her about Will's father.

"My father will not like you."

"Why? He does not know me."

"As if that matters. He will dislike you simply because you are my wife. He hates anything associated with me. Not even my dog fared well after I left England. He disappeared shortly after I did."

The words he spoke were too horrible for her even to comprehend. "Your father would take revenge against your dog?"

"He is capable of such. As I said, anything that belongs to me does not deserve recognition in my father's eyes."

"Perhaps this time, it will be different. Perhaps he will see that you have taken a wife and will give him grandchildren, that you have changed."

"But I have not changed."

"You have married and you are going home. A change in your life means there has been a change in you."

"There has been no change. I did not marry you for love. I am not going home out of a sense of honor."

"Then why are you going back? Why did you marry me?"

"I married you to save you. I thought you understood that."

"You did not have to marry me. You had already bought me. I belonged to you. You could have given me my freedom."

"It grows cold. I think you should go back to your cabin. I don't want you to get sick." His words sounded kind and gentle, but there was an element of evasiveness there as well. He took her hand in his. "Some day you will understand, and when you do, try to remember that it was never my intention to hurt you."

"But why . . ."

The closed expression came over his face and he turned away from her. "I don't want to talk about it anymore. "Go back to your cabin. It grows cold."

"I will see how Dan is feeling."

"Yes, seek out Dan's company. He is a far better companion for you."

"But you are my husband."

"A condition you will soon come to regret."

He turned away from her then and walked toward a large coil of rope where his sketchbook lay. He picked it up, sat down, and began sketching. He retreated into that private world that only he knew, a world where all the pain and suffering he felt expressed itself in remarkable beauty. How she envied him that — his ability to retreat into himself, like a turtle draws into his shell, both of them doing so for protection. While all she could do was conform like the winter hare, whose fur turns white in the cold so it will blend with the snow.

As she turned and walked toward her cabin, she wondered if there would ever come a time when she no longer felt she had to adapt, a time when she could be a black rabbit surrounded by the brightness of snow.

Will took care to avoid her as much as possible for the rest of their journey, but a week out of London he made the mistake of looking through his sketchbook while he was drinking. It was filled with pictures of her.

Margery and whiskey. A bad combination.

He looked down at the sketchbook he had filled with her likeness. It was only when he looked at these that he could see her as a person and not as an object of his revenge. Here, she was brought to life, charcoal to paper providing him with a medium to study her. He flipped through the pages until he came to the sketch he had done of her that day they had talked — one of the few times they had a real, honest-to-God conversation. He studied her face, the perfect fullness of her mouth, the incredible openness in her eyes. Here, he had captured the essence of her trust, a trust that would soon be broken.

✓ He stared down at her likeness. She with her open ways, her lovely, honest face, the green eyes that took in everything — eyes bright with curiosity and sparkling with wit — he had never met anyone like her. She was uncivilized, and yet there was a humanness that verily glowed within her. She was nothing more than a savage, with no knowledge of cleanliness or table manners, but there was a gentle submissiveness to her that was missing in those he considered to be the most cultured and refined.

Her like was not to be found anywhere. She was as rare a find as Pharaoh's tomb. He had purchased a pearl of great price with a string of wild ponies. The thought scared the living hell out of him. He saw his father's face then, red with fury, spewing his never-ending string of criticism, his unforgivingness, his harshness, his anger, his bitterness, and Will remembered what he was about.

He closed the sketchbook with a vivid curse and swept his arm across the table, sending charcoal and brushes clattering to the floor. He did not love her, but there was something about her that drew him, something about her quiet understanding, her gentleness. He admired her strength, her endurance, her ability to see a logical pattern to life when he saw everything in terms of hopelessness. How strange that she, who had lost everything, was such a happy being, while he, who had it all, was miserable.

He finished his drink and stood, making his way to his bunk when he stepped on something. He looked down and saw the sketchbook. Margery's face, her eyes round with surprise, her mouth closed in a kissable pout. He rubbed his thumb across the fullness of her lower lip and could almost feel the texture of it. His mind went back to the night she had come to him.

He did not remember all the reasons why she was his wife, he only remembered the way she looked when she stood naked before him, the way she felt when he moved inside her.

He felt his body harden, dryness suck at his throat. Desire for her coiled about him like a beautiful snake, brilliant and seductive, luring him with all the colors of a rainbow and the promise of a pot of gold at the end. He fought against the urge to go to her, telling himself that to do so would show his weakness, and if he admitted that, all was doomed.

He poured himself another drink, but not even whiskey was effective against the memory of her that seemed to cling to him like an exotic fragrance. His mind went blank. Nothing was there except the memory of that one night with her. Margery. His body told him how badly he wanted her. Margery. He took another drink and saw her body, wet with sweat and wrapped in damp bedding. Margery. He threw the glass across the room and went to the porthole and opened it.

A surge of cool, sea air washed over him, but not even that could overpower the feel of her hair covering him, the sounds she made, the scent of their lovemaking.

He crossed the room and watched his hand turn the doorknob. He had not willed it any more than he had willed himself to go to her, but his feet were moving now, of their own accord. She was drawing him to her, like something from another world with powers no mortal could resist.

He walked to the door of her cabin. His desire surged, overriding his ability to think, while something within him said she could heal him, that making love to her would make the pain go away.

His hand came out to close around the handle to her door. He felt disconnected, as if he had come from another time, another place — like he had traveled a great distance and for a terrible length of time just for this one moment. The moment when he would open this door and seek the forgiving solace of the warmth between her legs.

He opened the door a fraction. A deep, warm, inviting fragrance curled around him, luring him inside. He fought against it. But her warm flesh was inviting. And he was so terribly weary.

She watched him come into the room.

He brought with him the smell of the sea and a cool, damp breeze that swept into the room, touching her heated skin like a chill. She had never seen him looking like this, for there was a certain disarray about him, a looseness of clothing, a wildness to his hair, something that made him appear more human, and much more a man.

Perhaps she should be wary of him. He looked like a stranger, his long hair loose and hanging down, instead of neatly tied back. Yet, he was her husband, and she had, on a previous occasion, come into his room in much the same manner.

Was that what he was about then? Had he come here to sleep with her, to come into her with the strength of his need?

He paused, just inside the door, as if trapped with indecision. He looked at her and then at the open door and she knew he was torn as to what he should do. He stood there, silent and anguished, for some time. Finally, he reached out and gave the door a shove.

When he turned back toward her again, there was something compelling in his eyes, something that made her breath catch like a trapped bird in her throat. She knew then what he wanted, why he had come.

Her first thought was to throw back the covers on the bed, to show him that she had nothing on, to tell him that she had been lying here, in the dark of her room, her thoughts on the night he made love to her.

But that would have made it too easy for him.

She said nothing but continued to watch him, seeing the play of emotions across his face, feeling his torment, his anguish. He began walking toward her now, and she could sense the heat in him, but it was the weariness, the pain, the hunger to belong that touched her soul.

Suddenly, he was beside her and bending down to kiss her like a shy fawn coming to the edge of a river to drink, with slow, cautious steps, the warmth and scent of him closing around her as gently as the long fingers that touched her face and stroked her cheeks.

She opened herself to him, a delicious sensation spreading swiftly downward. She felt the weight of his knee on the bed and then he was lying beside her, his arms holding her close against him, her naked flesh pressed against his, and she realized that he had somehow managed to remove his clothes.

His hands seemed to be everywhere, touching her, stroking, sliding over her body with the finesse and rhythm of a canoe that skims the rapids of a river. She gasped, the breath rapidly leaving her throat, and she wondered if she was going to faint.

"Love me. Heal me. Make me whole."

His words were like a song, possessing a rhythm and melody that flowed out of him and into her. He kissed her again and again, his hands touching her breasts, her belly, his mouth pressed against the hollow of her throat. Her whole body tingled with awareness. Each place he touched, she burned.

There was a wildness in his actions, a certain kind of insanity that drove him on and swept her along with it until she became as driven and as frantic as he. Her hands came up to caress him, to learn the textures of his skin and hair. He was a man, with manly urges and a manly feel. That pleased her and she felt engulfed with a thrilling sensation as he came swiftly into her and her body began to move.

A beautiful spasm. Then another.

On and on they came, one after the other, each one building on the promise of the next, like a wave is followed by another, until she began to pant and writhe.

"Yes, come with me. Show me your fire. Burn for me."

He rolled completely over her, putting her beneath him, the wildness of his hair falling down about them, brushing her face, cool and smooth as autumn on a placid lake.

And then she felt the power of him coming inside her with a violence that seemed appropriate for this man and this moment. He covered her mouth once more and she felt the hot warmth flow into her. And she knew love. "Give me your child," she whispered.

But all he answered was, "Forgive me."

CHAPTER
◈ FOURTEEN ◈

Dan stopped by Margery's cabin and asked her to take a walk with him on deck.

The weather was cold and damp, and he apologized for dragging her out in weather such as this. She laughed at that. "I lived in weather such as this."

She took her cloak from the peg by the door and followed him outside.

"I asked you to walk with me because I knew Will might return before I had a chance to talk to you."

"You want to talk about something you don't want Will to know?"

"I think it would be best, yes."

They reached the railing and she stopped. There was an almost pensive tone in his voice, and she turned to search for confirmation in the golden depths of his eyes. The melancholy she heard had come from the heart, for it had stolen the fire from his eyes.

She waited for him to speak, and yet it was his silence that spoke to her. "You search for the words, but they are as slippery as a fish in troubled waters. You must strike, but you look for a way to soften the blow."

The wind ruffled his brown hair as he turned toward her. "Never think of yourself as uneducated. Whatever you lost in knowledge, you have gained in wisdom. It is not easy to hide things from you. You sense what others overlook."

"You are leaving."

"Yes. When we reach London, I must return home. I have not seen my family for quite some time. I wanted to tell you, so you would understand."

"You will not come later for a visit?"

"No, I think it best if I do not."

"I do not understand."

"I know you don't, and for that reason I ask you to trust my judgment. I must stay away."

"Why?"

He leaned his head back and stared up at the sky overhead. "I knew you would ask that, but somehow, I was hoping that you would not." He closed his eyes for a moment, and when he opened them, their eyes met and held. "I have come to care for you a great deal, Margery . . . more than I should. Will and I have been friends since we were boys. I will not allow my feelings for his wife to come between us."

"I did not know."

"I know, and for that, at least, I am thankful."

"Are you going to tell Will?"

"No."

"I think it best that you do not." She watched

the play of emotions on the face of the only true friend she had ever had. She was so accustomed to his presence, his gentle guidance, his quiet teaching, the encouragement when she thought she could not go on. How had she so foolishly thought he would always be around, as if by marrying one man, she would be blessed with two? She understood what Dan was saying, why he had to stay away, but the thought of losing his friendship was difficult to accept.

"I shall miss you."

His mouth twisted into a smile that she knew he had to force. "It is ironic, isn't it? . . . that I must sever my friendship with one of you in order to keep it with the other."

"You must love him very much."

"I do."

"I will never forget you and all you have done."

"Nor I you," he said, then kissed her softly on the cheek. "Be happy."

"I will try," she said, and wiped away her tears with the back of her hand.

They arrived in London two days before Christmas. Margery saw Dan only once since the day they talked. She knew they would be leaving the ship at any moment, and she searched the faces of those leaving the ship, hoping to find him. She could not leave without telling him good-bye.

She was standing quietly next to Will, feeling apprehensive and frightened. Will seemed like a stranger to her and she could not help wondering if he would continue to avoid her now that he was home.

Will was giving directions concerning the removal of their baggage from the ship when Daniel walked up. "I wanted to say farewell."

"You are leaving now?" she asked, trying to keep the sadness from her voice.

"Yes, my coach is waiting."

"You won't change your mind and come with us?" Will asked.

"No, I find I have a sudden urge to hurry home to my family."

Will and Daniel shook hands then embraced briefly before Will left the ship to see about their coach.

Dan turned to Margery, tilting her chin upward. "Don't look so forlorn. This isn't the end of the world . . . it's the beginning of a new life. You won't have me there to act as your tutor, but you will have Octavia, Will's mother, and right now, you need the things she can teach you much more than you need someone like me."

Margery nodded because she could not speak, too many feelings seemed to jam in her throat.

"Don't worry. You will do fine. Will isn't a cruel man, just a pigheaded one. One of these days, he will come to his senses and he will realize what he has in you. Just remember everything I've taught you."

She did her best to blink back the hot tears that spilled down her cheeks. "I remember. Take my time. Do not rush things. Slow and easy wins the race."

Delight danced in his eyes. Then he reached out and took both of her hands in his. "How like winter will your absence be, with December bareness everywhere." He gave her fingers a squeeze, then turned, and without a backward glance, left the ship.

She moved to the rail and watched him go.

It was only when he closed the door of the coach that he looked out the window and waved.

Margery waved back.

Will, who had just joined her, nodded his head and raised his hand a fraction.

A moment later, the coach bearing the crest of Daniel Boardman, Lord Waverly, pulled out of sight.

"Don't look so downtrodden. You haven't seen the last of him."

Margery said nothing.

Another coach pulled up and Will said, "That one is ours. They are loading our baggage now."

Margery followed him down the plank to where the coach waited. As they walked toward it, she saw two beautifully dressed women stepping down from a nearby carriage, their clothing as fine and bright as a bird's plumage. As they passed, the two women looked at her, then exchanged glances. When they were past, they broke into laughter.

Will did not seem to notice, but Margery looked down at her worn buckskin dress and wished that her foolish pride had not prevented her wearing the dresses Will had bought in New Orleans. She pulled he cloak more tightly about her, feeling the soft green wool, thankful that she had not been too stubborn at least to wear that.

It was such a dark winter day that the fog appeared yellow, colored by the lit lamps that glowed in the streets of London as they passed by. On either side of the street, the walks were crowded with people and the shop windows blazed with the light of gas lamps, as if it were night.

She sat stiffly on the seat, her feet tucked beneath her, her bundle in her lap as she stared out the coach window, seeing things she couldn't name, with a look of expectancy upon her face.

"There is no need for you to hold on to your bag all the way to Emberly," Will said, taking the bundle from her and tossing it into the corner. "You might as well rest. We've a long journey before us, and we won't be stopping at an inn for the night. We will have to drive straight through if we are to be home in time for Christmas."

In time for Christmas . . . She had no real understanding of this special time, although Father Marc had told her the story of the birth of the Christ child. But the things Daniel spoke of — Yule logs, mistletoe, holly, stuffed goose — were still foreign to her. She turned her face toward the steaming pane of the window and gazed out at the thickening fog. Before long they crossed a bridge and left the city of London behind, the journey ahead stretching out before them like a length of lonely road. Although there was nothing for her to see, she continued to watch steadily until all the black and grayness that surrounded the coach grew as heavy as her eyes, and she fell asleep.

She had no idea how long she slept, but when she awoke, Will gave her a basket and told her to eat. It was filled with cold chicken and tea, which he purchased at the coach's last stop. She held the basket in her lap and looked out the window. It was dark now, and she could not see any more of England, but the damp cold that seeped into her bones told her it was there.

After a while, she ate the chicken and drank a bit of the tea, which was bitter and dark, then she settled back in the seat. For the rest of the journey, Will devoted his attention to a bottle of whiskey, while she kept her head resting against the window as she stared out at the dense darkness. Just ahead, the coach lamps cast a tight circle of light in front of them, and she saw something familiar to her at last. It was snowing, and she found comfort in knowing not everything here would be alien and unknown. Gradually, her apprehensions began to ease and she felt herself awaken to what was going on around her.

The first thing she noticed was the softness of this strange land to which William Woodville had brought her. Here, the harsh bite of winter snows seemed but a pale and distant cousin to the violence and ruthlessness of the winters in the valleys near the Yellowstone River. In spite of its coldness, the air seemed surprisingly soft, caressing her face with a gentleness she did not expect; the snowflakes were not hard and frozen or driven against her skin with the wind's stinging force, but soft and weightless, fluttering with the grace of a butterfly to melt kindly upon her face.

Across from her, William slept, and she closed her eyes and listened to the steady cadence of the coach horses — the sound of their hoofbeats the only familiar sound she had heard in many weeks. Unable to sleep again, she stared silently out into the darkness, watching the snowflakes swirl and dance in the yellow circle of light just ahead.

Sometime later, she heard the sound of cork popping out of a whiskey bottle, followed by a hearty swallow, a satisfied sigh.

"Close the window. Your hair is getting wet. I'll not have you catching your death your first day here."

She closed the window, shutting out the cold and, along with it, the reminder that she had spent most of her life living out-of-doors, no one minding if her hair was wet, and no illness coming because of it.

She felt uneasy under Will's gaze. She thought about Dan and how different it would have been if he had only chosen to accompany them, for the coach would be filled with the sound of his voice as he told her about the countryside through which they were passing, or taught her the names of towns and rivers and a thousand other things she would need to help her through the time ahead.

Her husband's gaze was still upon her and she stared down at the two long braids that lay across her breasts. Beneath those braids, her once fine antelope-skin dress was showing signs of wear, many of the prized elk teeth having been lost during the long journey to England. Her knee-high leggings and moccasins were dirty and worn. But, like the snow, her clothing gave her a sense of home in this foreign land.

Will lifted the flap over the window next to him and poked his head out, sending a cold blast of air rushing across her face. "We are almost there. I can see the gates."

She looked out the window and followed the direction of his gaze to glimpse a dim light shining just ahead. A moment later, they passed through two great iron gates, which were thrown open by a man carrying a lantern and wearing a long black cape.

Once they were through the gates, they drove for quite some time through a tunnel made by many tall trees that seemed joined overhead.

"We are there?"

"Close. It's a little over a mile from the gates to the house. You aren't getting anxious, are you, little savage?"

"No."

He laughed and held the whiskey bottle up in a salute, then tipped his head back and drank.

She looked past him, her attention drawn now by the lights of a great, hulking house just ahead. The coach rattled over a stone court before coming to a heaving stop before the immense house. To her, it was a house the size of a mountain, slumbering in a bed of soft snow — a great bear in the midst of his winter sleep. Her husband's family must be as large as the clan of the River Crow, she thought, for the light from more than a dozen windows illuminated the snow.

CHAPTER
❂ FIFTEEN ❂

The door to the house opened and a man trotted down the steps. "Ho! Who is about at a time like this? 'Tis Christmas Eve!"

"It is I, William."

Margery watched William climb out of the coach and tumble from the effects of too much whiskey. Without a backward glance, he motioned for her to follow.

The man standing on the steps gasped. "Lord William?"

William stepped into the light and removed his hat.

"Oh, your lordship . . . I beg your pardon, your lordship. I had no idea you were coming home for Christmas. Your mother did not say she was expecting you."

"Nor was she. I fear she will be as surprised as you, Jenkins. I did not send word that I was coming, nor that I was bringing home a wife."

Jenkins's gaze traveled toward the coach where Margery still sat patiently. His expression left little doubt as to the exact moment he saw her, for his eyes seemed to bulge and his mouth dropped open. "Your . . . your . . . your wife, your lordship? You are married?"

"Come, little savage, it is time to meet my family."

She rose obediently and started down the coach steps.

Will stumbled back to her, grabbing her hand as she came off the last step. "This is my wife, Lady Margery Woodville, the Viscountess of Linwood." Amazingly, Will did not slur his words this time. He spoke without a hint of emotion showing upon his face.

"Welcome to Emberly Hall, my lady," Jenkins said, his voice formal and stiff. Jenkins did not move, for truly he seemed as frozen as the ground upon which he stood. He looked her over and it was difficult to tell if he was horrified at her appearance or simply stunned at the revelation that Lord William had taken a wife. Perhaps it was both.

Whatever the reason for his stupefaction, he took his time, his gaze lingering at length upon the long antelope-skin dress, taking in every detail before it dropped down to the moccasins on her feet. At last he stared at her long braids.

William released her hand, then led the way toward the entrance to his home. She followed him up the stone steps. The great carved doors opened to an enormous hall, which was decorated with greenery and ribbon. The lamps were so numerous and bright that the suits of armor fairly shone, and the portraits along the wall and staircase looked new.

"I will inform your family of your arrival."

"That won't be necessary, Jenkins. I will inform them myself."

"Very well, your lordship."

Margery stood in the hall, uncertain and shy. Everything around her seemed unfriendly and aloof — from the hard stone floors to the dark polished furniture. Two red chairs that stood on each side of an old, carved chest looked so stiff and uncomfortable that they reminded her of Jenkins. Behind her, the slow, steady tick of a tall clock caught her attention, and she studied it for a moment, finding even the moon face, with its smiling mouth and red cheeks, had a rather severe look to it.

But the hall was warm and it smelled delicious, for it was filled with wonderful scents — greenery, bayberry candles, and the aromas of apples and nutmeg, cinnamon and mince — fragrances for which she had no name. Yet there was something hauntingly familiar about them, something that made her insides ache for someone she longed for but could not remember clearly. Her mother.

Beyond the hall came the sound of music and of many voices . . . happy voices . . . and she decided then that she liked this thing they called Christmas.

William stood before her in the glow of many candles, the snow on his coat melting into little puddles that reflected the candlelight. "Jenkins will take your cloak."

She removed her cloak and handed it to Jenkins.

William turned at the same time she did, and their eyes met and held. Wings fluttered in her chest. For a fraction of time, he stood looking down at her, his face illuminated by the same bright lights she saw shining in his eyes. He had not looked at her like this since the night he had made love to her on the ship.

Whatever it was that had tormented him since then appeared to be gone, and she felt the joy of it. This might be a foreign land filled with strange people, but this was her husband, and he had brought her to his home. They would live here and raise their children, and the thought filled her with a wonderful feeling of security.

The look in his eyes was tempting, almost tender. He was so handsome, his features so beautiful. He reached out his hand and lifted one of her braids, his hand brushing her breast lightly. She could see his face so clearly, more than she ever had before. His gaze did not leave her face, and she could see now the hunter in him, the desire for her that gleamed in the depths of his eyes, flickering like a blue-white flame. Pinpricks of anticipation danced along her spine. For a moment she thought he might kiss her, but the blue flame grew suddenly dim, flickering once before going completely out. He dropped her braid, and the features that seemed so beautiful a moment before retracted into a hard mask.

"Come, little savage. I want my family to meet you."

Margery's heart fluttered then fell with the mockery of his words. He turned and led the way down the long hallway. Humiliation stealing her color, she followed him, passing many servants who stopped what they were doing and turned to stare at the strange sight.

She followed him into a room that captured the power of the sunlight, for it was flooded with warmth and brightness.

It was also full of people.

The sound of music reached her ears. A child's shrill laughter pierced the air. The warm current of delicious aromas she had smelled earlier was stronger now, swirling around her head and reminding her of how long it had been since she had eaten.

She was suddenly aware that the room had gone terribly quiet and that the twenty or so people there had all turned to stare, as if they were looking at the spirit of someone long dead.

Amid the gasps of surprise, the whispers of speculation, the shocked looks, Will spoke not a word but strode purposefully to where a man stood, a man she knew had to be the Earl of Warrenton, William's father.

As she stood next to her husband, she allowed her gaze to quickly skim the room, hastily taking in the people gathered there. This would be the rest of the family that Daniel had spoken about — Will's four sisters, their husbands and children, and a few other relatives and friends. Daniel had spoken of Christmas as a time when families and friends gather together.

The room spoke of things she was learning to identify with Christmas, for it was wreathed in swags of greenery, holly, and mistletoe, and in one corner, standing in front of a great window, stood a magnificent tree, much like those she had seen many times in the land of the Crow — only this tree glittered with the light of many candles, with beautifully decorated dolls and ornaments dangling from its boughs.

Glancing at his family again, she could see the clothes they wore were fine and befitting a special occasion. And yet the laughter, the merriment, the beautiful singing she first heard when she came were gone.

At last the silence was broken when William's mother, Octavia, stepped forward. Except for his great height, which William inherited from his father, William Woodville was the image of his mother.

It did not take Margery long to see the affection he felt for his mother, for the moment he looked at her, the pain that was always present in his eyes was transformed by a look of true delight.

While it was apparent his mother was glad to see him, it was obvious his father was not. Heated words were exchanged. The children were led from the room. No one dared to speak — no one, save William and his father.

Margery's palms were wet. A weak trembling

began in her knees. Fear leached into her spine, and she knew by the coldness that settled like a chill about her that all the color had fled her face. She looked at William's mother, expecting to see her meekness, her respect of her husband's authority, and therefore, the honoring of his anger toward his son. She saw none of this.

Octavia looked from her husband to her son as if she fought some inner battle of loyalty between the two. Then, without a word, she stepped forward and put her arms around her son and hugged him to her. A moment later, he introduced Margery as his wife.

Octavia gave her a kind look. "You said her name was . . . Walks Fast?"

William's gaze was still on his father. A muscle worked in his jaw. "That is what the Crow call her."

Octavia looked as if she did not understand. "The Crow?"

"Indians."

"Oh, she is Indian. . . ."

"The American kind."

Charles almost choked. "An Indian? You have married an Indian? A savage?"

A hard smile seemed to grip Will's mouth. "I have married a woman. What she is, I don't find important."

Charles slammed his hand down on a table. A crystal decanter rattled against two glasses. "I'll not stand for it. I'll not have my son and the heir of my title marrying a savage."

A triumphant gleam flashed in Will's eyes. "It's a little late for that, I'm afraid."

"You did this on purpose."

"Think what you want," Will said, striking like a snake and releasing his venom. "And the next time you think about sending me an ultimatum, I hope you remember this: My life is my own, to do with as I please. . . . ."

As the kindness in her eyes had led Margery to believe, Octavia had no difficulty accepting her, but the reaction of William's father was violent. "How dare you come in here, among your mother and sisters and their families, looking like the heathen you have become."

Margery stood in silence, but her mind whirled with thought. Although she had wondered at his purpose for marrying her, it had never occurred to her William's sole reason for doing so had been revenge. How wrong she had been to give it a nobler purpose. She had been wrong to think of him as her rescuer, her savior, and yes, even her loving husband. His motives had been far more selfish.

She wanted to flee. She wanted to get away from these people and this place. She wanted to run and keep on running until she was out of his life and England, until her legs would no longer carry her and the pain in her chest was more than she could bear. Only then would she be able to stop. Only then, when the physical pain was too intense to bear, would she be able to think about what he had done.

Gradually, she became aware that the angry exchange between William and his father continued.

"I cannot believe you have done this," Charles said. "It is unforgivable."

"You did say you wanted me married."

"Damn you to eternal hell! You know what I meant. I told you in my letter that I had already arranged the betrothal between you and Lady Jane Penworthy."

"Except you forgot one minor thing. Lady Jane Penworthy is not a woman I wish to marry."

"And this unrefined" — he waved an arm in Margery's direction — "uncultured, uneducated savage is? Just look at her. She is a disgrace to the hallowed halls of Westminster . . . unfit to tread upon English soil." He paused a moment, then continued. "This is not the end of it." He stepped closer, until he was no more than a hair's breadth from William's face. "I will see you burn in hell before I will allow this."

Octavia stepped between them. "That is quite enough. If the two of you don't have enough sense to stop this, then I will. It is Christmas Eve. We have family present. Mind your language."

Ignoring his mother, William stepped around her, pausing just in front of his father. "I will not allow you to run my life. Not now. Not ever. You may not approve of me or the woman I have married, but at least *I* made the choice."

"You sure as hell didn't do a very good job of

it, laddie. Blind drunk, I could have done better than that."

Margery did not need to look at the others in the room. She could feel the heat of their stares, could hear the shocked whispers behind her back. Her face felt hot. The candles in the room seemed to blur before her eyes as she gazed sightlessly across the room. Nothing in her past had prepared her for this. Not even when her dress had been ripped from her had she known the depths of degradation that she felt now.

Her gaze was drawn once again to her husband who had suddenly turned toward her. She looked into the familiar blue eyes and saw the truth. Her trampled heart fell to her feet.

So it was true. All of it. The look, the apology in his eyes was all the confirmation she needed. He had rescued her from the savagery of the Indians only to submit her to a newer, more brutal form called civilization. Now she was married to this man, joined to him by a bond that could not be severed, a bond that held her more tightly than any amount of captivity had done.

How foolish she had been to think of him as her savior, when, in truth, she was only something he used to cause his family pain. She was an instrument of revenge, something to be despised and hated, and judging from the expression on his father's face, William had accomplished his goal. Never had she seen anyone look at her with such loathing, such hatred. Not even the most ruthless Comanches hated without reason.

She closed her eyes for a moment, remembering Will had introduced her using her Crow name. There was no question now as to why he did it. The answer was sharply clear. He had used her Crow name as an added insult. He wanted them to think she was bred a heathen and not just raised as one. In spite of her pain, she resented the warm trail of tears on her face. She wished there was some place for her to go. Some place she could hide. Was there never to be a place of refuge for her, a place she could call home?

Suddenly, she was filled with a longing for the wild country, where the sky and the water would heal her wounds. Like a captive bird, she had been separated from her wildish nature. She would have to learn to fight and fight hard in order to preserve her integrity. She must remember and find her strength in the memory of green sprouts pushing through the snow, in the vision of the she-wolf running hard, eyes scanning the ground, ears pricked forward in readiness. She had nothing more than her instinct to guide her now — instinct that had been handed down to her from all the women who had come before her.

Just when she thought she might break down and cry, William's mother moved to stand next to her. Octavia's arm slipped around Margery's shoulders, and she turned to face her son and husband. The moment Octavia touched her, Margery felt the strength and power of countless women reaching out to her from across time, instilling her with a wild essence that preserved, a female tradition that would see her through the dark days ahead.

"Enough! Have you no shame!" Octavia's voice rang out sharp and clear. "Regardless of who she is, or what she is, she is William's wife and she is a human being. She will be treated as such."

Charles gave Margery a spiteful look. "Human? Surely you exaggerate. She is a mammal. Beyond that, I dare to speculate."

"As we are all mammals . . . *some* of us having been elevated to a higher plane when we developed the capacity to feel." She looked from Charles to William. "I am ashamed of you . . . both of you. How could you be so cruel? She obviously has feelings and they have been trampled flat as a sixpence. Have you none of the milk of human kindness? Not even on Christmas Eve?"

Octavia turned then and picked up a silver cup filled with something she called wassail. She offered it to Margery. "Drink this. It will warm you, but more importantly, it will remove some of the sting of such poisonous words."

Without looking at Will, Margery took the cup, watching as Octavia turned and picked up two more cups, which she thrust into the hands of both William and Charles.

"Now, we will have a Christmas toast . . . a drink to the return of our son and the gaining of another daughter."

In response, Charles threw the wassail. Wine

flew in all directions as the cup rolled across the floor before it came to a stop at the base of the brightly lit Christmas tree.

Charles turned upon his son. "I rue the day you were born. If it takes the rest of my life and every farthing I have, I will see that you come to regret it as well."

"Then be of good cheer, Father. It will take neither time nor coin. Your wait is a short one, for I have regretted being your son for as long as I can remember."

"Regardless of your feelings for me, I am still your father, and as such, I will not let you get away with this. Tomorrow I will send for my barrister. What has been done can be undone."

Octavia spoke up. "Tomorrow is Christmas Day, Charles."

Charles glared at her, then mumbled something about the day after.

"That is Boxing Day."

His voice quivered with rage as Charles almost shouted, "By God, I will have this marriage annulled and quickly, and neither Christmas nor hell will stand in the way."

William, whether intentionally or not, kept his voice smooth and firm. "Not even the powerful Earl of Warrenton and all his money can end this marriage, I am afraid. No matter how badly you want to, there is nothing you can do."

"What do you mean, I won't be able to end it? You of all people should know that I have long been in the habit of doing as I damn well please."

William shrugged. "Go ahead and try . . . if trying gives you some sort of satisfaction. But, sooner or later you will have to face the fact that no one, not even you can annul this marriage."

"I'd like to know why not."

"Because it has been consummated . . . and more than once, I might add."

A unified gasp echoed from wall to wall. Octavia waved her hand and many of those remaining left the room.

William continued. "And to save you the trouble of having to prove what I have said . . ." He reached into his pocket and withdrew a document, which he held up for his father to see. "A legal, binding document, for a legal and binding marriage, performed by an ordained minister."

"You bastard!" Charles slapped the document away.

William folded the paper and put it into his coat pocket.

He glanced at Margery. As if sensing her pain, he broke eye contact and looked away. She tried to think of Dan and what he would tell her to do in a situation like this. She took a deep breath, hoping to slow the furious pounding of her heart as she reminded herself that Will was drunk and filled with revenge, two emotions that were older and far stronger than any concern or pity he might have for her.

Suddenly, he cursed, then strode across the room, leaving her standing alone with his parents.

Charles shouted after him. "Where do you

think you are going? Nothing has been settled. We aren't through with this."

"Yes, we are." William paused in the doorway, uttering the words that shattered all hope for her. "I have been the dutiful son and have taken a wife. My obligation to you and the future of your title is fulfilled. That done, I am returning to America."

"I'll see you in hell first!"

He gave his father a salute. "Save me a place when you get there," he said, then turned away.

His father's voice shook with rage. "Come back here."

William did not stop.

"I order you to come back!"

William kept walking.

"You bastard."

"Alas, everyone says I am the image of my father."

"You forgot something," Charles called out, giving Margery a hostile glare. "Leave if you like, but take your heathen wife with you."

William's voice shot back. "My wife stays."

"Like hell! You aren't going to dump her on us. I'll toss her out the moment you're gone."

"You will do nothing of the sort. William's wife stays," Octavia said, the tone in her voice declaring an end to the fight.

Charles lowered his voice as he spoke to his wife. "She is a savage, Octavia. A heathen."

"Apparently you have forgotten what it says in *Hebrews.* 'Be not forgetful to entertain strangers:

for thereby some have entertained angels unawares.' "

"Angels? You cannot compare her to an angel. She is a viper waiting to bear her fangs."

"She is William's wife and my daughter-in-law. I will see to it that she is treated with respect."

The sound of a door's opening could be heard. In unison, Charles, Octavia, and Margery turned to look, as William Woodville, Viscount Linwood, the only son and heir of the Earl of Warrenton walked out of Margery's life.

CHAPTER
⊞ SIXTEEN ⊞

Octavia ran after him.

"William," she called out. "Please wait. It is Christmas Eve. Can't you delay your departure for a few days?"

"No, Mother, I cannot."

"At least don't leave until I can say good-bye properly."

Will stopped. He turned around slowly. He could never resist anything his mother asked of him.

Octavia reached his side. "I beg you not to leave tonight. Stay for a few days at least."

"You know I can't, Mother. It was wrong . . . a mistake to come back here. I can see that now."

"Just a few days, Will. Surely that can't hurt too much. You've been gone so long."

He looked down at her, and his hand came out to touch her cheek. "You know I could never deny you anything. It grieves me that there must be a first time."

"Please stay. I beg you. It's Christmas."

He felt moisture collecting in his eyes. Agony

twisted his insides. He wanted nothing more than to put his arms around his mother and to tell her that he would stay, but he could not. "I can't. If I do, one of us may end up killing the other. I can't let him destroy me. You know that. You've always known that."

Octavia sighed. "What about her? What about your wife?" she asked, nodding in the direction of the grand salon. Will followed his mother's gaze, through the open doors to the place where Margery stood, her pale, white face stricken, her eyes huge and full of uncertainty. He felt his heart wrench painfully. He had never before in his life hurt anyone intentionally.

Yet he could not give in. He gritted his teeth, his jaw hard and determined. "She is better off here . . . without me."

"How can you say that, William? She is your wife."

"And for that, I pity her."

"You can't just abandon her here, without staying at least a few days. We are complete strangers to her. She needs you."

His eyes never left Margery's face. When he spoke, his voice was low, full of regret. "What she needs, I cannot give her."

"You owe it to her, at least, to stay . . . if for nothing more than a few days. Give her time to adjust, to get to know us."

"She does not need me. She is filled with an ageless wisdom and the instinct to survive. She has not been *civilized* by society and forced into its rigid roles. She is a wild creature, filled with the instinctual nature that culture and sophistication have not yet tarnished. She will teach you as much as I know you will teach her. Right now, she does not realize it, but her captivity will prove to be not the cause of all her travails, but the source of her survival. Removed from our corrupt world, she has grown up in the wild, possessing a keen sense and a playful spirit. She is deeply intuitive and a master in adapting to a constantly changing set of circumstances."

"She will be changed when you come back. If you leave her now, you will never . . ."

Will took his mother in his arms. "I can't stay. As for Margery . . . don't worry about her. Listen to her, to her story, then you will understand why I can't give her what she needs. The thing she needs now, more than anything, is the love of a family."

"And you think she will find that here, in spite of your father's wrath?"

"I know she will because I know you, and I know my sisters. Once I am gone, you will have Father properly chastised and playing the role of loving father and husband. Then you will busy yourself with Margery. She has lost a great part of her life. I would like to see that she finds it. There will be much to learn about being a civilized woman. Those are things I cannot give her." He paused a moment. "They are the things I would not give her, even if I could, for there is a part of me that regrets what I have done. I should have left her in the wild. But, since I did not, it is my responsibility to see she has the skills to survive in captivity." He kissed Octavia's cheek. "Care for her, Mother. Care for her as if she were your own."

This time, when William left, Octavia did not call him back.

However, she did motion for a small, dark-haired man standing by the piano to join her.

When Guy Montgomery reached her side, she said, "He is leaving, Guy. What shall I do?"

"Perhaps it is better this way. He has not yet learned to deal with his pain."

"I know, and I cannot bear to think of him all alone over there with nothing but his suffering. Go with him, Guy." Octavia took a deep breath, feeling suddenly exhausted. She put a hand on Guy's arm. "You understand him better than anyone."

Guy glanced toward the door, obviously considering Octavia's words. Then he nodded.

"You were always more than his tutor, you know. You were more like his father. He will listen to you, Guy. Watch over him, and if it is in your power to help him drive away the devils that torment him . . ."

Octavia's voice broke and she withdrew her handkerchief from beneath her cuff. "Go. Go quickly. And please . . . write to me, Guy. Let me know how he is doing," she said, "because I know he will not."

"I will write when I can," Guy replied, then

turned and hurried in the direction William had taken.

Charles poured himself a drink and tossed it down, then poured himself another one. When Octavia walked slowly back into the room, he said, "He is no son of mine."

Margery stood there, not knowing what she should do or where she should go. She watched William's father toss down the rest of his drink before he placed the empty glass on a silver tray and walked from the room, leaving only Margery and Octavia behind.

She glanced at Octavia and saw the weariness in her eyes. Octavia gave her an apologetic look, then lost the composure she had maintained throughout the evening.

Without a word, Octavia collapsed into a chair and softly wept.

Margery stood there, listening to the sound of Octavia's crying, feeling lonely and afraid. She could not help wondering what would become of her. Now that Will was gone.

Her heart swelled up with grief. All the light seemed to have gone out of her life. William was gone.

And then she reminded herself that he had left of his own choosing, and that he had used her selfishly and for his own purpose. Do not weep for him. Weep for what he has done. For the deception. The betrayal . . .

She sat down next to William's mother, wanting

to give her comfort, uncertain as to how she should do it. At last, she put her hand on Octavia's shoulder.

Octavia sniffed and raised her head, then took up her handkerchief to dry her eyes. "Well, I do feel better. I am like a beaver hat. I improve with rain."

"To cry is good?"

Octavia smiled at her. "So I've been told. A tear on the cheek, or a wrinkle on the face . . . although I think that no grief was ever equal to all those tears." She sniffed again, then picked up Margery's hand. "You poor, dear child. You must be terrified and feeling quite alone. However, I want you to know that it is past midnight and this is Christmas Day, and I do believe, without a doubt, that you are the grandest Christmas present anyone has ever given me."

Octavia sighed deeply and rose to her feet, then stood looking down at Margery. "I don't know what to say. I know our ways must seem strange to you, but I hope you will believe me when I say this really isn't our normal way of doing things. Will and his father have never gotten on, and unfortunately, it is the innocent who often pay the most. I cannot undo what my son has done, but I can do all I can to make you feel welcome. I know you won't believe it now, but in truth, I think you will come to love England and our family. We really aren't such a bad sort."

"Will's father . . ."

"Is an ass . . . I am sorry to say that on our

first meeting, but why hide the truth? Oh, he can be a perfectly charming dear, but when it comes to matters with his son, he is beyond stubborn. I will not lie to you and say it will be easy for you around Charles. He is stubborn and opinionated, and he does not choose his words carefully. I tell you this now, so you will know it will be in your best interest to avoid him completely — at least until you feel comfortable standing up to him."

Octavia paused and looked at Margery's face, obviously seeing the confusion, the threat of tears. "Oh, my dear, dear child. I am sure you have had more than your share of sorrow. We will talk when you feel up to it. Until then, I will see what I can do to ensure you a brighter future. You are Will's wife and that makes you another one of my daughters. Do come with me. I'd like you to meet the others."

Octavia tugged at her hand.

Margery stood, but she remained steadfast, staring down at her clothes. She could not help wondering if Octavia understood how she felt, how she could not bring herself to go in the presence of others who were so finely dressed while she looked as she did.

Octavia smacked her forehead with the palm of her hand. "I am so thoughtless. Of course you don't want to meet anyone without cleaning up first. Besides, it is late, and the others have probably gone to bed. Come with me, I'll take you to your room."

Margery followed her upstairs, where Octavia

told the maid, Dotty, she would put Margery in the corner room. "Go into Emily's room and see what you can find in the way of a nightgown that might fit Margery."

Dotty bobbed her head, the streamers on her white cape flapping as she set off down the hall.

"For the next few days, you will have to settle for whatever clothing we can rummage from Emily's closet. We won't have much luck, I'm afraid, trying to find clothes for you during the holidays. Once they have passed, we will set about getting you a complete wardrobe."

"William bought me English clothes in New Orleans."

Octavia started down the hall in the opposite direction from the one Dotty had taken. "Then we will go through them tomorrow." Octavia opened one of the doors and led Margery into a large, corner room with many windows. "This room has a lovely view of the countryside. It is one of my favorites. I think you will come to like it as much as I do. Now come and sit down with me while we wait for Dotty. I want to hear about your life. All I know is what Will said, which is precious little."

Margery's heart began to beat wildly. Once she told Will's mother everything, would they turn her away?

Octavia must have seen the fear in her eyes. "I am not asking this of you to make you uncomfortable but to help you. The more I know about you, about your past . . . what you have experienced . . . the things you know or don't know, the better I will be able to teach you the things you need to know. It is obvious your English is quite good . . . remarkable, in fact, for one raised by primitives."

Margery was not certain where she should begin, but since this was Christmas, she decided to tell her about Father Marc. Once she started talking about that, the conversation seemed to flow quite naturally into the events of her life. It was an emotional experience for her and by the time she finished — Dotty having come and gone some time ago — both she and Octavia were crying.

Octavia handed Margery her handkerchief and encouraged her to "blow."

Margery blew her nose, finding the procedure quite strange and without purpose, but she did not tell Octavia that.

When Margery handed the handkerchief back, Octavia waved it away, telling her to keep it. "Dear child, I cannot undo what you have suffered, but I can promise you that I will do everything in my power to see that you never feel unwanted or unloved again." She paused, shaking her head. "It is a good thing for Will that he returned to America. I fear that if he were still in England, I would find him and give him the worst dressing down he has had since he was in short pants. In spite of what he said, I think it would have been much better for you if he had stayed . . . at least for a while."

Octavia stood, smoothing out her skirts, then looking at the watch pinned to her bosom. "Dear me. It is late and you are exhausted. I have talked overlong. Forgive me."

"It is your right to know my story."

"I did not ask it of you because it was my right but out of concern for you. Go to bed now and sleep well. We will talk again tomorrow."

"Tomorrow is Christmas?"

Octavia frowned. "Yes . . . well, as I said earlier, it is after midnight, so it is already tomorrow, but that is a confusing concept, so suffice it to say that tomorrow is Christmas Day." She paused. "Do you understand what Christmas is?"

Margery nodded. "I am Christian. Father Marc taught me about Christmas, and Dan told me more about it on the ship."

"Dan? Oh, Lord Waverly? He and Will have been friends for as long as I can remember. I always approved of Daniel. Such a sensible lad. He is such a dear, isn't he?"

"He is my friend. He was very helpful. I will miss him."

"Then we shall invite him to visit." And with that, Octavia was gone, leaving Margery to settle herself into the corner room that would be hers for some time to come.

Margery removed her clothing and pulled the soft, white gown over her head. Like everything else in this house, it smelled lovely.

She climbed in bed and turned out the light. As she lay there in the darkness, she thought about her unbelievably long day. She liked William's mother and planned to stay far, far away from his father. As for the rest of the family, she would withhold judgment until she could meet them. It was only after she had decided all of these things that she allowed herself to think about Will and his betrayal.

The first rays of morning peeped around the draperies in her room when Margery closed her eyes to sleep. William was gone, but he had left behind the pain of betrayal.

To love someone and not have them love you was a pain that would eventually mend. But to love someone and have them betray you . . . It was an unforgivable agony, something deep and regretful, like the loss of limbs or the sight in both eyes.

A wound would heal . . . but loss was eternal.

For a moment she wondered if she would ever be able to survive his breach of faith, and yet, at the very moment when she thought she would never be able to overcome this, the heart she had thought broken beyond repair began to beat again.

As she listened to it, she could feel it growing stronger and harder. Where there had once been a heart that whispered the sound of his name with every beat, there was nothing left but a cold, hard stone.

Stones did not feel. . . .

CHAPTER
◼ SEVENTEEN ◼

He wasn't the cold-hearted bastard he made himself out to be.

A cold-hearted bastard would have walked away from her without another thought. Will had another thought. In fact, he had several thoughts. They were all about her. About Margery. The wife he left behind.

When he could not seem to shake the nagging feeling that he might have made a mistake in leaving her, he realized he wasn't the consummate villain, no matter how black he painted himself. It was encouraging to know the conscience he thought long ago lost was still intact, and yet discouraging to realize that he had done something he was beginning to fear he would regret.

Sitting in the coach across from him, Guy cleared his throat.

Will gave him a quick glance, then said, "What made you decide to come with me? And don't tell me it was because my mother asked you. You never had any difficulty changing my mother's mind before."

That got a chuckle out of Guy. "I came because

I've been waiting for an opportunity like this all my life. For once, I want to do something on impulse, something that seems a little daring. I want to walk down a passage I did not take. I want to open a door that I have never opened. I want to know what is on the other side."

"And what do you think you will find? Darkness? Despair?"

"I don't know. A rose garden, perhaps."

"Perhaps, and then, perhaps not."

"I know you probably don't understand someone's having a longing to do something like that. You've followed your impulse and taken a chance on life many times. You've seen half the world because of it. I don't want to wake up an old man one day, feeling life has passed me by."

Will understood. "Then, I suppose we need to gather your belongings. Where do you live now?"

"I've lived with my sister, Elizabeth, since her husband died two years ago. Her townhouse is in London. We can stop by there on our way."

Will nodded, then turned his head to stare out the window at the first gray hint of dawn. In the distance, he could see the spires and rooftops of the city of London. They would be there before long.

He closed his eyes and tried to rest. Sleep would not come. Thoughts of Margery did. Margery, bold as innocence, full of wisdom, giver of love. And he had left her.

Would she ever understand? Could she find it

in her generous heart to forgive him? He should have explained things. It would have been the right thing to do. Certainly, he owed her that.

But he had never considered it until now. Only, now was too late. Too late, and he would not get a second chance. He cursed this omission, his insensitivity to what she might have felt. But most of all, he was ashamed of allowing a consuming passion with getting even with his father to turn him into someone who was both thoughtless and indifferent.

The sound of the horses' hooves striking the cobbled streets reached his consciousness and he opened his eyes to look out. They had been in London for some time now, for already he could see the masts of the ships riding anchor in the harbor just ahead.

"You regret what you have done? Or what you have said?" Guy asked.

"Neither. I find it is the things I might have said that fester."

" 'Your eyes shall be opened, and ye shall be as gods, knowing good and evil,' " he quoted. "Once you have tasted of the tree of knowledge, there is no going back."

"And hindsight is only good for telling me where I've been. It cannot tell me where I need to go."

"Ahhh, the burden of choice. And now you seek guidance."

Will gave him a sad sort of smile. "You were ever the soothsayer."

"It was not difficult. You are looking as lost as an Englishman without his umbrella. Want to talk about it?"

"No."

Guy nodded. "Perhaps you are wise to keep your own counsel. It is said the silent bear no witness against themselves."

Will said nothing. His feelings were too new, too fresh, and too sensitive to lay upon the table for dissection.

Guy rested his head against the wall of the coach and closed his eyes. His words came with the gentle stirring of a released breath. "Know that I am here . . . whenever you feel like talking."

"I know."

He opened one eye. "You realize, of course, that whatever troubles you will be made manifest until you can no longer ignore it. Problems, like heavy cream, always rise to the top."

"We will talk then, when the cream has risen."

Guy chuckled and said no more.

It was a short while later that Will stood along the railing of the ship, watching it drift farther and farther from the docks, until London was as distant and gray as the fog. A terrible sadness began to settle over him, and he knew that he had passed the halfway point . . . that twinkling of a second when he could have stopped what he had put into motion.

But he had not acted, and the moment had

passed, like footfalls that echo in the mind, reminding us of the path we did not take, the door of opportunity we did not open.

CHAPTER
◼ EIGHTEEN ◼

When Margery opened her eyes the next morning, an eerie light penetrated her room. She climbed out of bed and crept across the floor on bare feet, tripping on the hem of her long nightgown. She went to the window and parted the draperies to stare out at the world below for her first glimpse of her new home in daylight. What she saw was a surprise, for everything outside her window was hushed and white.

A soft mantle of snow lay across the fields and orchards — snow that was still falling, steady and gentle, roofing the gabled wings of the house in white, and dusting the branches of the chestnut trees with a light powder. Below the trees, she could see the tracks of many birds, their prints looking very much like the ancient drawings she had seen in caves near the Yellowstone.

Everywhere she looked, it was cold and still. The world outside had settled down with a quiet sort of patience to wait for spring. How like her life it was, and she wondered, as she stared out at the frozen world below, if there would ever come a time when the cold shroud of winter would slip away, and she would see spring once again.

A few minutes later Will's youngest sister, Emily, and her mother came marching into the room, followed by an army of maids carrying a tub and buckets of hot water, which looked suspiciously like the torture she had undergone in St. Louis.

"We will start the day off with a bath," Octavia announced. "I must see to things downstairs, but Emily will stay with you, to make sure that everything goes smoothly."

Octavia departed.

Margery eyed the steaming tub of water. "Well hell!"

Emily gave her a startled look then collapsed, falling across the bed, consumed with laughter. Margery decided then and there that she liked this sister of Will's. She did not understand her and she had never seen anyone who looked as she did. Although Emily had hair about the same color as Margery's, Emily's hair was very, very curly. She was quite small and graceful, her movements as quick and effortless as a deer's. Never had Margery seen anyone so happy, so prone to laughter. Her eyes fairly sparkled with life and something else, something she could only think of as an urge to be naughty.

When Emily had recovered enough to speak, she asked, "Where did you learn to say that?"

"From William."

"I should have known," Emily said. "It was

always Will's favorite expression. Just be careful where you say it." Emily glanced at the tub of water. "Your bath will be cold if you don't hurry."

Margery was soon in the tub, and before long, she finished her bath, finding it went much smoother than it had the first time. She did balk, however, when Emily went through her trunks and showed her the things she was to wear.

Never in her life had she seen so many things that had to be worn at one time. She wasn't convinced she had enough places to hang all of it. However did one manage to remember where it all went and what went on first?

"Go ahead," Emily said. "Put them on."

Margery eyed the garments with suspicious trepidation. They looked like more torture to her.

Her first instinct was right. They were more torment, especially the contraption called a corset, a device of supreme torture garnished with whalebone and an immense busk that laced up the back. Once it was on, she couldn't breathe. "Well hell . . ."

Emily was unconcerned. "No one can breathe in them, but it's the fashion, so you learn to endure."

"Why?"

Emily looked puzzled. "Goodness! I don't know why, it's just something we do . . . without thinking."

That didn't make much sense to Margery, who had always thought there had to be a reason for what one did. You built a fire when you were cold; ate when hungry; sought shelter when it rained. But you wore clothes that made you miserable for no reason? Strange, these English . . .

Once Margery was dressed, and her hair arranged on top of her head, it was declared that in spite of her inability to breathe, she was the loveliest thing to grace the Midlands, nay, England's shores in many years.

"Mother will never believe this," Emily said, taking Margery's arm to escort her downstairs.

By the time Emily and Margery arrived downstairs, the rest of the Woodville family was gathered around the Christmas tree, where the children were receiving their Christmas boxes containing money.

Amid the clamor and joyous shouting of children, Margery was introduced to the rest of Will's family, which consisted of three older sisters, Elizabeth, Caroline, Marianne, and their husbands — a viscount, a marquess, and an earl — who all complimented Margery on how lovely she looked. Next she met the children and a few visiting cousins.

Looking about the room, Margery saw that Charles, the ass, was absent, which suited her just fine.

As if reading her thoughts, Octavia gave her a knowing smile and announced to everyone: "Charles went to have breakfast with your uncle. Poor Rand is under the weather with a bad case of the sniffles."

"Then that means John won't be coming either," Emily said, sounding disappointed.

Margery remembered Dan telling her about John, Will's cousin who was a doctor, and decided this must be the same John of which Emily spoke.

"No, John won't be coming, but Charles will be back for dinner," Octavia said.

Margery didn't care if he never came back, but she nodded and moved closer to the Christmas tree, having never seen anything quite so lovely before. Caroline and Marianne came to stand beside her.

"Do you have Christmas trees in America?" Marianne asked as she leaned over and pulled the thumb out of the mouth of her two-year-old daughter.

"I don't know."

"That must be very sad for you, to have no memory of such things," Caroline said.

"Perhaps it wasn't so sad," Marianne said. "You can't miss what you can't remember."

"Is that really true?" asked Emily, who had just joined them. "Have you never seen a Christmas tree before?"

Margery looked at the tree. "I don't remember having seen one before."

"That is highly possible, since we have not had them in England overlong. Don't be forgetting that it was our own Prince Consort who brought the tradition with him from Germany," said Elizabeth, who also joined them. She was balancing a plump, smiling baby on her hip.

"Oh, that's right. I had forgotten," Caroline said. "It seems as if we've had the tradition forever."

"Elizabeth knows all about it, because she is the only one old enough to remember," Emily said, and everyone laughed.

"I am not that old," Elizabeth replied. Then to Margery she said, "It must have been very difficult for you to survive such an ordeal."

"Yes, it was very difficult."

Elizabeth shifted the baby into her arms. "Did you always know you would be rescued one day?"

"It is hard to know if I really felt that way, or if I simply wanted it so badly that I believed it. There were many times that I came close to giving up hope."

Caroline was about to say something when Octavia joined them. "It is almost ten o'clock."

"Time for breakfast in the dining room," Emily whispered to Margery, "but we have a few minutes, since my sisters will have to rid themselves of the children before they go to breakfast."

Margery glanced around the room, looking at the children and thinking the sisters had a monumental task. Clustered around Elizabeth Chatsworth were two of the four Chatsworths, whom she was ardently trying to keep from harassing the little Landsdowne girls, who numbered three and were tearfully clinging to mother Caroline's skirts. Marianne de Burgh was handing her baby over to the nanny, while her husband, Hugh, the

Earl of Chillinghurst, separated the two younger de Burgh boys, who were arguing over a bit of tinsel that had fallen from the tree. Not far from them, the two eldest de Burghs were harassing two of their cousins, who were cutting out silhouettes. In the midst of this were the remaining children, plus two cousins — who circled the room, waving banners of brightly colored ribbon tied to sticks. Competing with the clamor of children were the yapping of three dogs and the snapping and crackling of a roaring fire.

Once the children were led from the room, some semblance of order returned. Even the fire seemed somewhat tame, having burned down a bit, its popping reduced to nothing more than the occasional pop of dry wood.

At three minutes past ten, Margery walked with Emily to the breakfast parlor, a small, feminine room with walls of pale peach and green set off with white plasterwork and gilding. From where she was seated, she could either stare at her reflection in a large pier glass that hung over a coordinated table or look out into the circular conservatory that opened into both the breakfast parlor and dining room. If anyone had cared to ask her, she would have said she preferred to look into the conservatory, with its half-naked statue rising out of a fountain, surrounded by lush, exotic plants.

As far as meals went, she would have to say that her first meal with her husband's family did not go as smoothly as she would have liked.

Upon entering the breakfast room, Emily whispered that the "cold dishes are on the sideboard," whatever that was.

Once they were seated, Octavia poured cups of coffee, while to her right, Elizabeth served hot chocolate. While that was being done, Margery looked about the table. What Emily identified as crumb muffins, oat cakes, crumpets, breakfast cake, bannocks, Sally Lunns, and scones, were arranged along with an assortment of fancy breads, one of which, she noticed, was green. There was also an assortment of butter, marmalades, honey, and preserves.

Next to her plate stood a silver egg cup and small spoon, and while she wondered what she was to do with that, the butler stopped next to her and inquired as to what she would like to eat.

Not knowing what the choices were, she answered, "I will have whatever you are serving."

Having no clue as to what she had just ordered, Margery got a pretty good idea that she had done something wrong when Emily almost strangled, trying to keep from laughing.

While Emily choked, the footman dished up "whatever you are serving" and handed it to the butler, who served it to Margery. With a look of horror, Margery stared down at the plates set before her containing an array of foods, some of which Emily identified as rissole, minces, bacon, sausages, fresh fruit, baked mushrooms, smoked kippers, chicken, fried rabbit, roast partridge, pigeon, woodcock, quail, quenelles, game pie, mar-row toast, curry of mutton, cromeskies, and cow heel in tomato sauce.

Margery, who had never sat down to a meal such as this in her life, stared hopelessly at the food before her, then just as hopelessly at the arrangement of glasses, dishes, and eating utensils. She had never seen so many choices. How would she ever know what to do?

She recalled Daniel's advice. "Take your time. Watch what others do and follow their lead, doing what they do."

She tried that. With disastrous results.

Taking her time, she watched Octavia pick up her knife and fork to cut the fat, round sausage that lay on her plate. When Margery tried this, the sausage went shooting across her plate, sending the mushrooms rolling across the tablecloth, where one fell off the table and another landed in Viscount Downley's bread plate. While that was happening, the sausage, which was airborne by this time, knocked over the egg cup, the egg bouncing once before landing in Emily's cup of hot chocolate, just as the sausage shot across the plate of the Marquess of Handley, causing him to drop his spectacles in his gratin. While the marquess fished his glasses out of the gratin, the sausage barely cleared the salt cellar to land in Caroline Landsdowne's lap, where it came to rest at last.

"Well hell," Margery said.

No one laughed outright, but there was a mad scramble for napkins as everyone seemed to be in need of clearing his throat.

His throat apparently cleared, the Earl of Chillinghurst said, "I suppose that is one way to clean your plate."

While the footman and the butler raced to set the table to rights, Octavia, obviously trying to distract attention from what had happened, changed the subject. "Tell us, Margery, what kind of foods the Indians you lived with ate."

"Buffalo."

"Buffalo?" Octavia repeated.

"I have seen pictures of this buffalo," Simon, the Marquess of Handley, said. "It's a big animal with horns and a hump."

"I, too, have seen it," Marianne said. "In Will's sketches."

"That is all you eat?" Octavia asked. "Just buffalo?"

Margery nodded. "Occasionally we would have rabbit, but buffalo is the main food of the Crow."

"Don't you grow tired of eating the same thing all the time?" Elizabeth asked.

"There are many different parts of the buffalo, and many different ways to prepare it."

"What kind of parts?" Emily asked.

"The favorites are tongue, brains, raw liver, kidneys, and a dessert made from berries mixed with blood."

Three people left the table.

CHAPTER

❈ NINETEEN ❈

Charles surprised everyone when he returned home by bringing his nephew, John.

Margery was in the gothic library with the rest of the family. It was a large room with a first-floor gallery that contained tables and chairs, where the three sons-in-law, Simon, Hugh, and Robert, were talking quietly over a game of cards. Down below, on the main level, Margery sat with Octavia and her daughters, with all the younger grandchildren playing about their feet.

Everyone looked up when Charles and John entered the lower level. When he saw Margery, Charles went directly to the first-floor gallery to speak with his sons-in-law, but John, after speaking briefly with the men, came back down to the main level to greet the women.

After kissing each of them in turn, he looked at Margery and said, "So you are William's wife?"

Margery felt her body stiffen. She could not help but wonder if Charles had turned him against her before she even had the chance to meet him. "Yes, I . . ."

"How neglectful of me," Octavia said. "John,

this is your cousin by marriage, Margery."

"I've always said that Will has the devil's own luck. Who else could travel in the wilderness as he has done and come back with a beautiful wife." He bowed low over her hand. "I am charmed already."

"Shamed, you mean," Emily said. "I have never heard you speak with such eloquence, John."

"John is the misguided one in the family," Caroline said. "He is a surgeon, but he should have been a poet."

"Heaven forbid!" Elizabeth said. "One brooding, artistic person in the family is enough. Spare us more." She gave Margery a wink. "You aren't an artist, are you?"

Margery could not help laughing at the thought. "I have difficulty drawing a straight line."

Marianne leaned over and patted her hand. "Then you will get on nicely with the women in the family. There isn't a dram of artistic ability in the lot of us."

"And that is as it should be," said Octavia, "for we've more than our share of moody, sensitive men who would rather sulk than eat."

"Ouch!" John said, clutching his shirt in the vicinity of the heart, and everyone laughed.

Margery liked him immediately.

The rest of the day passed pleasantly. The children were sent upstairs with their nanny, and Hugh announced that yesterday's snow had almost melted. That was all the men needed to send them tramping into the gun room. When they emerged properly outfitted and carrying more guns than they could possibly shoot, they went out for an afternoon of target shooting.

Luncheon was informal and served to the women only, since the men were still out-of-doors. Later in the afternoon, the older children played games, while the women retired to the sitting room to visit and do a little sewing.

By the time the men returned, the women were all upstairs dressing for dinner.

When she was dressed, Emily stopped by Margery's room and knocked on her door, telling her it was time to go downstairs. Apprehension about seeing Charles again made Margery nervous, but Emily, who chatted gaily, did not seem to notice.

Margery tried to join in the conversation with Emily as they went downstairs, but her heart sank like a leaky canoe when they walked into the dining room and she realized they were the last to arrive. Everyone else was seated, including Charles, who took his proper place at the head of the table.

Octavia kept her gaze on Charles, who glared at the women as they entered the room but said nothing as Emily indicated what chair Margery should take.

Emily sat down next to her.

As they took their seats, Charles's voice

boomed, slicing into the murmur of conversation, which immediately stopped. "This is a family gathering. What is *she* doing in here?"

Octavia knew Margery could feel every gaze at the table upon her. Even from where she sat, she saw the girl's breaths become shallow, and judging from the red flush on her face, she was probably growing quite warm from embarrassment. It was obvious that she wasn't certain as to what she should do. As Octavia saw it, Margery had three options: to say something in her own defense, apologize, or simply leave.

Octavia decided to take the decision out of her hands. "Of whom are you speaking, dear?"

"You know as well as I do. That Indian savage . . . who should be eating with the help in the servants' hall or by herself in the kitchen."

Octavia glanced around the table. "I don't see any savage, Charles, only members of our immediate family."

"Don't try to sidetrack me, Octavia. I may have to suffer her presence at Emberly Hall, but I don't have to endure her sitting at the same table. I don't want her eating with us. I don't want to look up and see her every time I take a bite."

Octavia glanced at Margery, who obviously understood everything and knew that she was not welcome. If Octavia had her pegged right, she would not want to cause a confrontation between members of the family. As Octavia suspected, Margery looked for the path of least resistance, apparently deciding her best course of action was to do as her father-in-law requested and get out of his sight. Octavia did not say anything when Margery pushed back her chair and rose to her feet. Nor did she speak when Margery walked toward the door, too shamed and too humiliated to look at anyone.

Octavia waited until Margery had almost reached the doorway before making her move to show her support of her daughter-in-law. A moment later, Octavia stood, her chair scraping silently against the Turkish carpet on the floor. "Very well, Charles." She tossed her napkin on her chair. "I shall see that your wish is granted."

And with that, Octavia picked up her bowl of soup and turned, walking toward the door.

"Octavia!"

Octavia kept on walking, pausing only when she reached Margery's side, then she turned and said, "Yes, dear?"

"Where are you going?"

"Why, I am going to the kitchen to eat with Margery so you won't have to see her face every time you take a bite."

Charles muttered something, but it was drowned out by the harsh sound of chairs being pushed back across the Turkish rug. As Octavia passed through the doorway that led from the dining room, bowl of soup in hand, she saw that all four of her daughters had risen to their feet. As Octavia had done, they each picked up their soup bowls and turned to follow their mother from the room, leaving their husbands sitting at the dining table, looking not anywhere near as astonished as Charles.

Octavia glanced back once to see that Margery had fallen in line with Emily, who was bringing up the rear.

As they walked behind the others, Emily looked at Margery and said, "You should have brought your soup."

"Why?"

"Mother says revolt is always more effective when you use props."

Once they were all seated at the kitchen table, Caroline asked her mother what she intended to do about their father's attitude toward Margery.

Octavia looked at Caroline and decided it was time to let them in on what she had decided. "I intend to show him just how wrong he is."

Elizabeth paused, her spoon halfway to her mouth. "How do you plan to do that?"

"By showing him that she can be every inch the refined lady . . . as much a refined lady as any nobly born woman reared in England."

Marianne let out a gasp. "You can't mean you are going to take on a challenge like that?"

"Of course I do, silly girl. Why shouldn't I?"

"Mother, you cannot mean to do that to Margery."

"Do what?"

"Make her into something she is not," Marianne said.

"And how do we know what she is, if we don't experiment?"

"What do you intend to do with her?" Caroline asked.

"I shall make a refined lady out of her and then we shall take her to London and show her off to the ton during the Season."

Caroline almost dropped her glass. "That would be cruel."

"Caroline, I cannot fathom whatever gave you that idea. What would be cruel about it?"

"Humiliating her in front of the ton."

"It wouldn't be humiliating to show them what a lady she is."

Elizabeth, who was always considered to be the reasonable one, said, "Do you realize what you would have to teach her in order to expose her to a Season with the ton? To ride, to dance, to speak eloquently, to walk, to discuss the latest topics, to curtsy, to correctly address the peerage . . . it's impossible."

"Nothing is impossible," Octavia said, her voice evoking the same qualities she imagined God would have used when He gave Moses the Ten Commandments.

Marianne leaned back in her chair and began to fan herself. "I cannot believe it."

Octavia gave her a stern look. "Believe it."

Marianne asked, "Mother, what if you fail? What if she isn't ready and she does something awful to embarrass herself . . . to embarrass all of us?"

Emily brightened. "You and Hugh can always disown us."

"This is not the time to be impertinent, Emily," Octavia chastised.

Marianne's hand came to her head. "I think I'm going to faint."

"Emily, get your sister a glass of your father's brandy."

Emily came to her feet.

"I don't need any brandy," Marianne said.

Emily sat down.

"Perhaps you could have Margery ready in time to try her out at the hunt at Uncle Rand's in February," said Caroline.

"February!" exclaimed Marianne, grabbing her head. "Where's the brandy?"

Emily was on her feet in an instant. "I'll get it. I know exactly where Father keeps it."

Octavia raised her brows. "Oh, and how do you know that?"

Emily looked down at her feet. "I spied on him."

"Emily Justine! If you are going to partake in the sisterhood, then you must learn to be careful. Never, ever spy . . . unless there is a lookout. Now, go fetch your father's brandy."

Emily gave Octavia a bright smile, then darted from the room. Octavia glanced at Margery, who, by this time was looking utterly terrified. She patted Margery's hand. "Oh, my dear, dear child. There is no need for you to look so panic-stricken. I have all the faith in the world in you.

Under my tutelage, you will shine."

In spite of Octavia's words of optimism, Margery did not look like she believed a word of it.

CHAPTER
▣ TWENTY ▣

By the time the voyage was half over, Will knew that by leaving Margery in England and returning to America alone, he had committed a grievous sin. He realized, too, that he had erred in his reasoning. Time had not changed the way he felt.

Time, if anything, had only served to make him more and more aware of what he had walked away from. How strange life could be. Here he was, thinking he had done something to make his father's life miserable, when he had dished up that portion for himself. In trying to hurt his father, he had wounded himself.

He was dazed from the shock of it. He missed her. He really, really missed her. *She!* The savage with the savage ways. *She!* The uncivilized one who taught him more about being a human being than he could learn if he read a million manifestos.

Even now, he was astonished to realize how much he had come to care, how much he had begun to admire her understanding, her wisdom. He was reminded of her quiet ways, her shy presence. He knew now that he had been right to keep his thoughts from Guy, at least in the beginning, for his feelings were still too new, too tender, and too bewildering to expose to another.

His self-banishment had produced an unquenchable desire: to be with her. The unfulfilled desire produced its own punishment: complete separation.

The more he desired her, the more he punished himself. If he was consoled by anything, it was in knowing the kind of woman his mother was. In his heart, he knew Margery would not be mistreated. He knew Octavia would welcome her into her nest as surely as she did her own chicks. The mothering instinct ran deep in Octavia's veins. Margery would be a challenge Octavia could not pass up. Soon, Margery would be basking in the attention she would receive.

✓ That did not mean she would understand the reason he left, or that she would not be hurt by what he had done. Nor did it mean the pain would lessen. Ironically, he began to welcome his pain, to look forward to it, for it was the pain he suffered that gave him the strength to endure. And now, he found his endurance tested beyond what even he thought he could withstand.

Guy had not been feeling well during the entire voyage, so he had remained in his cabin a great deal of the time. He was plagued by fever and an increasing loss of appetite. Thin and pale, he grew weaker day by day. He came topside only when the weather was calm and he could find a place to soak up the sun's warmth.

Today, Will found him in such a place.

He was stretched out, near one of the dinghies, his head resting upon a coil of rope, his frail body blanketed with sunlight.

Hearing Will approach, he opened his eyes and squinted up at him. "You always know" — he paused a moment, consumed by a fit of coughing — "where to find me."

Will frowned. In spite of Guy's efforts to conceal it, Will saw the blood on the handkerchief before he tucked it away.

"It isn't difficult," Will said at last. "All I have to do is listen for your coughing and wheezing. It is growing worse, by the way. I think we should find you a doctor when we reach Boston."

"Let's not discuss my ailments. Tell me why you have come. To wile away the time in endless chatter or has the cream risen?"

Will grinned at him. "To the top, just like you said."

Guy smiled and indicated with his hand that Will should sit down.

Will took a place across from him. "I've been thinking."

"Lord deliver us."

Will was not in the mood for humor. "Do you want to hear this or not?"

"Yes, in spite of your doleful tone."

"Well, as I was saying, I've been thinking."

"You never did master the art of getting to the point. You've been reflective since we began this journey. Tell me the source of all this reflection. Is it your wife?"

Will shook his head. "I don't know why I should. I have a feeling you know even the answer to that."

"Perhaps I do, but I want to hear it from you . . . confession being good for the soul and all."

"I am beset with guilt . . . consumed by it. Does that surprise you?"

"No, but more importantly, I don't think it surprises you either. Am I right?"

Will nodded. "I knew that guilt would come. Even that day . . . before we reached London, I could feel the first weak stirrings of its presence, like the disquiet that precedes an illness."

That much was true, for since that day in London when he had suffered his first taste of regret, his thoughts had been on her. Only her. He longed for her with an intensity that burned like an eternal flame within him, and he accepted it willingly. It was his punishment, the penitence he must pay for the wrong he had done her. He took an odd sort of comfort in knowing beforehand that guilt would rush to pay tribute to its complement, punishment. Therein lay his satisfaction.

In spite of his propensity for seasickness, the thing that had really upset his equilibrium was a sickness of another kind: a sickness of the heart.

As if he had spoken the words aloud, Guy said simply, "You care for her."

"Yes."

"Is it love?"

"I like to think it is, but I don't know for certain. I call it love, but there is a voice inside my head that keeps asking, is it guilt . . . or is it love."

"Sometimes it is easier to interpret the feelings of others than it is to understand yourself."

"I did not realize it would take this long. My first feelings were of regret. I was sorry . . . not so much for what I had done, but because of the way I handled it. Gradually, I began to realize my sorrow and regret had turned into guilt. Whenever I thought about her . . . really thought about the way it was between us, I was . . . I'm not certain what I felt. Confused would be a good place to start."

"So, you didn't know if your feelings were borne of love or pity?"

He looked Guy straight in the eye. "If it's pity, I cannot go back."

"And love? What of that?"

"*If* I go back, it will be because of that and for no other reason. It will be because I know beyond a doubt that I love her, that I have loved her for some time."

"But you are not certain?"

"No." Will grew silent for a moment. After a period of reflection, he said, "Tell me, Guy. Tell me how I can know the true motivation for this longing inside me. Is it love? Or is it guilt?"

"Only you can answer that."

Will sprang to his feet and turned away, thrusting his hands deep into his pockets. He could hide his expression, but he could not conceal the frustration in his voice. "I cannot! If it were possible, do you not think I would have realized it by now? It's impossible, I tell you! I cannot know for certain. How will I ever know?"

"You will simply know. When the time is right. Not before."

"*Time!* Always time." He seemed to snarl the words. "Time may be the one thing I do not have."

As it turned out, time was the one thing William had aplenty, for Guy was quite sick by the time they reached Boston. As soon as Will had him resting in his hotel room, Will went to find a doctor.

After the examination, Will was stunned by what the doctor said.

"Tuberculosis? Are you certain?"

"I am certain, but if *you* are not, I would recommend that you have another doctor examine him. Boston is fortunate enough to have many doctors."

Will brought three more doctors to examine Guy. Their replies were all the same: tuberculosis.

Other than bed rest, there was not much the doctors could prescribe. Their first concern was to get him eating so he would regain his strength, along with the lost weight.

At first, Will pushed thoughts of Margery aside, as his primary concern became Guy's health, but as Guy began to improve and regain his weight,

Will found his thoughts turning more and more to Margery. It had not taken him long to realize what Guy had said was right. It had taken nothing more than a little time for him to realize that his guilt was a product of his feelings for her, not the cause of it.

But Will was uncertain of just what his feelings for Margery were. He only knew that the way to find out once and for all was to return to England and face her. He should never have left her. He would go back as soon as Guy's health would allow it.

As soon as he made the decision, Will ran all the way back to the hotel to tell Guy.

When he reached the third floor of the hotel, he headed for Guy's room on the corner, profound enthusiasm in his step. Even from the opposite end of the long hallway, he could see the door to the room was ajar.

Will was no more than halfway there, when he recognized the rich baritone of Dr. Rutherford C. Bernard's voice. "I said you would be well enough to resume a normal life. I did not say you could hop on the first ship you saw. I do not consider sailing to England normal for someone who almost died doing it once before. The damp sea air was not good for your lungs. Try it again, and you will kill yourself. Is that what you want?"

"We can't stay in Boston forever."

"Nor would I want you to. Besides New York, Boston has one of the largest outbreaks of consumption in the United States. While no one is certain as to the cause of it, we feel it might have something to do with the climate. Go out West, where the air is dry, like you planned. I don't think this damp sea coast is any better for you than sailing across the Atlantic was. A trip out West has helped many others with your condition. Most decide to stay once they get there."

For a moment, Will stood outside the door feeling as if his life was a long line. His dream of having a life with Margery was at one end. His fear that he would never attain his dream was at the other. He saw himself standing in the middle.

Without a thought as to which direction he would turn, Will stepped into the room. He greeted Guy, then spoke to the doctor as if he had heard nothing. Once the doctor was gone, he sat beside Guy's bed, much as Guy had sat beside his own bed many times, when Will was just a lad. "So, what did the good doctor have to say?"

"He said that at the rate I was going, I should be healthy enough to sail around the world in a week or so. The way I figure it, we could have you back in England before summer's end."

Will did not miss Guy's inadvertent slip with words. *Have you back* . . . Yes, *Will* might make it back, but Guy obviously knew he would not see England again.

Will wanted nothing in the world more than to take the first ship back to England. He had so much to make up for; there were so many wrongs he had done that he wanted to set right. He knew the cost might be high. He had not counted on it being his friend's life. For a moment he felt as if he hovered between two worlds: between darkness and dawn; between heaven and earth; between a woman and a friend.

In the end, there was no choice to make. Not really. The answer had been as clear as Margery's conscience from the beginning. Will had known from the moment he heard Dr. Bernard's voice what he would do. Life was far more precious than happiness, more sacred than love.

"Did you hear what I said?"

Will focused his attention upon Guy. "I heard."

"You don't seem too elated with the prospect of going home."

Will shrugged. "I just got here. Why should I be elated about going back?"

"What about your wife? Have your feelings for her changed?"

"Whatever my feelings, she will be there when I return."

"Just what are you trying to say? That you don't want to go back?"

"No, just that I'm not ready to go back right now."

"I don't understand."

"I've been thinking that I must be absolutely clear in my resolve to return or I will just be making an even greater mess of things. I still want to do all we set out to do."

"What are you suggesting? That we stay here in Boston? Maybe open a hardware store?"

Will chuckled at that. "You can open a hardware store if you want to, but as for me, I'm heading for St. Louis. I want to paint again. I want to go West one last time, and then I will know if my future lies there or back in England with my wife."

Guy's look turned sober. "You are certain this is what you want?"

"I have never been more certain of anything in my life."

"You haven't allowed something else to sway you?"

"Nothing has swayed me — nothing save the uncertainty of my feelings."

"If you change your mind . . . you will tell me?"

"I will tell you."

"On your word of honor?"

"On my word of honor," Will said.

CHAPTER
▨ TWENTY-ONE ▨

The next afternoon Octavia sat in the sitting room with Margery, wondering how she was going to proceed. There were many things she needed to say to this new daughter-in-law of hers, but Margery's background made it a very delicate thing to handle. She sighed and looked at William's lovely wife, and her heart went out to the girl for all that she had endured, for all that she would still endure.

Octavia prayed for wisdom. How could she explain William to anyone? — William, the child of her heart, the child only she seemed capable of understanding. She was about to say something, hoping and praying the words she needed to utter would come, when suddenly she realized an explanation of William was not what this young woman needed.

Margery needed a family more than she needed a husband. She needed love and security more than explanations. She needed time to discover the world about her, time to find out who she really was. She needed to be pampered and treated to a lavish life. She needed to realize how very lovely and how utterly unique she was.

Octavia remembered William's saying much the same thing the night he left. Perhaps her son knew his wife better than Octavia first thought. In a way, it was best that things had happened as they had, for there was little doubt that William's being gone would give Margery time to become the woman she was destined to be.

But there was one thing that bothered Octavia and that was the girl's shyness. She would not last five minutes if she continued to do everything she was told without question and regardless of how she felt or what she wanted to do.

"Do you love my son?"

The question was meant to give Margery a jolt and it obviously did. "I . . . I loved him when I arrived. Now, I am not so certain."

Octavia rose to her feet and went to stand before her son's wife. "Tell me how you feel about all of this."

"How do you mean?"

"You were abandoned by your husband, the man you loved. How does that make you feel?"

"At first, I was hurt and sad. Now, I try to understand why he felt he had to leave me."

"I see."

"That was not the right answer?"

Octavia sighed. "There are no right answers, child. You should be angry, Margery. You should be very, very angry at William for what he has done."

"But I understand why he did what he did."

Octavia raised her brows at that. "You do? Well, that is remarkable, indeed, for I am his mother — I have raised him since he was born — and I don't understand." She waved her hand. "Oh, of course I understand the problems between Charles and William, but there are other ways to solve differences besides running away. I am not saying William has not been hurt, for he has, and deeply. Nor am I saying Charles has not been dictatorial, unforgiving, rigid, headstrong, and a fool to boot, for he most assuredly has. I am simply saying that William has always had a choice: He could either stay here and stand up for his right to be himself, or he could run away. It is not your fault that he chose to run away."

Octavia paused, thinking things over, then shook her head. "And to bring you here for the sole purpose of slapping his father in the face is unforgivable. However, I will say in his defense that I truly believe William cares for you more than either of you know. I suspect he will realize that before too long, and when he does, he will be back. In the meantime, you have a lot to learn and a great deal of work to do on yourself."

"What kind of work?" Margery asked, looking up as Caroline and Elizabeth walked in. They each took a seat nearby but said nothing.

"My dear, this meek-and-mild pattern, the subservient attitude will not cut it. Try that with William — or any man — and he will get the bit between his teeth and you will never be able to rein him in. Start out easy and amiable and you will have to stay that way. Start out firm and independent and you can switch to easy and amenable when it pleases you, without losing ground. A woman must be like a grain of sand in an oyster. You don't make a pearl by being quiet and satisfied."

Elizabeth laughed. "Mother, you make it sound like a battle."

"That is precisely what a marriage is — a battle. A battle of wills, if you please. That is why a woman must learn warfare tactics before she marries. Pardon the analogy, but men are like dogs: train them right and they will be faithful and lifelong companions. Do it wrong and they will snarl and growl and bite you every chance they get."

Margery smiled, her eyes bright, her mind obviously sifting through Octavia's words.

"Mother," Elizabeth said, "when did you first decide things were so unfair between men and woman?"

"I was seventeen . . . or was it eighteen? . . . Well anyway, it was when I went to the first ball of my coming-out season. I was dancing with Geoffrey Tutberry when it suddenly occurred to me that there was no logical explanation for why a woman had to spend the rest of her life dancing backward."

Caroline joined her sister's laughter then paused to tell her mother, "You have done much to change the unfairness of it all, but women are still dancing backward."

"I know, but I haven't given up yet."

"Would the vicar love to hear what you are saying," Caroline said. "He would think you didn't appreciate the role of a husband."

Octavia replied, "Since Adam, the role of a husband has been misconceived by men."

"Since Adam?" Elizabeth asked. "I had no idea it went that far back."

"The scripture reads, 'Adam knew Eve his wife, and she conceived.' It is a sad thing to admit, but many men have no more knowledge of their wives than that."

"She is right," Caroline said. "Meek and mild is not part of the wifely profession. A wife is her husband's equal, not his possession."

Octavia blinked and looked at her daughter. "Why Caroline, that was downright poetic . . . not to mention true."

"Why, thank you, Mother."

Octavia paused a moment here, in order to cast a quick glance in Margery's direction, just to see how the girl was handling all of this. One look told her that her new protégée was not only accepting what was being said, she was even smiling at the mere *thought* of becoming independent and in control of her life. What a wife she would make William. It was common knowledge that men adored variety. That's why so many of them took mistresses. If a wife was wise, she would be a woman of variability. Then her husband would dwell in a state of bliss, a sort of spiritual harem.

Octavia smiled. How wonderful independence

was. Oh, what a pleasure and delight this was going to be. This dear, dear creature was a rare find, indeed. Her mind was sharp and as clear as a summer day. She was honest and forthright, and as eager to learn as anyone Octavia had ever seen. Armed with the right tools for survival in a man's world, she would be the kind of wife to keep herself and William happy and content for the rest of their days.

Elizabeth asked, "Mother, what are you thinking?"

"What? Oh . . ." Octavia laughed. "Well, actually I was thinking of a poem by Tennyson.

" 'He will hold thee, when his passion shall have spent its novel force, / Something better than his dog, a little dearer than his horse.' "

The four of them laughed, then Elizabeth and Caroline departed, having been called up to the nursery to tend to their babies, who were now awake and howling with hunger.

After they left, Octavia's thoughts turned serious. She thought about Margery and realized that if she failed, if Margery remained this accepting, passive little thing that she was now, William would take a mistress within a fortnight of his returning home. "I want you to do something for me."

"Of course."

"I want you to think about being angry at William for what he has done."

"Angry? How could I be angry at him? He rescued me from captivity."

"Something you do not have to pay for with your own personal happiness. I am not asking you to be angry with him for the good he has done but for the wrong. You must learn to separate the two. Now, do you think you can make yourself sufficiently angry at him?"

Margery looked amused. "I will try."

"Good. I want you angry at him because it is the normal way to feel when someone has wronged you. Get angry. You can be forgiving later. Now why don't you sit there and think about things for a few minutes. Remember the callous way he treated you, how he used you for his own purposes. He was not honest with you, Margery. He bought you, then treated you as if you were his possession, something he owned, which makes him no better than the savages from whom he bought you. He brought you to England, never telling, never even hinting about his intention to abandon you the moment you arrived. My dear, he left you here . . . among strangers . . . without even staying long enough to introduce you to the rest of the family. And you say you understand, that you love him? That won't do. That simply won't do."

"You don't wish me to love him?"

"You can love him *after* you get angry with him; *after* you learn to take care of yourself and to stand up to those who try to use you. You must always remember, child, that a heart can be broken many times, but it keeps on beating."

Octavia rose to her feet, amid a rustle of silk

231

skirts. "I will leave you for a few minutes. When I return we will see if you are sufficiently angry."

She walked toward the door, paused, then turned to give Margery an understanding smile. "And while you're at it, if you want to get angry at anyone else who has hurt you or used you, go ahead. You have had many wrongs done to you in your life and you have learned to suffer in order to protect yourself. I understand why you learned to be submissive and biddable, but you no longer have to behave that way. You do not have to sell your flesh to survive any longer. There are other alternatives besides suffering."

"I will try."

"You better do more than try, my girl. You married William for better or for worse. And if you don't want worse, you must learn to take care of yourself. And when you do, I promise you that you will feel ever so much better."

With that, Octavia walked from the room.

After she had gone, Margery sat there in stupefied silence. She understood the words Octavia said to her. But she did not understand why they were said. It didn't make sense. What would make a woman do something against her own son? Especially a woman like Octavia, who obviously adored William. And then it occurred to her that what Octavia was doing would, perhaps, not only make Margery happy, but William as well.

Margery thought about the way she had learned

to protect herself, by being or doing whatever others chose. She was good. She was obedient. She was loyal, faithful, and devoted.

She acted like the dogs in the Crow village.

Those that were submissive were often mistreated. Those that growled and showed their fangs were treated with respect. Was that the secret then? To growl and show your fangs, just as Octavia said?

She thought about the packs of wolves that would sometimes follow the Crow from camp to camp, lingering near the village. Often two wolves would engage in a fight, which continued until one of the wolves realized he was losing. The wolf who was losing would then show its submission by lying down and baring its throat to the other wolf. Most of the time, this sign of submission was victory enough for the winning wolf, and the loser would tuck his tail and slink away. She realized then that in her own dealings with those who had captured her, she was like the submissive wolf, always baring her throat instead of her fangs. When a person bared his throat in submission, humans were more savage than the wolves, for rarely would the victor allow the loser to tuck tail and slink away.

It seemed so simple when she put it in those terms. She had been guilty of baring her throat and accepting whatever punishment or cruelty was given to her. She began to think of the way she stood meekly to one side while William argued with his father, then walked out of her life without so much as calling her aside and saying good-bye. What he did was, as Octavia said, unforgivable. And what had she done about it? Ignored her heart so that she would not feel the pain.

The thought of it made her so angry, she wanted to kick herself. Instead of doing that, she transferred the anger to where it belonged — to William — for treating her as he had. The more she thought about it, the angrier she became.

By the time Octavia came into the room, carrying a tray of tea, Margery's fists were curled in her lap.

Octavia put down the tray and poured two cups of tea, handing one to Margery, noticing the clenched fists as she did. Taking her own cup of tea, she sat down in the chair opposite Margery. "Are we angry yet?"

"Yes. *Very* angry."

"Good. And who are we angry at?"

"The Comanche, the Cheyenne, the Crow, my parents, William."

"The first three are Indian tribes, I gather?"

"Yes."

"Why are you angry at your parents?"

"Because they didn't protect me better; because I was kidnapped and deprived of the childhood and life I should have had; because they didn't find me and take me back home; because of what I had to suffer."

"Excellent!" Octavia put down her cup and scooted to the edge of her chair, as she was wont to do whenever she was excited. "Now, the first thing we must do is separate things into two groups: those we can do something about, and those we cannot. In the first group, the one we cannot do anything about, we will put the Indians and your parents. In the second group goes William, because he is someone we can certainly do something about."

"But William is not here."

Octavia smiled. "True . . . but he will be. Now, tell me, why are you angry at William?"

"Because he treated me no better than my other captors; because he married me for selfish reasons; because he abandoned me here for revenge; because he never told me the truth."

"Can you tell me more?"

"I wish *he* was here right now."

"Why?"

"So I could . . ." Margery paused, looking up at Octavia.

Octavia smiled and took a sip of her tea. "What would you do, Margery, if he was here . . . right now . . . in this very room?"

"I would like to punch him in the face."

"That's a good start."

"It wasn't very nice, what he did to me. He used me."

"I could not agree more. The question is, what are we going to do about it?"

"I don't know."

"Now, the way I see it, we can either sit here feeling angry and sorry for ourselves, or we can find a way to deal with this anger and then get on to the business at hand."

"What business?"

"Why, the business of making you the toast of the ton. You don't have time to grieve for him, my dear. You will be far too busy. You have a lot of catching up to do, you know . . . much was taken away from you when you were kidnapped. You have a whole, entire life to find. You are young. There will be time enough to deal with William. You are his wife and that guarantees you the right and the chance to make him fall in love with you . . . if you haven't completely given up on the oakwit by then."

Then, Octavia leaned forward and took Margery's face in her hands and kissed her forehead. "I feel I should thank you, you know."

"Thank me? Why? For driving your son away?"

"Oh, my dear, dear child. You didn't drive William away. William is searching for himself, like a holy man who goes into the desert to fast. He will find what he is searching for. In the meantime, we will busy ourselves with preparing you for that day."

With a shot of energy she had not felt in years, Octavia practically marched across the room and gave the bellpull a healthy yank.

A moment later, Lucy came bounding into the room, her wild red hair flying in a hundred different directions, the freckles on her face seeming to jump from her pale, white skin. She gave a quick curtsy. "You rang, your ladyship?"

"Yes, thank you, Lucy. Will you find Emily and send her to me, please. And when you've done that, find Mrs. Singleton and tell her I need her straightaway."

"Yes, your ladyship." Lucy bobbed again, another wild lock of violent red hair escaping a confining pin.

"And do something with that hair of yours. You look like someone has frightened you out of your wits."

"Yes, mum." Lucy hurried from the room.

Octavia said, "You know, I feel positively youthful! You are exactly what this family has needed: a cause to rally around, and by heaven, the women in this family have rallied."

Emily, who had come into the room during this outburst, paused in the doorway, mouth agape. "Mother? Are you feeling all right?"

"Come in, Emily, and shut the door. I have never felt better in my life."

Emily, bless her, obeyed, but there was a suspicious look in her eye.

Octavia did not hesitate to address her obvious concern. "Don't be such a silly goose! Your mother has not taken leave of her senses. You are on the verge of being inducted into that age-old society known as Women-Banding-Together-for-a-Cause."

"I have never heard of it."

"Well, you have heard of it now. It is something of a ritual, a mother-daughter thing that is passed down, generation to generation, and right now, you are the lucky daughter this generation has chosen to pass it down to."

Emily gave her a skeptical look. "What do I have to do?"

"Nothing but be a good observer . . . save for those occasions when you feel swept away by the moment or compelled to exercise your womanly right."

"What right would that be?"

"Why, the right to be yourself, to stand up for the things you want, things you believe in — to face the adversary. In other words, it means learning to take care of yourself so that you don't end up miserable because someone else is making the decisions in your life. You must believe me when I say there is nothing worse than being forced to creep when one wants to soar."

"Oh dear," Emily said with a sigh as she dropped down into a chair next to Margery. "Father isn't going to like this."

"No, he won't . . . he never has, but he might as well gird himself up for it, because he has a revolution on his hands."

"He will order us *all* out of the house . . . or have us shot in our sleep."

"Merciful heavens! I do believe there is a coward in my midst. Tell me, Emily, would you rather be the horse running in the front with nothing but the wind in your face, or the one bringing up the rear, eating the dust of all who went before you."

"I would rather be on your side, Mama. I want to be strong like you. I don't want to be weak and mindless . . . but I don't want Father to be mad at me either."

"Have you seen me stand up to your father?"

Emily nodded furiously. "Lots of times."

"And have you ever . . . even once, seen your father raise a hand to me, or have me thrown out of the house?"

"No."

"You are either with us or against us, Emily. What is it to be?"

"I am with you." Emily's face took on a downtrodden cast. "Now I'll never get married."

"Oh, fiddlesticks! What makes you say a silly thing like that?"

"Because Father will brand me a traitor as sure as a goose has liver, and he will never give me a dowry or his blessing."

"Oh piffle! Your father is mostly bark, a throwback to the days when men were hunters and chest beaters. Pay him no mind. You will inherit plenty through me and from your grandmother, and there is always elopement, but never you mind. Your father is more concerned with gaining a noble son-in-law than he is with keeping a daughter who has turned independent."

Emily sniffed and rubbed her nose. "I guess I am in this thing whether I want to be or not. Where do I go to enlist?"

Octavia looked at Margery, who was watching what was going on with a puzzled frown. "You look as lost as a cat in a counting house, but don't you worry. I have everything under control. When

239

I'm finished with you, you will think me a wizard . . . or would that be a wizardess?"

Emily gasped. "Mother! What are you going to do to her?"

"Transform her, of course. Make her independent. And when I'm finished, there will not be a lovelier, more gracious, better educated woman in the whole of England. The more I think about it, the more I am convinced that Caroline had an excellent idea: to let Margery participate in the hunt at Uncle Rand's in February."

"But that isn't much time," Emily wailed.

"Nonsense. You must never underestimate the power of your determined mother. Margery will be the envy of every woman there, and there won't be a bachelor in attendance who won't curse the day she married someone else."

The downcast expression vanished from Emily's face. "Can we do me when we finish with her?"

Octavia smiled. "Why, of course we can."

Octavia took in Emily's bright countenance and then Margery's apprehensive one. She went to Margery and, taking her by the hand, pulled her to her feet. "Come along now, we've work to do, my pet. When William comes back . . ."

Margery shook her head. "He won't come back."

"Nonsense. He will be back, and when he does, someone will be in for a big surprise."

Someone was in for a big surprise, all right, but it wasn't William.

CHAPTER
▣ TWENTY-TWO ▣

The fourth time Margery threw up, she knew she was going to have a baby.

The fifth time, Octavia knew.

Margery worried about the reaction of her father-in-law so much that it cast a gloomy cloud over her euphoria. She was going to have Will's child, but she did not want Charles to know. Because of this, she begged Octavia not to tell Charles.

"But he will know, sooner or later."

"Please, let it be later. I would like to have time to become accustomed to the fact myself, before I have to defend it."

Octavia nodded in sympathy. "I understand. What you ask makes perfect sense. Of course we can keep it a secret. I will have to speak with the staff, of course, but do not worry. I have their loyalty."

When Octavia left to have a few words with the staff, Margery, who remained in the morning room, sank wearily into the plump cushion of an elegant Grecian chair.

"When is the baby due?"

Margery jumped a mile, her hand flying up to her chest. She turned to see Emily standing behind her, beaming. "Well hell."

Emily came around the chair to sit beside her, smiling broadly.

"You oughtn't to sneak up on people like that, Emily. You frightened me. I'm sorry for what I said. It is a bad habit, I am afraid."

"I've heard you say it before. But don't worry. I say it sometimes, too." Emily looked down at the floor. "I'm sorry I frightened you."

"It's all right. It's just that I didn't hear you come in."

"Oh, I didn't come in. I was already here. I was hiding behind the chair. I heard you and Mother talking. That's how I knew you were going to have a baby."

Margery gave her a chastening look.

Emily looked adequately chastened. "I know, Mother told me to never snoop unless I had a lookout."

Margery softened. "You will keep it a secret, won't you?"

"Oh yes! I shan't tell a soul."

Two days later, William's cousin, John, came by for a short visit, bringing with him a longtime family friend and neighbor, Lydia Lancaster.

After being introduced to the lovely, dark-haired Lydia, Margery watched her go outside with John and Charles to see the new gelding Charles had just purchased for the upcoming hunt.

As usual, Charles ignored Margery and did not invite her to join them.

As they walked away, Margery whispered to Emily that Lydia was quite the most beautiful woman she had ever seen. "I cannot believe Will grew up with her and did not fall in love with her."

"Lydia was in love with our brother James," Emily said.

Margery's expression seemed to freeze on her face. "Your . . . your brother? I knew about James, but I had no idea that he and Lydia . . . I mean I had only heard he died, I did not hear how."

Emily suddenly looked as if she had said something she shouldn't have. "Oh, I talk too much."

Emily glanced at Octavia, who said to Margery, "James was our youngest son. He was killed in one of the first battles of the Crimea."

"Oh, I am so sorry. Will never told me about him, you see. What little I knew came from Dan."

"That is to be expected. The wound is still fresh for him . . . even now, it is still painful for us to speak of it."

"I am sorry for being the one to call back a time of such sadness."

"Do not worry overmuch. If the world were filled only with happiness, we would never learn to be patient or brave."

Margery did not mention James again.

Lydia and John returned a few minutes later, but Charles did not. They paused a moment to speak with Octavia, then John came to sit next to Margery. "I understand you are coming over to Wiltshire Manor to join us for the fox hunt in a few weeks."

"Yes, I am looking forward to it."

"Have you ever done any hunting?"

"No."

"Not even in America?"

"Indian women do not hunt."

"Then this will be a new experience for you. Do you ride well?"

"The groomsman says I sit a horse quite naturally, although the sidesaddle is a bit of a challenge." She looked off, trying to sound disappointed.

"Of course, you are not doing much riding these days."

Margery stole a quick glance back at him. "You did not know?"

John was staring at her with a knowing smile and a delighted look in his eyes. "Yes, Octavia mentioned it just now, but I thought it best not to mention it until you did. Now you must permit me to offer you my congratulations. Children will be yet another adventure for you. I know you are pleased."

"Yes, very pleased." She smiled. "If for no other reason than it will keep me from having to go on this bloody hunt. Riding is not my favorite pastime."

John threw back his head and laughed. "I see why Will married you. You are really delightful, did you know that?"

Margery's light mood left her. "Will did not marry me for my wit. He married me for revenge."

"I have heard the story, but I don't believe it."

"You don't believe it? Why?"

"Not for a minute. I know my cousin quite well. We were always very close when we were growing up, you see. I know Will would have never married you purely for revenge. There had to be something else, some other reason attached to it."

"You forget that he brought me here to abandon me."

"I can almost promise you that the thought to do that came after the decision to marry you."

"You really believe that?"

"I would lay my life on it."

"Thank you for telling me."

"I am happy I did, especially if it makes what he did easier to bear."

"It does not, but it does make it less humiliating."

It was a few weeks later, to the day, that everyone went to Uncle Randolph's home, Wiltshire Manor, for the big fox hunt. Since she would not be riding, Margery did not wear her fashionable riding dress, which was already getting too tight. Instead, she wore a blue-and-green plaid day dress of fine wool, trimmed with dark green silk fringe. The skirt was very full, in three flounces, requiring a number of crinolines and a stiff horsehair underskirt to give it fullness.

Upon their arrival, she stopped to visit for a while with John's father, Rand, who was as gentle and kind as Charles was rude and boisterous. After talking with Rand, she made her rounds among the neighbors, pausing for some time to visit with Lydia.

After talking with Lydia, Margery went to stand with Octavia in the yard, admiring the scarlet coats of the riders, which she learned were called pinks, but was unable to fathom why. Suddenly, Octavia took her by the arm. "Come along. We will ride out in the open carriage so you can get a closer look. It is quite a spectacular sight to see the hunters come running over the hills in hot pursuit of the wily fox."

Margery had heard much about the English fox and she was anxious to see if it was any different from the fox in America. Excited about seeing her first hunt, she went with Octavia. Just as they settled themselves in the open carriage, a horn sounded and the riders were off.

Margery expressed her disappointment over not getting to see the fox.

"Perhaps they will pass close to our carriage and you can get a look," Octavia said.

They rode on in silence, Margery listening for the sound of horses galloping and the barking of dogs.

"This looks like a good spot to wait," Octavia said, and gave instructions to the driver to stop. "We've a good view of the open fields on the edge

246

of the woods, which is where the fox, if he's a smart one, will head."

Margery waited, and listened, and watched. The tension she felt was much the same as she had felt in the Crow village during a buffalo hunt, only there it was a few hunters chasing hundreds of buffalo, while here, it was many hunters chasing one fox.

After a few minutes, she turned toward Octavia. "Would it be all right if I got out?"

Octavia nodded. "Of course. I don't see what it would hurt."

Margery left the carriage and walked around a bit, stretching her legs. She was just on her way back to the carriage when her reverie was interrupted by the loud barking sound of the approaching dogs.

A split second later, she saw a pitifully small animal come racing over a low hill. Not far behind it came the dogs and then the riders, the hooves of their horses tearing up clumps of sod as they raced across the fields.

"Is *that* the fox?"

Octavia looked in the direction Margery was pointing. "Yes."

"But it looks the same as the fox in America. I had no idea they would be hunting something so small. Do they eat the fox here in England?"

"No, the fox is hunted for sport."

Margery frowned. She had never heard of this hunting for sport. The Indians hunted, but they made good use of every bit of the animals they hunted. Hunting was a manner of survival, not sport. She turned toward Octavia. "It doesn't seem right to hunt such a beautiful animal for no reason other than to see it die."

"Yes, well, that is what I've always thought, and for that reason I have never been a champion of the hunt, you see."

Margery did not answer, for at that moment, the fox made a sharp left turn and began running toward her, obviously heading for the screen of trees behind them. As it drew closer, she could see it was beginning to slow down, showing obvious signs of exhaustion.

The pack of dogs was almost upon it.

Not really thinking about what she was doing, Margery was suddenly swept away with the tension that mounted inside her. Over the field the fox came, running for its life. The dogs were coming on stronger.

Suddenly, Margery screamed, "Hide your bloomin' arse!"

Some twenty or so feet away from her, the fox faltered and collapsed, panting hard.

"Oh my stars!" exclaimed Octavia.

A second later, Margery took off running, not heeding Octavia's shouts to stop. She reached the fox only moments before the hounds did. She looked frantically around for something with which to hold the dogs off, and finding nothing, she did the only thing she could think to do: She lifted her skirts and stepped next to the fox, then dropped her skirts over it.

As far as disrupting a fox hunt, that just about did it, for suddenly there was mass confusion everywhere.

Within minutes, the dogs were circling her, barking and yapping, pawing at her skirts and trying to poke their heads beneath her hem. With only her parasol in her hand, she took a few swipes at the dogs. "Go away! Get back, you little gudgeon!"

John, who was one of the first riders to reach her, was trying his best to stay in the saddle, but he looked so weak from laughter that it was difficult to speculate on whether he would make it. Charles and Rand rode up next, followed by Lydia and Emily and a dozen or so others, mostly men.

Everyone stared at Margery for a moment, then, one by one, they began to laugh, all save Charles, who ordered her back into the carriage.

"I will not move until you call the dogs back," she said, giving another one of the dogs a thump beside the head with her parasol. "Back, Satan!"

For a moment it was a standoff, with Charles ranting and making threats, and Margery ignoring him, going after the dogs with her parasol, standing in the same spot as if she had put down deep roots.

Charles's voice shook with rage and he threatened to have her on the next ship bound for America.

And still Margery would not budge.

"You move, or by God, I'll throw you over

my shoulder and carry you to the carriage myself."

"Charles," Rand said.

"You stay out of this," Charles replied, dismounting.

Suddenly, Octavia was standing beside Margery.

Charles came toward them.

"You will have to move both of us," Octavia warned.

Charles stopped and stared until his face turned purple. "Octavia, I am warning you."

"Yes, dear, I know you are."

"It does not suit women to be headstrong and rebellious."

For a moment Charles and Octavia stood there, staring at each other, and Margery knew by the look in Charles's eyes that Octavia was doomed. Charles would not back down if Queen Victoria herself ordered him.

"I should have listened to my father. He warned me about marrying an educated woman and he was right. A man is happier with a wife who has his dinner on the table than with one who can speak Greek."

Octavia stared at him. "I won't say you are being pigheaded, Charles, but *one* of us is being pigheaded, and it isn't me."

Suddenly, and without a word, he turned and stomped back to his horse, mounted, and jerked the poor gelding around so hard and fast that he almost went down. Digging his spurs into the horse's sides, Charles went thundering back across the field.

Rand followed his brother's retreat with his eyes, then looked at John and said, "Women, you know, seldom fail to make the most stout of men turn tail."

As the two of them laughed, Octavia faced Margery.

"I am sorry," Margery said, feeling wretched.

"Once you make a stand, Margery, do not back down and do not apologize for it."

Margery nodded. "Thank you for helping me."

"Women are a sisterhood, and that is as it should be, considering the men have the law on their side."

"I hope I have not caused problems for you. Will he get over what happened, do you think?"

Octavia looked off in the direction Charles had taken. "He will learn to live with it. A man never forgives a woman for having the wit to outwit him."

"Wits aside, I would say the hunt for today is over," Rand said, giving Margery a wink. "Tell me, Octavia, what does this daughter-in-law of yours eat for breakfast? I would like to have a bowl of it on the morrow."

"Nails," Octavia said. "By the pound."

Rand laughed and guided his horse into a wide turn as the master of the fox hounds called the dogs away.

A few minutes later, only John, Lydia, and Emily remained with Margery and Octavia.

Emily dismounted. "Oh, I do wish I had come in the carriage with you. That was the bravest thing I have ever seen anyone do."

"And the most foolish," Octavia said, turning toward Margery. "What would you have done if one of those dogs had gotten under your skirts?"

"Move, I suppose."

With that, the entire group burst out laughing.

Margery stepped away then and looked down at the small red fox with its heaving sides and tiny pointed nose.

"What should we do with it?" she asked John.

"Leave it. It will rest a while. When it recovers, I would imagine it will go on its merry way."

"You are certain?"

"If you like, I will come back later to make sure."

"Thank you," Margery said, then turned toward the carriage.

"By the way," John called after her, "what was it, exactly, that you yelled to the fox?"

"I told him to hide his bloomin' ar—"

"Margery!" Octavia said. "Remember your manners. A lady does not speak indelicately."

Then to John she said, "Just you wait until Will comes home. I will pin both of his ears back for this. Teaching a young, impressionable woman to speak so horribly. It is unheard of."

"Oh, it wasn't just Will who spoke that way," Margery said. "Daniel did it also."

"Then I have reason to be twice as mad."

John, who was grinning widely, crossed his

arms and leaned over his horse toward Margery. "Are you certain you're married?"

"Of course, I'm married. Why would you ask such a thing?"

"Because I think I'd ask for your hand myself, if you weren't already taken."

"You might want to reconsider," Margery said, "for I am going to be independent."

John laughed. "I would say you were off to a good start." Taking Margery's parasol from her, Octavia gave John a thump beside the head. "Mind your manners, you ruffian. This is the mother of my grandchildren you are being flirtatious with."

"Beg pardon, Aunt . . ." Then looking at Margery, he winked and said, "And yours, Margery."

"Accepted," Octavia said. "Now, help me into the carriage as part of your penitence, you lazy rogue."

CHAPTER
❖ TWENTY-THREE ❖

Will and Guy traveled with a band of Cheyenne for two months, and during this time, it amazed Will to see how fast Guy adapted to the life of a nomad. More than once, Guy had said something about spending the rest of his life out here, where a man learned what it was to be really free.

The more Guy talked about it, the more Will began to think that Guy might indeed settle here. If he did, then Will would leave him and return home to the woman he married.

Yet the closer Will came to suggesting they find a place to build a cabin for Guy, the more he feared that moment would never come. There was little doubt that their decision to travel west had been good for Guy, but in spite of Guy's robust look, Will was concerned.

Guy's health might have improved, but his cough was growing worse. Whenever Will questioned Guy about it, his only reply was, "A little cough never killed anybody."

"We both know consumption is considerably more than 'a little cough.' "

"Well, humor me then. Call it a little cough.

Perhaps I don't like to be constantly reminded that I am dying."

Guy, dying?

Somehow, Will had overlooked that possibility. He had simply assumed, in what he realized now was a very naive manner, that Guy would be fine, as long as they did not sail for England.

That night, long after Guy had gone to sleep, Will sat before their campfire, stirring the coals with a stick and staring into the flames. Not long before dawn, he cursed and threw the stick into the fire. A few minutes later, he spread out his bed and lay down. He still couldn't sleep, so he lay on his back, his arms folded beneath his head as he looked at the blanket of bright stars overhead.

As he did this, he could not help wondering if there was something beyond his control, something out there in the vast universe, something beyond even those stars that controlled their lives — his and Margery's — that called all the shots. He was inclined to think so, for like Job, misfortune seemed to smile upon him.

Was it written somewhere that he and Margery were destined to spend their lives apart?

Will closed his eyes. It did not matter. There was nothing short of his own death that would keep him from going back to her.

CHAPTER
❖ TWENTY-FOUR ❖

It did not take long for Margery and Emily to become close friends. It was only natural that, in exchange for the many things Margery was taught about England and English ways, Emily wanted to learn a bit about the past Margery had left behind. For to a young woman of seventeen, a life with savages in a raw and untamed land was quite the thing.

Soon it was obvious to everyone in the household that Emily was more than fascinated with Margery's unusual background.

"I would not be surprised to see her wearing war paint and feathers in her hair," Octavia remarked to Lydia and Margery over tea one afternoon.

Margery was to wonder later if perhaps Emily had been hiding behind the Grecian chair again and overheard her mother.

It was one afternoon in late March that Margery smelled something so delicious and so familiar that she followed the scent of it and ended up in the kitchen. When she first walked in she saw Octavia talking to Cook. Cook was busy leaning over a large bowl filled with a yellowish mass Margery could not identify. As she stood there observing, Cook picked up a bit of the yellowish lump and rolled it around in another bowl that was filled with sugar. Once the round lump was covered with the sugary mixture, Cook placed it on a flat pan.

Fascinated, Margery watched Cook put the pan into the oven, removing another pan from the oven at the same time. Warm, delicious smells reached out to her and she stepped closer. Something about the round, flat objects in the pan seemed so familiar to her. "What is it?" she asked.

"Cookies," Cook said. "Would you like to try?"

Margery indicated she would and Cook moved aside. Margery picked up a bit of the lump Cook identified as dough. She rolled it in her hands until it made a round ball, then rolled it in the sugar, which Octavia said was mixed with cinnamon. She was just placing the round ball of dough in the pan when suddenly she looked at Octavia. "I have done this before, I think."

Octavia hugged her. "I am certain that you have. It is a source of great joy to a mother to bake cookies with her children. You must have done the same thing with your mother."

Margery could not remember if that were true or not, but oh, how the thought warmed her.

After she left the kitchen, she wandered around the house a bit, stopping by the conservatory, which was her favorite room, with its abundance of windows and lush plants. It felt like the cheery warmth of summer had been trapped indoors.

She moved to the window, still fascinated with the countryside and how different it was from the hills around the Yellowstone. The weather outside was what Octavia called "dreary," and Margery now knew that word meant hours of heavy fog and rain, which soon turned the fields and roads into a quagmire and sent the rivers gurgling and churning on their way. The last clinging remains of flowers were lying flat on the ground, looking battered and quite forlorn. Even the birds that perched on the bare branches of the chestnut trees seemed to be waiting patiently for spring. They sat with their backs to the wind, the rain running off their feathers, as if they had nothing better to do.

Once she left the conservatory, she went to her room to find Emily standing in front of the mirror, wearing one of Margery's doeskin dresses that she had pulled from the trunk.

"I hope you don't mind my trying it on." Her voice sounded different today than it normally did, as if she were pinching her nose together when she spoke. "You will have to pardon me. I have a touch of the sniffles," she said, then took a handkerchief out of her pocket and blew her nose like a cavalry trumpet announcing the charge. She stuffed the handkerchief in her pocket and turned to look shamefully at Margery.

Margery smiled at the sight. "Of course I don't mind."

Emily rushed toward her. "Will you show me how to braid my hair and put these feathers in it?" She held up a handful of feathers, offering them to Margery.

"Where did you get these?" Margery looked down at the ragged feathers in her hand.

"From the feather duster."

Margery smiled at that, then walked with Emily to the dressing table, instructing her to sit down. After braiding her hair, she inserted the feathers into the long braids, smiling at the enraptured way Emily looked at her reflection in the mirror.

"Do you think I look . . . exotic?"

"Definitely exotic."

"Oh, thank you!" Emily jumped up. "I want to show Mother."

Margery followed her, pausing midway down the stairs when she saw Emily had encountered three of her friends who had just come to pay a call.

The three horrified girls took one look at Emily and almost fainted.

"You look like a heathen," Josephina exclaimed.

"I wouldn't let anyone see me like that if I were you," advised Jane.

"You should be more careful of who you choose for your friends, Emily. If the ton ever gets word of this, you will be ruined."

Emily, who had obviously had all she was going to take, ordered the three from the house. As soon as they left, she burst into tears.

Margery came down the stairs. "I'm sorry. I had no idea something like that would happen."

"It isn't your fault," Emily sobbed. "I should have chosen better friends."

"People of the ton ridicule what they don't understand."

"Excuse me," Emily said, and ran up the stairs.

A moment later, Margery heard her door slam.

It was two weeks later that Margery was invited to ride with the family to church. When Charles heard she was going, he refused to accompany them.

"Then we shall pray for your cantankerous soul, dear," Octavia said as she went through the door.

"Perhaps I should stay here," Margery said.

Octavia stopped dead. "Stay here? Whatever for?"

"So he can join his family at church."

"Nonsense. Charles is being difficult because he is afraid."

"Afraid? Of what?"

"The idea of women banding together makes a man nervous, my dear. It isn't so much your going as it is the three of us."

"Civilization is very complicated," Margery said.

"Yes, it certainly is. Perhaps I should have been born a savage," Emily quipped.

"You are a savage," Octavia said, giving Emily a shove so that she toppled into the carriage and landed in the corner, a fluff of petticoats and giggles.

Once church was over, Emily, Octavia, and Margery walked outside. Octavia paused a moment to speak to the vicar. Margery and Emily walked on, for Emily was hoping to catch up with Lydia to invite her over for tea, but Lydia was gone by the time they were outside. They stopped to visit with John and Rand a bit, then walked toward their carriage.

They passed a neighboring coach and a voice called out, "Oh, Emily, I'm so glad to see you." It was Frances Overmyre and Sarah Freeman. They both looked at Margery but didn't acknowledge her. "Do come over. I have something to ask you."

Margery waited as Emily stopped by the Overmyre carriage. She could not hear what was being said, but she could see by Emily's expression and the way the two girls kept taking covert glances at her that she was the subject of their conversation.

A second later, she heard Emily exclaim, "I don't care! If you're an example of the kinds of friends I'll be losing, it will be no loss."

Breathless and red-faced, Emily returned to Margery's side. "Come on," she said, taking Margery's arm. "Mother will be waiting for us."

"They were talking about me," Margery said.

"Actually, they were talking about me. Seems they heard about my little escapade with the feathers in my hair. Sarah said it was all over the countryside that I was becoming as heathen as my sister-in-law."

"What did you say to her?"

"I told her she was probably right, that my mother said I was a savage."

Margery managed to keep the news of her being with child from Charles until the following Tuesday. That was the day Emily blurted the news like a bleating sheep at dinner. The moment he heard it, the earl went into a rage. He directed his cold stare upon Margery, his words cruel and biting. "So, tell me, whose child is it?"

Margery, who had been quite ravenous, suddenly lost her appetite. She was so stunned that her first inclination was to leap from her chair and bolt from the room. In truth, she might have done just that if she had not glanced up and seen the observant, almost expectant expression on Octavia's face. It shocked her, for she would have expected to see anger, displeasure, or even rage upon Octavia's face.

It occurred to her then that Octavia was waiting to see what Margery would do, how she would defend herself. It was as if Octavia were telling her that she would not come to her rescue anymore, that it was time Margery learned to stand up for herself.

Margery knew that running away was not the independent thing to do, and if she had learned anything in the past three months, it was that she was expected to take a stand and be strong. The kind of woman who could "face down an avalanche," as Octavia so aptly and so often put it.

Margery faked a calmness that she did not feel. "I am not certain about the father, but when I decide, I will see that you are the first to know."

"You'd like me to believe that, wouldn't you? You'd like nothing better than to have me thinking I was forced to accept grandchildren that I had my doubts about. Fortunately, I know William better than that." He turned to Octavia. "I'll not have her giving birth here in this house. Have you given any thought as to what people will say?"

Margery sat very still, very stiff, and very, very silent, afraid to even breathe. All of the independent thinking she had been taught seemed to fly right out the window, and the old way of adapting to please rushed to the forefront.

She focused her gaze on a crystal candelabra, blinking when the prisms began to blur before her very eyes. She made no sound, but she could feel the tears on her face. She knew Octavia was looking at her, knew, too, that Octavia would let her cope with this new rush of emotion in her own way. It was part of learning to take care of one's self, and if that meant crying at the dining table, so be it.

Octavia put down her water glass. "They will think she has given birth while her husband is away. It happens all the time, Charles."

"Not to me, it doesn't."

"Well, what would you have me do? Send her outside to give birth in the flowerbed?"

Charles sprang to his feet and threw his napkin in his plate. "She can give birth in the stables for all I care. If Will can't live here, I see no reason why she should."

"There will come a day, Charles, when you will regret ever saying such a thing."

"Not in this lifetime," he said, and strode from the room.

Octavia looked at Emily, who appeared to be adequately admonished. "I'm sorry, Mother. I didn't mean to cause trouble. It's just that I was so excited."

Octavia smiled and put her hand over Emily's. "Of course you were. We are all excited. This is a blessed event for this household. I only wish there was some way to get word to William, but it serves him right, dashing off into the night like he did, and on Christmas Eve . . . hauling himself out of here as if the devil himself were after him."

She looked at Margery. "I know what you must be thinking and you are wrong. No matter how great an ass Charles makes of himself, you mustn't forget that this is your home, Margery. This certainly is not the time to be thinking about leaving. You have your child to think about now."

"But I am not welcome here. . . ."

"Balderdash! You should know by now that it is Charles's way to make everyone feel uncomfortable. The best way to cope with someone like him is to give it back to him as good as you get. Stand up to him when he is being perfectly ridiculous. A woman is not born. She is made. If you sit around waiting for a man to hand you power all done up in satin ribbons, you will find yourself waiting for the rest of your life. In other words, it will never happen. Power is something to be taken, not given. That is something I learned the hard way."

"I don't understand."

"Just how do you think I've managed all these years? Well, I can tell you. The first time he blustered at me I went crying to my room. The next day, I went flying home to my mother."

Emily's eyes grew round. "You left Father and went to Grandmama?"

"I most certainly did."

"And what happened? Did he come after you?"

"No, much to my chagrin, he did not."

"Then how did you get back together?"

"I came home . . . or rather, I was *sent* home by my mother . . . after a stern lecture, mind you."

"What did she tell you?" Emily put her elbows on the table and rested her chin in her hands.

Seeing how comfortable Emily looked, Margery did the same. "Tell us what she said."

Something about the way the two of them looked must have amused Octavia, for she smiled and said, "She told me I had better get some backbone and quick, because if I ever allowed Charles to run over me again, my life would be pure hell."

"Grandmama said hell?"

"She did, but that does not give you permission to say it."

Emily looked downcast.

Octavia went on talking. "I will never forget the way my mother sat me down and told me a story about her and my father — a story that was quite similar to the one I am telling you about Charles and myself."

That surprised Margery. "She did?"

"Yes, she did. She told me I needed courage to stand up for myself and courage to keep on doing it until Charles learned that I was not going to be his whipping post. She said if I didn't learn to defend myself that I might as well lie down in front of a speeding carriage, because I would feel about the same way after living with an overbearing husband for years."

"And you went back home to Father after that?"

"Yes."

Margery was dying to find out more. "Was he glad to see you?" she asked.

"Glad to see me? My gracious, no. He was as belligerent as ever — perhaps more so. He even went so far as to tell me he had not even been aware that I was gone."

Emily gasped. "He didn't!"

Octavia nodded gravely. "He most certainly did."

Margery leaned forward so far one of her curls dropped into the water glass. She pulled it out and gave it a squeeze. "What did you do then?"

"I picked up a vase of roses and I bashed him over the head with it. It was a lovely vase, too. One of my favorites."

"You hit Father over the head with a vase of roses?"

"Yes, and I told him that he might not have been aware I was gone, but I would bet him money that he was aware that I was back!"

At that, Margery burst out laughing, for the image of Charles dripping wet — his hair plastered to his scalp, a rose drooping over his ear — was just too funny to pass up.

Octavia and Emily joined in the laughter.

After a bit, the laughter died away and the room grew quiet.

"I wish that wasn't the end of the story," said Margery.

"It's not," replied Octavia.

"There is more?"

Octavia nodded. "I don't mind telling you that there were times those first few years that we were married that I wished I had married Rupert."

Emily, who had been gazing off at nothing in a rather dreamy manner, snapped her head to attention.

Margery forgot all about her earlier woes. In unison, she and Emily asked, "Who is Rupert?"

"Rupert was my first love. He was killed in the war with Napoleon. I grieved for him for quite some time and never planned to marry . . . probably wouldn't have, if my father had not betrothed me to Charles."

Emily fluttered her eyes in a seizure of infatuated bliss. "Oh, that is so romantic. Poor Rupert, to die so young." Emily sighed. "How unfeeling it was of Grandpapa to affiance you to someone else and deprive you of the honor of mourning Rupert until you joined him in the grave."

Margery remained quiet, trying to understand why it was romantic and noble to mourn a dead person for the rest of your life. Perhaps that was the English way. If she had learned anything since coming here, it was that the English had strange ways. Perhaps this was simply another part of their strangeness.

It was not until a few months later that she learned the war with Napoleon had been fought some forty-three years prior, and that would have made Octavia ten years old at the time, and far too young to have been in love with Rupert or anyone else, for that matter. However, it was a remarkable story and it illustrated a point. A mother did what she had to do, Margery supposed.

By the time she realized this, her own twin sons had been born, and with their birth came a deep and profound mothering instinct. It was only then that she was aware of what a truly remarkable woman Octavia really was.

CHAPTER
▣ TWENTY-FIVE ▣

After the birth of her sons, Robert Charles and William Daniel, Margery was so busy she did not have time to think about William or his blustery father, but there were times when she did wonder what possessed her to name one of her adorable baby boys after such a cantankerous old man.

Giving birth did not change things for Margery around Emberly Hall. As she had done since her arrival, she arose each morning to be presented with a long list of daily activities that had to be checked off before she went to bed that night. Besides the hours she spent with her sons, there were fittings with dressmakers and lessons in deportment, as well as hours spent on the piano and with an embroidery needle, not to mention her riding lessons. After a late lunch, she painted and spent four hours with her tutor. After months of training, it was reported that she excelled. . . .

Except in one area: dancing.

Her dancing master, Mr. Gerard, threw his hands up in surrender more than once. When Octavia made the mistake of inquiring as to the reason he was quitting, for the fifth time, he replied, "Madam, it is impossible to teach her to dance. She acts like she is in a race. She leads when she should be following. She counts in my ear. I could teach a horse to dance faster than I could teach your daughter-in-law."

"Do try just a little harder, Mr. Gerard. I am confident Lady Margery will get the hang of it before long."

Mr. Gerard bowed low over Octavia's hand. "Only for you would I take on such a monumental task." He sighed. "I will try."

Turning to Margery, he nodded for the pianist to play. "Again, Lady Margery, if you please. Try to remember you are a feather, and a feather floats. You are not a barge that must be pushed up the Thames. A feather . . . one, two, three . . . a feather, one, two, three . . ."

On and on they went, spinning around the room, with Margery reciting the lilting phrase to herself: *a feather . . . one, two, three . . .*

Wanting to please Octavia, Margery tried harder, and soon she began to believe she was a feather.

It was at that point that Mr. Gerard declared her to be as light on her feet as a feather floating on an updraft. "By heaven! I think she's gotten it. At last, I think she's gotten it!"

Margery turned toward Octavia and beamed.

Octavia was apparently thrilled with the news, for she said, "I think you are ready for London, my dear."

Once it was announced that they would be returning to London in preparation for the Season, Charles, who had refused even to see his new grandsons, announced that he would not be going.

"We will miss you, dear," said Octavia.

"You cannot mean you are going on without me?"

"Of course. There is no reason for me to miss the Season, simply because you have chosen to miss it."

"But . . . but . . ."

"Yes, dear?"

"How can you possibly get on without me? What about an escort?"

"John will be there. I am certain he would be happy to fill in for you."

"Octavia, London is a dangerous place for a woman alone. You cannot . . ."

"I will be careful, dear," Octavia said, rising up on her toes and giving Charles a quick kiss.

Once she related what happened to Emily and Margery, Emily looked a bit concerned. "We have never been to London without Father."

"Emily, don't fret over what your father said. Men would like us to believe our world is flat, that if we sally forth we will fall off the edge. It is all a ploy. You will not fall."

Several days later, they arrived in London.

It took them three days to get things in order in the townhouse on St. Charles Street. Margery settled herself in a lovely room just a few doors away from the nursery, so she would not be far from her babies, even though there were two nurses and a nanny to care for them.

A week after their arrival in London, Octavia, Emily, and Margery were joined at the theater by Caroline and Robert. It was Caroline who introduced Margery to the Duchess of Grenville and her beautiful black-haired daughter, Annabella, the Duchess of Dunford, who was visiting from Scotland.

After the duchess left, Lady Ashford joined them. "I saw you speaking to the Duke of Grenville's daughter."

"Yes," Octavia said. "She is a lovely woman. I understand her husband, the duke, is an American."

"Yes, he is," Lady Ashford replied, then she stopped short, as if she was considering something. "You know, that reminds me. I remember hearing . . . of course this was a few years back, but the story was, I believe, that the duke's parents were murdered by Indians, and that his brothers were scattered to the four winds."

"Oh, how terrible," Emily said.

"Yes, but there is more," Lady Ashford said. "I also remember hearing that he had a sister who was captured by Indians." She paused and patted Margery's hand. "Just as you were captured, my dear. Can you believe this sort of thing has happened twice? Have you ever heard of such?"

"It is a fairly common occurrence, I am afraid. It would be impossible to know the exact number, of course, but it would run in the hundreds. I would often find myself with other captives."

Lady Ashford was aghast. It was obvious that this only raised Margery in the old lady's eyes. "Oh, you poor, poor dear. Please do come to my home for tea on Thursday. I want to hear more about all of this from you."

About that time, the theater lights blinked, leaving no time for conversation. After bidding Lady Ashford good evening, Margery went with the family to their box.

Once they were there, Emily exclaimed that she liked going to the theater with women ever so much better "than when Father is along. He is such a fusspot."

"Yes," Octavia said. She gave Margery a wink and whispered, "There is something contagious about demanding freedom."

When intermission came, Margery did not go downstairs with the other members of the family. It was her first experience in a theater and she was overwhelmed by the sheer size of it and the magnificence of the gilt decor and breathtaking chandeliers.

It was while she sat in the abandoned box that she overheard two women talking in the adjoining box.

"I do feel sorry for poor Octavia, forced to drag such a burden around with her."

"Did you hear she wears Indian feathers in her hair?"

"No!"

"It is the truth. I had it straight from Lady Penworthy, who heard it from Lady Marberly."

And that is when Margery hit upon an idea.

A week later, Margery dressed for her first ball. Her gown was the loveliest thing she had ever seen, a pale green silk that rustled when she walked. The low-cut neckline was edged with tiny pink satin roses — the same roses that graced her skirt.

Taking a last look at herself in the mirror of her dressing room, Margery remembered the night she attended the theater. With a fluid motion, she removed the pink roses from her unswept hair and tossed them on the dressing table. She went to her trunk and opened it, digging through it until she found her feathers.

Back at the mirror now, she selected several downy white feathers and a few longer ones tipped with an iridescent green. These she worked into her hair with a few of the roses.

There! They thought her a savage, so why try to hide it.

From the moment she entered the ballroom, Margery was an instant success, for everyone seemed to think she was exquisite. The fact that she had feathers in her hair did not seem to bother anyone, for Octavia reported to her that everyone said they found her grace, her poise, her openness captivating and quite refreshing.

The Dowager Duchess of Dudley remarked,

"There is just enough exotic aloofness in her to make her intriguing. I saw her the moment she entered the room, like a cool breeze from opened doors that rushes into a stuffy, smoke-filled room." Then she folded her fan and clipped Margery on the arm. "The feathers are the very thing! What a clever puss you are to flaunt them in the face of society. The ton was prepared to whisper about them behind your back, and now you have taken all their fun away."

"Oh, I am sorry, your grace."

"I'm not! This is the most fun I've had since Lady Marsley poured her drink down the front of Caroline Lamb's dress."

"When was that, your grace?" Emily asked, always eager for a bit of gossip.

"Why it was some forty years ago . . . or was it fifty?"

The next evening Margery, Octavia, and Emily went to the opera. The moment they entered the doors, the three of them came to an immediate halt, for they were quickly surrounded by ladies of the ton, each and every one of them wearing feathers in their hair.

Soon it was the rage of London.

Three weeks after she first arrived in London, Margery accompanied Octavia and Emily to a garden party at the Duchess of Shrewsbury's. It had been raining, but the rain cleared the day of the party, and with the clearing came the heat.

London was stifling and humid.

Margery knew before she arrived at the party that she had made a mistake in the dress she had chosen. It was quite lovely, a soft blue silk, but it was the long sleeves and the overly tight corset — combined with the heat and the fact that she had not eaten that day — that threatened to do her in. Once they were in the garden, with the crowd of people and poor air circulation, she felt a bit nauseated.

"Do you want to leave?" Octavia asked.

"No, perhaps if I could just sit down for a moment and get some fresh air."

"There is a gazebo at the end of that path. Why don't you go sit there for a while? You will be out of the crush and there is a nice breeze, for the gazebo faces a lovely pond."

Margery excused herself and hurried down the path to the gazebo.

Unbeknownst to her, Freddy Hardcastle, the Marquess of Harrinton, followed her.

She had no more than made her way into the gazebo and sat down, taking out her fan to cool her face, when Freddy came to join her, taking a seat uncomfortably close to her.

"Would you like some company?" he asked.

"I prefer to be alone, if you don't mind. I don't feel well," she replied. "That is why I came down here, to get some fresh air."

"Perhaps I should remain then. It wouldn't do for you to fall ill with no one around to help you."

"I can take care of myself."

"Yes, I have heard that you were an independent sort. I suppose that is because you don't have a man around to take care of you."

"I don't need a man to take care of me."

Freddy removed his gloves and put them down beside him. Turning back to Margery, he drew one finger down her bare arm. "A woman always needs a man to take *care* of her, if you know what I mean. Your husband has been gone for a long time. A woman like you must get very lonely."

Margery picked up his hand and shoved it back at him. "I have William's family and my two sons to keep me from being lonely."

"But there are . . . certain things his family and your children cannot do for you."

Margery jumped to her feet. She had taken no more than a few steps, which barely put her outside the gazebo, when he stepped in front of her, blocking her way.

She turned and tried to go around him on the left side.

He sidestepped and blocked her way.

She turned, going to the right.

He sidestepped again, blocking her way for the third time.

He looked down at the low-necked gown she was wearing. "You are an exciting woman and a beautiful one. Do you know what it does to a man to look at you like this?"

"Yes, it makes him hurt," she said, slapping his face hard.

He acted as if he didn't feel it and went on telling her how lovely she was. Then, before she could realize what he was about, he ran a finger along the edge of the bosom of her gown, telling her as he gazed at her that she had "something there that interests me."

She smiled seductively at him and stepped back. "And I have something here, that might interest you even more," she said, lifting her skirts to expose a long length of leg.

He gave her a sly smile and released her. "I knew you were the woman for me. I knew it the moment I first saw you."

She said nothing but went on to raise her skirt a bit higher. Freddy swallowed. Just as he reached for her, she jumped back and yanked a knife out of her garter. Her skirts dropped back into place.

He made a grab for her and they went down to the ground, wrestling together. He was bigger than her and heavier, but she was quick and light, and after a few rolls, she got on top of him.

Before he could push her away, she had her knife at his throat. "Listen, you mealy little duffer, I've had just about a bellyful of your groping. Put your hand on me again and I'll slit your slimy throat from ear to ear and hang your scalp on the duchess's gatepost."

He gave a choking gasp, and she wondered if he would try something, but she needn't have fretted; the shock of having the sharp point of her horn-handled knife pressed to his gullet had almost caused him to faint, and for a moment he could do nothing but lie there, panting, his eyes bugging, his face as white as a sun-bleached bone.

By the time Margery sheathed her knife in her garter, she noticed a crowd had gathered. She ignored the crowd and released Freddy just as she came to her feet.

Lady Lovett said to no one in particular, "I suppose barbarism is to be expected from a barbarian."

Octavia, who had witnessed the entire incident, said proudly, "Yes, Freddy did behave like a beastly savage, didn't he?"

Everyone laughed, a few of them breaking into applause when Freddy staggered to his feet and departed.

Emily, Lydia, and Octavia rushed to Margery's side. "You were spectacular," Lydia said.

About that time, John appeared. "I just heard what happened." He looked her over. "Are you all right?"

"I am fine." She looked down at her dress and saw the dirt smudges, the grass stains. "Apparently I fared better than my dress."

"A dress given over to a good cause," Lydia said. "I have never seen anything like it."

"Me neither," chirped Emily. "Will you show me how to do it? Egads! You sure put old fondling Freddy in his place."

Octavia almost fainted. "Emily Woodville, where do you come up with these things that you say?"

"I —"

"Was snooping," Lydia and Margery finished for her, and the four of them laughed.

In the coach a short while later, they continued their discussion.

"I apologize for what happened," Margery said. "I suppose I have ruined your chances for any further invitations from the ton."

"Nonsense," Octavia said. "When you are the darling of the ton, they are willing to forgive." Then she squeezed Margery's hand. "Besides, I have never witnessed anything more magnificent, nor have I been more proud of anyone in my life. I only wish William had been here to see it."

At the mention of William's name, Margery's heart stilled. As if sensing her change of mood, no one said anything for a long time. At last, Octavia said, "I should love to visit America one day and see these Crow Indians of yours.

"Oh, yes," Emily said, "I want to go, too." To Margery she said, "I want you to show me how you got the best of Freddy." With her next breath, she turned to John and said, "Will you get me a knife like Margery's?"

John laughed. "Why? So you can take it after poor Freddy?"

"Poor Freddy, my foot!" Lydia said.

"Freddy deserved what he got," Emily said. "He is always lurking about, trying to find a woman he can corner so he can quote his dirty little quotes from Ovid."

Up went Octavia's brows. "And just how would you be knowing about Ovid?" Seeing Emily's mouth open, Octavia said, "No, never mind. I know how. Emily, you have got to stop this snooping."

"Well, then how am I ever going to learn anything?"

Octavia hesitated. "Well, if you are going to snoop, Emily," she said at last, "you must learn the first rule of snooping."

"What rule is that?"

"Don't get caught," she said, and this time the coach shook with laughter.

CHAPTER
❈ TWENTY-SIX ❈

Charles died of apoplexy a week and a half later.

Margery, Emily, and Octavia had just returned to the townhouse from making a round of calls when John arrived, the bearer of bad news. They left for Emberly Hall immediately.

Charles was buried two days after they arrived. Octavia did her best to keep her composure, at least when she was around everyone, but the evidence of her tears was always present whenever she came out of her room.

The family mourned Charles, everyone wearing black, none of them liking the color. "It makes my face look like I've fallen in a flour barrel," Emily said to her mother.

"It isn't my best color either," Margery said.

"Why don't the two of you take a walk down through the orchard? The trees are in bloom. The sunshine and fresh air would do you good. It might put a little color in your cheeks."

As they walked, Margery told Emily how sorry she felt about the hard feelings she had harbored toward Charles.

"You mustn't feel guilty, Margery. Although I

loved my father, I recognized he was far from perfect. The problems he had with members of the family he brought upon himself. He was always overly hard on Will, and after James died, he was even worse. He was never able to get over Lydia and Will . . ."

Emily snapped her mouth shut. "Let's talk about something else. I am tired of talking about dead people. I am tired of mourning, and I am especially tired of black."

This was the second time Emily had almost blurted out something about the relationship between Lydia, James, and Will. Margery decided she would not press the issue now by asking Emily to tell her more. It would be better to wait until she could ask Octavia.

Later that evening, Margery had the perfect opportunity when she and Octavia were in the library, writing notes of thanks for the many kindnesses that were shown to them by friends and family during the weeks that followed the death of Charles.

Octavia paused, rubbing her fingers. "The last time I did this was right after James died. I had forgotten how cramped your fingers get."

"That must have been a very difficult time for you . . . I cannot fathom the pain of losing a child."

"It was devastating . . . something that took me a long time to get over. Even now, there are times when the pain seems as fresh as the day I first heard the news. They buried him there, you know. They did not send his body home. That made it even more difficult to grieve. There was no physical evidence that he was gone, no body to say farewell to at a funeral, no grave to visit and ease the burden of grief with flowers and tears."

Margery put the pen down and took a deep breath. "I have to ask you something. You may tell me it is none of my business, or that it is something you do not want to talk about. That is your right. But the question has been with me for some time. It will not go away, and so I must ask. I hope you understand that."

Octavia was looking down at her fingers. She stopped rubbing them and looked at Margery. "I understand, more than you realize, perhaps."

"You know what I am referring to?"

"I have a good idea. It concerns Lydia and James, does it not? Lydia and James, and William."

"Yes."

"Has Emily spoken of this to you?"

"No. It is only that there have been times that she came close, but she always managed to catch herself and divert the conversation."

Octavia gave her a half-amused smile. "Emily has such enthusiasm. It sometimes overrides her better judgment. Did you ask her about it?"

"No. I did not want to put her in an awkward position. That is why I waited to ask you."

"You did the right thing. I don't think Emily understands the situation completely. For that reason, I preferred to keep it from her, but

Charles was in such a bluster that keeping it from her was impossible."

Margery did not say anything.

"James was our youngest son. The one with no title to inherit. Because of this, I think he felt passed over, as if life had cheated him and left him without honor. He adored his brother, and William was very protective of him, yet there was always this need to prove himself and his value. It was important to him to be seen as William's equal, or better. When James and Lydia announced they wanted to marry, I hoped it would have some calming effect upon James, that it would turn his attention away from his inferior feelings to more productive things. But I was wrong. Neither his love for Lydia nor their engagement could stop his need to prove himself. When the war in the Crimea broke out, he saw this as an opportunity to achieve glory, a chance to rise above his station in life as a second son. I will never forget the day he came home and announced he was going to war. James knew what he wanted, and he saw the war in the Crimea as a way to get it. He enlisted immediately. Word came three and a half months later that he was killed."

"I'm so sorry. I know it was devastating for all of you. . . ."

"Yes, it was. Charles locked himself in the library and tried to drink himself to death. William blamed himself for not being able to talk his brother out of going. Lydia, of course, was heartbroken. When she first heard the news, she went crazy . . . throwing and smashing things, until her family sent for John, who gave her a sleeping draught. Afterward, she seemed to withdraw into herself. She would not leave her room. She barely ate. She lost so much weight, her family feared for her health. But the thing that concerned them the most was the fact that she could not cry. She could not grieve."

"I cannot imagine her like that."

"Grief does strange things to people."

"Did she gradually come out of it?"

"No, she was going downhill . . . day by day, getting a little bit worse, until one day, Lydia's father rode over to speak with William. In desperation, he had come to ask William to talk to her. Will and Lydia were always close as children, closer really, than Will was to any of his sisters. It was Lord Lancaster's hope that this strong bond of friendship could be used to heal Lydia, but he needed William's help."

"To do what?"

"He wanted Will to spend time with her, to try to pull her out of the deep hole she had slipped into. He wanted her to accept James's death, instead of denying it. He wanted her to cry, to grieve, and then to get over it."

"And he needed Will to help."

"Yes, but none of us realized then just how James's death had affected Will. If we had, we would have realized Will could not deal with his own grief, and therefore was not capable of dealing with Lydia's. But we did not know, and Will began to visit the Lancasters. Gradually, he began to get Lydia out of the house. They would take long walks together, but Lydia would not let him mention James. If he did, she would go home, refusing to see Will for several days. But, one afternoon, Will was a little more persistent. He walked her down to the gazebo at the edge of the Lancasters' pond. Once she was inside, he began to talk about James, and when she tried to leave, he wouldn't let her go. He held her there, like a trapped animal, talking and saying things about James until Lydia broke down. At last, she cried. Only when she started, she did not seem to be able to stop. Will went to her and sat down beside her, taking her in his arms. She cried on his shoulder until his shirt was wet. She was consumed by her grieving, and Will suffered because he had caused it. He tried to comfort her, to ease her pain. One thing led to another, and the next thing they knew, they were making love to each other on the floor of the gazebo."

"Will and Lydia?"

Octavia shook her head. "That's what we all thought. In fact, I don't think anyone was more surprised than the two of them, when it was all over."

"How did you find out?"

"Will told us."

"How did Charles react?"

"In his usual manner. He blamed Will for James's death, for committing the ultimate dishonor to his brother by taking the virginity of the woman he was to marry."

"But why? James was dead. Couldn't Charles understand?"

"He did not *want* to understand. He thought Will should have been able to stop his brother, to keep him from enlisting."

"How was Will taking all of this?"

"He was shattered. Whatever slim thread of sanity he had found to hold on to after James died was lost. He had already blamed himself for the death of James."

"And Lydia?"

"Whatever it was that had kept her from grieving was gone. She mourned James as she should have in the beginning. She accepted her part in what happened and never tried once to blame Will. Gradually, she began to improve. She never looked at what happened between herself and Will as betrayal or disgrace. It was a necessary part of her healing process. She refused to feel guilty or less virtuous because of it. She said later that she was glad it happened, glad that it was William, because in a way, he was a part of his brother. If anything, she accepted most of the blame, for it was her grief that brought William to her in the first place."

"And William? Did he leave after that?"

"Not right away. Always wanting to do the honorable thing, he went to see Lydia, ready to do what was right. He had taken her virginity. That made him accountable. She was also the daughter of a nobleman. He asked her to marry him. Her answer was, 'Dearest William, I cannot take from you the rest of your life. You have already given me more of yourself than I had a right to.' "

"That's when he went to America."

"Not long after that, yes. At first he began to have horrible nightmares where he would see James with half of his body blown away, swimming in a sea of blood. He was so tormented by this, that he began to stay up all night, drinking until he was too numb and too exhausted to feel much of anything. He began to imagine he had James's blood on his hands. One night, he locked himself in the attic. He stayed up there for three days, without anything to eat, and nothing to drink except whiskey. I sent for John. He had to break the door down, and when we went inside, the attic was filled with paintings, all of them half-finished pictures of James, all of them painted over with crimson, as if the canvas had been dipped in blood. He had found the trunk where I had packed away all of James's things, and we could see he had pulled everything out. Nothing was damaged, except the front of each shirt, which he had slashed with violent strokes of a brush dipped in crimson. Afraid he might harm himself, John locked him in his room. The next morning when he went in, William had escaped. He left a simple note that said he had to get away, that he needed answers."

"And he thought he would find them in the uncivilized West?"

"I think he harbored the idea that time and distance would eventually reveal to him just why it was that James had to die, why he could not keep his brother from such a fate."

Octavia glanced at her, then put her hand on Margery's. "And you? How are you taking all of this?"

"I understand the words of suffering, even though they never make a sentence. I know the torment of dreams scalding the heart, the anguish of wrestling with what is past, the agony that comes from having to accept your fate, the hopelessness of not being able to do anything about it. As for what happened between Will and Lydia . . . I don't blame either of them. In their separate ways, each has paid dearly for what they lost."

"You are wise beyond your years. Not many wives would be capable of such understanding."

"Perhaps that is because I hear one word and understand two."

CHAPTER
❈ TWENTY-SEVEN ❈

It was a particularly fine morning, and Margery dressed quickly. Emily was visiting her Uncle Rand, and Margery was in a hurry to invite Octavia to ride with her to fetch Emily home. It wasn't so much that she needed Octavia's accompaniment as that Octavia needed to go. Octavia needed to get out more.

Margery was about to reach for her bonnet when she was informed that she had a caller waiting downstairs.

Lucette giggled and flashed her dimples. "A gentleman caller, your ladyship."

Completely bewildered over who it could be, Margery went downstairs, trying to think just who could possibly be paying her a visit. By the time she reached the door to the sitting room, she had come up with no names. She paused a moment outside the door, squared her shoulders, then opened the door and walked in.

There sat Daniel, talking to Octavia.

She was completely flabbergasted and stood there for a flat minute before she exclaimed, "Daniel!"

When he saw her, he stood up, a smile a mile wide upon his cherished face.

She flew into his arms. "I can't believe you are really here," she said, pulling back a little to look him over, as if trying to compare the reality with the memory. "I simply cannot believe it. You are really here."

"I find it hard to believe myself, but I had some business in London, and decided to stop by here on my way home."

It was difficult to tell just who was more surprised: Margery, at seeing Dan for the first time since she had come to England, or Dan, when he saw the changes in her.

He held her at arm's length, just so he could look at her. "I always knew you would turn into a beauty, but I had no idea. What a transformation you've made."

Margery smiled at Octavia. "I have my mother-in-law to thank for that," she said. "Octavia has been wonderful."

"I never had any doubts on that score," he said. "Octavia is a remarkable woman." His face softened. "I was sorry to hear about Charles."

"Thank you. It took us all by surprise," Octavia said. "I can only be thankful that it came quickly and he did not suffer."

"Yes, that is a blessing in itself. Have you sent word to Will?"

"No. William will come home when he is ready. His father's death will not change that."

"No, I suppose it won't."

"How is your mother?" Octavia asked.

He chuckled. "She is suffering from acute loss of sleep, having just returned form my sister's home in Sussex. Julianne became the proud mother of a baby girl three weeks ago, and my mother has not slept since."

Margery sprang to her feet. "Oh, that reminds me. I have something to show you," she said, and hurried from the room.

A few minutes later, she came back, carrying her two sons. "I'd like you to meet William and Robert," she said proudly.

This time, Margery definitely had the best of him. It was the first time she had ever seen Dan speechless.

"I don't know what to say."

After Dan fussed over the boys for a while, Margery put them down. While the three of them talked, the boys played about Margery's feet, drooled on Daniel's trousers, and picked the pearls out of the buckles on Octavia's shoes.

When Robbie became so cross that he began to cry, Margery rang for Nanny Goodpenny, who took the boys back to the nursery with her.

Dan winked at Octavia and said, "I hear the strangest fashion has hit London — something that has every man fearing for his life."

"Oh?" Octavia said. "What fashion is that?"

"The women in the ton have taken to carrying knives, which they slip in their garters."

"Oh?" Margery said.

"I wonder where they got the idea?" Dan was heard to comment.

"I wonder," was Margery's reply.

They invited Daniel to stay for lunch, then he and Margery went for a walk.

"I still can't get over the change in you. Will is going to be shocked beyond belief. Do you ever hear from him?"

"Did you expect that I would?"

"No, I don't suppose I did," he said. "He hasn't written then?"

"Not a word."

"Then he doesn't know about his sons?"

"No."

"What will happen . . . between the two of you, I mean . . . when he returns?"

"I don't know. I suppose that all depends upon whether or not he comes back."

"He'll be back."

"I wish I had your optimism, but then, it really doesn't matter."

"It doesn't matter, as in you have learned to live without him?"

"My life is very full, and now my sons have made it rich. I do not need William to make my world complete. Men are like the earth and we are the moon; all they ever see of us is one side, so they think they know us. But there is more to us than they can see."

"I am not surprised to see that you are so multifaceted. I always knew you were a strong woman, but something has happened . . . some-

294

thing that has made it all the more obvious."

"Octavia says, 'Women are like tea. It is only when you put them in hot water that you realize how strong they are.' "

He laughed at that, and she turned to look at him, enjoying the sound of his laughter, the sight of the familiar brown hair, the smiling eyes. It reminded her of just how much she missed his company. "I will never forget what you did for me. Your friendship will always be something I treasure. I don't think I would have managed as well as I did, if it hadn't been for you."

"I can think of nothing I would like better than to take responsibility for what you've become, but I cannot. What you are was always there, I just helped you look for it. I know this has been hard for you."

"It wasn't easy to go through it alone. If it hadn't been for Octavia, I don't know what I would have done."

"You would have survived. I think Will knew that."

Her tone turned cold. "I doubt Will took the time to think much about me one way or the other."

"I think you are wrong."

"I don't know how you can say that. It's been almost two years . . . not that time matters when the heart is not involved."

"And whose heart are you speaking of? Yours or his?"

"His, of course."

He chuckled at that. "Of course. And what makes you think his heart is not involved?"

She was amused. "The simple reason that he dumped me unceremoniously on his father's doorstep and returned to America as fast as his long legs would carry him."

"What he did had nothing to do with his feelings for you. I doubt that Will was even aware that he had feelings. He was too consumed with his own misery to think about the misery he caused others. However, I do think that he has realized by now how you were always more to him than he knew."

"What on earth could make you say that?"

"I was on the ship with you, remember? I saw his moods, the devil's own time he had of keeping his distance from you, the nights the liquor would not completely drug his need to go to you."

She was amused at that. "He did come to me . . . I have two sons to prove it."

"Do you love him?"

She did not have to think about that. "I did once."

"But no longer?"

She shrugged. "I don't know. I would have to see him again to know the answer to that, I suppose. Even if I did discover I loved him, it is not something I would tell him. He will not find me so gullible, so easy to infatuate this time. He was my savior, my knight in shining armor, the beginning and ending of everything. I pinned all my hopes on him."

"And he hurt you."

"He broke my heart, but now, whenever I look back, I think it was for the best."

He chuckled. "I am looking at the result and I would say it was definitely for the best. I think he will see that as well . . . if you give him half a chance."

"I am not the same girl I was. The stars are gone from my eyes. Things might not work for us. I am stronger now, more determined, more capable of standing on my own two feet. His being my husband does not give him much advantage with me, contrary to what the law says."

"I can see he will have a fight on his hands, but who is to say it won't be worth the effort? I cannot help thinking that is just what Will needs, something to fight for, something to believe in, a reason to go on. If a wife and two sons won't do that for him, then there isn't much hope, is there?"

"No," she said, "there isn't."

"I've been hearing a lot of stories about you."

"You have? What kind of stories?"

"It seems Lady Ashford has been telling everyone in the ton that you knew the Duke of Dunford's sister, that you were captives together. You never told me that you had a captive friend."

Margery's color faded. "But that isn't true. I never told her that."

"You didn't?"

"No. She mentioned his sister's being kidnapped and found it amazing that it happened to two people. I informed her that it had happened to hundreds of people, that I had encountered other captives from time to time. I never mentioned the duke's sister. No one I ever met could remember where they came from, just as I couldn't remember. I cannot fathom what possessed Lady Ashford to say such a thing."

Dan chuckled. "Age," he said. "It comes with old age. Often the elderly find they have to add a bit of color to things, just to get others to listen. It is a sad fact but true. I am certain she meant no harm."

"I am sure she didn't. I only hope the duke does not hear of this. A story like that . . . why, it could get his hopes up, and then I would have to be the one to disappoint him."

"I doubt he will hear. After all, he lives in Scotland. He rarely comes to England."

"But the duchess's family might tell him."

"The Grenvilles of all people wouldn't believe a word Lady Ashford said. She once told the duke that she was the twin sister of the queen of France."

Daniel turned up the graveled drive. "Well, here we are, back at your front door. The time passed too quickly."

They went up the steps and walked to the door. She turned. "Will you come in?"

"No, I must go, but I do want you to promise to send for me, if you ever need me for anything."

She smiled, and rising up on her toes, kissed him on the cheek. "Dear, dear, Daniel. You are always close to my heart. Of course I would send for you."

"I can ask for no more," he said, then turned away.

She stood on the steps and watched him drive off. As she went inside, she wondered why it was that they spent the good part of the afternoon discussing the possibility of a reunion with a man who had forgotten that she even existed.

CHAPTER
▨ TWENTY-EIGHT ▨

There was never a day that went by that he did not think about her, a night when she did not haunt his thoughts. . . .

William had not the slightest illusion that by leaving her he had made the most regrettable mistake of his life. He understood, but it did not make accepting the delay in returning any easier. He could not have Margery, but he had his memories and his dreams.

He knew dreams were not reality, but it was as close to the real thing as he could get. He had to be satisfied with that. At least for a while. Whenever he thought about it and fantasized about it, he would often find himself thinking that everything might be erased, transformed somehow, by the magic of reunion. In reality, he was not so naive.

He wanted to go back . . . had always wanted to go back. It was something that burned within him passionately. Still, it was beyond his control. Having Margery was something that always lay just ahead, something that would happen tomorrow, but somehow tomorrow never came. He was like a man walking in the desert who spots an oasis, only to find that it always hovers just ahead, shimmering and mystical, just beyond his reach: a vision in the sand, a distortion of light, an illusion of water. Margery.

Will had tried to concentrate on Guy's illness. But now he couldn't. The fire that was ignited when she lay in his arms now threatened to consume him with its heat. Never was he at rest — no, not even when he lay on his blanket at the close of day, waiting for sleep — for she would be there, in the sound of her breathing faintly in the darkness, in the smell of the wind and sea that was in her hair, in the wisdom of a hundred generations hidden behind the softness of her eyes.

Will figured the best way to stop the thoughts of her was to keep busy. So he and Guy moved around a lot, never remaining in one place very long. They traveled from Indian village to Indian village; Will obsessed with filling sketchbook after sketchbook, always on the run, trying to leave the pain of the past behind him, trying to outrun the shadow of her smile.

Until there came a day when fate intervened, and he couldn't run anymore.

They were camped near a band of Ogallala Sioux that they had been trailing for over a week now. It was dark, but neither he nor Guy were asleep. Sitting by the campfire, Will picked up a stick and stirred the dying embers to life. A shower of sparks rose, crackling and popping in protest of their imminent demise.

Guy, who was sitting across from him, heard the noise and looked up.

"You're thinking about her."

Will poked the fire again, his expression sullen. "Would you deny me that? It's all I have left."

"Then, perhaps it is time to go back. I find myself growing a bit homesick as well."

"I thought you liked it here, that you might even consider making your life out here."

"It's a possibility." He started coughing again. Of late, he had been coughing more and more, and when he did, the blood was always there.

Guy closed his eyes, as if waiting for the weakness to pass. The good color he had during the summer was gone along with the robust spurt of improving health. His weight had been dropping for weeks now, and the paleness of his skin was ghostly, unnatural. A week ago the fever had returned. As a result, Guy's face was now constantly waxen and covered with a sheen of perspiration. Two days ago, Will noticed the purplish color of his lips. For the first time since they had come out here, Will began to fear Guy was dying.

"You're sick. I think we should go back to St. Louis." Will tossed the stick into the fire, then fell silent.

Guy did not say anything, so Will asked him again. This time Guy replied, "I will die in St. Louis. I'm in no hurry to return."

"Don't talk like that. You don't know where

you'll die any more than you know when."

"But I do know. I have known since we passed through there on our way out here. Remember that bluff that overlooked the Missouri? The one we camped upon?"

"Yes."

"And do you remember my telling you that it would be a fitting place to be buried?"

Will nodded, because he could not speak.

"I meant that. I have put off going back, because I know once we do that it will be for the last time."

"Then we won't go back."

Guy smiled. "Such logic takes me back . . . you sound so much like you did when you were a lad. You always challenged life. You refused to accept defeat. You were ever optimistic and filled with an assurance that no matter what went wrong, you could somehow fix it."

"I'm not a lad anymore . . . nor am I optimistic. I've replaced that with a strong dose of reality. Of late, I find I'm saturated with it."

"Then you should understand the reality of what is happening here. This is something beyond our control, something neither of us can fix. I have done what I wanted to do. I have seen a part of the world I have never seen. Few are so lucky. Strange as it may seem, I am ready to die. I grow weary of this coughing, weary of life. It is a good time to go back. Tomorrow is a good time to leave. I am ready."

After Guy fell asleep, Will was consumed with

morbid thoughts. He tried to think about his father, but somehow he couldn't recall his father's face. Only Margery's vivid eyes seemed to fill his mind.

He knew he had made a mistake, just as he realized his decision had been a rash one. He was haunted by what he did to her. How strange it was that although he left her behind, her memory was always here, with him.

He did not need to ask if it was madness. He knew that it was. Every brown-skinned Indian face he looked at, every profile he sketched was hers.

"Don't blame yourself for any of this."

The sound of Guy's voice caught him off guard. "I thought you were asleep."

"I was, but I never sleep for long. I meant what I said. I don't want you to think any of this is your fault."

"I made a mistake in allowing you to come. If I had known you were ill . . ."

"No one knew, not even your mother. I think this happened because it was part of a bigger plan, and I can tell you truthfully that I am proud to have played a part in it, however insignificant."

"I don't call dying insignificant."

"Well, that is not the first time our opinions have been different."

"What are you trying to say?"

"I am saying that you often have to make mistakes in order to make discoveries."

"What does that mean?"

"Well, it could mean that I would have never seen all of this if I had remained in England. Or, it could mean that if you hadn't made the mistake of leaving Margery in England, you wouldn't have discovered you loved her."

"Did I say I loved her?"

Guy laughed, but soon it turned into a fit of coughing. He was winded and should have rested, but he wanted to talk. "You didn't have to tell me you loved her, you know. I have known you since you were eight. I have taught you everything. I think it safe to say I know you better than anyone, save your mother. I have seen you in love before, but even that was different."

Will felt the old dread creeping back into his bones. It had been a long time since he had thought of Bess . . . Bess, the miller's black-eyed daughter. Bess, his first love. "And how was it different?"

"It was the love of a youth, heated by the fires of youthful passion. You are a man now. Your feelings run much deeper."

"I was inexperienced."

Guy chuckled. "Inexperience is a term that makes our mistakes seem more palatable."

Will picked up a cup that he had wedged into the dirt earlier. He threw the remains of his tea into the fire. Steam rose with a cloud of thick smoke and a hiss. He came to his feet. "I don't want to discuss this anymore." He turned away. For him, the conversation had ended.

But the memory of her had not.

They broke camp the next morning. It had been decided, without either of them discussing it further, that they would return to St. Louis. Will figured it was just as well. The Sioux had begun to resent their presence. Guy had, more than once, advised they should move on to friendlier territory. Up till now, Will had refused.

Later, whenever he was to think back upon it, he could never come up for a reason for his stubbornness, and yet, there had been a reason there, in the circle of pain within his head — a reason that he had struggled with, trying to justify his action to himself.

Such was the hell of make-believe and the reality of fate.

He was confronted with this reality later that afternoon, when he and Guy had mounted their horses. They were camped not too far from a Sioux village where Will had been working on a series of sketches he was doing of the chief, Iron Fist. Just as they rode away from camp, they were met by a band of Sioux led by Hungry Wolf, the eldest son of Iron Fist. Before Will had a chance to say anything, Hungry Wolf raised his rifle in the air.

A moment later, Will and Guy were running for their lives, chased by a band of hostile Indians.

Half a mile from their camp, Will's horse began to tire and slow down. He waved Guy on, but his lifelong friend dropped back to ride beside him. A moment later, Will felt a burning pain stab into his thigh. His horse stumbled, and Will was thrown to the ground. He landed on his back, hard enough to knock the wind out of him.

Guy was beside him in an instant. As he pulled Will to his feet, he saw a bright red blood stain soaking the leg of his pants.

The Sioux were almost upon them when Guy helped him in the saddle. They rode like hell after that.

Even when they were certain Hungry Wolf and his band did not follow, they continued to press on. It was only when it grew too dark to see, that they stopped and made camp. Once they did, Guy removed the bullet and cauterized the wound with a hot knife. For three days, Will was delirious with fever.

On the fourth day the fever broke.

It was while he recovered from this wound that his entire past began to catch up with him, and once it did, Will could not run from it. He was forced to confront his actions. For the second time since leaving Margery on his parents' doorstep, he had to think about what he had made of his life up until then.

One night he told Guy, "You know, this is the first time in my life that I've realized I have to face what I have been running from. James didn't die because I couldn't stop him. And my father can only hurt me if I allow him to."

Guy almost dropped the rabbit he held over the fire. "I never dreamed I would hear you say that, Will."

"I suppose I was always running too fast for the realization to catch up to me. Perhaps this leg wound was what I needed."

"It slowed you down, that's for sure."

"And it kept me down, so all I could do was think."

"Why don't you get some sleep? You can think tomorrow."

"Tomorrow we need to break camp. I won't rest until we put a little more distance between us and Hungry Wolf."

"I don't think you're in any condition to travel."

"I'm not in much condition to do anything *but* travel." He shook his head. "I remember you told me once that it was better to remain still than to rise to meet the devil. Perhaps that's what I've been doing all along, rising to meet the devil."

"Well, you are as still as a widow's bed now."

Will put a dramatic emphasis on his next words. "My heart lies as still as a pool of limpid water."

"Ever the poet."

" 'Badly done' is what you used to say."

"True. Some things never change. Only our perception changes. Now get some sleep. We need rest if we're going to leave at first light."

Will was almost asleep when he heard Guy say, "If you are lucky, you can be home by Christmas."

"Christmas," Will said, closing his eyes and feeling suddenly weary. The pain in his leg was throbbing now. He did not want to think about pain or Christmas. For to think of either one of them reminded Will that Guy would be dead soon.

And he was.

Guy died three days after reaching St. Louis. The last thing Will did for his friend and tutor was to bury him on the bluff that overlooked the Missouri River.

Because of the infection in his leg, Will remained in St. Louis for three weeks before he was well enough to catch a boat for New Orleans. A week after he arrived in New Orleans, he set sail for England.

It was a month before Christmas when Will arrived in London and stepped upon English soil. He had been gone almost two years.

Two long years he had waited to see her again, dear, damned, distracting woman. And now the moment had come.

CHAPTER
❖ TWENTY-NINE ❖

He did not send word that he was coming home. He wanted it to be a surprise.

He also wanted to find a doctor. Since he wounded his leg, he had been experiencing some numbness in his arm. While he could see no connection between a gunshot in the leg and a numbness in his arm, he wanted to have it checked out. He did not want the possibility of anything happening to ruin his reunion with his wife.

Dr. Arch MacAllister was reported to be the queen's own physician, so Will figured if it was good enough for old Victoria, it was good enough for him.

He was in a lighthearted mood when he went into Dr. MacAllister's office. It was a mood that did not last long.

When Dr. MacAllister walked into the examining room, Will rose to his feet. Dr. MacAllister was a blustery old Scot, with white bushy eyebrows and a voice as rough as a cob. "What seems to be the problem with your arm?"

"Occasional numbness."

"When did it start?"

"I was shot in the leg by Indians a few months back. It started shortly after that." Anticipating the doctor's next question, Will told him about the accident in America.

Dr. MacAllister frowned. "I can't see any connection between the two, but I'll have a better idea after I examine you. Take off your shirt and have a seat on the table there."

Shirtless, Will sat on the table while Dr. Mac-Allister poked and punched around on his back. "Tell me if this hurts."

Will sat quietly, waiting for the doctor to finish playing doctor so he could get dressed and get home. Suddenly, he felt a sharp, stabbing pain that nearly doubled him over. "Hellfire! What are you doing? Poking me with hot needles?"

"Did that hurt?"

"Well hell. I had forgotten doctors like to be such comics. You're damn right it hurt. Want me to punch you in the jaw so you can see just how much it hurt? What did you do?"

"I'll tell you when I'm finished."

After concluding his examination, Dr. MacAllister sat down and began to scribble a few notes in a small leather notebook. "You can put your shirt on."

"Thank you, doctor."

"Did you ever have this numbness before you were shot in the leg?"

"Not that I remember."

"Tell me about the wound, how you got it,

what you did for it, how you felt . . . leave out nothing."

Will went on to relate the particulars of his accident and how, after being shot in the leg, his horse stumbled and fell, throwing him to the ground.

"So you fell after you were shot?"

"My horse went down, what other choice did I have? . . . Of course I fell."

"Was it a hard fall?"

"Was it a hard fall? . . . Look, if you are asking me if the ground was hard, yes."

"Did you notice anything different after you fell?"

"Hell yes! I was hurting all over and my leg was bleeding a bloody river. I was so numb, I couldn't even move for a few minutes."

"Ahhh, let's talk about the numbness."

"There is nothing to talk about. I just felt numb, that's all. I had just had the breath knocked out of me and my head was swimming and all I could think about was that I was probably about three minutes from being scalped."

"Well, you still have your hair, so let's get back to the fall. When you felt this numbness, was there any pain?"

"Of course, I had just been shot in the leg, remember?"

"Anywhere else?"

Will thought a moment. "My back hurt."

"Your back. You did not tell me about the bullet wound over your spine. Judging from the

312

scar, I'd say it was an old wound."

Will had completely forgotten about it. "I was shot by a childhood friend. We were hunting. It was an accident. It happened a long time ago. I couldn't have been more than fourteen or fifteen . . . maybe not even that old."

"You were under a doctor's care, I presume."

"Yes. My father brought me to London."

"I saw no surgical scars. Did they remove the bullet?"

"No. They were afraid it might cause paralysis."

"And you had no trouble with it . . . until you were shot?"

"None."

"A moment ago, when you felt pain, I was pressing on that old bullet hole. I think the fall you took in America jarred your back and caused the bullet in your spine to move a bit. That's why you never experienced this numbness before."

"Well, if that's all it is, there is nothing to worry about."

Dr. MacAllister's expression did not change. "You are wrong there. Unfortunately, there is everything to worry about. These spells of numbness and temporary paralysis will continue, only they will get longer each time until finally the paralysis will come and it won't leave. When that happens, you will not be able to use the left side of your body."

"For good?"

"For as long as you live. The bullet in your

spine has to come out. The sooner, the better."

"You make it sound serious."

"My boy, that is because it *is* serious. You need to have that bullet removed right away. I could schedule you for the latter part of the week and . . ."

"I'm not having an operation."

He and Dr. MacAllister butted horns over the surgery issue for a bit, but in the end, Will's stubbornness proved stronger than Dr. MacAllister's.

Admitting defeat, the good doctor said at last, "If you won't have the operation, at least be careful."

"What do you mean?"

"Stay off your horse. Don't do anything that would jar your back. No sudden, jerky movement. No lifting heavy objects. In other words, don't do anything that would jolt your body or strain your back. If that bullet moves again . . ."

Will did not say anything for several minutes. When the full impact of the doctor's words hit him, he took a deep breath, then said, "I understand. I'll be careful."

Will spent the next three days being fitted for clothes. Unlike the last time he put in an appearance at his home, now he wanted to make a good impression.

A week after his arrival, his coach loaded with trunks of new clothing and gifts for everyone in the family, Will headed home. He thought it appropriate that he was on his way to Emberly Hall, to the Midlands, for it was the very core of romantic traditions: Sherwood Forest, Warwick Castle, Chatsworth. Then there was Shakespeare's Forest of Arden and the graceful crosses raised six centuries ago by Edward I on the funeral route of his adored wife, Eleanor of Castile.

Soon, he was passing by the ever-twisting River Wye, then crossing Sheepwash Bridge, where the river meandered through Ashford. He drove up the narrow streets, passing the limestone houses and the church of the Holy Trinity.

An hour later, he drove through the iron gates of Emberly Hall, then through the tunnel of trees, until he saw the house in the distance, looking as it did when he and James returned home from school, just before Christmas. It was the first time Will thought of how good it was that some things never change.

The early morning mist had not completely lifted by the time the coach arrived at the front door. Combed, oiled, polished, brushed, dressed to the nines, and smelling like the worst London dandy, Will made his grand entrance.

Octavia was descending the stairs when Will walked into the house. For a moment she looked so stricken that Will feared she might drop in a swoon right before his very eyes. And his mother was not a woman given to swoons.

"William," she whispered. "After all this time . . . dear, dear beloved William. How I have longed to see you."

Will opened his arms and cradled his mother against him, kissing the top of her head. "I have missed you, too, Mother. More often than you could know."

Octavia dropped back and looked him over, much in the same manner Will figured she must have done all those years ago, on the day he was born. It was obvious to him that she wanted to see for herself that everything about him was hale and hearty.

"All in working order," he said, realizing there was a part of him that he had not exercised in so long, he really had no idea if it still worked or not. But that wasn't a part his mother would have been interested in, anyway, so he did not mention it.

Satisfied, Octavia then glanced around and asked, "Where is Guy?"

"He's dead."

"Dead? Guy? What happened?"

"He became ill on the voyage to America. The entire time we were there, he was dying with consumption."

"I never knew."

"He didn't want anyone to know."

"When did it happen?"

"Over three months ago."

"Oh, dearest Guy, how terrible that you had to be laid to rest in a foreign land."

"Actually, he was quite taken with America. I buried him in a place he had seen before, a place that he said he wanted to be his final resting place.

He told me once that if it was his fate not to die, that he would not return to England. He is where he wanted to be. He was ready to die. We have to accept that."

Octavia let out a long sigh. "I always took him for granted. I never thought he wouldn't be around. He wasn't that old."

"You were the first one, I believe, to tell me that death favored no one, that he took young and old alike."

"You have an unbelievable memory for some things."

"Some things? You mean, like unimportant things?"

"Wear that shoe only if it fits. I will say no more on the subject."

Not much later, Will posed the question he had been waiting to ask for a long time. A question he had once wondered if he would ever have the opportunity to ask. He uttered the words slowly, savoring the sound, the feel of each of them upon his lips. "Where is my wife? Where is Margery?"

"Margery is . . . out. She's out."

She said the word *out* just a little too brightly for William, and he narrowed his brows suspiciously. "Out? What do you mean out? Out where? Out with whom? How long has she been out?"

"Why don't you come into the salon? We can have a nice cup of tea."

"What is going on here? What are you trying to hide, Mother? Isn't she here?"

Octavia sighed. "I see two more years of wandering did little to temper your impatience."

"Where is she? How long has she been gone? What have you done to find her?"

"I said she was gone, William. I did not say she was lost."

Will stared at her but said nothing.

"Calm yourself," she said. "If the prodigal son had given his family any notice of his coming, we would have killed the fatted calf."

"To hell with the fatted calf! Where is my wife?"

Octavia raised her brows. "Wife? Did you have a wife, William? One that you have misplaced perhaps?"

"Mother, this isn't the time to be flippant."

"Well, at my age, one takes her pleasures where she finds them. Now, before you rupture something vital, Margery isn't . . ."

At that moment, Emily walked in with a young boy balanced on her hip. Seeing Will, she stopped with a sudden jerk and stared, openmouthed, as if she had just glimpsed someone long dead. "Will! I can't believe that is you! When did you get home? Why didn't you send word that you were coming? Why haven't you written? Are you going to stay for Christmas?"

"Long-winded as ever, I see," he said, opening his arms.

She hurried toward him, then realized she couldn't hug him with the child in her arms, so she settled for a kiss on his cheek. "What a marvelous surprise. Welcome home, dearest brother."

Will looked at the little boy who stared back at him. "When did you get married?"

Emily gave him a confused look. "Married?"

"Don't tell me the child is illegitimate."

She glanced at her mother and her face turned a bright pink. "I'm not married, and he is *not* illegitimate."

Will's heart seemed to ice over. "Then whose child is he?"

Emily looked down at the boy. "Robbie? Why he's Mar—" Emily snapped her mouth shut and her eyes grew round. "Oh!" she said, and then again, "Oh!"

"Margery? He's Margery's child? My wife, Margery?"

Emily nodded, her head bobbing violently.

"And where, pray tell, did she get a child?"

Octavia gave him an exasperated look. "For heaven's sake, William. What do you mean where did she get it? She got it the *usual* way. . . . She gave birth."

Will's fists clenched at his sides. "And who is the father? . . . Or does she even know?"

Octavia looked Will in the eye. "I believe Margery said something about the father being a pigheaded brute who married her for all the wrong reasons, made love to her only to make the marriage irrevocable, then dumped her with a lot of pomp and little ceremony, in a foreign country to reside with a group of complete and idiotic strangers before abandoning her completely. *You* wouldn't happen to know anyone who fits that description, would you?"

At that, Emily burst out laughing, but Will wasn't listening. He was too overcome with emotion. His son . . . this small, perfect little being was his son. "My son," he whispered. "You mean this is *my* son?"

Octavia nodded, looking at Robbie. "Every dimpled, stubborn inch of him, although I must say you don't deserve to have such a fine son, or such a splendid wife. You have behaved like a complete ass, if you don't mind my saying so. But then, I don't suppose you could help it. Your father was an ass. And his father before him. Apparently, asses run in the Woodville family." She looked at Robbie and sighed. "I suppose it is only a matter of time until you become an ass, too."

Will looked at his mother and grinned like a fool. "Why should I mind being called an ass? I suppose I deserve it." He glanced at his son again, then held out his arms. "Here, let me hold him."

Emily held Robbie out, but Robbie had a mind of his own, and he wasn't having any part of this stranger. His face wrinkled up like a prune and he let out a wail that you could hear in Brighton. A moment later, he whipped around and put his arms around Emily's neck so tightly, her words came out in a strangled whisper. "He isn't accustomed to strangers."

Will's face turned scarlet. "I'm not a stranger. I'm his father."

"Explain the difference to *him*," Octavia said,

nodding in Robbie's direction.

"I'll explain it to him later. Right now, I want to see my wife, and if you don't tell me where she is, I will take this place apart, stone by stone, until I find her."

Octavia sat down with a sigh. "This is what makes mothers old before their time."

"I am waiting."

"As she has been, only longer."

"I am aware of that and I fully intend to make it up to her."

"Lost years are difficult, if not impossible, to recapture."

"Mother, I want to see Margery and I want to see her now."

"I think you should at least let me tell her you are here. She . . ."

"I will tell her myself and I prefer to be alone with her when I do. Where is she?"

"In the kitchen seeing to Robbie's breakfast."

"Don't we have help to do that, or has my wife become the scullery maid?"

Emily chortled. Will gave her a hostile look.

"Sorry," she said.

"Margery is treated like one of the family, because she is part of the family," Octavia said. "She enjoys cooking and does it often. I saw no reason to deny her the privilege, but if you prefer to have her confined to her room, I will make immediate arrangements."

"Why is everyone making light of something quite serious?"

"Maybe it is because we are all furious with you, and that is the only alternative we have, except shooting you square between the eyes, which is certainly appropriate, considering what you have done, you reprobate."

Will shook his head. "Thank you, Mother, for those kind words." A second later, he crossed the room with quick steps and disappeared around the corner.

Emily watched him go, then turned to her mother. "Shouldn't we go to the kitchen?"

"You heard Will say he wanted to be alone."

"But . . . what about Margery? She might need our protection."

Octavia's brows raised in surprise and then she smiled, as if recalling something humorous. "I think our Margery is more than capable of taking care of herself. It would serve him right if she lifted his scalp."

"Mama!"

"Oh hush up, Emily Woodville. How many times have I told you not to take things so seriously? Now, go fetch me a cup of tea, and lace it with brandy."

"Brandy before breakfast?"

Octavia nodded. "And afterward, too, if I need it. Now hurry."

"You don't usually have brandy with your tea."

"I don't *usually* have Will marching through the front door looking as dangerous as a rapier. Now, get me that tea and be quick about it."

CHAPTER
◉ THIRTY ◉

Will walked into the kitchen and paused in the doorway, looking around the room. And then he saw her, Margery, his wife, the object of his tortured mind for two years, looking nothing like he had seen her last, or for that matter, nothing like he thought to find her now.

She looked even more beautiful than he remembered. She had been a beauty as an Indian. She was exquisite now.

The dark blue dress she wore fit her to perfection. And what perfection! Maturity and motherhood had been generously kind to her. She was getting close to thirty, and yet, her face and body, while not completely youthful, held a ripeness that captured the vitality and energy of youth, as well as the maturity that comes from experiencing life's joys and sufferings.

She did not look surprised to see him or too happy about it either. Her calm reaction, her exquisite appearance, her overall refinement left him speechless, and he looked her over, taking in her appearance, trying to salvage the moment by searching his brain for something appropriate to say.

After a quick glance in his direction, she turned her attention back to the pot on the stove. She picked up a large spoon and began to ladle what looked to be porridge into a juvenile bowl.

He searched for something to say . . . anything. . . . "Hello."

She ignored him completely.

He frowned. This wasn't the way he had things planned. Where was that worshipful look that was supposed to be in her eyes? Where was the throwing herself into his arms, the breathless exclamations, the joy over his return, the scattering of a hundred misplaced kisses? Didn't she understand that he was her conquering hero returned home?

She had done very well for herself without him and he began to get angry. She could have suffered just a little — as he had done — or at the very least, missed him. But the only thing she did was to look right through him. It was her distance, her aloofness, that threw him off balance.

"I gather you aren't too glad to see me?"

She picked up the bowl of porridge and walked toward the table.

She passed the basket of fruit. She passed the cooling loaves of bread. She passed the butter churn. She passed the table.

Well hell. Where in the devil is she going?

Then she turned and walked toward him.

Will smiled. She was coming around now. In a moment she would be in his arms. Right where he wanted her.

She stopped in front of him.

He made a move to embrace her.

Before he could touch her, she upended the bowl of porridge against his stiffly starched shirt-front. The slimy mass oozed in grayish clumps downward, then slid across his trousers. He looked down just in time to see some land with a heavy *shlump* on the polished toes of his new shoes.

He was just about to lift his head to glance back at her when she placed the porridge bowl on his head. Before he could react, she rapped it once, hard, with the wooden spoon she held in her hand, then she dropped the spoon at his feet, stepped around him, and was gone.

For a full minute he stood there with the porridge bowl on his head, his ears ringing as he looked down at his ruined new clothes and the spoon balancing across his toes. It was difficult to believe that this was the woman he had bought . . . a woman he had purchased with a few ponies. The woman who was submissive and obedient. The one who looked at him with quiet adoration. The one who had come naked to his bed, wanting him to make love to her.

He was a man who opened an oyster and found a pearl. Only now the pearl was gone and nothing was left but an empty shell.

Margery found Octavia and Emily in the salon.

"Will is back," Emily said. "He went looking for you."

"He found me."

Emily blinked. "Did you argue?"

"Emily, that is none of your affair," Octavia said, "but since you have raised the question, we might as well stick around for the answer." Turning to Margery, she asked, "Well, did you?"

"No."

Octavia's surprise was evident. "You didn't argue?"

"No."

Emily's curiosity seemed to be growing. "What did you do, then, if you didn't argue? What happened? What did you say?"

"I didn't say anything."

It was Octavia's turn. "If you didn't say anything, then what did Will say?"

"He said hello."

"Hello?" Octavia repeated. "Just hello? Is that all?"

"I believe so."

Emily looked bewildered as she glanced at her mother. Octavia appeared intrigued with something she saw through the window.

"Will just said hello, and then you walked out of the room?" Emily asked.

"After a fashion."

Octavia turned back to Margery. A slow smile began to form on her face. "Where is William now?"

"I believe he is still in the kitchen."

"What is he doing?" Emily asked.

"Last time I saw, he was into Robbie's porridge."

Emily looked doubtful. "But Will doesn't like porridge. He wouldn't eat it even as a child."

"Well, he's feeling his oats now," Margery said, holding out her finger and smiling as Robbie grabbed it.

At that moment, someone knocked at the front door, and they listened as the butler answered it. A few seconds later, they all turned to stare as Lydia and John walked into the salon.

"And here we thought we might be a bit early," John said.

"Oh, I'd say you arrived just at the right time," was Octavia's reply.

Lydia looked around the room. "What is this we hear about William's return?"

Emily dimpled. "It's true. He just arrived a short while ago."

John glanced at Margery. "Where is he?"

"I believe he is in the kitchen," Margery replied, calm as a summer wind.

John started for the door. "I can't wait to see him."

"I can't *wait* for you to see him," Margery replied.

Everyone followed John out of the room. Even Margery followed, but she was not going to the kitchen. She trailed behind a bit, planning to go upstairs. She was not ready to face Will again. At least, not yet.

In the kitchen, Will was still trying to recover. As he attempted to wipe the gooey mess from his clothes, he almost laughed. Of all the responses he had imagined . . .

Porridge . . .

He told himself that she was angry because he had hurt her feelings when he left her behind. That was understandable. She did not know him. She had not seen him in two years. She had given birth to his child. All alone. Of course she had to redeem herself. Well hell, she had made her point, he thought. *Now we can get down to basics.*

After he had gotten the worst of the porridge off his clothes, he left the kitchen. He would change his clothes and then he would find her. They needed to talk.

He was walking down the hall, heading toward the stairs when Octavia, Emily, Lydia, and John walked out of the salon, with Margery lagging a little bit behind.

Will had been thinking that all he and Margery needed was a little time together, then she would come around. Somehow he knew that was not to be, for there was something in her eyes that said this was not a shy, retreating woman. What he saw instead was confidence, intelligence, self-assurance, and something that horrified him: the strength to survive without him, the ability to take care of herself.

That sounded dangerously like someone else he knew . . .

With slow, precise movement, he paused to stare at his mother.

Octavia was not looking at him but had turned

to glance at Margery. Pride was in that gaze. Hers was a feeling he knew well, for he felt it himself from time to time — whenever he finished a painting that went beyond even his own expectations. He called it a sense of accomplishment.

John and Lydia were staring at him with bemused expressions, neither of them daring to ask what everyone was dying to know.

Emily was doing her best to look properly horrified.

Will skimmed over the faces of everyone gathered there to center his gaze upon the face of his wife. He knew he should say something, but he couldn't think of a single thing, and it would not do to start off on their next encounter with his babbling like an idiot, or saying something equally as asinine as *hello*. He did not think she would appreciate his telling her how beautiful she looked or how well she had matured. Or for that matter, how much he desired her.

Robbie began to squirm and call, "Mama . . . Mama . . . Mama . . ."

Margery gave him a smile that lit up the hallway; a smile warm enough to wrap one's self in. Will felt the first searing pain of jealousy and instantly hated himself for it. How could he, a grown man, be jealous of his own son?

"Mother is here," Margery said, her voice low and cultured. She held out her arms and Robbie tumbled into them. "It is time for you to have your breakfast, my little man. Where is Nanny?"

Robbie squirmed and said, with much conviction and obvious practice, "Nanny, no!"

The response made William smile, but only briefly, for he realized then that Margery had turned away from him and was carrying their son from the room, without even acknowledging his presence or saying good-bye.

He could not let her go, at least not this way. "Aren't you going to say anything to me?"

Margery paused, then turned slowly. "Why should I?"

"Well, for starters, unless you've obtained a divorce, I happen to be your husband. And when a husband returns from a trip, it is customary for the wife to greet him."

"Then you must forgive me. I have had no practice at being married, and therefore have no knowledge of its customs."

"I see. I am going to have to pay the price — make full restitution for having left."

"Nothing of the sort. You did what you wanted to do. I had no hold over you then . . . just as you have no hold over me now."

"Why didn't you say something when I spoke to you in the kitchen?"

"You did not speak to me when you left. I saw no reason to speak to you now that you have returned."

Will's anger began to simmer. He had made an effort to ignore her chilly reception, the oatmeal, but this was too much.

She wanted reasons?

By God, he would give her reasons. He opened his mouth to tell her in so many words just why she should have responded to him.

No words came forth.

For the life of him, Will could not think of even one solitary reason, save the fact that she was his wife, which she obviously did not consider a valid point. His anger boiled down to frustrated steam. "Well hell!"

"William! Not in front of your own child!" scolded Octavia.

"Beg pardon." Will stood there, his hands shoved deep into his pockets, his clothes mottled with porridge, looking as whipped as a beaten dog, wishing he could back up and start this homecoming all over again.

He had bungled and bungled badly, but only because he had been taken so off guard. Never, even in his worst nightmare, would he have expected her to react this way. For months he had dreamed of nothing but her gentle, caring way; the love for him he remembered seeing in her eyes; the desire she had to be a good wife; the pleasure she took in his pleasure; and most of all, the way she looked that night when she first came to his room, naked, and wanting only him.

He wished he could change the way things seemed to be going between them, that he could have some time alone with her, away from his family, away even from their child.

And yet, things did not change. There was no way for him to turn back the clock. He was left, all alone, in the painful present. No one moved. No one said a word.

Only the hall clock made any sound at all — a slow, ominous ticking that reminded him that with each breath he drew, precious time was slipping away.

The silence was driving him insane. He wanted to smash something, to drive his fist through a door or beat his head against a brick wall. *Just look at her, standing there so blessedly beautiful, so regal, so in control: Madonna and child.*

But he could do nothing but stand there, feeling remarkably like Judas Iscariot.

Robbie began to fuss and squirm again.

Margery cuddled Robbie close and placed a kiss on his nose, whispering endearments. The boy quieted for a moment, then began to wail in earnest. "Please excuse me." It was obvious she spoke to no one in particular. A second later, she turned around and walked from the room, Robbie balanced upon her hip.

Will looked at Emily then at his mother, avoiding the stares of John and Lydia. "Well, I cannot say that was exactly the homecoming I expected."

"She'll come around," John said, and stepping forward, clapped him on the back. "It's good to have you home, Will. How does it feel to be back on English soil?"

"Like hell, but if that changes, I'll let you know in a few days."

Everyone laughed — more to relieve the tension than from anything humorous.

Will turned to Lydia, and taking her hands in his, he kissed her cheek. "You are looking as lovely as ever. How have you been?"

She glanced at John and her face turned pink. Will raised his brows at his cousin. *John and Lydia? Well hell. Why hadn't he thought of that? They were a perfect match.*

John gave her a reassuring smile and Lydia took a breath, then said, "Thank you, Will. It's so good to have you home again. Are you visiting, or is this permanent?"

Will was staring at the door Margery had just walked through. "From the looks of things, I'd say it had better be permanent."

"I am inclined to agree with you," Lydia said.

John cleared his throat. "You heard about your father?"

Will felt like someone had hit him. *You heard about your father?* He knew immediately what John was talking about, not because anyone told him that his father was dead, but because something inside of him simply knew. He was not certain how the news made him feel.

Will shook his head. "No, no one told me, but I gather you are trying to tell me my father is dead."

Octavia cut in. "I did not tell Will because I did not want to ruin his homecoming."

"Oh," John said, "I am sorry. I should have kept my big mouth shut."

"It's all right," Will said. "My homecoming was ruined shortly after I returned. I am wearing the proof of it still."

Everyone looked down at his soiled clothes.

"When did my father die? How?" Will asked John.

"We can tell you later, Will. You've just arrived. Let's not talk about sad things now." Emily slipped her arm through his. "Come sit down. I want to hear all about your travels. Did you bring back as many sketches as you did before? Where did you go? What adventures did you have? What made you decide to come back?" She jerked to a halt and dropped his arm quite suddenly. "Perhaps we should talk later."

As if that was the break they needed to ease the strain, everyone began to laugh — even Will, who excused himself a moment later and went upstairs, going to his old room to change.

As he dressed, Will barely paid any attention to what he was doing. He was too distracted. He couldn't get over the fact that he had a son.

He had left a husband and come back a father.

A father . . . he had a vision of a critical, controlling man, a man who always seemed to prefer the company of his nephew to that of his son. A cold fear settled in his stomach: a fear that he would turn out just like Charles, that he would ruin his son's life.

CHAPTER
▨ THIRTY-ONE ▨

Octavia massaged her temples, trying to rub her headache away.

Will was back, and although Octavia was deliriously happy to have him home again, what a misadventure his homecoming was turning out to be. The distance between Will and Margery was problem enough. Of course, Will had learned about only one of his sons. How would he react when he learned there were two?

No wonder she had a headache. Her life was a boiling pot that threatened to bubble over at any minute. Being a wife was a commitment. Being a mother was a full-time job. Being a matchmaker was exhausting. Righting all the wrongs in this family was a nightmare.

"Mama, are you feeling all right?"

Octavia turned to greet her daughter. Dear, sweet Emily. How long before she fell in love? How long before she would need Octavia's help to smooth out the wrinkles in her life? "I am fine, dear. Just a little headache."

"And small wonder. Actually, I am surprised your headache is a small one."

"To be truthful, it is not. Right now it is a dandy with promise of developing into something more."

"What are you going to do about everything?"

Octavia thought a moment. "I don't know as yet. I'm still cogitating about that. William will always be Charles's son and heir. Nothing can change that. However, if William and Margery don't find some common ground and decide to live as man and wife then their marriage could be as gone as a Christmas goose."

"What can I do to help?"

"For starters, we need to take advantage of every opportunity to get the two of them together. . . ."

"Alone," said Emily.

"Yes, alone, and that includes keeping Robbie and young Wills occupied. This is a delicate situation and must be handled carefully, or we could do more damage than good."

Emily swore her dying devotion. "I will do everything I can. Cross my heart." She crossed her heart to seal the pledge before turning to leave the room. Just as she disappeared around the door, she called out. "Don't worry, Mother. Everything will turn out fine. I know it will."

Octavia smiled at Emily's youthful optimism. Perhaps she was right. Perhaps all would be well. "But not until I have a few more headaches."

Octavia's next headache came later that very afternoon.

William returned from a ride with John. After leaving the stables, the two of them walked toward the house. Will's arm was tingling and he rubbed it absently, forgetting about it completely when they stopped by the garden where Lydia sat on a stone bench, reading to Robbie, who seemed more interested in the thumb he was sucking.

Will looked at his son, still finding it difficult to believe this miniature human being was part of him. "Well, hello," he said.

Robbie pulled his thumb out of this mouth with a loud *thuck,* then left a drooling trail across the pages of the book until his chubby finger pointed at a picture. "Horse."

"Two horses," Will said, pointing at the other horse in the picture and feeling a jolt of warm current when his hand brushed the tender skin of his son.

"How old are you?"

Robbie held up two wet fingers.

Lydia laughed and grabbed his fingers. "He is perfecting the art of getting *close* to the truth early. You won't be two until June, you little gudgeon." She tickled him and Robbie collapsed in a fit of giggles.

Will walked toward the house then stopped, noticing John wasn't coming with him. He glanced back at John. "Are you coming?"

"I'll be there in a minute. I wanted to speak to Lydia for a moment."

Will's gaze went from John to Lydia, and he couldn't help remembering their trial by fire. He was happy for her and nodded his approval. She gave him a warm smile that was full of understanding. Their friendship had withstood the most difficult and trying times and persevered. He was glad they had been able to talk things through after what had happened all those years ago between Lydia, James, and him. It said a lot that she could put what happened behind her and not allow it to ruin her life. How he wished he could have done the same thing with his father. He and Lydia had sinned and wronged his brother, but they had recognized it for what it was and gone on from there. Their friendship had proved stronger than their infidelity. Looking back, he understood now that it had been their deep bond of friendship that had drawn them together, only they had allowed their pain to override their common sense and had let things go too far. They were young then and irrational. Time had painted a different perspective on things. He gave her one last glance and knew she understood what he was thinking. A current of forgiveness seemed to flow between them. Love was blind, but friendship closed its eyes.

He walked on. He was thinking that he couldn't think of a better man for Lydia than John, and after what she had been through . . . well, she deserved the best and now it looked as if she was going to get it.

A few minutes later, Will walked upstairs and passed the nursery. He glanced inside and saw Robbie riding a rocking horse — one that had been his when he was a young boy. He didn't waste any time coming up here, Will was thinking. He was surprised the boy's short little legs could move that fast.

He rubbed the tingling in his left arm and walked on.

Margery stood at the window of her bedroom watching Will talk to Robbie in the garden. She marveled at the miraculous nature of fate. She had never thought to see this moment, and yet it had come to pass. William with his son. At last.

She studied Will. He was thinner than she remembered him, but perhaps that was due to the leg wound Octavia had asked John to take a look at earlier. Margery had to act indifferent, of course, but she did manage to grab John and pull him aside for a bit to hear him say Will's wound looked perfectly healed.

Her heart seemed to swell at the sight of him, and she had a memory of what it had been like to lie in his arms, to feel the force of his passion, the heat of his desire. Her body grew warm and limpid at the thought. If there had been any doubt in her mind as to whether she felt anything for him, it was laid to rest. Oh, yes, the feeling was there.

But she was different.

"What are you thinking?" Octavia's voice came from behind her, and Margery turned around.

"Forgive me for coming in without knocking,

but the door was open and I saw you standing here."

"You are always welcome and you know it."

Octavia joined her at the window. "He hasn't changed much, has he? A little thinner and the slight limp, but other than that, he seems unchanged."

"Do you think he will stay this time?"

"Do you want him to?"

"It would be best. Robbie and Wills need a father."

"And what about you, Margery? Do you need a husband?"

"No, I don't *need* one. I can be happy without a man in my life."

Octavia smiled at her, obviously pleased by Margery's answer. "But you would not be opposed to having Will back in your life?"

"I would have to say that depends."

"On what?"

"On the reason why he came back. What his plans are. How he feels about me. Whether or not he is committed to being a husband and a father."

"That is all?"

Margery thought a moment, wondering if she should tell Octavia the rest. After all, she was her husband's mother. Yet, she was also the woman who had taught her independence. "No. The biggest factor will be his expectations of me. I am not the same meek and mild, grossly overinfatuated woman he left behind. He bought me, but he does not own me. I will not be stabled in some country manor house like a horse put out to pasture while he spends his time in London. I will not tolerate a mistress. I will not be married to a dictator."

"Excellent."

"You do not think me too harsh?"

"Nonsense. You could never be as harsh as he was — leaving you here as he did. It would serve the rapscallion right if he had to walk on hot coals just for the right to live with you as man and wife."

Margery sighed and turned away from the window, letting the curtain drop back into place. "We may be doing all of this to no avail. He may not want to live with me. After all, he was not so tied to me that he could not abandon me before. I doubt anything could have happened to change his feelings toward me."

"You never know."

"I suppose not, but I do know one thing. If William Woodville wants me as his wife, he will have to work for it. I was easy before. I will not be so again."

"Good. That is the right thing to do. Anything worth having is worth fighting for. Poor William, he has no idea what he is in for."

"No, he doesn't."

Will came into the salon where his mother was sitting by the window, an embroidery frame in front of her.

She looked up as he entered the room. "William, what on earth are you doing inside on such a lovely afternoon?"

"I was looking for Margery."

"Have you talked with her yet?"

Will scowled. "No, but not because I haven't tried. Believe me, I've had the devil's own time of it."

"Oh? What seems to be the problem?"

"Most of the time I cannot find her, or when I do, she is surrounded by family or friends and I can't get her alone."

Octavia gave her attention to her embroidery. "She is alone now."

"What?"

"I said she is alone now."

There were times when Will wanted to shake his mother for her subterfuge. This was one of those times. "Thank you for being so helpful. Now, do you suppose you could tell me just where she is, or don't you know?"

"Of course I know where she is."

"Then why didn't you tell me before now?"

"For heaven's sake, Will. Mothers are many things, but one thing we are not is mind readers. If you wanted to know where Margery was, why didn't you ask me?"

"Mother, that is the first thing I did when I came in."

"I beg your pardon. You did not ask me if I knew where Margery was. You said you were looking for her."

"If you knew I was looking for her, then the logical assumption would be that I did not know where she was, in which case you would volunteer the information."

"There are two things wrong with that statement. First, and most importantly, women are not logical creatures. We are guided by instinct and feelings, not logic. Secondly, I never volunteer information. Information is power . . . something we women have little of. . . ."

Octavia went on talking, but Will was not listening. How had he grown up with the misconception that it was a mother's place to look after her children? He was shocked beyond belief to discover his own mother was not a "mother woman." A mother woman would have fluttered around him from the moment he returned, surrounding him with her protective wings. A mother woman would idolize him; she would consider it a devout and holy privilege to efface herself as an individual in order to put him first. She would have done everything in her power to get him and Margery together as soon as possible.

He stared at her, waiting for her to grow the wings of a ministering angel. She did not. He felt positively terrified to stand there watching the mantle of idolization — which had always enveloped her — slowly slip from her shoulders. He blinked, as if making certain this was his mother, the embodiment of grace and charm, the protector of her precious offspring.

She was the same woman, for there were the

golden combs holding up her hair, just as they always had, the diamond pin at her breast, the blue eyes that were like no other eyes he could remember, which always looked at him with devotion and undying love. And yet, she was different. Or was he the one who had changed?

"William, are you feeling well?"

"Yes, Mother, as well as can be expected, considering I have just suffered a tremendous loss."

"Well, I am certain you will find a way to recover. You were ever a resourceful boy."

"Mother, are you going to help me?"

"I don't think you need any help, William. After all, you have managed thus far without my help."

Will nodded, clenching the corners of his mouth, then walked from the room.

"She is in the kitchen, I believe."

"Thank you," he replied, mumbling to himself as he walked away. "Well hell, if your own mother won't help you, who will?"

Moments later, he heard someone playing the piano. As he passed the music room, he saw it was Emily who played, while Robbie sat on the bench beside her.

CHAPTER
⊞ THIRTY-TWO ⊞

Margery and Wills were in the kitchen making gingerbread men. As Margery placed the cut shapes on the baking pan, Wills, who was standing on a chair beside her, decorated the face with currants.

"When you finish making the face, you must give the gingerbread man a shirt. Now, watch me." Margery took three currants and placed them in the proper place. "See? He has a shirt now, and here are the buttons. One . . . two . . . three . . . three buttons."

Wills looked down at his own shirt and poked his buttons with one finger. "Buttons!"

Margery reached over to give him a kiss. When she raised her head, she saw Will standing in the doorway. He was rubbing his arm and looking quite perplexed. "How did he get in here so fast?"

She glanced around and saw no one. "Whom are you speaking of?"

"Robbie," he said. "How did he get in here so quickly?"

"I don't understand. What do you mean, how did he get in here so quickly?"

"I mean, I just passed the music room, and Robbie was playing the piano with Emily."

"Yes, Robbie loves to play the piano."

William looked at Wills and then down the hallway. "Something strange is going on here," he said, "but that isn't why I came in here."

"No?"

"May I join you?" he asked, coming into the kitchen and stopping next to Wills.

She did not look at him but went on cutting out cookies — which was difficult, considering how good he looked and just how close he was standing. In that regard, her memory had not failed her, for he was every bit as handsome as she remembered. She could not help wondering what he thought about her — not only the way she looked, but the other changes she had undergone as well. Her pride wanted to show him just how much she had accomplished, how much she had learned, how many topics she could discuss with ease. But the woman in her wanted to wait. Caution, her mind warned her. Do not make it easy for him. Easy women do not have an easy time of it. What men have to work for, they appreciate. She hardened herself, keeping her tone cool, detached, emotionless. "Since you've come in anyway, I don't need to answer that question, do I?"

"I thought I'd help Robbie decorate."

Margery opened her mouth to correct Will, to tell him this was not Robbie, but Wills was quicker to respond.

"Robbie, no!" Wills shouted, standing staunchly in the chair. He grabbed a fistful of cookies and hugged them to his chest. "My cookies."

Margery smiled and stroked his cheek. "Yes, love, they are your cookies. But don't you want to give Robbie one?"

"No! My cookies!"

Will looked from Margery to Wills and back to Margery. "What in hell is going on here?"

There was such venom in his words that she turned to look at him, feeling the old attraction, the same strong, magnetic pull when she met his eyes. "I don't know what you are talking about."

"I think you do. I want to know what kind of joke you are playing on me."

"I was not aware I was playing a joke on you. I have been baking cookies, and although I am not the finest cook, I would not say my talents could be called a joke."

"Did you think you were being clever? Did you think it would be great fun to trick me, just so you could see how long it took for me to figure out I was being duped?"

"I have not done anything to dupe you. I don't know what you could possibly be referring to."

"Him!" Will said nastily, pointing at Wills.

Wills started to cry.

She picked up her son and cradled his head against her shoulder. "There, there. Don't cry." How dare William think this child was not his son. That he would think she would stoop so low as to name another man's child after him made her furious. "Wills is your child. Whether you choose to recognize him as such is entirely up to you. However, since you seem to feel so strongly about it, I can assure you that we can be out of this house in a few short hours."

"And just where do you think you would go?"

"I could go to the townhouse in London."

"Which belongs to me now that I am the earl."

"Then I will stay with friends. I have plenty."

"Oh, I'm sure you do."

"I don't have to stay here and take this." She started to turn away, but his hand came out to grip her upper arm.

"What is his name? And don't lie to me again."

"I never lied to you. His name is Wills."

"Then why was I told his name was Robbie?"

They were interrupted by the sound of a child's crying. A sound that grew closer. A second later, Emily walked into the room. "Robbie wants his mama. He smashed his finger when he closed the cover on the piano."

Seeing Robbie, Wills put his hands more tightly around Margery's neck. He wasn't about to be rooted out of his comfy spot by his brother.

Margery kissed him on the head. "Go to Aunt Emily."

He hugged her more fiercely. "No!"

Margery shook her head and walked to the kitchen table. She took a chair and sat down. She shifted Wills to one side of her lap, then held out her arm for Robbie. Emily giggled and deposited

Robbie on the other side. Sitting there, with both of her sons in her lap, Margery cast hot, furious eyes at her husband, ignoring the dumbfounded look upon his face.

Will turned to his sister. "There are *two* of them?"

Emily laughed and, reaching out, curled her fingers under her brother's chin, then closed his astonished mouth. "They are commonly known as twins. Don't tell me you've never heard of twins before?"

He ignored her comment. "Why didn't someone tell me? I had a right to know."

Margery raised a questioning brow. "Oh? And by what right? You abandoned me when I carried them."

"I didn't know."

"Neither did I, but you had to know that my being with child was a possibility."

"I never thought . . ."

"No, of course you didn't. From what I understand, you've thought of precious little but yourself for years."

"That is not true, but even if it were, things are different now. I have changed."

"I have seen no evidence of it. As I see it, you are still the same arrogant, self-centered man I remembered you to be."

The boys had grown quiet now and tired of their mother's comforting presence. Almost in unison, they slid from Margery's lap.

Emily held out her hands. "Come along, you

two. How would you like to go for a ride in the pony cart?"

The boys showed their enthusiasm by each taking one of Emily's hands. Without a backward glance, the trio left the room.

Will could not take his eyes off of them. "I still can't believe we have twins."

"I have twins," she corrected. "You had precious little to do with it."

He smiled. "True, my role might have been a small one, but vital, nonetheless. You couldn't have done it without me."

"Oh, but I could have. I just couldn't have done it without a man."

"As in any man will do?"

"Exactly."

"I suggest you do not try it."

"Don't worry. I have decided two children is enough."

He found his anger evaporating. He really liked her better this way, damn if he didn't. He gazed at her thoughtfully for a long while before he spoke. "I cannot get over the change in you. You are not the same woman — which I expected — and yet, you are nothing like I imagined you to be."

"Nothing stays the same, not even people."

"I know, but surely you must realize that your progress in such a short time has been remarkable. Try as I may, I can find no trace of the savage in you."

She laughed. "There are those who would disagree with you."

He raised a curious brow. "Oh? For what reason?"

She raised her skirts just enough to show him the knife in her garter. It amused her to see the astonished look on his face.

"Surely you don't go around showing that to anyone."

"Only when I intend to use it."

"You have actually used it?"

"When I had to."

"When?"

"For protection."

"You shouldn't be going places where you have to draw a knife to protect yourself."

She laughed at that. "Actually, I was at a garden party the first time I used it." The amusement in her voice died. "Ask me no more questions about it, for I will not answer them."

He nodded in agreement. "I can always find out from Mother or Emily."

"You will do what you feel you must do. I cannot stop you." She went to the sink and washed her hands.

He followed her from the room. "Where are you going?"

"I have some Christmas gifts I have been making that I need to finish."

"Do it later. We need to talk."

She paused at the foot of the staircase. "I thought that is what we have been doing."

He took her hand and tugged her along behind him. "I mean *really* talk." He stopped in front of the ballroom where the Christmas tree stood near the fireplace. "In here." He led her into the room and shut the door behind them.

She took a seat.

He remained standing behind her. "Wills. It is short for William?"

"Yes."

"You named him for me?"

"Contrary to what you think, you are his father and he was the firstborn."

He put his hand on her shoulder. "I did not mean . . ."

She shrugged, pulling away from his hand. "Yes you did."

"Thank you for doing me such an honor as to name my firstborn after me, even when I did not deserve to be honored."

"I didn't do it for you. I did it because it was the traditional thing to do."

"I never meant for you to think I didn't believe they were mine. I never doubted that. It was simply the shock of discovering there were two."

"You were no more shocked than I."

He could not help smiling. "You had no idea?"

"None of us suspected there were twins. Not even John."

"Was it a difficult time for you?"

"More difficult than all the years of my captivity. At least with the Indians, I always knew where I stood. I did not have even that when I first came here. From the very beginning your father resented me."

"He was cruel to you?"

"Octavia would not have allowed that. He made cutting remarks or simply avoided me. Whenever we were forced to be in the same room, he would act as though I was not there. I saw very little of him, actually."

"Even after the boys were born?"

"Especially then. He referred to them as offspring of the devil. He wanted nothing to do with them."

"I am sorry."

"Why? Surely you must have known how it would be for me . . . how your father would react to having a savage for a daughter-in-law."

"I am ashamed to admit I did not think that far ahead."

"As I said, you rarely think beyond yourself."

"In the past perhaps, but in the years I have been gone, I have thought of little else but you."

"You cannot expect me to believe that. If you thought of me at all, it was as an annoyance, someone you were lucky enough to get rid of."

"That is not true, but even if it were, you cannot truthfully say that you are not better off now than you were. At least I saved you from a life of slavery and gave you freedom."

"You did not have to marry me to do that."

"I don't remember your putting up any fight when we were married."

"Because I thought you intended for me to be your wife . . . in every sense of the word."

"I do. Believe me, I do."

"Now perhaps, but not then."

"And I ask you to forgive me for that. I never meant to hurt you or cause you pain. I honestly thought I was helping you, that I was making your life better. I can't believe that I didn't achieve at least some of that. Look at you! You are every inch the refined lady. You live a life of luxury, wanting for nothing."

"Except a husband and respect. Have you ever thought about what it was like for me? Oh yes, your home is quite lovely, but it is not mine. I am a guest here. I do not belong. I am dependent upon your family for every bite I take. Do you know what it is like when I go out? Because I have no husband to defend me, I am considered a fair target for every lecher in the ton. Rumors have circulated about the parentage of my sons. The kinder women look at me with pity; the others whisper behind my back, treating me like the abandoned wife that I am. And you say I want for nothing. How deluded you are."

"But I am back now, pleading . . . begging for the chance to make up for all the wrong I have done."

"It isn't that easy."

"Why not?"

"Because I have suffered a great deal. Because I am not certain I even care for you anymore. Because I have seen nothing to show me you have changed, only your words. Because I don't trust you."

"And if I can prove myself trustworthy? If I can

prove that my feelings have changed, that I have changed . . . if I show you how much I love you, will you give us another chance?"

"I cannot make any promises."

"If you believe in marriage, you will try."

"If you love me, you will be patient and give me time."

He put his hands on her shoulders and she closed her eyes, allowing herself to feel the exquisite sensation of being touched by him once more . . . but only for a moment. Remembering all the reasons why she could not give in to him, she rose to her feet and went to stand by the fireplace, praying that he could not see how his nearness, his touch had disturbed her.

"If I love you? . . . You have no idea how I have never been able to forget you — the way we were together — especially that last time, on the ship. It was when our sons were conceived. It pleases me to think they were born of a moment of such wild desire. Two sons given to us as a blessing. Two complete human beings that have come from the fusion of our souls. If I love you . . . You are the object of a thousand sleepless nights, the mother of my sons, and yet you wonder if I love you. . . . How could I not?"

She felt herself melting at the sound of his voice, the rhythm of his words. He was seducing her, bending her to his will. Oh, he was a sly one. But she was wise. "You have no way of knowing when our sons were given to us."

"I know, because there was something special

about that night, something different that has carried me during all the time we have been apart."

"Then it can carry you a little longer." She sprang to her feet and started from the room but found her way blocked by him. She backed up as he began advancing toward her. "No," she whispered. "Stay away from me. Do you hear? Leave me alone."

"You know I can't do that. I have to know."

She retreated until she felt her back against the wall. "You have to know what?"

He was just inches from her now and he lifted his arms, placing his hands to each side of her head, trapping her between them, the wall, and his body. She felt the warm strength of his body pressing against her, heard his voice low and throbbing with desire. "I have to know what happens when I kiss you."

"No." She turned her head away.

He did not let her show of resistance deter him but went on. He placed slow, nibbling kisses along the line of her shoulder, giving special attention to the sensitive skin around her ear before dropping lower to kiss his way along the lines of the low-cut bodice of her lavender dress.

Her body was betraying her will, and she clenched her fists at her sides, reminding herself how important it was that she show no reaction to him and what he was doing.

"I have wanted you . . . wanted to be with you like this for so long. I was tormented by it —

waking up at night in a cold sweat, thinking you were beside me and finding it difficult to accept at first that it was only a dream."

"It does no good to talk like that. We can't go back."

"No, but we sure as hell can go forward."

He pushed his body closer, his knee pressing against her intimately. There was no denying the invitation and she found her body growing weak, her legs too limp to hold her. She shook her head from side to side, all the while whispering, "No . . . no . . . no."

"Your mind says no, but your body wants me. Kiss me, Margery. Kiss me like you used to, when you cared."

"I cannot . . ." The rest of her words were lost when his mouth covered hers. It was a long kiss and deep, probing for the answers she would not give him. She knew the moment he found what he was hoping for.

How could she push him away?

But she did. A moment later, she hurried from the room, his words trailing behind her.

"You can't run forever. Now that I know, I won't give up. I will be here, forever, if that is what it takes. You may continue to deny it for a time; you might even be successful in keeping your distance. But one thing is certain: you cannot run away from yourself. I will have you. And it will be soon."

CHAPTER
◈ THIRTY-THREE ◈

The numbness in his arm woke him.

Even in his sleepy state, he rubbed the numbness, trying to massage it away. It was worse today than he had ever experienced, for along with the numbness came a creeping sort of paralysis that left him unable to move his hand.

By the time he sent for his valet and dressed, the paralysis was gone, but the tingling numbness lingered for a good part of the day. When John came over that night, the family gathered in the grand salon to light the lights on the Christmas tree, much to the delight of Robbie and Wills.

Drinking in the sight of his sons, Will was not aware that he rubbed his arm intermittently, until John, ever the physician, noticed and said something.

"Is your arm bothering you?"

Will looked away from his sons to stare blankly at John. "What made you ask?"

"I've been watching you. You've been rubbing your arm off and on all evening — for the past thirty minutes you've done it without stopping."

"It's nothing."

"Let me be the judge of that. When did it start? What does it feel like?"

"It's just a little numbness, that's all."

"Hmmm. Numbness . . . no paralysis?"

Will shook his head. "Well, not until this morning."

"What happened this morning?"

Will went on to tell him.

"Come with me." John put his hand on his shoulder and walked him from the room.

"Where are we going?"

"Into the library. I want to examine you."

"I was examined in London."

"And?"

"And what?"

"What did the doctor say?"

They walked into the library and shut the door.

"Do you remember that hunting accident —"

"When you were shot in the back?"

Will nodded.

John grimaced. "Of course I remember. I remember that idiot, DeWitt Burford, who shot you. He didn't know one end of a gun from the other. You were damn lucky he didn't kill you or leave you paralyzed."

"That could still happen."

John's look was grave. "If I remember right, the bullet lodged in your spine and was never removed."

"Yes, it's still there." Will went on to tell him what the doctor in London had said.

"It makes sense. Are you going to have the surgery?"

"I don't think so."

John began telling him the same thing the doctor in London had said, then ended by saying, "You cannot take such a risk."

"I don't want to talk about that right now."

"All right, but you better start thinking about it soon. In the meantime, do as the doctor suggested. You've got to take it easy, Will. No horseback riding. No —"

"I said I don't want to talk about it."

"Very well," John said, then clapped him on the back. "Let's join the others."

Two days before Christmas it snowed, a beautiful blanket of white that covered the ground. Wills and Robbie were driving everyone in the household crazy with requests to go outside and play.

At last, Margery could stand their whining no longer. "I'll tell you what. If you two will behave yourselves and take your naps without any fuss, I'll have the pony hitched to the sled and we can go for a sleigh ride."

Wills and Robbie raced upstairs as if they could not get into their beds fast enough.

Once they were up from their naps, the pony was hitched to the sleigh. The boys, watching the excitement from the window, were jumping around so much, Margery and Emily had a difficult time of getting them into their warm clothes. The moment they finished dressing them, the boys shot from the room.

"Don't climb into the sleigh until I get there," Margery called out.

"I don't think they heard you," Emily said.

"They never hear anything they don't want to hear." Margery hurried down the stairs and took her woolen cloak from the peg by the back door. "Are you coming, Emily?"

"No, I thought I'd let Will go with you."

"I don't think Will cares anything about going for a sleigh ride."

"I think you are wrong. In fact, he went up to get his coat."

"I thought he was playing billiards with John."

"Apparently they finished. Right now, John is having a cup of tea with Mama."

Margery did not try to hide the fact that she was a bit put out. "If he isn't there by the time we're ready to go, we will go on without him."

Emily walked outside with her. A moment later, Margery paused to look at Wills and Robbie, who were standing near the sleigh, urging her to hurry.

She watched Robbie throw snow at his brother, hitting Wills in the chest and leaving a white circle of snow on his dark blue coat.

She watched Wills grab a handful of snow. "Behave yourselves. Wills, do not throw that snowball at your brother. I'll be right there," she said, and she started toward them, pulling her gloves on as she went.

The words had no more than left her mouth when Robbie suddenly climbed into the sleigh, followed by Wills. Before she could call to them to get out, Wills let fly with the snowball. It missed Robbie and hit the pony on the rump.

With a startled squeal, the pony leapt ahead, taking off in a dead run.

Margery screamed and ran after them. As soon as she reached the corner of the house, she saw Will running through the snow trying to head off the pony. He must have come out the front door, she thought as she came to a stop. Gasping for each painful breath, she realized there was no way she could catch up with them. Will was the only chance they had of stopping the sleigh before the pony was through the gate.

With her heart in her throat, her eyes moved from Will to the boys and back to Will. He was only a few feet from the pony now. As long as the pony kept running in the same direction, Will had a good chance of catching up to her.

"Oh my God!"

Margery heard John's voice and turned to look at him. Octavia was standing near the back door, her face white, her hand spread across her breast.

Her voice wavered as she said to John, "I think Will can stop the pony, if she doesn't turn off in another direction."

"I pray he tries to get inside and get the reins, instead of stopping the pony himself."

Margery heard the concern in his voice. She was about to ask what it meant when the pony spotted Will coming toward her. Suddenly, she made a sharp turn to the left. Will, as if knowing he had only one chance, took a dive toward the pony, colliding with her as he made a grab for her bridle.

Margery's heart nearly stopped beating. She took off, running through the snow, John passing her a moment later.

Will had his hand on the bridle and he held on as the pony began to slow down, dragging him along with her. Margery and John were almost to the sleigh by the time the pony came to a complete stop. Will collapsed into the snow beside her, his body twisted with pain. Without wasting a moment, Margery snatched the boys from the sleigh and handed them to Emily and Octavia.

The moment she turned back, she saw John go down on his knees beside Will. "Dear God in heaven, Will! Why are you so bloody stubborn?"

Before she could say anything to John, she watched him gather Will into his arms. To keep from crying out, she brought the back of her hand up against her mouth. Her heart pounding, she watched as her husband was carried into the house.

CHAPTER
◼ THIRTY-FOUR ◼

Will lay in bed, feeling nothing, for as the numbness on his left side increased, the pain decreased.

John finished his examination. "It's growing more severe. Soon the entire left side of your body will be completely paralyzed."

"Paralyzed?" Octavia asked. "I don't see how. William has taken harder blows than this one and walked away from them."

John was quick to reply. "He didn't have a bullet lodged in his spine."

Octavia looked astonished. "You mean from that old wound?"

"What old wound?" Emily asked.

Margery, Octavia, and Emily stood beside the bed across from John. It was Margery who spoke next. "Paralyzed? You mean it will be permanent?"

John shook his head. "I don't know for certain, but it is my guess that it will be."

Margery rubbed her hands as if they were cold. "What can you do?"

"Operate . . . and the sooner we operate, the better his chances."

Octavia wasted no time. "Then operate. What are you waiting for?"

"No operation," Will whispered.

Margery gasped. "You can't mean that, Will. Surely you understand what John is saying. If he doesn't operate soon, it may be too late."

Will felt tired. He didn't want to fight for every little scrap that came his way. It just wasn't worth it. His entire life had been nothing but struggle: the struggle for a father's love; the struggle to find out who he was; the struggle to deal with his brother's death; the struggle to realize his true feelings for his wife; and now the struggle to keep her. Weariness crept into his very bones. "It may be too late anyway."

"But you have to take the chance," Emily said. "It would be foolish not to."

Will turned his face away. "I am tired now. I don't want to talk anymore. I want to rest."

Octavia and Emily turned to go. Margery did not move. "I will stay here with him."

"No," he said, not caring if his voice sounded as cold and empty as he felt. "I don't want you here. I don't want any of you here. Leave me be. Can't you see I don't care anymore. I'm tired. I don't have any fight left in me."

"It's the opium talking," John said. "Let him rest. You can visit him again tomorrow."

Margery let Octavia and Emily go on ahead. She lingered just outside the door to Will's room, waiting for John.

A moment later, John appeared. He seemed surprised to see her. "Are you still here?"

"I wanted to talk to you."

"If you want to know if his condition is serious, it is."

"No, it isn't that. I know it is serious because I know you. You take medicine quite seriously. You would not say something if it were not true."

"No, I wouldn't, especially to Will. He has always been like a younger brother to me." He took her arm and they walked down the hallway. "What did you want to talk about?"

"This afternoon, right after Will fell, what did you mean when you said, 'Why are you being so bloody stubborn?' Did you know about his condition before he stopped the sleigh? Did Will know?"

"Yes . . . to both questions."

Margery did not say anything. She was busy thinking.

"You are wondering why he used his own body to stop the horse, knowing it would very likely paralyze him?"

"How could I not wonder? He saved my sons' lives."

"They are his sons, too."

She fell quiet. At last she said, "I am not accustomed to thinking of them as his sons."

"What he did today . . . it was not only noble, it was a very fatherly thing to do — putting the lives of his children first."

"I know, and that is what has me so puzzled.

How could he feel such fatherly instinct, when he did not even know they existed until a week ago?"

"You think you must be around your children before you can love them?"

"I don't know. It sounds more reasonable, I suppose."

"Being a parent is anything but reasonable. You should know that."

"I do, but . . ."

"If I remember correctly, you told me once that you did not know what you would do if the baby you carried did not live. Do you remember?"

"Yes, I remember."

"Then tell me something. Why would you have been so distraught? The child was unborn. You had not been around it. How could you love something you did not know?"

"Because it was mine, a part of me."

"Exactly. Did you ever stop to think that might be the way Will feels?"

She felt ashamed of herself. "No. I was so busy looking for the wrong motives that I overlooked the right ones."

"Maybe that is what you are doing between yourself and Will."

"I don't get your meaning."

"Do you think it is possible that you are so obsessed with finding reasons why you should not allow yourself to care for him again, that you ignore all the reasons why you should?"

She sighed heavily, feeling suddenly tired herself. Everything seemed so clear to her when Will was gone. Only now that he was back, everything was as muddy as a just-crossed stream. She had no peace. All was confusion. She didn't seem to know her own mind anymore. Part of her wanted to believe him, to forgive him and live with him as his wife, in every sense of the word. Yet, another part of her could not let go of the memory of the way he abandoned her, the selfish reason he married her. "I am so confused, I don't know what to do."

"Why don't you try loving him, or at least being supportive? He is going through some tough times and it is going to get worse. He needs you, Margery. More than you know."

"I will try. I cannot promise any more than that."

"Then it will have to be enough."

"I only hope I will be able to talk him into letting you operate. How long does he have before it is too late?"

"I have no way of knowing that, but every day he waits is another day off of the time he has."

She wiped the tears that fell away from her face. "Then I will see what I can do. There must be some way to convince him."

"I hope you are right, because I firmly believe that if you cannot do it, no one can."

She realized then that they had reached the front door. John took his hat and coat from the butler then kissed her cheek. "I will be back to see how he is doing tomorrow. In the meantime, send for me if you need me."

"You know I will. Thank you."

"I love him, you know. Like a brother."

She nodded. "I know. I love him, too." She gave him a watery smile. "But not the same way."

After John left, Margery stood next to the door. She was not going to let Will destroy himself. There had to be a reason, something to make him care, something to give him hope, something to make him go on. Something to make him have the operation.

But what?

Christmas arrived. All of William's sisters came with their families, and they all tried to talk some sense into his stubborn head, with no more luck than Octavia and Margery had had. His obstinate refusal to listen to reason — and the dreaded consequences that would follow if he didn't — seemed to absorb all the gaiety and celebration from the Christmas season. All in all, it would have been a wholly uneventful holiday if it had not been for the children. Because of Robbie, Wills, and their young cousins, everyone went through the motions of observing Christmas, but it wasn't the same. Now the numbness in Will's arm was getting worse.

Everyone in the family had done everything he or she could to convince Will to have the bullet in his spine removed. John talked to him, and even Lydia and Uncle Rand came to do what they could, but Will proved himself capable of going "beyond stubborn," as Octavia put it.

It was several days after Boxing Day that Margery reached the point where she was about ready to give up. That was when she was struck with a bit of divine inspiration. It came to her one particularly sunny afternoon when she returned from a long ride, dismounted, and led her mare into the stables.

Damascus, the groom, was having a devil of a time with Napoleon, a beautiful stallion who wasn't ridden much anymore, since he was used primarily for breeding purposes. Napoleon was as temperamental as they came, and on this particular day, he was feeling especially cantankerous.

By the time Margery put her mare into the stall, she could see that Damascus had just about used up all of his powers of persuasion and cajoling. As if sensing this, Napoleon began jerking his head back, trying to yank the reins out of Damascus's hand. Suddenly, and without warning, Damascus whopped the stallion beside the head with his hand — a hard blow that echoed with a loud pop.

Almost immediately, Napoleon began nuzzling Damascus, wickering softly.

For a moment, Margery was dumbfounded. She had never seen anything like it, for here was a horse who would not respond to any amount of kindness, gentleness, or bribery, who suddenly became as meek as a lamb when he had his ears boxed.

Would that same philosophy work on stubborn husbands as well?

She was not sure, but she intended to find out.

Shortly after changing out of her riding clothes, she went to Will's room with a large pitcher of hot water, which she deposited on the table beside his bed. Next, she went to the windows and tied back the heavy damask draperies, letting the low, winter sun into the room.

"I don't want the windows open. Close the draperies."

"If you want them closed, you will have to get up and close them yourself."

"You know damn well I can't."

"Then they will stay open . . . unless you decide to cooperate."

"I'm not having that bloody operation, if that's what you mean."

"Did I mention an operation?"

"What happened to the sweet, eager-to-please woman I married?"

"You didn't want her."

He mumbled something under his breath and Margery studied him for a moment, wondering what happened to the handsome man she married. In his place was an unkempt, shaggy-haired, and bearded ogre.

But he won't stay that way for very long. . . .

Without saying anything to him, she went into his dressing room where his valet cowered. "Phillips, my husband is sorely in need of a bath, a haircut, and a shave. Where do you keep the things that I will need?"

Poor Phillips almost jumped out of his skin to

accommodate her. She supposed it was out of gratitude that she had not asked him to perform the task. A moment later, he placed the items she needed in her outstretched hands.

"Thank you, Phillips."

"You are welcome, my lady. Do you . . . that is, would you . . . Can I be of service to you, my lady?"

"No thank you, Phillips. I think it best if I attend to this matter, don't you?"

He swallowed and his Adam's apple bobbed. "Unequivocally."

A few steps and she was back beside Will's bed. Will glowered at her, but said nothing as she put down the scissors, razor, soap, brush and comb. She whipped up a lather in his shaving cup and reached toward his face.

He jerked his head around. "I don't want . . ."

Plop! Right into his overactive mouth went the brush.

He gagged and sputtered, but by the time he had the soap out of his mouth, she had shaved half of his face. He did not give her any trouble when she moved to the other side of the bed to finish the task.

An hour later, Will was cross and sullen, but he looked infinitely better and much more like the man she married. She did not tell him that, however, for fear she would set his temper in motion. She simply said, "You should rest much better now."

"I was resting fine until you came in here."

She ignored that and began fluffing his pillows.

"Stop it! Can't you understand I don't want you in here?"

She said nothing but reached for the pan of water, intending to carry it from the room.

"I don't want your pity. I don't want your understanding. And I most assuredly don't want you in here, wasting your time, trying to talk me into that operation. I am not going to have it and there is nothing you can do about it. I want you out of here. Stop mothering me and smothering me! I can take anything but that!"

"Very well," she said, and dumped the basin of water over the top of his head.

CHAPTER
🏵 THIRTY-FIVE 🏵

Will sat in his soggy, squishy bed and blinked two or three times to clear the water from his eyes. Through a hazy blur he saw his wife's retreating form.

"Don't you dare leave this room."

Margery's spine stiffened and she stopped, but she did not turn around. "If you want me to stay, you will ask me in normal, respectful tones."

"And I suppose what you did showed respect?"

"It was honest. Ogres deserve no respect."

"All right. Honest. So let's be honest with each other, shall we? You have been in here every day since the sleigh accident, doting on me. Why?"

"It is my duty . . ."

"Stuff duty! Why were you here? And remember, we are being honest."

"Very well. I was here because I was sorry you were hurt. I wanted to make you comfortable."

"Why? Because you care?"

"Yes."

"Well, now we are getting somewhere. If you

care, then you must have some feeling for me. Right?"

"I . . ."

"Yes or no."

"Yes."

"If you care and if you have some feeling for me, then it does not seem unrealistic to expect you would be willing to give our marriage a try. Am I right?"

"I don't know."

"Let me put it another way. What would you say if I said I would be willing to have the operation if you were willing to live with me as my wife, in every sense of the word, for a period of one year?"

"You should not use your physical well-being to make bargains."

"But I have used it and I am waiting for your answer. An operation for a commitment? Do we have a deal?"

"I . . ."

"A deal, Margery. Do we have one or not? Agree or disagree?"

"Agree," she said softly, then fled from the room.

For a long time after she had gone, her image haunted him. He felt like the worst kind of unfeeling brute. He could not believe he had propositioned her like that, that he had used his illness to bribe her into staying with him.

He turned to his side, wanting to go to sleep, but the bed was wet and he was damned uncomfortable. He couldn't sleep. The more he thought about it, the more he realized that her dumping that pan of water on him had been just what he needed to shock him out of his wallow of self-pity.

"Margery . . . Margery . . . Margery . . ." he said, remembering the way she had been when he first married her — sweet, submissive, and subservient, eager and willing to please. She had been nothing more than a servant, a slave he bought and paid for. The memory of that did not seem as sweet as it had before.

Perhaps that was because he didn't really want sweet, submissive, and subservient. Maybe he wanted a woman who stood up for what she wanted, a woman who would not take the easy way simply because it was expected of her or because it was the easiest.

A woman like his wife . . .

He realized then that he liked her better the way she was now: strong, independent, brave, confident. How he wished he could have known her family, the stock she came from, for much of what she was had to have come from them. She was an overcomer, a survivor. Had this come from her family as well?

He also realized he could not use her empathy to force her to remain with him. He was ashamed that he had ever considered anything so low. He knew just what he had to do, for if he didn't, he could not call himself a man.

Margery was sitting in the morning room with

Wills and Robbie the next morning when Octavia and Emily came in. Octavia carried a large hat-box.

"Emily, take the boys outside for a walk, will you? I have something I want to show Margery."

Emily left with the boys and Octavia took a seat on the sofa next to Margery. "I should have shown you these a long time ago." She removed the lid and withdrew several bundles of letters, all tied up with red satin ribbons.

She handed the bundles to Margery.

"What are these?"

"The night Will left you here, I asked Guy to go with him. I knew Will would not write. He was in too much pain to do so. For that reason, I asked Guy to write me so I would know how he was getting on."

"And these are Guy's letters?"

"Yes."

"But why are you giving them to me? They were written to you."

"Because they are so insightful. Guy always knew Will better than anyone. He could see through the pain to what lay beneath."

Margery took the letters to her room. After dinner, she went upstairs to begin reading. When she looked at the box upon her bed, she saw a stack of Will's sketchbooks, a note folded on top. She opened the note. It was from Octavia.

I think you should look through Will's sketch-books. What you find there might surprise you.

Read Guy's letters first. When you look at the sketches, try to remember that they were drawn by a man who can express himself much more eloquently through art than he can with words. You will know what to do, for I have always known your heart was in the right place.

Margery put the note down and changed into her nightgown. She began reading the letters as soon as she was in bed. She stayed up all night, finishing them just before daybreak. She was astounded by what she learned.

Guy was not a man to gloss over detail, for each letter was lengthy, often a composition of letters written over a long period of time. Looking through Guy's eyes, she saw Will as a deeply sensitive man, a man who loved and missed her, a man who carried her image before him for two years. In every page, she gained insight into the man she married and the devils that tormented him. She began to feel the pain Will felt over his father's rejection, his criticism, his obvious favoritism for John, and even more intensely, the death of James.

When she read the last letter, she tied them with the red satin ribbons, then returned them to the box. She sat there thinking about what she read for quite some time before she picked up the sketchbooks.

Page after page, book after book, she found her likeness — various images of herself, the dates they were sketched written below. She realized what Guy had written was true, for Will had to have cared a great deal to have sketched her so often and in so many different poses. She was touched with a bittersweet sort of poignancy when she saw that in some of the sketches, he had tried to imagine what she looked like, back in England, dressed in the proper English way, going about her day in the customary English manner.

The last book was obviously newer than the others, for it did not have the worn, stained cover that the others did. When she opened it, she understood why. Inside this book were dozens of sketches of her in various stages of her pregnancy. The last few pages were filled with sketches of her holding her newborns in her arms, of the boys crawling across the nursery floor, taking their first steps, their first pony ride. How did he know these things as well as if he had been here? How like him to try and capture the part of her life that he had missed by drawing it. It was obvious to her now that her pregnancy and the birth of the twins was far more important to him than he had let on.

Will was feeling worse about his treatment of Margery, and it was her obvious absence that caused this. The numbness in his arm was worse this morning than it had been last night. He wondered how long it would be before he lost the use of it altogether.

The door creaked, then opened, and Emily

stepped inside. "Are you asleep?"

"No, I was just lying here, thinking."

"About having the operation, I hope." She came into the room and took a seat beside his bed.

He could see the concern, the love for him in her eyes. "You are making your house calls awfully early, aren't you? Have you had breakfast yet?"

"I was just on my way down. I thought I would stop in and see you . . . in case you might want me to bring you something."

"I had a few bites of the usual. Oatmeal. You know, I never liked oatmeal. Now I remember why."

She laughed. "I could slip you a biscuit or two."

"With sausage?"

"With sausage and eggs."

"Well, what are you waiting for? Go, before the biscuits are all gone."

Emily rose to her feet and started to turn away but caught herself and turned back toward him.

"What is it?"

"I'm glad to see you are doing better."

He raised his brows. "Am I?"

"Yes. Your spirits are ever so much better. Why, you haven't yelled at me once."

"Was I really that bad?"

She shook her head until her curls bobbed up and down. "Worse."

"Well, I promise to be the model patient from here on out."

"You have agreed to the operation?"

He frowned. "I haven't gone quite that far, but at least I'm not behaving like an ogre."

She kissed him on the cheek. "It's nice to have my brother back."

A moment later she disappeared through the door.

After breakfast, Margery met Octavia coming down the stairs. "If you are looking for the boys, they went outside with Emily a few minutes ago."

"I was going to see Will."

"Wait a moment. I have something to show you before you go to visit him."

Margery went outside with Octavia, the two of them walking along the gravel path to a small gamekeeper's cottage that was no longer in use. Octavia took a key out of her pocket and unlocked the door. A moment later, it swung open.

Margery stepped inside. As soon as her eyes adjusted to the dim light within, she could see that this must have been where Will went those many times he seemed to have disappeared, for there were a few canvases stacked about the room and the smell of paints and turpentine was strong.

Octavia lit a lamp and carried it to a table. "Go on. Look at them," she said, indicating the paintings that were stacked against the wall.

Margery began to look through them and saw several paintings in various stages of completion, many of them done from the sketches she had seen earlier. There were two he had started of the boys, one of them with Margery.

But there was one painting in particular that brought tears to her eyes.

Over in one corner stood Will's easel, a canvas in place. Walking around it so she could see what he was painting, she could only gasp with surprise. There, staring back at her from the canvas, was a picture of her with one of her babies at her breast. The image moved her, for there was nothing lewd or vulgar about it; it was obvious he meant it as a tribute to what he had missed — the parts of their lives that he had never seen.

As she stood there, looking at the painting before her, as well as those stacked around the room, she realized it was as if he had tried to capture each stage of their lives while he was away.

She turned to Octavia. "Thank you," she whispered, close to crying.

After leaving Octavia to lock up the cottage, Margery went to see Will. Before she could say anything, he told her he was glad she had finally come to see him.

"I have a terrible weight in my heart, something eating at my conscience that will give me no rest until I ask your forgiveness."

"But I came to tell you . . ."

He shook his head. "Hear me first. It has taken me days to get my courage up and I have been practicing what I would say to you for hours. I realize now that I was the one at fault, and I ask your forgiveness."

"There is no need."

"Oh, but there is. I was terribly wrong to think that I could own you, that I could always count on you to be there, like some obedient dog awaiting me with my slippers. I used you, without really realizing that I did. I must have been so consumed with my own pain that I could not see the pain I caused others. Again, I ask your forgiveness. What I did to you . . . God! Leaving you here like I did . . . it was unforgivable."

"I no longer hold that against you. I will not lie and say there were not times that it was very difficult for me, but never, ever did I think I would have been better off the way I was when you found me. In spite of the years I spent with the Indians, I never became one of them. I think that is why it was so hard for me; why I was never completely accepted. After you left, your mother treated me like a daughter. She taught me all the things I could not learn from books. It was strange how some things came so easily to me, as if I had done them before."

"That does not make up for what I did."

"Don't you understand what I'm trying to tell you? Not only did your bringing me to England give me my culture back, but it also created a thirst in me . . . a thirst to find out who I really am, where I came from, who my family was. I never felt that way during my captivity. Perhaps that was because I knew, in some way, that to feel that way would only make it more difficult for me. Whenever I thought about the family I had lost, it was only in terms of loss, a way of feeling sorry for myself and all I had been deprived of."

"I am glad something that started out so wrong has turned out right, but we are dealing with two different things here. You are discussing the benefits of coming to England. I am talking about the callous way I used you to get back at my father. I had no right to force you to marry me, no right to bring you to England and abandon you. I want you to know that from the deepest part of my heart, I regret what I did. I cannot change it. I cannot make up for my lack of empathy or understanding. The only thing I can do is give you the freedom I should have given you then. Whatever you want, I am willing to give to you. If you want a divorce, I will comply. You will never have to worry about money or a place to live. I will not try to take the boys, although I would hope you would not take them so far away that I could not see them. A boy needs a father . . . a father who will love, guide, and nurture him. I can be that kind of father. . . ."

His voice broke, and she thought she might cry, but that was something she was determined not to do. Thankfully, he went on talking.

"Also, there is the matter of Wills being my heir and the next earl. He will have to be taught much about the role he is to assume, and that would mean he would have to come here to live with me, when he is older, of course."

"And if I don't want a divorce?"

"Then the conditions I described will remain the same. I will support you wherever you choose to live." He paused a moment, searching her face, and she could tell by the look in his eyes that she was something dear to him. He gave a little half laugh and shook his head. "It is strange, is it not? In the beginning I did many things to cause you pain; now I seem to have no purpose in life, except to make you happy."

She started to speak, but he cut her off.

"I have made arrangements with my solicitor. There is an envelope on your dressing table with my solicitor's name and address. You may contact him to have your money sent wherever you decide to go."

Margery came to his bedside and leaned down, kissing him lightly on the mouth. "Such a long speech and so unnecessary. I have been trying to tell you for the past half hour that my feelings for you have never changed. I fell in love with you before you brought me to England. My love grew deeper on the way. But it was a love I had to give freely. I could not be owned again."

"You don't have to tell me this."

"Don't you see? All I ever wanted was for you to love me enough to trust me, enough to believe I would stay with you of my own free will and not by force. If you had only told me about England, if you had given me the choice, I would have stayed here."

Will looked at her as if he could not believe what she was saying. She knew he was probably asking himself how she could possibly love him after the way he treated her. He probably couldn't even come up with one logical reason why she should even like him.

"How?" he asked. "How could you possibly love someone who abandoned you?"

"I never stopped loving you, but I did not realize it until I read Guy's letters. I opened the bundles of letters, untying each ribbon, and that is how it came to me: a ribbon at a time." She kissed him again, and this time he kissed her back.

"Say you will have the operation, Will."

Will looked like a burning spear had been driven through him. "So it was all for this? All those pretty words you knew I wanted to hear were nothing more than a ploy."

"No . . ."

He pushed her away. "I won't have the surgery, and I don't need you sacrificing yourself for me. I don't want your pity, and I don't want you to lie that you love me in order to get me to agree. It will be easier for you to divorce an invalid. No one would blame you. I would be only half a man. I could expect nothing more than half a life."

"What you have is half a brain. How could anyone be so stupid?"

He could see that she was furious, and he found himself thankful that there was not another pot of water sitting on the bedside table.

Without saying another word, Margery turned and left the room.

She slammed the door so hard, a picture of a

flock of grazing sheep fell off the opposite wall.

Margery returned a short while later, Wills on one hip, Robbie on the other. With all the ceremony of a royal parade, she marched across the room and deposited his sons right on top of Will. He was baffled. What was she up to now? He was not certain, but it did warm his heart to see her fighting for a cause in which she believed. He did not say anything, but simply lay there, his sons patting and pulling at him, waiting to see what she would do next.

"Now," she said, hands on her hips, "you tell me, in front of your sons, that you are too pigheaded to have an operation that would allow you to be a father to them."

Before he could speak, Wills and Robbie put their arms around his neck and began planting wet, sloppy kisses all over his face. Somewhere beyond all this action came the sound of her voice: "If you won't do it for me, then do it for them."

Will was being choked into surrender by his overeager sons, so he couldn't say anything, but he did manage to disentangle one arm to reach the bedside table. He picked up the small, white towel lying there and began to wave it.

It was the first time in a long, long time that he heard her laugh . . . really, really laugh.

They took Will to London for the operation. While he was in surgery, Margery paced back and forth with the rest of the family. Hours passed and she began to worry. Was it supposed to take this long? Was this a bad sign? Was he going to be all right?

The moment she saw John walk into the room she knew the operation was over.

She ran toward him, grabbing him by the arms, looking into his eyes for assurance.

"He is doing fine. The operation was a complete success. I feel certain Will won't have any more problems. He should regain full use of his body. All he needs is a little time and a lot of love."

She looked at John, knowing he could see the gratitude she felt. "The love," she said, "has always been there."

CHAPTER
❈ THIRTY-SIX ❈

Three weeks after his surgery, Will showed signs of being completely recovered. He was staying up for the entire day now, save for a short rest in the late afternoon, which John ordered, and the women in the family saw that he complied.

Late one afternoon, Will was looking for Octavia when he approached the salon and overheard his mother and Margery talking. He paused a moment, ignoring the saying that eavesdroppers never hear any good about themselves.

Margery was saying, "I cannot believe how well things are going between us."

"What do you mean?"

"We have argued only once since his surgery."

"What was the argument about?"

"It was over a trivial matter . . . something that I cannot even remember."

"That is a promising sign. Tell me, how are *other* things between the two of you?"

"What other things?"

"I am referring to the particular procedure necessary for the conceivement of children. There. Did I phrase it adequately, without giving you cause to blush profusely or to laugh yourself silly?"

Will leaned back against the door and crossed his arms in front of his chest, resisting the urge to burst out laughing over the words his mother chose. *The particular procedure necessary for the conceivement of children?* Never had he heard it put that way. She made it sound like surgery.

Apparently, Margery hadn't either, for the sound of her laugh drifted out of the salon. Will was startled at his reaction — a sudden and intense longing. He closed his eyes and began to remember the way she had come to him that first night. Even now, the way she had looked, her nakedness called out to him. He wished his mother was not in there with his wife. He wanted to go to her, wanted to take her in his arms and whisper to her all the things he had been longing to do. He could hear her short breaths, the soft moaning sounds, the footsteps . . .

Footsteps?

He opened his eyes and saw John strolling down the hall toward him. What in the hell was John doing here now? Will signaled him to be quiet, then motioned for him to join him.

John paused, gave him an amused look, then made a big to-do about tiptoeing down the hallway, before flattening himself dramatically against the wall. In keeping with the occasion, his voice was a mere whisper. "You're a little old for hide-and-seek, aren't you?"

Margery said something, but Will could not

understand what it was. *Well hell. Just when the conversation was getting good, I have to miss the best part.*

Before Will could respond to John's childish comment, John glanced downward. Apparently, he saw something funny, for his entire body began to shake with laughter. Will gave him an elbow to the ribs to put an end to his amusement, and when that did no good, he looked to see what in the blue blazes John found so comical.

A moment later, Will stared down at his own erection. He shrugged. "It is a common circumstance among *normal* men."

"It isn't the phenomena, but the place of occurrence . . . in the hallway in the middle of the afternoon, in broad daylight?" He chuckled, shaking his head slowly. "Having lustful thoughts, were you? Oh, to be a country earl, with nothing but fornication on his mind."

"It isn't fornication. She happens to be my wife."

"I suppose one takes his erections where he finds them."

"I'm warning you."

Suddenly Octavia's voice cut through the air. "You mean to tell me that Will has not been to bed with you since his return?"

Will strained to hear Margery's reply, but John, who was overcome with theatrics again, slapped a hand over his chest and did his dramatic best to look aghast.

Will never wanted to punch anyone more in

his life. "Don't you have something to do?"

"Nope."

Will would have responded to that, but the sound of Margery's voice cut him off.

". . . anyway, that's what I think," she finished. *Well hell.* He'd missed everything. Will glared hotly at John, but when she started speaking again, Will turned his back on John and put his ear closer to the door.

"Having Will up and about is pure pleasure, but having an ailing male underfoot is exhausting."

"That is an understatement, my dear. Men, when it comes to any sort of illness, are notorious for being the world's worst patients. They are worse than babies."

"Yes, they are."

"What you need is a good night's rest. You have exhausted yourself these past few weeks, devoting yourself to Will."

"It was for a good cause."

"But not one that paid dividends. Will should have come to you long before now. There is simply no excuse for it . . . unless of course, he was . . . how shall I say it, incapacitated?"

"Incapacitated?"

"When a certain part of the male anatomy is unable to function."

John leaned over to whisper. "Want me to march in there and tell them I can attest to the fact that it's been standing at attention in the hall for quite some time now?"

"What I want is for you to get yourself lost."

"And miss all the excitement?"

"I suppose you were right about one thing," Margery said. "I am quite tired. I think I will take your advice about going to bed early tonight."

"I am glad to hear it. A good night's rest will do you a world of good."

"What did she say?" John asked.

"Will you lower your voice?"

A chair creaked. Clothing rustled.

Margery's voice penetrated the silence that followed. "What is it?"

"Someone is listening outside the door."

The sound of footsteps approached.

Will looked at John and the two of them tore down the hall, pausing just long enough to open the first door they came to, which happened to be the music room. A bad choice, actually, since there was not a featherweight of musical ability between the two of them.

"Now we're in a fine fix," John said as he shut the door. "What will we do if they come in here?"

"They won't come in here. Why should they?"

"But what if they do?"

"Then we will play something. You take the violin. I'll take the piano."

"Will, I don't know which end of the violin to pick up."

"Then we are well matched, because the only thing I know about a piano is how to sit at the bench."

Out in the hallway, Octavia and Margery were

just passing the music room when Octavia paused. "Did you hear that?"

"What?"

"I heard voices. Someone is in the music room. Do you think that might be our eavesdropper?"

"It has to be. Aside from the two of us, no one ever goes in there."

Octavia opened the door and gasped. "What are you doing in here?"

"Who is it?" Margery asked, up on her toes now, trying to see over Octavia.

Octavia moved to one side as Margery stepped forward.

Will looked up to see his mother and Margery standing in the doorway. "John and I felt like a little music before dinner."

Octavia narrowed her eyes suspiciously, looking from one to the other. "And when did you become the Prince of Music?"

"Recently," Will said, hearing John's groan.

"I see. 'Music hath charms to soothe a savage breast, to soften rocks, or bend a knotted oak.'"

Will swallowed and felt his Adam's apple hit bottom, a sound remarkably close to a wooden bucket dropped down a dry well.

Octavia looked at John. "Your violin is upside down."

"It's more of a challenge this way."

Will groaned as John glanced down at the violin, then put the bow beneath it, drawing it across the strings.

Will had heard a sound remarkably like that

only once in his entire life: when his father accidentally slammed the door on his mother's parrot. He closed his eyes and groaned again. To think that he had let this man operate on him.

Before Will could take another breath, Octavia turned on him. "Don't look so relieved. You aren't out of the line of fire yet."

"Was I looking relieved?" Will asked, hoping for a diversion, but his mother was a wise old bird who wasn't about to be duped with a trick as old as that one.

"I think you will find the piano sounds much better when played with the keys exposed. Open the keyboard, dimwit."

She turned to Margery, who stood looking quietly amused during the entire exchange. "Come, my dear, let us leave these two buffoons to their folly."

As the two of them left the room, Will heard his wife say, "Octavia, you know you were right. Fools do grow without watering."

Later that evening, Margery was determined to stick to her plan to go to bed early. Once dinner was over, she read the boys their bedtime story and led them in their prayers. After kissing them good night, she turned out the lamp and slipped quietly from their room.

On her way to her bed, Margery passed Will's room. She stopped, staring at the door, remembering how quiet he and John were at dinner. She smiled and shook her head. Men. They could be such children. She knocked softly.

"Who is it?"

"Margery."

"I'm asleep."

He sounded just like Wills and Robbie and her heart warmed at the thought. "May I come in?"

"Why? Do you feel the need to laugh some more?"

"No, but I detest talking through doors."

"The door's open."

Margery went inside.

Will was standing beside the bed without a stitch on, naked as a needle he was, and it didn't seem to bother him. But, oh, did it ever bother her. The sight of him standing there in so much masculine muscle and smooth skin fairly took her breath away.

She had seen him naked, of course — before they came to England, and during his illness, but this time was different. This time she found his nakedness unsettling. A warmth seemed to suffuse her, and she felt as if she were floating in one of the warm pools not far from the Yellowstone River.

He made no move to cover himself. "You don't have to knock when you come to see me. You are my wife."

She heard what he said but couldn't seem to find a response. Her thoughts were jumbled. All she seemed to comprehend was his nakedness, how very beautiful the sight of his body was, the pale slimness, the curve of muscle, the hair on his body, the very manliness of him.

Perfection, she realized, occurs not when there are no more clothes to put on, but when there is nothing left to remove: a body in its purest form, utter and complete nakedness.

She studied him. She knew the strength of that arm, the unspeakable suggestions of tenderness that lay in those hands with their nicks and calluses, and all the varied muscles, the rock-hard curves, down to the most vulnerable part of him. He was like the mountain, born of energy and force, full of expression, mystery, passion, and strength.

"Are you enjoying yourself?"

Her thoughts vanished and she met his gaze. "Yes."

"Why doesn't it embarrass you to look at a naked man?"

"You are my husband. I have seen you naked before."

"That was a long time ago."

"I have the memory."

"With no desire to replace it with the actual fact?"

"I came to you once. I will not do so again."

"Why not?"

"It is not the English way."

"And you do everything the English way?"

"I try to."

"Why?"

"I have been taught that the English way is the right way, the superior manner. But, in my heart,

397

I don't always believe it. I am a woman with many pasts. I think I am richer because of it. I do not intend to lose my past and replace it with total Englishness. To do so would mean that Margery, as I know her, would no longer exist. I cannot give up what I am. I can only add to it with the hope that I will become a better person. I will add the English pieces that please me and discard those that do not. That is why I don't succeed very often. Because my heart isn't always in it."

"I think that is one of the wisest, most beautiful things I have ever heard you say. You cannot imagine how it pleases me to know there is still a part of you I recognize and admire, a part of the woman I learned I could not forget."

"What parts are those?"

"Your honesty, for one. When you wanted me, you did not hide it."

"I do not hide it now."

"Are you trying to tell me that you want me? That you suddenly find me desirable?"

"Why would I stand here looking at you as I am if I found you ugly and undesirable. I look because I like what I see, because I like the way it makes me feel. Whenever I look at you, I find you desirable. I have never stopped wanting you."

"If that is the truth, I cannot help but wonder why. Surely it was not the sight of my pitiful body with its pale skin, jutting bones, and many wounds."

"And if it was?"

"Your eyes deceive you." He turned his back

to her and braced his hands on each side of the window, staring out at the blackness beyond.

She looked at the red scar that ran along his spine and counted the wounds — the gouged hole of an Indian lance, the puckered scar of a bear's claw, the flat smoothness of a burn, the round shape of a bullet.

Without realizing she had moved, she found herself standing behind him. She reached out and touched him. He flinched and she felt the muscles contract. "I have often wondered if the hand is not more sensitive to beauty than the eye."

Her hands swept down the length of his body, then traced the red scar until it stopped. Dropping down, she followed the hard curve of his buttocks. "It is majestic . . . there is such power in you, in the flow of the lines and curves of your body."

She closed her eyes. Her voice was low and fluid. "How much more subtle they are when felt, rather than seen."

She placed the side of her face against the smooth warmth of his back. "I can feel the heartbeat of a thousand sculptures, the warm flesh of ancient Greeks."

Her hands came around him then, and she took his penis in her hand, ignoring his gasp, the way his body jerked, the thrown-back head. "And here, I can feel the perfect rhythm of muscle, even when you stand as still as a marble god. I want you, Will. So much I wonder if I am no longer sane. If you don't feel the same . . . if you don't want me, I don't know what I will do."

"Not want you . . ." He turned and took her in his arms. "It was always your honesty . . . your frank, unaffected honesty that was my undoing. I remember sitting by the campfire at night, listening to you and Dan talk. Even then, your honesty called out to me."

"You wanted me then?"

He kissed her softly. "I have always wanted you . . . from the moment I first saw you, standing there with your white dress of antelope skin down around your waist, your beautiful breasts standing as proud as you were shamed."

"I . . ." He covered her mouth with his, stopping her words, telling her how he felt in a way that could not be misunderstood, and she was glad, for she liked his way ever so much better.

The taste and smell and warmth of him flowed through her, as surely as the fire in her blood hummed a rhythm, as wonderfully as her thundering heart felt, for it was near to bursting with a joyful rhythm that she could not keep quiet. She felt drunk. His very presence filled her. Time had no motion. There was only forever. Only the heat of his body spoke to her, the hardness of the muscle pressing against her, the breathy warmth of whispered words as his tongue worked its magic.

The pins fell from her hair, releasing a soft fragrance that seemed to hover over them like a blessing. Her clothes fell away from her body and she groaned at the feel of nakedness against nakedness, the smooth sensation of skin touching skin.

He lifted her in his arms and carried her to the bed, where he lay her down and covered her with his body. "I have waited a lifetime for this."

"As I have." She opened to the quest of his hands, feeling the tightly wound coil of desire low in her stomach.

"I love you," he said, and entered her slowly as he spoke.

She could not answer. She could only go with him, carried along as a leaf on a mighty raging river, tranquil now, then swept out into the fierce power of a mighty current, rushing heedlessly through rapids, unable to stop or to slow the mounting speed, then hurtling out over the deafening roar of a waterfall, flying for a moment, out of touch with the world below, then floating on a current of air, spiraling downward until the surface of what was real glittered like all the stars of the universe and she felt herself land safely, the water no more than a ripple beneath her, a ripple that carried her to the glassy smoothness of a tranquil lake, and there she drifted . . . drifted . . . drifted. . . .

From out of the stillness of her mind came the sound of his beloved voice. "Sleep here beside me. Now and forever. I am here. I will always be here. I will never leave you again."

CHAPTER
◙ THIRTY-SEVEN ◙

She awoke to William making love to her once
more.

When she was as sated as he, they lay together,
limbs intertwined, his hand stroking her softly. "I
want to take you to London. I want to take you
everywhere — to the theater, the opera, the ballet,
to the finest restaurants. I want to buy you jewels
and the finest clothes . . . your own carriage with
a pair of perfectly matched horses. For once, I
am going to treat you like the beloved wife you
are, and I want the whole bloody world to know
just how much I adore you. I want to give you
everything your heart desires."

"You already have."

She was thinking how difficult it would be to
leave the twins behind, not because she worried
about their safekeeping, but because it would be
the first time she would be away from them overnight. It was something she shared with Will.

"It will be good for them. It will reinforce their
learning, their understanding that their mother is
not the whole universe . . . although she is to
me." He kissed her softly, his arms drawing her

against him as he held her close.

"But they are so young. I will feel lost without them. To whom will I read bedtime stories?"

He chuckled. "You can read to me, little mother."

She punched him. "You are poking fun at my misery."

"You didn't mind my poking last night . . . or this morning either, if I remember right."

"Oh, you are wicked."

"Only around you." He kissed the top of her head. "I'll tell you what. If you promise to be a good girl, I'll do everything in my power to give you another baby . . . one that is even younger than the two you have."

She warmed at the thought. "I like the sound of that."

"What? Gaining another child, or my sworn devotion to the task."

"Both, but especially the latter. I love you William."

"William? Want me to start calling you Walks Fast?"

She was silent for a moment. Reflective. She had not thought about that part of her life for some time. "That name is strange to me now. Sometimes I feel as if I have lived here in England, all my life."

"Perhaps that is because your life here is more like your life in the beginning — before you were taken."

"But isn't it odd that I spent such a large part

of my life roaming the plains with one tribe or another, and yet I rarely think about it? Do you suppose that is the mind's way of healing — to allow the painful past to fade into oblivion?"

"I suppose so. There is no reason for you to relive the past. You are in England now, and you are my wife and a mother. Your life is full and rich." He kissed her softly. "You are loved. You have become the woman you were destined to be. Why should your mind take you back?"

"I don't think it can. Even now, when I try to think about it, the memory is almost as shadowy as the memories of my own family. Even the name Walks Fast seems foreign to me now. It is as if she doesn't exist anymore."

"It isn't that she doesn't exist anymore. She never existed. You were never an Indian. You were always Margery, just as you were always my fate."

"Your fate. I like the sound of that."

"I like the reality better." He leaned across her, taking both of her hands in his. "Come here and make love to me."

She glanced at the clock. "It's getting late. Don't you think we should get up? Everyone will wonder where we are."

"They *know* where we are. Now, come here. I want to make love to you and there isn't a snowball's chance in hell that I will let you out of this bed until I do." He kissed her. Once. Twice. Three times. The fourth time, she moaned and put her arms around his neck.

The sound of running feet echoed down the hall, followed by the frantic cries of a voice that sounded remarkably like Nanny's.

A door slammed. Outside, a dog began barking, followed by the shrieks and laughter of the twins.

Will raised his tousled head. "What the devil is going on around here?"

Margery laughed and looked toward the window. "It snowed last night. Don't you remember what it was like when you were young and it snowed, and no one wanted to let you go outside to play?"

"No," he said in a grumpy voice, looking down at himself. "All I can remember is when I was an adult and ready to make love to my wife, and my equipment failed."

"Well," she said, rolling from the bed, then reaching for him to coax him to his feet, "I suppose this means we will just have to go outside and throw snowballs."

Will took her to London two days later and kept his promise to take her everywhere. The first two days they were there, he accompanied her to the finest dressmakers and ordered the latest Paris fashions. The third day they visited three jewelers and he bought what Margery said were, "more jewels than I could possibly ever wear." Her new carriage and matched grays were delivered the fourth day after their arrival. But it was seeing Dan step out of the carriage that seemed to thrill her the most.

Will smiled when she greeted Dan with laughing eyes and a kiss on the cheek. "It is so good to see you, although I should be quite angry with you for not coming to see me."

Dan held her at arm's length and, looking her over well, let out a slow whistle. "New clothes and a new life, and both of them agree with you."

"You were always a flatterer." She slipped her arm through his and walked with him into the house.

Dan stayed for dinner, and the three of them talked far into the night. When he announced that it was time for him to leave, Margery said, "Only if you promise to visit us again. Soon."

Will walked him to the door, extracting a promise from Dan to ride with him the next morning.

The rest of their evenings were spent at the theater, the opera, the ballet, and afterward he would take her to the finest and most fashionable places to eat.

Once word was out that they were in residence, invitations began arriving. Will walked in one afternoon as Margery was opening an envelope.

"Another invitation?"

She nodded as she scanned the invitation. "It's for a ball at the home of the Marquess of Pemberton."

"I know Pemberton only slightly. I know you are tired. We can skip that one, if you like."

"Yes, I think I would like an evening at home."

"Is the Duke of Norfolk's ball tonight?"

"Yes."

"I suppose we should arrive a little earlier than normal for this one. It will be large and well attended."

She put the Marquess of Pemberton's invitation on a silver tray with a pile of others, then turned toward him. He was shocked to see that she had been crying, for her face was blotched, her nose red. "Sweetheart, what is wrong?"

The tears began to flow again, as if they had just been waiting for him to notice. "Oh, Will, I am so homesick. I miss our life in the country. I miss our quiet evenings with your family. I want to see my sons."

He took her in his arms and kissed her forehead. "You are my life. Whatever makes you happy makes me happy. If you are ready to go home, then we will go home."

She threw her arms around his neck. "That means more to me than all the clothes in Paris. Can we leave now?"

He chuckled at her excitement, the way her face was turned up to him. It was the first time he had ever looked at her and seen the child in her. He could see now how she must have looked on Christmas morning, with her eyes bright and eager. "It's a little late in the day for that, but I will alert the staff to begin packing our things. I'll tell you what. We will go to Norfolk's ball tonight and leave for home in the morning."

"Do we have to go to the Duke of Norfolk's? Couldn't we stay home?"

They could stay home every night, if that

pleased her. He had only brought her here in the first place because he thought she might prefer the excitement of the city to the country life many found exceedingly dull. It pleased him immensely to learn that she favored life in the country, just as he did. It was also a relief to know he would not have to spend a great deal of time in London, involving himself with the ton.

"You know I would do anything you asked, but I have promised someone we would be there."

The mystery seemed to put a sparkle into her eyes. "Who? Oh, Will, don't keep me waiting in suspense."

He sighed. "I can see I will never be able to keep a secret. Daniel asked about you and I promised him we would be there tonight. I know he would be greatly disappointed if we did not go."

"Of course we will go. A promise is a promise. Besides, it is always good to see Daniel."

Margery and Will finished their second dance and were on their way to speak to Dan, who had just arrived, when they paused to hear the announcement of another arrival.

"The Duke and Duchess of Dunford."

Margery watched as the handsome duke and his beautiful wife were received. She must have stared overly long, for Will asked, "Do you know them?"

"I am not certain, but I think I have met the duchess before. Perhaps it was when I came to London with your mother. Do you know them?"

"No, nor am I familiar with the title."

Margery watched them being greeted by several couples. "Apparently they are familiar to some, for they are well received."

"What . . . oh, yes, I suppose they are."

"You know, the strangest thing happened the night I met the Duchess of Dunford. Lady Ashford came up right after the duchess left and had the strangest story to tell. She said the duke was from America and that his parents had been killed by Indians and his brothers all scattered. She said he had a sister that was taken captive, just like I was. Poor Lady Ashford. She was amazed that there were two of us in the world who had been captured by Indians."

"I feel certain you set her straight on that score."

"Of course I did." She paused a moment, reflective. "I remember something else. It was shortly after we returned from London that I saw Daniel. He mentioned that Lady Ashford was telling the entire ton that the Duke of Dunford's sister and I were captives together. Can you imagine?"

Will was looking at something, but he had been listening, for he said, "I suppose it is possible. You did say you encountered other captives from time to time, if I remember correctly."

"Yes, I did, but the chance that any of them were the duke's sister . . . why it would be nothing short of a miracle if I had met her."

He put his arms around her. "I believe in miracles."

"You do?"

"You are my miracle."

She punched him. "The only miracle was that I still loved you after what you did."

He chuckled. "No, the real miracle was that you loved me at all."

"Perhaps we are both right," she said, seeing that Will was suddenly distracted.

"I don't believe it."

"What?"

"Grenville . . . the Duke of Grenville and his duchess. He must be seventy, if he's a day. What the deuce is he doing here? He gave up coming to functions like this over ten years ago."

"Which one is the duke?"

"The old one, over there, talking to the Duke of Dunford."

Margery looked in their direction and whispered to her husband behind her fan. "William, they are *all* old, save one. Which one is the duke, pray tell?"

"The one in black."

"Thank you. Let me see, I count one, two, three . . . seven, eight . . . nine in all. That makes nine men dressed in black in one small group, not to mention the other hundred or so in the room. Do you think you could be more vague?"

"What?" He turned to look at her. "Oh, I'm sorry. What was it you asked?"

"Never mind. Let's . . ."

"Have another dance," Will said, and whisked her out onto the dance floor. "Have I told you how lovely you look?"

"Yes, but I wouldn't mind hearing it again."

"Green is definitely your color. You should wear it more often."

"Now that you've given me these lovely emeralds, I will."

"You are by far the most beautiful woman here . . . with or without emeralds."

"I don't know. The Duke of Dunford's wife is quite striking with all that splendid black hair." As she spoke those words, she glanced toward the duke and duchess as they danced past. For a flashing moment, her gaze and that of the duke caught and held. A cold shiver passed over her and she could not seem to break the contact. But then, William turned her and the duke's face passed in a blur. She glanced back in the duke's direction. He was still looking at her. Margery missed a step. Had he felt the strange sensation, too?

"I prefer blondes."

"What?"

"I said, I prefer blondes."

"You are prejudiced," she said, feeling inexplicably strange. She wished they had not talked about Indians and captives. Now she would think of little else. She made a mental note to shove that thought as far back as she could, to the place where the memories of her past lay.

"I am only prejudiced where you are concerned."

They danced four more dances, then Will went to have a cigar and brandy in the library with

Dan, while Margery went upstairs to powder her nose.

When she entered the room, several women she knew were there. She spoke to them all, stopping to chat for a moment with the Countess of Upton and Lady Fitzpatrick. When she turned around, she saw the Duchess of Dunford touching up her hair in front of a gilt mirror festooned with cherubs.

The duchess looked at Margery in the mirror and tilted her head to one side. "Don't I know you?" she asked, turning around to face Margery. "I feel as if we have met before. Your face is very familiar to me, although we live in Scotland and don't get to London very often."

"We have met before, your grace. It was in London, I believe. About a year ago."

Annabella smiled. "I remember now. Forgive me for not recalling the time sooner."

"I have heard much about Scotland. I do believe you are the first lady Scot I have met."

The duchess laughed. "Then you shall have to wait a bit longer, for I am not a true Scot. I am English, but I have lived in Scotland since my marriage. I am the Duchess of Dunford, by the way, but please call me Annabella."

"I am the Countess of Warrenton, but you must call me Margery."

"Margery. What a lovely name. You know, my husband . . ."

"Annabella, will you walk down with me?"

Annabella turned and nodded. "Just a moment,

Mama." She turned back to Margery. "I am sorry to cut our visit short, but I must go now. My mother is getting old. She isn't as patient as she once was. I do hope we will see each other again."

"I hope so, too, although it may be a while. My husband and I are returning to the country tomorrow."

"Perhaps we shall meet again, the next time we are both here."

"I look forward to it."

"As do I. Good-bye."

"Good-bye." Margery watched the duchess leave the room, resplendent in a shimmering dress of darkest blue.

CHAPTER
❈ THIRTY-EIGHT ❈

Margery and Will were having dinner with Lydia and her family, Lord and Lady Lancaster. There were twenty or so people seated at the long table, all of whom were neighbors that Margery and Will knew, save two men who were houseguests of Lord and Lady Potterford. The younger gentleman sat far down the table from Margery, but the other gentleman, who sat across from her was a middle-aged man with a stout build. His hair was a color she had not seen before, a very dark red, streaked with gray. They had not conversed as yet, and the only thing she knew about him was his name, Dr. Davidson.

All in all, it was a lively group and the room fairly hummed with conversation.

Margery, who was sitting on Lord Lancaster's left, was discussing their last trip to London with him.

"I heard the Duke of Norfolk's ball was quite a bash."

"Oh, it was. I have never seen so many people I did not know."

Lord Lancaster's booming laugh caught the

attention of everyone at the table, and they all turned, in unison, to look at him. Lord Lancaster looked at Will. "Your countess was telling me about your recent trip to London. Sounds like old Norfolk had another room stuffer. I've been told he invites everyone in England who possesses a title."

"I am inclined to agree with you," Will said.

Margery looked from her husband to Lydia's father. "Oh, but it isn't just England, Lord Lancaster. There was at least one duke from Scotland there."

Lord Lancaster seemed amused by that. "A Scottish duke, you say? I probably don't know him, since I am not exactly up to snuff on my Scottish titles. He must have had English relations; otherwise, I cannot imagine what would prompt a Scot to come to England for Christmas. They have never been that fond of the English, you know."

Margery nodded. "So I have heard, but this duke has English relations, just as you said. His wife is English, and quite the most beautiful woman I have ever seen."

"An English wife. Hmmmm. I wonder what family she is from. She didn't tell you that, did she?"

Margery felt her face grow warm. "She told me her father's name, but I must confess that I have forgotten it. I do remember that she said her father was a duke."

"The Duke of Grenville," Will said. "Margery

415

told me who it was after she talked with Grenville's daughter."

"I do remember that her name was Annabella."

"That would be the Duke of Dunford's wife," Dr. Davidson said, and everyone turned to look at him.

"Yes," Margery said. "That is the name. The Duke of Dunford. Do you know him?"

"I am from the Isle of Skye, where the Duke of Dunford resides."

Margery leaned forward. "Then you must know Annabella."

Dr. Davidson smiled. "You might say that, since I have delivered all six of her and Ross's children." Dr. Davidson paused, then said, "I forgot to mention that the duke's name is Ross."

Margery frowned. *Ross . . . An unusual name, yet oddly familiar . . . Obviously a name I have heard before, but where, I do not know.* "Six children. Why, she doesn't look old enough to have six children."

Dr. Davidson fought a smile. "She is old enough, but still, as you said, quite lovely. Did you by any chance meet the duke?"

"No, the duchess and I only visited a short while when the men were smoking cigars. I saw him from a distance."

"That's too bad. He's an American, you know."

"I have heard that he was, but I was never certain if the story was true."

"Oh, it's true all right," Dr. Davidson said. "I

can personally vouch for that."

"If he's American, how did he end up with a Scottish title?" asked Will.

"His grandfather was the old duke. His father, although Scots born, had emigrated to America, where he died. When his health began to fade, the old duke sent for his grandson."

Margery picked up her wineglass just as Will said, "It's a pity Margery did not get to meet him, then. She doesn't have the opportunity to meet too many Americans."

"Well, there are plenty of them in Scotland, when the duke's kin come for a visit," Dr. Davidson said. "I think there must be more members of the Mackinnon clan in America than there are in Scotland."

Margery dropped her wineglass.

The glass struck her plate, spilling wine all over her ivory satin gown before it fell to the floor and shattered. Her breathing was shallow and her chest seemed too small, making her fight for each breath. Her body was suddenly warm and she could feel a clammy dampness across her brow. A loud droning noise buzzed in her ears. The room seemed to spin and grow black. She was afraid she was going to faint.

Mackinnon . . . Mackinnon . . . Mackinnon . . .

The name echoed through her head, and each time it did, it grew more and more familiar to her. She closed her eyes briefly, and behind her lids the images danced in the shadows before her, just as they had for as long as she could remember. She could see the same shadowy pictures she had always associated with the family she did not know. She opened her eyes but did not see anything. She was only aware of the terrible shaking of her hand as she brought it up to lay flat against her chest. "Mackinnon," she said giving her husband a desperate look. "Mackinnon."

Suddenly, Will was crouching down beside her, his fingers on her upper arm as he shook her gently. "Margery . . . Sweetheart, what is it? What's wrong?"

She put her hand to her head, feeling dizzy.

From somewhere far off, she could hear the sound of Will's voice. "I think I better take her home." She felt his arms go around her as he helped her to her feet.

"Mackinnon," she whispered. "My name is Mackinnon." The light in the room turned suddenly black and she felt herself falling down a long and dark tunnel.

Early the next morning, Will opened the door to Margery's room and saw her sitting up in bed, a look of bewilderment upon her face.

He stepped into the room and closed the door behind him, then crossed the room to sit beside her on the bed. He touched her forehead. "How do you feel?"

"Like I don't remember much of what happened last evening."

"Dr. Davidson accompanied us home. He said you had suffered a great shock. You kept saying the name Mackinnon and then you fainted. Do you remember anything about it?"

She swallowed, then closed her eyes and leaned her head back against the pillow. The shadowy vision swam before her eyes — dark shapes of her family, with no faces, but at least now they had a name. "Mackinnon," she said. "My name is Margery Mackinnon, but my real name was Marguerite."

The color drained from William's face. "My God! Do you know what this means? Are you certain?"

She nodded. "I would stake my life upon it."

"Well, it is a start. At least we have a name to look for. Now, if we just knew where to look."

"Start with the duke."

"The duke? You mean the Duke of Dunford?"

"I remember when Dr. Davidson said his name was Ross that there was something oddly familiar to me about that name, but I had no idea at the time where I had heard it." She paused. "Ross . . . Ross Mackinnon." She shook her head. "I have heard that name before. Ross. Ross and Alex. Ross and Alex Mackinnon!"

"Alex? Who is Alex?"

She put her hands to her temples and pressed, as if her head pained her. "I don't know. It just came to me when I said the name Ross Mackinnon." She stopped rubbing her temples. "Do you suppose Ross could have a brother named Alex? If they are Americans, then it is possible they could be related to me . . . possibly brothers."

419

Will leapt to his feet. "Brothers? Are you trying to tell me the Duke of Dunford might be your brother?"

She recalled the night at the ball when she danced with Will and her gaze had locked with the duke's. She knew it wasn't much as far as proof went, but she would die before anyone could convince her that there hadn't been something about the incident that left the Duke of Dunford just as unsettled as she had been. "I don't know, Will, but it is a place to start. We can go to Scotland and see the duke. It won't take long to see if there is a connection, if he has a family member named Alex."

He could see how important this was to her and the thought of not taking her to Scotland was heartbreaking. But how could he take her to the Duke of Dunford's home and start prying and asking questions about his past? That sort of thing just wasn't done. He sat back down and put his arms around her. "Sweetheart, I think all of this is a mere coincidence."

She looked hurt and the sight of her pained expression cut him to the heart. "You don't believe me?"

"I do believe your name was Mackinnon and the part about your name being Marguerite, but the probability of you and your brother coming to Great Britain and becoming peers of the realm is a bit farfetched. Even I have trouble believing it."

"But he is an American, and I am certain my

420

name was Mackinnon. Isn't that enough? That and the name Alex . . ." She paused. "Alex is for Alexander," she said, not knowing where that had come from. "Alexander and Adrian."

It was getting more confusing by the minute. "Adrian? Where did Adrian come from?"

"I don't know. It just came out of my mouth."

"You must remember the name Adrian from your past, just as you did the others."

"Alexander and Adrian," she said. "I don't know why the two seem to go together."

"Maybe someone in your family was named Alexander Adrian Mackinnon."

She wrinkled up her nose. "It doesn't have much of a ring to it, does it?"

He smiled down at her. "No, I don't suppose it does. How about Adrian Alexander Mackinnon?"

"Better, but I think they are two separate people."

"Well, at any rate, you have a last name and three first names. I think that is more than enough for a good start."

"We will go to Scotland then?"

He stood and took her hand, patting it.

She pulled it away. "Don't try to humor me. This is important to me."

"I know it is, only I think you have punished your brain enough. Get some rest. Whatever names are locked inside there are safe. If you've held on to them this long, then a few hours of rest won't drive them away. Who knows? After a good rest, you might recall even more. Hell, you might even discover you are old Victoria's sister."

"William, don't you dare make fun of me at a time like this. You . . . of all people! You are my husband. You are supposed to support me."

"Sweetheart, I do support you . . . when you will let me. The rest of the time it's damnably difficult to get you even to admit you are my wife. I don't know where that stubborn, independent streak in you came from. Maybe you are a Scot. You sure are as stubborn as one."

"Do you really think there is a chance that I might be a Scot?"

"There is always a chance," he said, bending low and kissing her softly upon the mouth before walking quietly away.

"I will still want to go to Scotland when I wake up," she said, just as he closed the door.

Will smiled and walked downstairs to look for his mother.

"Of course you should take her," Octavia said upon hearing the story of what had just transpired. "What can it possibly hurt?"

Dr. Davidson walked into the room. "Is your wife awake?"

"Yes, I was just with her."

"How is she feeling this morning? Was she able to remember what happened?"

"She is much better. A little shaky still but composed. She did remember what happened . . . at least most of it."

"I would like to talk to her. I am convinced she was suffering from some kind of severe shock."

"Oh, she was shocked, all right. When you mentioned the name Mackinnon, it seems that triggered some long-forgotten memory that made her think her name was Mackinnon."

Will noticed the confused look on Dr. Davidson's face just as Octavia said, "I think you should start from the beginning, William."

The three of them sat down and Octavia rang for tea as Will began to recount the story of his wife's life. As he spoke, the doctor's face changed, as if he knew something about the story Will was telling.

When William finished his story, Dr. Davidson drank the last of his tea and returned the cup to the saucer. "I find your wife's story quite fascinating."

"But you don't believe it."

"Quite to the contrary. I not only believe it, I think there may be every reason to think the connection she feels between herself and the Duke of Dunford might be a valid one."

Will's heart began to pound. "What makes you say that?"

"It is actually quite strange. You see, I have known the family for many years and the duke and I have had abundant opportunities to talk. One particular story he told me might be of interest to you. I recall that we spoke of his family in America only once. I never brought it up again, because there were many things that obviously disturbed him, things that I could see were quite painful, even after so many years."

A mouth as dry as desert sand followed the pounding heart, and Will began to have a suspicion that something big . . . something very, very big was about to happen. "What did you speak of?"

"The duke told me about his family . . . the deaths of his mother, father, and eldest brother by Indians."

"Indians?"

"Yes, the same Indians that captured his only sister . . . a sister Ross and his brothers have never found."

"My God!" Octavia said. "You don't suppose . . ."

Will interrupted. "Margery told me the name Ross was familiar to her, and then two more names came to her. Alex, which she later said was for Alexander. The moment she said Alexander, she said Adrian."

"The Duke of Dunford has a brother named Adrian. I know this because Ross found Adrian a Scottish wife. He stood in for his brother to marry Maggie Ramsay by proxy. I was one of the witnesses to that wedding. As for the names of his other brothers, I cannot recall his telling them to me."

"There are other brothers, then?" Will asked.

"Yes. Four or five brothers, I think . . . not counting the one killed by Indians."

Octavia's cup rattled and she set it down. "I

remember Margery's telling me once that she had a feeling she had several brothers and no sisters. And then there was the time when she first met the duchess, and Lady Ashford started spouting off all that stuff about the duke's sister being kidnapped by Indians. At the time, I thought it was all a bunch of Lady Ashford's poppycock. She is getting old and her mind has bouts of lavishness."

Will nodded. "Perhaps she wasn't being lavish this time, for what she said certainly fits."

Dr. Davidson rose to his feet. "So far, I'd say everything we've heard fits." He turned to Octavia. "I thank you for your hospitality, Countess."

"You are leaving?" Octavia asked as she stood.

"I am returning to Scotland two days hence. I must get back to London to attend to a few more things before that time." He turned to Will. "If you don't think I need to look in on your wife, then I will be on my way."

Will walked the doctor to the door. "I don't know how I can ever thank you. You have no idea what this information you have shared with me means."

"Oh, I have a pretty good idea," he said, putting his hat on his head with a plop, "seeing as how I was an orphan myself." He started down the steps. "Good day to you then, your lordship. I trust you will be taking your wife to see the Duke of Dunford?"

"You can bet your sweet life on it."

CHAPTER
❁ THIRTY-NINE ❁

Five days later, Will and Margery arrived on the Isle of Skye. Two hours after their arrival, they sat in the salon of the aging castle where the Duke of Dunford resided, awaiting the duke's entrance.

Margery had never felt this nervous in her life. What was only a few minutes seemed an eternity to her. Why didn't he hurry? Didn't the duke understand how important this was to her? Then she remembered the duke had no inkling as to why they had come.

Will, as if sensing her nervousness, placed his hand over hers and gave it a squeeze. "Everything will be fine, my love. I am certain of it."

"I hope you are right. I have built my hopes up to such a point . . ." She turned to him. "Oh Will, if this proves to be a false lead, I don't know if I will ever recover from the disappointment of it."

She said nothing more, for the sound of footsteps coming down the hall were becoming louder. A moment later, the Duke of Dunford walked into the room. He was a tall man and regally slim, with kind eyes and thick dark hair that was turning gray at the temples. She searched his face for something to remember, some clue to her past, but there was nothing in that face that spoke to her.

After greeting each other, Will introduced her to the duke, who indicated two chairs. "Sit down, please."

The duke took a chair across from them, then leaned back in his chair. "I understand you have something consequential to discuss with me."

"Yes, your grace, we do."

"Please call me Ross and I'll call you William."

"Will is even easier."

Ross let his amusement show. "That it is."

Will glanced at Margery. She was sitting statue still. One look at Will told her he was having difficulty figuring out where to start. She decided to give him a little help by getting the duke's attention. "I think you may be my brother, your grace."

As far as an attention getter, that was the ultimate, for Ross looked as if someone had just slapped him in the face. "What did you say?"

"If I might intervene here," Will said, "I would like to back up a little and start a little earlier in the story."

Ross looked agreeable to that. "How about the beginning?"

Will nodded. "I spent several years traveling in America. Most of my time was spent out West, where I went from one Indian village to another, sketching pictures of the Indians and tribal life.

It was in a Crow village that I saw a woman being bartered to some Mandan warriors. My men and I could tell that, although she was dressed as an Indian, she was white, so I bought her."

Margery sat quietly as Will explained the circumstances of their marriage, admitting how he had used her to get back at his father. He went on to relate how Margery spoke English and knew her first name, having no memory of her family at all . . . save the shadowy images that she would see from time to time. "I took her to England. We arrived at my home on Christmas Eve, and I left her there. I returned to America that night."

Ross looked at Margery. "Will said you remembered your first name. What is it?"

"All I ever knew was Margery, but a week ago, when someone mentioned the name Mackinnon, suddenly I knew my name was Margery Mackinnon, and that Margery was not my real name, but Marguerite."

Ross seemed stunned, yet he spoke with caution. "My sister's name was Marguerite, although we never called her anything but Margery, and like you, she had blond hair."

Margery's heart was beating triple time, and she felt as if she might float right out of the chair. She tried to contain her joy, which seemed near to bursting.

"However," Ross went on to say, "my brothers and I have come across many captives who thought they were our sister . . . and many of them insisted their name was Margery." He paused a moment, looking from one to the other, before his gaze rested upon Will. "When did you decide I might be your brother?"

Will explained their trip to London and the Duke of Norfolk's ball. He mentioned Margery and Annabella's meeting for the second time.

Ross looked at Margery. "At that time, you had no inkling that your last name might be Mackinnon?"

"I did not know Mackinnon was your name until after we returned home." She gave the details of the dinner party they attended at Lord Lancaster's home, and how Dr. Davidson mentioned the name Mackinnon, then she told him about her reaction when she heard him say the name.

"And you fainted?"

"She fainted dead away," Will said. "I can't tell you how thankful I was that Dr. Davidson was there. He accompanied us home and stayed the night, just to be nearby."

"While I admit I am a bit shaken by your revelations, I am afraid that isn't enough to prove you are my sister. I don't mean to be harsh, but you must understand how many times I have gotten my hopes up, only to have them dashed. As I said before, you aren't the only white captive to come forth."

About that time, the duchess, Annabella, walked into the room. "I am sorry to have taken so long to join you. I am keeping two of my sister's children and their nanny was having a bit of difficulty with them."

Ross and Will took turns talking in order to bring Annabella up-to-date on what had transpired thus far. It did not take Margery a minute to see Annabella was much more sympathetic to her cause than her husband. "I am glad you came to us straightaway," she said. "I know how terrible it must be to keep something like this inside of you without knowing."

When Annabella finished, Ross said, "I was just explaining to them how many times my brothers and I have been convinced we had found our sister, only to discover we were wrong."

Annabella looked at the three of them. "You aren't going to send them home, are you?"

"There just isn't enough proof, Bella."

Margery knew she had this one chance and this one chance only. "The morning after I fainted at the Lancasters', Will came to see how I was feeling. We were talking about the Mackinnon name, when suddenly another name came to me."

Ross's eyes glittered with interest as he asked, "What was the name?"

"The name was Alex, but when I said the complete name Alex Mackinnon, I suddenly heard myself say, 'Alexander. His name was Alexander.' And then the strangest thing happened. I had no more than said that, when I said, 'Alexander and Adrian.'" She shrugged. "I have no idea why I said the names together, or why they came to me as they did. I thought at first that perhaps Alex might be your brother."

430

She looked at Ross and saw the raw play of emotion upon his face. His voice shook as he said the words, "Alex *is* my brother . . . and so is Adrian. They are twins."

"Twins," she repeated. "Then that must be why I linked the two together." She suddenly remembered something and smiled. "I have twins," she said. "Twin boys, William and Robert."

"There are several sets of twins in the extended family. It seems to run in the Mackinnon blood."

"Well, that should prove who she is . . . even to a staunch old doubter, like you," Annabella said, rising to her feet. "I think I should ring for Alice and have her bring us a bottle of wine . . ." Annabella stopped talking and stared at her husband, who she must have decided looked far removed from a celebrating mood. "Ross Mackinnon, you aren't still doubting this . . . after all you've been told?"

"I have to be certain, Bella. You know that." He spoke to Margery. "Isn't there anything else? Anything you remember that wouldn't be easy for anyone except members of our family to know?"

Margery felt her heart sink, felt, too, the burn of tears behind her eyes. "No," she whispered softly, "nothing."

Annabella threw up her hands and began pacing the room. "Do you remember anything that happened . . . anything special, like Christmas or another holiday?"

Margery shook her head.

Annabella paced. Back and forth. Back and forth. Suddenly, she stopped. "I've got it!" She turned toward Ross and took his arm. "Try to remember if there isn't anything you remember about your sister . . . anything that would prove beyond a shadow of doubt just who she is. Something no one else would have. Something like a birthmark . . . or a scar."

Ross shook his head.

"Not even a blemish?"

"Not even that."

She looked at the ceiling. "I cannot believe it! How could anyone go through life without having at least *one* accident that would leave a scar. You would think . . ."

Annabella stopped dead in the middle of her sentence. "Ross, what is it?"

Margery looked at Ross. His face was as white as the alabaster statue on the table behind him. While she was still looking at him, he came to his feet and walked toward her, stopping just in front of her. "Take off your shoes."

Margery blinked. "My shoes?"

Annabella came to stand beside him. "Ross, are you sure . . ."

Ross held up his hand and Annabella grew quiet.

Margery began to remove her shoes. When she was finished, Ross dropped down in front of her. He picked up her left foot and looked it over. He released it and picked up the right one. "Dear

432

God!" he whispered, his thumb rubbing over a small circular scar on the top of her foot.

Margery looked down at the scar. It was old, the top shiny and white and smooth.

"How did you get this?" Ross asked, his voice shaking.

"I . . . I don't remember. I have always had it."

"What do you mean, always?"

"It has always been there, for as long as I can remember."

"Was it there when you were captured?"

"Yes."

He closed his eyes for a moment, but even with them closed, Margery could see the tears that began to slip beneath his lids. When he opened his eyes, they were shimmering with tears. "I can tell you how you got it," he said, his voice dry and cracking, overcome with emotion. "When you were three years old, you jumped off a wagon and landed on a board with a nail in it. The nail went through your shoe, piercing the bottom of your foot and coming out the top. I reached you first and carried you into the house."

Margery realized all of a sudden that she was crying softly. She could not believe this was happening. No one deserved to be this happy. No one.

Not even her.

Ross stood up and she wondered if he would be able to speak again. "I remember the day it happened so vividly, I can almost hear our father as he looked at it and said it would leave a scar.

My brothers and I teased you and called you Scarfoot." His voice broke and it was obvious he could not go on. He did not need to, for when he opened his arms and Margery stepped into them, she could feel all the things he wanted to say.

And that is how it happened that, almost thirty years after she was kidnapped, Margery Mackinnon Woodville found herself in her brother's arms.

The Crow would have said it was a fitting end, but in truth, it was only the beginning.

❖ EPILOGUE ❖

It was one of those rare times that comes only once in a lifetime; the kind of time families talk about for generations, whenever they come together.

Margery stood between Ross and Will, looking out upon the fulfillment of a lifetime of dreams: the expectant faces of the family she had always had but never known.

Later in the day there would be speeches, introductions, cheers, the sharing of memories, the shedding of tears. There would be a picnic and games to play, and children to bounce upon one's knee. Then a band would strike up a song and there would be a time for dancing beneath a string of colored lanterns, swaying against the backdrop of blackest night. And when it came time for her to retire for the night, the brothers gathered here would be as familiar to her as they had been that day so long ago, when she was carried away.

She thought of her own restless wanderings and of the joy that presently filled her heart. She slipped her hand through the arm of the man standing beside her and felt her husband's strength flow into her. Tears began to spill down her cheeks as the brothers she had not seen since she was six years old came forth, bringing their families for her to meet.

Mackinnons all.

There were over thirty of them now, counting her five brothers, their wives and children: Alex and Katherine from Texas, Tavis and Elizabeth from Nantucket, Nicholas and Tibbie from Cape Cod, Adrian and Maggie from California, and standing next to her, his feet planted firmly on Scottish soil, her brother Ross, and his wife, Annabella.

She looked at each one of them, studying the faces that had been nothing but dark, mysterious shadows for so long, and thought about the missing parents and brother, whose lives had been taken by the same fierce Indians who captured her.

As she studied each of them, their features began to blur and grow dim. From out of the distance she could hear the thundering sound of hoofbeats as she watched a band of hawk-faced Comanches, with black braided hair and war feathers, ride across her mind, their war cries penetrating and strangely prophetic.

At last, the memory that had been locked away was free.

She saw herself as she had been that day in 1836, a little girl of six, clinging to her mother's hand. She watched the Comanches with their high cheekbones and coppery skin smeared with paint, red ribbons tied in the tails of their ponies, as they swooped down on the small stockade, armed with lances and bows.

Her mother's scream reached out to her, echoing across time. A brave's strong arm came out and swept her up, throwing her over a blanket as his pony thundered out of sight. The last thing she heard were her own terrified cries for her mother. Then the memory began to fade.

She blinked and saw the faces of her brothers again, and she knew her life would never be the same. Time would give her other memories to hold dear, just as time had given her Will, a new life in England, and their two beloved sons.

Overhead, a falcon cried out. In the distance, the mountains rose out of the earth, rugged, majestic, and shaded with blue. She felt somehow insignificant as she stood there, very silent and very still, surrounded by a past as solid and enduring as the gray stone walls of Dunford Castle, home of the clan Mackinnon. A sadness overcame her. Soon, it would be over, and her brothers would all be gone.

But never again would she be alone.

The comforting cycle of life would continue — the birthing, the growing, the deaths that would come one day. Margery turned and buried her face against her husband's chest, soaking his shirtfront with tears of joy.

Life went on and was still beautiful.

She would hold the memory.

Dear Reader,

Two years ago when the fifth and what I thought was the final Mackinnon book, HEAVEN KNOWS, was published, I included a letter, very similar to this one, in the back of the book. In that letter I shared with you how I always knew there would come a time when I wrote what I thought of as the last of the Mackinnons, and how difficult it was to let them go.

Your response was overwhelming. I have never received so much mail! Over and over you expressed your disappointment because you were not going to find out what happened to the sister, and how you felt somehow deprived knowing you would never get to read Margery's story.

How could I resist? I was ever a softy — and you were all so persuasive. Some of the pleas were downright despondent. "We have got to know what happened to the little sister!" "What about Margery?" "You can't stop now!"

Well, for each of the six-hundred-plus people who wrote asking for Margery's story, I can only say thank you for loving the Mackinnons as much as I do. And for those of you who still feel a loss, even after seven books, let me simply say, remembered joys are never past. The Mackinnons will never end. They live on, in each of your hearts.

And now, it is time to move on, so I might give you other books. Other memories . . .

P.O. Box 11674
Washington, DC, 20008
ecoffman@erols.com

F   26.95
Coff   G.K. Hall & Co.
Coffman   LARGE PRINT
        If You Love Me.

DATE DUE

AUG 27 2001	APR 0 7 2005
SEP 2 1 2001	2005
	JUN 2 0 2006
OCT 1 8 2001	NOV 1 9 2007
APR 0 3 2002	SEP 1 2 2008
JUN 1 3 2002	OCT 0 2 2008
APR 2 0 2004	
SEP 1 4 2004	

R

WM

MJ

GAYLORD M2